I

The hours after the battle passed in a blur. Torn from the routine of maintaining her vessel and crew, Maia fell into a strange state, caught between full wakefulness and dreams. Some part of her was still aware of the changes of watch and the shouted commands of the *Imperatrix*'s officers, but her detachment had thrown up a barrier that she had to struggle to pierce. Her sisters' voices ebbed and flowed around her in a murmuring tide, as if she still rode at anchor on the breast of the waves, everything around her dim and remote.

She could see faces through the haze - Pendragon, Raven, Leo, but it was easier to block everything out and drift. Her responsibilities had disappeared along with her vessel and she had no wish to be reminded of them.

It was her Captain's command that dragged her out of torpor. "*Tempest?*"

His voice was in her head and her ears, demanding her attention.

She opened her eyes and the world rushed in. Noise and colour momentarily overtook her until she blinked herself back to readiness and focused on Leo's worried face. Maia checked her internal chronometer. She'd been out for precisely fifteen hours and eight minutes.

"Good, you're back with us. I was warned this might happen. It's the shock of first detachment."

Maia was immediately alert, the soft fogginess that had enveloped her blown away in an instant. Part of her wanted to crawl back into it, but she knew that that wasn't an option. She had to forcibly override the automatic urge to go through her vessel checks and every sense ached with the loss, as if from the phantom pain of an amputated limb. There was no point in reaching for something that wasn't there any more.

"It feels strange," she told him.

"I can only imagine. We're about to hold the service for the dead, and I thought you'd rather be awake."

Now that she looked at Leo more closely, she could see the shadows under his hazel eyes and the stubble on his chin. He was wearing borrowed clothes too, which was understandable as everything he owned had gone down with her vessel. She realised with a sudden pang that this would have included the miniature of her father, which had kept watch over both of them from the Captain's desk and it was all she could do to restrain a sob.

It was all she had had of him and now even that small comfort was gone.

"How many dead?" she asked.

"Too many, including Sabrinus."

A cannonball had ended his young life in an instant and now the sundered body of her second-in-command was lost to the deep. She immediately reproached herself. Here she was wailing over a picture, when men's lives had been lost.

"Damn Albanus to Hades!" she retorted bitterly. The Admiral's pride had cost him his only son. She hoped that the proud man would grieve when he found out, for who would carry on the family name now? Likewise, his daughter had been sunk in spectacular fashion.

"I hope he rots in Tartarus for his perfidy," Leo agreed, scowling. "Sabrinus deserved a better father. His shade is in the hands of the Gods now, but we can at least try to send him and the others on their way with prayers and a payment for the Ferryman."

It was only then that she began to fully register their surroundings. They had found some shelter off a rocky coast framed by towering cliffs. To the east a headland jutted out into

E. M. KKOULLA

THE BATTLE
FOR
BRITANNIA

SHIPS OF BRITANNIA,
BOOK 5

ISBN: 9798345757215

PublishNation
www.publishnation.co.uk

BY THE SAME AUTHOR

SHIPS OF BRITANNIA, BOOKS 1-4

WRATH OF OLYMPUS

PREY OF THE HUNTRESS

THE TRIALS OF NEPTUNE

THE TRIUMPH OF MARS

SON OF THE SEA: A SHIPS OF BRITANNIA
NOVELLA*

available through emkkoulla.com

BRITANNIA

PICTS

CALEDONIA

MARE GERMANICVS

GAELS

HADRIAN'S WALL

LVGVVALLIVM

LON

ISLE OF
MANANNAN

EBORACVM

OCEANVS
HIBERNICVS

MONA

DEVA

LINDVM

LETOCETVM

HIBERNIA

GLEVVM

VERVLAMIVM

ISLE
OF THE
DEAD

OCTAPITARVM
PROMONTORIVM

ABONA

AQVAE
SVLIS

THAMESIS

LONDINIVM

DVBRIS

MALVADVM

DVRNOVARIA

PORTVS

ISLES OF
SILLINA

KERNOW

ISCA

NOVIOMAGVS

VECTIS

MERIDIANVM

OCEANVS
BRITANNICVS

GAVL

KRJB

CONTENTS

TIMELINE

AUC (AB URBE CONDITA) – from the founding of Roma, as Maia's dates are reckoned. Dates from our world in brackets – Before Common Era/Common Era

Year 1 AUC
(753 BCE)
Founding of Roma.
698 AUC
(55 BCE)
Julius Caesar visits Britannia.
743 AUC
(10 BCE)
Emperor Augustus makes a pact with the Sea God, Neptune.
Sacred oak branches begin to be grafted on to vessels.
796 AUC
(43 CE)
Emperor Claudius invades Britannia.
814 AUC
(61 CE)
Boudica leads a rebellion against the rule of Roma.
875 -881 AUC
(122 - 128 CE)
Building of Hadrian's Wall.
1146 AUC
(393 CE)
Birth of Artorius Magnus.
1163 AUC
(410 CE)
Roman Empire in crisis. Civil war in Britannia as rivals vie for the throne.
1165 AUC
(412 CE)
Civil War ends. Artorius acclaimed High King of the Britons and forms Britannic Legions. Merlin gathers Mages and forms Collegium. Artorius and Merlin lead the Legions on a march to Roma and rescue the Empire. Goths and Vandals bought off and retreat to the East.

1167 AUC
(414 CE)
Empire stabilises. Major Fae return to Britannia. Artorius returns
with his Legions.
1170 AUC
(417 CE)
Great Fae Wars. Artorius receives Excalibur.
1174 AUC
(421 CE)
Major Fae defeated at great cost and driven overseas to Hibernia.
Merlin disappears.
1210 AUC
(457 CE)
Artorius dies. His son, Gwydre Mordraut Britannicus Pendragon
becomes king.
1436 AUC
(683 CE)
Northern Alliance formed between Scandinavian, Baltic and
Germanic peoples. Hostilities increase.
First Ship, the *Britannia*, created.
1548 AUC
(795 CE)
HMS *Augusta* installed.
1567 AUC
(814 CE)
The Great Blight.
1579 AUC
(826 CE)
Battle of the Oceanus Germanicus
1730 AUC
(912 CE)
Jupiter's decree bans the creation of demi-gods.
2028 AUC
(1275 CE)
HMS *Livia* executed. Maia born.
2044 AUC
(1291 CE)
Marcia Blandina is killed. Maia enters the Naval Academy.

the grey sea, whilst the dark bulk of Mona protected them westwards. It was the best they could hope for at the present, she supposed. Across the water, the remains of the fleet rode at anchor, clustered together like the survivors they were. She could clearly see the damage the serpents had inflicted. *Unicorn* and *Blossom* looked particularly bedraggled, though the former had come off the worse. Great gouges along their flanks and missing rigging told of the mauling they had endured.

Maia sighed inwardly and opened up a channel to her sister Ships.

First to answer was her old friend and mentor. It was a relief to hear her familiar voice.

<*Tempest*! I'm glad you're back with us! How are you?>

Maia thought for a moment.

<Not bad.>

<Of course, it's not too long since you had a flesh body,> *Blossom* told her. <It's harder for those of us who've had a vessel for many years, though we become more accustomed to it if we've had a few moves.>

<It's not something I'd like to happen on a regular basis,> she admitted. <How are your repairs coming along?>

<I've lost some sail and my bowsprit because of that blasted serpent,> *Blossom* replied, <but I'm not as chewed-up as poor *Unicorn*. She gets repair priority as she's more or less crippled. If we do move on quickly, she'll have to heave-to until they get her seaworthy again. Ah, here's our friend! I'll leave you to it and catch up with you later!>

<*Tempest*! Welcome back!>

Patience's cheerful call broke into the conversation. Maia looked across the deck to see a waving figure. Both her own and *Patience*'s Shipbodies were now anchored to what remained of their vessels, unable to move from the spot where they were fixed. It was restricting and uncomfortable, but it would have been much worse if they'd had to rest directly on the *Imperatrix*.

Maia saw that the men were beginning to gather, forming into three groups: *Tempest*, *Patience* and *Imperatrix*. Her friend's was the smallest.

<I wondered when you'd come round. It's a strange sensation, isn't it?>

3

<Like you're drifting,> Maia admitted, <but I feel awake now.>

<We're never allowed to be out of it for too long.>

<Do you know what will happen to us next?> She found herself intensely curious as to what would become of them both.

<No-one's said anything. Look, the Admiral's coming to see you. He's just spoken to me, too. We'll catch up in a bit, after the ceremony.>

She was right and Maia was touched that Pendragon was taking the time to talk to his Ships personally. He hadn't yet had his earring replaced which must have been frustrating for him, but she was sure that would be remedied soon.

"Welcome back, *Tempest*. Detachment is something you'll have to get used to, but not under such dramatic circumstances, I hope."

"That's my hope too, sir."

He smiled at her.

"You acquitted yourself well, but now there's another rite of passage. Saying goodbye," he told her softly. "I know you'll be strong."

She saluted. "We lost too many brave souls," she replied, "but I know it's all part of being a Ship."

His sigh was almost imperceptible.

"Alas, yes. This won't be the last time, by any means. We'd better get on with it, then."

He glanced to one side where the Priests were waiting for him, and moved away to take up his position. Leo strode into the vacated space, with Amphicles at his shoulder. Automatically, she found herself searching for Sabrinus. His absence was something else she'd have to get used to.

<Are you all right, Maia?>

Blossom was checking in on her again. Of all the Ships, she was the one who'd lost her Captain so she'd be suffering too.

<It's strange. I keep looking for people who aren't there.>

<You've not been to many funerals then. Believe me, it's normal. It will be over soon, then it's back to work.>

The Priests had started invoking the Gods now, so *Blossom* slipped out of the link. Other voices echoed from nearby Ships who were also honouring the dead at their altars, though how

4

many bodies had been recovered in total she didn't know. Many had already gone to the depths of Neptune's realm, to be lost forever. Even the sacrificial animals were silent and no seabirds called.

A rattling of weapons in the silence told her that a party of marines were loading their muskets, ready for the salute. In her current state she hadn't been able to do a roll call, though she knew that Leo would have the list of casualties. She feared the worst, unless they had been picked up by other Ships. Maia debated asking him. Was it the right time, or even appropriate? Then again, she needed to honour her dead.

<Leo, who's missing?> she whispered.

His eyes flicked over to her in acknowledgement and began. <Caphisus and Batacarus.>

They'd been on the same gun crew and were inseparable in life. It seemed that the Gods in their wisdom had taken both of them.

<Egnatius.> The midshipman and senator's son. He'd not been popular, but had had a promising career ahead of him.

<Most of gun crews twelve to eighteen.>

This was hard too. They'd stayed at their posts until the end, vainly trying to pierce *Regina*'s shields.

Maia willed Leo to stop, listening in horror as he continued. Her cook, Pertinax. Corax, the purser, responsible for the monies. It was her duty to pray for each one and hope that they had found a safe berth, far from the troubles of the mortal realm. They'd been the unlucky ones, pierced by lethal shards of wood or trapped below decks where she'd been powerless to help them.

It was as the Fates decreed: Clotho drawing out the thread, Lachesis measuring it, Atropos raising her shears for the final cut. No pleas or prayers could ever stay their busy hands. Only Maia would remember them for as long as she lived, each face stored safely in memory and the first of many she would treasure.

She glanced around. The men of the *Imperatrix* were lining up in front of the Ship's altar, this one clearly dedicated to Neptune. The survivors of her own crew stood together, shoulder to shoulder. Hyacinthus, Big Ajax, Musca, her Master Gunner with his men, Sprout and Monkey, whose luck had held for once. Vestinus, her carpenter and Osric with a few of her marines.

5

Hawthorn and Rowan were below, tending to the wounded. The others had already been deployed to other vessels. It was a sad remnant of the family she had been given for all too brief a time. She felt panic rise within her as she searched their faces.

<Leo! I can't see Teg!>

Her Captain was quick to reassure her.

<Don't worry, *Leopard*'s crew picked him up. He's lost part of a leg, but their Adept says he'll live.>

That was a relief. The little crewman was greatly loved by his comrades, always ready to pull a face or tell a joke – and frequently to be the butt of one. She still didn't know what he thought of having a monkey named after him. Normally she'd have been in the Adept's domain to talk to her wounded, but that wasn't an option now she was stuck on deck. She'd have to rely on her officers briefing her as to their condition.

The boy Hyacinthus had rescued from the *Regina* stood close to his saviour, watching the proceedings with tear-filled eyes. He was the only one to have escaped his Ship's destruction. None knew if it was a mark of favour, or if the Gods had singled him out for yet more tragedy. That would be for the Priests to try and determine in the days to come. For now, he would stay aboard the *Imperatrix*, an object of both awe and fear.

The sweet smell of incense was already drifting on the breeze to alert any watching deities that worship was about to take place and she imagined them crowding around, unseen, eager to partake in whatever was being offered. She hoped that her mother was among them.

Imperatrix herself was already in position nearby as her Priest, head covered, gave orders to his acolytes.

<Ladies. I'm relaying to the other Ships in the Fleet, so you don't have to.>

<Thank you.>

Patience answered for the both of them.

It was time for the melancholy rites to begin. There were bodies, outlines shrouded in sailcloth and covered with the remains of naval flags. The image of Sabrinus's earnest face flashed into Maia's mind. He had been the best of them, dependable and loyal to the last, a Captain in the making. Cruel fate had snatched him away before any of them had been ready.

She knew that it was useless to rail against the will of the Moirai – even Jupiter couldn't change their decrees – but in this case, Atropos' shears had made the cruellest of cuts. All they could do now was raise their eyes to the heavens and make sure that dread Charon was paid enough to transport every last soul across the River Styx.

Imperatrix's Priest led the service, Danuco and others assisting when necessary. There was little to give, but animals had been procured from somewhere, probably when she was drifting in her somnolent state. They went to their deaths quietly, which was a relief to all. The men would dine well on their remains, while the Gods would be nourished by the smoke from their bones and fat. She watched as the offerings were being cast on the fire, greasy plumes ascending to the heavens as supplication. The Priests stood by chanting, red to the elbows from their butchery. Why the Gods liked the smell of death she could never fathom, but demand it they did and hopefully their prayers would buy the Fleet some time.

At the end of the ceremony, the crew of the *Imperatrix*, as well as the survivors from other Ships, came forward with gifts to tuck inside the burial shrouds. It wasn't right that their lost comrades should enter the Underworld with nothing to call their own, so the living gave the dead what they could spare: coins, trinkets, a spare comb or knife, whatever they had salvaged or put by. Their officers watched silently as Pendragon gave each a gold coin, to show that they had his special favour. A chest loaded with more would have to suffice for those who had gone to their doom with only the clothes they stood up in, though most would have had a gold ring on fingers or ears to carry them through. Nothing was left to chance.

Finally, before each body was carried reverently to waiting boats to be buried on land, the officer gave the order and a volley of shots rang out over the remains. These were answered from the other Ships and vessels, as the marines discharged their weapons. The smoke drifted over the deck, carrying with it the familiar tang of sulphur. Pendragon waited for it to clear, then stepped forward to make his farewell speech.

"And so we bid farewell to these brave men, both these whose bodies we commit to the earth and those who have found their rest in the depths of the ocean. I shall build a temple above their hallowed bones, so that all will remember their sacrifice down the ages. Furthermore, a Priest will keep the eternal light forever shining forth as a beacon for sailors everywhere and to glorify their memory. This I swear before the Gods and my people!"

There was a second of silence, before Captain Cornelius stepped forward.

"Gods save the King! Gods save Britannia!"

His cry was echoed by all, winging across the water from Ship to Ship, echoing off the cliffs and startling seabirds into flight. Maia joined in, adding her voice as fervently as she could and knowing that her sisters were doing the same.

*

Something startled Tullia from her stupor. Seabirds? No, the crying of many voices, carried on the wind like distant ghosts.

She jerked awake, suddenly aware of the waves' caress and a lowering sky filled with billowing clouds. Something bumped against her side and she reached out automatically to fend it off. A tiny shock of recognition tingled through her on contact and she raised her head to see what it was. Shattered planks drifted away on the current, but she knew instinctively that they had once been hers.

The memory rose up before she could stop it. Her vessel was gone, along with her rank and her pride. What had happened? One minute she'd been watching the wreck of the *Tempest* recede as she'd piled on sail, ready to deal with the rest of her traitorous sisters, the next, a flash, a rending and her world had exploded. What had done that? She searched her memory, but there was no clue. Whatever it was, it had evidently done for her vessel.

She paused, slipping into the Ship link to see what was happening. So, they were burying their dead. They could bury hers too for all she cared. She extended her awareness cautiously, seeking the whereabouts of her Captain. Gods help her if Silvius had somehow survived and was even now trying to find his Ship.

Her questing mind was met with nothing save a vast emptiness that told of a connection severed forever. A surge of triumph flooded her Shipbody. So, the dog was dead. It served him right for the way he'd treated her. She was still alive and he and his inhuman cronies were at the bottom of the sea, never to trouble her again.

She shut the link down hurriedly, throwing up mental barricades to wall herself off from any that might be seeking her. The last thing she wanted was to be found and recalled to duty. It seemed like freedom was finally within her grasp, something she hadn't felt for a very long time.

There was only one person she could trust now and that was her father. Her fate was linked to his ambition, of that she was all too sure. As for her sister Ships, she had literally burned her bridges there when she attacked *Tempest*. It was best that they all thought her gone. She considered her options, deciding it was time for her to act in her own best interests. The Navy be damned!

Her Shipsenses told her that she wasn't far from the coast of Mona, where her vessel had gone down. She shuddered. It was too far from civilisation for her liking, but if she swam along the coast there would be a port soon enough, at the entrance to the Dee. From there, it wasn't far to Deva, the main city. Failing that, there were other ways of travel that didn't involve land. Maybe she should go in search of an inanimate? A boat was all she needed to get to her heart's desire.

A promise was a promise, after all. Tullia wanted exactly what she was owed, and Hades could take anyone who stood in her way.

*

Their melancholy duty over, Pendragon, Cornelius and Leo, together with their senior officers, retired below to confer on their best course of action.

<He can't stay at sea indefinitely,> *Patience* remarked, watching the retreating backs. <Sooner or later, he'll have to make a stand.>

<With what?> Maia replied. <He'll need the legions, and it looks like Marcus has them on his side. Everyone still thinks that he possesses Excalibur and no-one will stand against him.>

9

They fell silent, contemplating the dire situation they were in.

<Has anyone heard anything of *Regina*?> Maia asked, eventually, if only for something to say.

A moment's questioning through the link threw up nothing but negatives.

<I don't think she's dead,> *Diadem* offered. <We'd know if she'd been destroyed. I'll bet she's laying low somewhere.>

<Very wise,> *Leopard* growled. <She'd better not come asking for sympathy around here. There'll be no Queen Whateverhernamewas while we exist!>

Angry murmurs supported her view.

<She's a fool if she thinks that Marcus will keep his bargain,> *Imperatrix* agreed. <Why would he marry the daughter of a mere Admiral?>

<The rumour is that Albanus has been made a Dux,> *Blossom* answered.

<Even so. Do you know of anyone who went back to their flesh?> *Imperatrix* pointed out. <I don't, at least not recently. Maybe back in the distant past, but there's none here who remembers it happening. Am I right?>

<You are,> *Diadem* chipped in. <It's all hearsay. I don't think it ever happened. Once the sacrifice is made, that's it. The Mother doesn't give up her own that easily.>

Maia cast her mind back to the Sacred Grove and the enormous oak that cradled them deep in its roots, binding their souls to their Shipbodies for as long as they lived. She couldn't see Tullia coming back from that, no matter what her erstwhile friend had been told, even though Raven had insisted otherwise. Unless Ceridwen, the High Priestess of the Mother, was to have a hand in it? That was another mystery she would like cleared up.

At the moment, though, there were more pressing concerns. A Ship without her vessel was merely an interesting piece of wood, or a communication device. Even movement was hard. She was only built for speed when she had her masts and sails. Furthermore, even if by some miracle she was offered her mortal body back she wouldn't want it, badly scarred as it was. It had been a relief to be rid of it. It wasn't as if there was another empty vessel for her to transfer to either. She would be at the back of the line behind *Patience*, *Farsight* and possibly *Unicorn* if she couldn't be repaired, for all she was technically a Royal.

Farsight had been quiet through the conversation and Maia wondered if she was still dozing. She had been through even more trauma than *Patience*, though Durus, her Captain, had survived. Maia was grateful to whichever God had been his protector, as she had fond memories of him from when he had been *Blossom*'s second-in-command. She Sent to *Blossom* to find out. If anyone knew, it would be her old mentor.

<Yes, she's recovering,> the Ship confirmed. <My bet is that they'll try to match you all with inanimates. It's not as good as having your own purpose-built vessel, but you can bend the wood to your will and at least be functional again. I daresay the crews will be happy enough to have your Potentia on their side.>

<I suppose so. But what can we do now? I only had the one torpedo, so we're helpless against Fae magic. Pendragon needs to challenge Marcus directly and expose the fake Excalibur. Surely that means going on land?>

Blossom sighed down the link.

<Yes, I suppose it does. He won't be without resources, though. Your Master Mage has a lot of contacts and he's been busy.>

<What do you know?> Maia asked her, curiously. The old Ship was keeping something back. What had Heron told her? She'd not seen Raven since she woke and he hadn't been at the ceremony. <Where is Raven, anyway?>

<Sorting things out ashore.>

<And?>

<And, we'll all have to wait to see what the Admiral decides, based on the information he receives.>

Maia resisted the urge to grumble at all the secrecy. She was tempted to contact the ancient Mage and demand to know what was going on, but that had been a less than successful strategy lately. She would be told of her fate when it was deemed necessary. It was easier to let her thoughts drift, anchored by the remains of her vessel and, far below that, the unceasing swell of the ocean as it rocked her to sleep.

Her rest didn't last as long as she might have hoped. Another order from Leo prodded her to wakefulness, so she was forced to gather herself together and pay attention once more. The first thing she noticed was his excitement. She focused on his face as he took up position beside her.

<You look happy.>

Her Captain gave her a knowing smile. <Oh yes. There have been developments.>

This piqued her interest.

<Please tell me Marcus choked on a fish bone.>

<Alas, no. If only! No, this is about us.>

Maia frowned. He was being as annoying as a certain Master Mage and she didn't like it.

<You woke me up, so you can tell me.>

<Fancy a new vessel?>

Now this was good news. In her current state, she'd have settled for a merchantman. Anything to get off the *Imperatrix*'s deck and back to independence.

<Let me see…that's a yes.> Maia searched her surroundings, wondering which of the two inanimates bobbing nearby would be the one for her.

<Don't bother looking here,> Leo told her with suppressed glee. <It's not one of these.>

<It isn't?>

<No. The largest vessel is to be given to *Farsight*, as she has seniority. *Patience* will have the smaller one.>

Maia ran an eye over first one inanimate, then the other. They weren't bad for their type – smaller patrol vessels that generally operated not too far offshore looking for smugglers and other ne'er-do-wells. They weren't of the same class as the Ships' former vessels of course, but, like her, she suspected that both of her sisters would be glad to have their own space again. Whatever names these possessed would be superseded by the Ships' own.

<So, where's mine then?> she demanded.

<We'll have to travel to it,> Leo told her. <It's a few miles away.>

<Along the coast? Why can't it come to me here?>

Leo's smile grew wider, but she could tell he wouldn't give her a straight answer and was enjoying knowing something she didn't.

<I bet Raven will tell me,> she reproached him.

<Shall we make a wager on that?>

Now she was really cross. Had Ship-baiting become a sport while she was out?

<Fine. Whatever you say, O mighty one. Captains order, Ships obey!>

She deliberately distanced herself from the link as a reproach. He pushed his way straight back into it.

<Seriously, I can't tell you anything else, because I don't know. It sounds strange to me too, though as Heron and Robin are involved it's probably something experimental. We're to set off tonight. You'll be transferred to *Leopard*, who'll take us up the coast with the rest of the Fleet. After that, we'll have to go overland.>

<So, we're all going to where – the Dee estuary?>

<Yes. The Fleet will receive a consignment of the new anti-Fae weapons and wait for more information. There's a feeling that the main force will be crossing shortly, so we need to be prepared.>

They certainly did. The new torpedo device was the only thing that had saved the Fleet from *Regina*'s murderous attack. Nobody had any doubt that she would have finished the rest of them off as soon as she'd been able.

<Are there any thoughts as to why our shot didn't penetrate their shields?>

Leo shrugged.

<No idea. It's clear that they've developed some kind of defence, but what it consists of nobody knows yet. I'm sure our people are working on it.>

The pace of events was starting to pick up again and Maia felt a qualm of apprehension.

<We'll meet Raven as soon as we disembark,> Leo said quickly, sensing her unease.

Well, that was one good thing. She was missing the ancient Mage's presence, especially in her weakened state. The sooner they were back together, the happier she would be.

<What of Pendragon?>

<He's staying here, aboard *Imperatrix*. We can't risk him going ashore until we know more about the current situation. Our

way leads us into possible danger, as there's a whole legion stationed at Deva which isn't far away. We're safer out here.>

That was true. Most of the Ships that had previously supported Marcus had stayed with them and declared allegiance to Pendragon. A couple had slipped away, including the *Justicia*. Maia speculated that they'd decided to take a long sea voyage for the good of their health. Some Captains were still hedging their bets.

<Right then. When do we board *Leopard*?>

<When the word is given. We'll be taking a few of our surviving crew as well, but I'm only taking volunteers. We shouldn't need more than half a dozen, plus marines. Any others will be supplied later.>

<But I'll need experienced seamen, surely?>

Leo threw up his hands.

<Who knows? This is all top secret and now you know as much as me. I guess we'll have to find out what's going on together.>

"Admiral on deck!"

They both straightened to attention as the familiar figure of Pendragon emerged. He made his way over to them immediately, returning their salutes. Maia was glad to see that he had another earring to replace the one that was taken from him. Unofficial King or no, Admiral Pendragon was back in charge.

"Captain. I take it you've brought *Tempest* up to speed with recent developments?"

"I have, sir."

"Excellent."

Though he still had the same commanding energy he always had, Maia thought Pendragon had aged over the past months. There was a haunted look in his eyes that hadn't been there before. The loss of his beloved *Augusta* had hit him hard, and his son's treachery doubly so.

"We await your orders," Leo answered.

Pendragon nodded. "I don't have to tell you that all communications will be restricted, even with your sisters, *Tempest*. You will be exposed to highly sensitive information and we can't risk it leaking."

"I understand, sir."

His eyes softened as he gazed at her. "You'll have the chance to serve your people and make us all proud. This is truly an age of wonders."

She was about to ask what he meant, when suddenly the link opened and a voice she didn't think she would hear again broke in. Pendragon and Leo stiffened as the message channelled through their earrings.

<This is Lucius Albanus Dio. I appeal to you as a father. Can anyone give me news of my son, Lucius Albanus Sabrinus?>

Silent outrage filled the link. Leo swallowed and looked to Pendragon, who listened, stony-faced. Maia froze, wondering who would answer. Technically Pendragon could reply directly, but she had the feeling he wouldn't and she was right.

Pendragon cleared his throat.

"*Tempest*, tell him what happened. Do not spare the details."

If she'd needed to, she would have taken a deep breath. The looks of controlled anguish on her officers' faces were almost too much to bear. She took a second to compose her thoughts, picturing the imposing, square-jawed man she'd met an age ago at the Academy. He'd seemed all kindness then as he tried to win her over to his side, giving her presents and fine promises as he was planning the murder of his King. Should he be treated as a grieving father, or as an enemy who hadn't deserved the fine son the Fates had granted him? It was as if he'd thrown the gift back at the Goddesses' feet. She took refuge in formality.

<This is His Majesty's Ship *Tempest*. I am authorised to tell you that my second-in-command, Lucius Albanus Sabrinus was killed during the battle by a cannonball fired from the *Regina*. His body was destroyed by the impact.>

The horrific vision flashed across her mind before she could stop it, but it just strengthened her resolve. Pendragon had been clear in his instructions.

<He was a fine Captain in the making, and his loss is felt keenly by those who knew and loved him. *Tempest* out.>

She slammed the link shut, knowing that her utter contempt for the man would have underlined every word. She neither knew nor cared whether he would grieve for Sabrinus as a son, or simply the fact that his male line had ended. Albanus had already carved out his place in Tartarus with the rest of the damned.

The three of them stood in silence for a few minutes, surrounded by the noise of the *Imperatrix*'s crew at work and a few crying gulls. Across the deck, *Imperatrix* and *Patience* looked stricken, remembering the young man who had given all he had in the line of duty.

At last, Pendragon spoke. "Thank you, *Tempest*."

He blinked the moisture from his eyes before turning and going below.

"Gods above," Leo muttered. "Well done. Especially the last bit."

"You don't think it was too much?"

He met her eyes. "Definitely not. The swine deserved it. I hope he's suffering, though I wish things were different."

He glanced towards the ladder. "I'll go and see if the Admiral has his orders ready."

Or wanted to talk. Across the deck, *Imperatrix*, who had heard him, nodded in agreement.

<He shouldn't be alone.>

<Our hostess agrees,> Maia Sent privately.

Leo set off and Maia became aware of the murmurings over the link.

<I can't believe he had the nerve!> *Leopard* had her claws out.

<Him? He's without shame!> *Diadem* said. <You wouldn't have thought they were of the same blood.>

<No, you wouldn't,> Maia replied. She felt wearied by it all. <I will miss Sabrinus very much.>

There would be extra prayers tonight on Sabrinus's behalf, though she hoped he was already in the Elysian Fields, the cares of this world forgotten.

She shook herself out of her sadness. Tonight, she would board *Leopard* ready to head off into the unknown and whatever was planned for her.

Let Clotho draw the thread as she would. Maia would be ready.

II

It was finally the end of the working day and the evening service was finished. Several acolytes were busy rounding up the last petitioners with a promise that yes, Jupiter would hear their pleas and respond in his own time but the temple was closing and they had to leave.

High Priest Aquila, facing the enormous statue of the King of Olympus, listened to the hubbub recede behind him and sighed to himself. Public attendance had dropped off lately, what with people attending the games for days on end, but there had still been a lot to do especially as many of his Priests had been arrested for speaking out against the new King. Aquila had kept his own counsel, but he knew his God. Jupiter wasn't happy with the state of Britannia.

After Marcus had been seen to pull out the Sword by most of Londin, Aquila had kept his distance. He had continued his duties at the Temple as if nothing had changed, but he knew that trouble was brewing. It was not only in the wind. The entrails of the last bull he had sacrificed had been so corrupted that they'd had to fumigate the premises. He supposed that Marcus knew of the God's displeasure, but so far nothing had been said. The network of spies and Government Agents had to have been disrupted by Favonius's hasty departure and it was rumoured that many departmental employees had decamped with their Spymaster or gone to ground.

It was only a matter of time before something unpleasant kicked off. He'd made representation to the new authorities about the incarcerated Priests, but was none the wiser as to their fates. They weren't in the main prisons – he had reliable spies of his own – so they had to be somewhere unofficial, or simply dead.

He had it on good authority that Bullfinch, the former Chief Mage, had been murdered, though by what means he didn't know. It wouldn't have been easy to kill a practitioner of his Potentia, but Marcus, or more probably those who were controlling him, had managed it somehow. Aquila had always suspected that the Prince was weak and vain, and here was the proof. If he hadn't met Marcus recently he would have suspected a changeling substitution, but it had simply been the man's weak and selfish nature that had led to his corruption.

He lifted his head and regarded the looming figure. Gold and ivory gleamed in the light of the lamps, cunningly wrought to represent the King of the Gods in the way of the ancients. The deity could appear as he pleased, whether as an eagle such as the one seated on the arm of the throne, an old man, a mighty bull or a shower of golden rain. Jupiter, Jove or Zeus, was endlessly inventive it seemed, though lately his favourite method had been to manifest through his servants, much to their discomfort.

Sometimes Aquila wished that he could change his shape at will, preferably to something a lot lighter, but he could never get around to denying himself the pleasure of good food and wine. It made up for the other duties he had been blessed (or cursed) with.

At that, his thought turned to the evening meal. He was mostly confining himself to temple grounds at the moment, but he had to admit that he missed the hospitality of his friends and the culinary delights that had always been on offer. He was just contemplating roast sucking pig in a rich sauce, when raised voices and the tramp of hobnailed boots on the marble floor caught his attention.

"I must protest! His Eminence has only just finished evening service…"

"Oh good. He won't mind coming with us then."

Aquila turned to see a detachment of legionaries marching towards him, four abreast, pushing past the startled acolytes. He recognised their leader immediately. There were some very nasty rumours going around about Marcus's chief enforcer, one being that he had killed Senator Rufus in cold blood. He decided to take the offensive.

"Greetings, Naevius Sutorius Macro! Welcome to the Temple of the God. I'm afraid that the evening service has finished, but if you want to make your own private petition, I'm sure it can be arranged."

Macro raised his hand, stopping the soldiers just short of the steps to the sacred altar. His face twisted into a smirk as he ran his eyes dismissively over both God and Priest.

"You mistake my purpose. You are summoned to the Palace, by order of the King."

So, no roast sucking pig for him tonight. Aquila sent up a silent prayer.

Lord, use my eyes and ears to witness this disrespect in your house.

Outwardly, he remained calm, motioning the attendants to leave.

"Very well. I will need my cloak, as the evening is chilly."

Even as he spoke, Macro was already issuing orders.

"Take him!"

The outer men of the front rank peeled off, jogging up the steps to seize an arm each. Aquila was dragged down the steps.

"You dare arrest me here, in the sight of Heaven?"

Macro grinned widely, thrusting his face into the angry Priest's.

"I dare. Your Gods have little power in these lands now. Their time is up, and unless you do as you're told, so is yours."

He cast a look of contempt at the statue. "There'll be some rich pickings here for sure, lads. We'll be back!"

Macro spat on the floor to emphasise his words, then Aquila was hauled out of the Temple and into a waiting carriage. It creaked alarmingly on its springs as it took his weight and he found himself wedged in beside his captors. A couple of thumps on the carriage roof and they were off, rattling over the paving stones towards the Royal Palace. Aquila kept his mouth shut, taking in the facts that the blinds were down and the streets had quietened. It appeared to be a non-military vehicle as well, so Marcus wasn't as confident as his henchman that there wouldn't be trouble if the population knew what was happening.

19

It was a short ride to the Palace, and all too soon the sounds of the horses' hooves echoed as they entered the huge gateway that led into the grounds. Instead of going up to the front steps however, the carriage turned down the side of the building towards what Aquila knew to be the rear, where he could be bundled in with the minimum of fuss.

Motion stopped and the door was opened. Aquila blinked at the sudden light.

"Get that out of my face!" Macro snarled and the lamp was hastily withdrawn. He exited and a hurried conversation ensued, before Macro appeared once more.

"Out!"

Puffing a little, Aquila heaved himself out and down the steps. Given the choice, he preferred a closed litter to travel in, not that he went far these days. They were easier to get out of than narrow doors. Grasping hands reached for him as soon as he emerged, all the better to hustle him inside.

It had to be nearly ten o'clock now and dusk had fallen. The shadowed doorway was lit with Mage lights and Aquila tried not to think of a mouth gaping wide to swallow him. He could only hope that his Priests had kept their wits about them and followed the instructions he'd left, just in case this happened. There were people who needed to know and he'd made preparations.

Several corridors later, Aquila was ushered not into a dungeon, but the throne room itself. It was unchanged from the last time he'd seen it, with the familiar inlaid marble floor and frescoed walls, though instead of the welcoming face of young Artorius he was greeted by the stony expression of his successor as he sat on the throne, a golden goblet in his hand. He was probably trying to look regal, Aquila thought, but Marcus couldn't hide the glee in his eyes as the Priest was thrust forward.

The legionaries turned and marched away to line the walls, leaving Aquila standing alone at the foot of the steps. Behind the daïs, the dragon banner of the Pendragons hung in solitary splendour, bereft of its Imperial eagle companion. Aquila wondered whether Marcus had had it burned.

"Well, Aquila, are you not going to bow before your King?"

The Priest inclined his head.

"Your Majesty."

He had no compunction in using the empty title. Anyone with a brain doubted what their eyes had seen outside the Basilica that day.

His words seemed to mollify the young man. Marcus's stiff posture relaxed a little and he smiled.

"Please forgive the abruptness of my summons at this late hour. I do hope Macro wasn't too demanding?"

Aquila returned the smile. "He was his usual charming self."

Marcus let out a bark of laughter. "That's one word for it. Now, you must be wondering why I wanted to see you."

Not at all, you murderous, unfilial creature. May the Gods strike you dead!

"It must be a matter of great import, Majesty. How may I assist you?"

Suddenly, Marcus was all geniality. He gestured and a stool was brought forward for Aquila to seat himself, though the Priest waved away the proffered wine. He wouldn't be eating or drinking anything here.

"I merely wanted to assure myself of your support, especially as I can't rely on my own family these days. My mother is refusing to speak to me and my father…well, you know how it is. My poor cousin Julia is heaven-knows-where, probably kept against her will, so I need your help in getting her back. Also, any information you might have about my father's movements."

Marcus's eyes narrowed.

"I know you have an extensive network of Priests and spies all over Britannia. They work for me now. Do you understand?"

Aquila beamed at him. "Naturally, Your Majesty. I will offer any help I can."

Marcus's smile faded. "You most certainly will. Starting now. What do you know?"

Aquila thought fast. He spread his arms in mock surrender.

"Only that your father is far away at sea. You have the loyalty of the people of Londin, due to Excalibur."

He gestured at Marcus's hip, where the jewelled hilt winked in the lamplight. "As to the Princess Julia, I fear I know no more than you do. There has been no news of her whereabouts since she was falsely reported sunk aboard the *Tempest* – a rumour which I am delighted to hear was totally unfounded."

Marcus chewed his lip. "I would hate to have to resort to more, *extreme* methods of questioning. Are you sure you know nothing?"

Now was the time to play his trump card. Aquila had already detected the subtle weaving of spell work creeping into the room like a noxious gas. It was this very reason that he had ordered Raven to tell him nothing that might be incriminating. He hauled himself to his feet and raised his right hand to the heavens.

"I do solemnly swear and aver that I have no information as to the whereabouts of the Princess Julia, or the intentions of Prince Cei. Jupiter, Best and Greatest, witness my words."

It was the undeniable truth. Marcus glanced briefly to the side, out of Aquila's view, then his eyes flicked back to the High Priest.

"Very well. If you hear anything at all you will tell me, on pain of punishment."

Aquila drew on all his acting skills, widening his eyes and looking aggrieved.

"Of course, Sire! I serve the interests of the people of Britannia, after all!"

For a second, he thought he'd gone too far, but Marcus merely nodded.

"As do we all. You may go. Oh, and I will be stationing a detachment of the Royal Guard at the temple, in case of any unrest."

Aquila bowed.

"Macro! Send Lord Aquila back to the temple. Provide an escort."

"Immediately, Sire!"

Macro saluted, arm across breast, then Aquila found himself surrounded once more. This time he didn't wait to be dragged, but stepped out as fast as he could for a man of his size, forcing the legionaries to hurry after him.

The carriage was waiting, and he clambered in with a sense of relief. He had been able to buy himself some time, but for how much longer he didn't know. As to what happened next, it was surely out of his hands. The threats had been overt and Aquila was under no illusion that Marcus wouldn't replace him in a heartbeat if he thought he could get away with it.

Judging from Macro's attitude, that moment would be coming very soon.

*

Marcus chewed on his lip, watching the High Priest's hasty exit. He had intended to imprison the old fraud immediately, but Kite had advised against it. Still, it rankled to see the chief link to the Olympians escape unscathed because he didn't have enough evidence to convict the man. Yet.

He took a swig of the wine. It was interesting that Aquila had refused to join him, which told Marcus exactly whose side he was on.

The door at the far end of the throne room opened and the Major-Domo took up his position.

"His Eminence, the Prime Mage!"

Kite swept in, boots ringing on the marble, stopping exactly five paces from the throne. Marcus regarded him with an interested eye. Had the man added extra charms since last time? There was certainly less of his face showing under more of those painted scrawls. He looked like something one of the old Emperors would have come across, back when Britannia was ruled by druids. Even though he knew Kite was loyal, Marcus couldn't shake a sense of uneasiness when he was in his presence, as if the man brought with him his own following of unseen spirits. He straightened up in his seat and fixed the Mage with what he fancied was an imperious eye.

"Well?"

Kite bowed. "Majesty. Aquila was telling the truth, so far as it went. If there had been any prevarication, the spell would have reacted instantly."

Marcus scowled. "It doesn't mean he isn't hiding something else."

"True," Kite agreed, "but we would have had to ask him more specific questions to find that out."

Was Kite meaning that they had missed their chance? Marcus frowned.

"Such as?" His tone was sharp, a reminder of who ruled here.

"Possibly whether he had been in communication with your enemies."

Marcus glared at him. "Too late now. Watch him. If he's passing messages, make sure they're intercepted."

"I fear the Priests have their own network, Sire."

Marcus scowled. He didn't know how it worked, and that was a liability.

"So? Get one of those idiots we locked up and force them to listen in, unless you've disposed of them all?"

"Not all, Sire."

"Good! Then get on with it! Keep me informed."

He stood up, stretching his back. Gods below, who would have thought that the throne would be so uncomfortable? It was a damned pain that it was a roughly carved stone bench instead of a more civilised wooden chair. Supposedly it was made from the sacred stone that had held the first Artorius's sword, but Marcus thought that was a load of rank superstition. Magic had its place, but the new scientific methods were far more interesting. When all this was resolved, he would be making some changes that his allies weren't aware of. If they thought they could rule forever, they were in for a surprise. The new machines were the future and he had already set their wheels in motion.

He gestured for a slave to come and rub his back. Sitting through hours of petitions hadn't improved his mood either. He could almost wish Artorius were still here, to shoulder the tiresome burden.

"Just one more thing, if I may, Sire," Kite said smoothly. "I have been told that your bride is even now approaching accompanied by an escort. She should arrive in a few days, then the marriage can take place within the month."

Marcus nodded absently, his mind already on his evening meal and the promised entertainment. So, he'd be married. It would further cement his grip on the Kingdom, and that was all that mattered. He would deal with the rest later.

"Excellent. See to it that all is prepared."

Now he was king someone else could sort out the details. As to whether his bride was even human anymore, it was of no consequence. It was the dowry of support and alliance she brought with her that was the main thing, and they all knew it. As to Albanus, he'd been bought so easily with the promise of wealth and position, more than willing to sacrifice his daughter and unaware that Marcus had never had any intention of marrying the girl. She'd be a Ship forever and do as she was told. If Albanus gave him any trouble, he would disposed of too. There were plenty ready to take his place.

He'd deal with more pressing matters first before worrying about the Britannic Royal Navy. His father could keep his stupid Ships, for all they mattered now.

The land took priority, and it would soon be his completely.

*

It was the hour before dusk and time to go. Maia and Patience enjoyed a quick hug, the sailors nearby marvelling at the pair of stately Shipbodies embracing like the human women they had once been.

"Look after yourself," Maia told her friend. For a short time, it had been like being back with Briseis again, free of duties and not separated by distance. She hadn't liked to admit to herself that she'd felt her absence after the months together at the Academy.

Patience smiled. "You too. I haven't a clue why you're going with *Leopard* and not getting a new vessel, but I suppose you'll soon find out."

"How strange for you, going on to an inanimate," Maia said. They both glanced over to where the two nominated vessels rode at anchor.

"It'll be fine. Sandpiper's going to help me bond, though I've been told that there will have to be some forcing to create channels for Potentia as they're not woven into the fabric. The existing crew are happy to have the protection and some of my own people will be there as well."

"I've got some of mine too," Maia agreed, "but it's hard when you look for familiar faces and they're gone."

"Yes, but they'll be safe with the Gods now, even if we couldn't give all of them a proper burial." She smiled. "Imagine that lot queueing up on the banks of the Styx!"

"They'll be telling Charon how to row," Maia giggled. She adopted a gruff tone. "Here, matey, you're doing it all wrong. Give us the oars! Right lads, pull away!"

There were quiet guffaws from some of the sailors within earshot. Maia raised her voice.

"Isn't that right?"

"Too right, ma'am. Knowing some of 'em, they'll be across the river in double time and give the Ferryman a day off!" It was Hyacinthus. The old sailor was grinning at his mates. "Caphisus'll be beating the stroke and Mr Sabrinus'll giving 'em what for if they slack."

It was a comforting thought.

"I see you're transferring with me, Hyacinthus."

"I am, ma'am. They couldn't stop me!"

"We've come a long way from that night in Portus, haven't we?"

"Oh aye. You were such a skinny slip of a girl. Who'd ave thought we'd be 'ere now, eh?'"

"I always wondered if you knew it was me."

He tapped the side of his nose. "I knew, but I didn't tell."

Patience looked puzzled, then her face cleared. "Well, fancy that. It's good to have friends."

Amphicles approached and waited for her attention.

"All's ready for you, ma'am. We're going to hoist you over, planks and all. The Captain and I will be following."

Maia thanked him and he hurried off to supervise the loading. She turned to her fellow Ship.

"Now, you look after Drustan. He's a very promising young man."

"Don't worry! Fabillus is looking forward to working with him, now your second is out of action."

The young officer had been promoted to *Patience*'s acting second-in-command. It wasn't dead man's shoes but a replacement for Tegwyn, who had been injured by flying shards and was laid up in the Adept's quarters. When he recovered, Fabillus would recommend that the latter be made Captain. There had been a lot of rearranging of ranks among the fleet.

"May Fortuna smile on you!" she told *Patience*.

"And I hope she keeps a special watch on you too," her friend replied.

Maia had the feeling they'd both need as much luck as the Goddess could dispense. She permitted the fastening of ropes and ties, trying to assist the crewmen to secure her in a makeshift cradle ready for transport. Finally, they were done. Maia felt like a joint trussed up for roasting but did her best to hide her discomfort, especially as Pendragon and her Captain were approaching. *Imperatrix* glided over, her face set in a gracious smile. Even though Maia knew that the older Royal would be delighted that she now carried the King and had seniority, Maia had to admit that she had been a considerate hostess.

"May the Gods smile on you, *Tempest*," *Imperatrix* said.

"And upon you, *Imperatrix*," she replied. "Thank you for your kindness to my crew and myself."

The Ship dipped her head in acknowledgment, then made way for Pendragon. She saluted, remembering with amusement when it hadn't been second nature to her. He returned it and spoke for the benefit of all.

"Farewell, *Tempest*! May the Gods smooth your path and give you strength to vanquish our enemies! You have my blessing."

His dark eyes met hers and she glimpsed the warmth in them.

"Thank you, Your Majesty," she answered, then raising her voice, "Gods save Britannia!"

The response was deafening, ringing across the sea and Maia felt a surge of pride. *Imperatrix*'s boat waited alongside to take them all across and Maia braced herself for the command.

A nod from Pendragon, and she felt the ropes take the weight of her Shipbody as the deck fell away beneath her. Guiding hands manoeuvred her towards the rail, ensuring that she wouldn't swing and damage the vessel, then she was free and dangling over the edge. She inched her way down the *Imperatrix*'s flanks, seeing faces pressed up against portholes and open hatches as the gunners watched her go. More hands helped her find a place in the boat and deftly secured her in place, then it was up to *Imperatrix* to send her over to the *Leopard*, where she would be winched straight over to the smaller Ship's deck. The remainder of her crew followed, settling themselves in the boat for the short trip.

On arrival, the process was reversed and they were greeted by the Ship herself, along with her Captain, Boduogenus. He was a man of middle years with an excellent reputation. To be honest, she'd thought she might have ended up with him herself, but there was clearly a strong attachment between him and his Ship and the Navy didn't like to separate a winning team without good reason.

She recognised him immediately. Maia was aware that *Leopard* was saying something and she was replying, but the rest of her was busy making connections. She'd seen this man before, when they had both been rescuing sailors from beneath the waves after the battle. So, he was some kind of sea-deity as well as being a Captain? Another of the Navy's secrets. She smiled and held her tongue, but the reason that she'd been assigned to this Ship was becoming more and more apparent. He gave her a knowing smile in return, acknowledging her realisation.

"*Tempest*, welcome! Please accept my sympathies for the loss of your crew."

"Thank you, Captain. I'm just glad that the majority survived."

It was a comfort that some of her men were accompanying her on her journey, Hyacinthus and Big Ajax among them, together with Osric and his men. To her surprise, Monkey had been included, though a tearful Sprout had been left on board the *Imperatrix*, being deemed too young. They stood to one side with her after saluting the *Leopard*, whilst Leo and Boduogenus went below to continue their conversation.

It was harder to judge expression on the feline's face, but from the sideways glances the Ship was giving her, Maia had the feeling that the *Leopard* knew all about the Potentia of her unusual Captain. It was something that could never be spoken of, even Ship to Ship, so she settled for giving her sister a nod. *Leopard* blinked slowly, reassured.

<Pendragon to *Tempest*. I trust everything is to your satisfaction?>

<Transfer achieved, sir.>

This time, they could use the regular Ship link. She hadn't enquired where he'd obtained his new earring from and hadn't liked to ask anyone else. Captain's earrings were taken from the wood of their Ship, forming the bond, but there seemed to be a different protocol for the higher echelons of the Navy. However he'd come by it, she was glad.

<*Leopard* will brief you as to the mission. Take care, and I hope to see you again before too long, in happier circumstances.>

What was he hiding? At least he seemed hopeful that they would meet again soon.

<Indeed, sir. I look forward to it.>

He slipped gently out of the link and she was left with the warmth of his feelings for her. He, like Plinius, had become a father figure. She bit her lip at the sudden stab of pain. Captain Plinius deserved to be remembered with as much loving kindness as he had always showed her. From never knowing a father she'd been lucky to have found two, even if one was now gone.

She thrust the sadness away and turned to the matters at hand.

"*Leopard*, thank you for taking me aboard. The King says that you'll brief me."

The big cat's eyes gleamed like emeralds. "I certainly will, sister. I hope you're ready for an adventure!"

"What, another one?"

The Ship's mouth parted slightly in the approximation of a smile, showing white fangs.

"Well, we can't have you being bored. Let's get you settled, then we'll have a nice long chat in private."

Her eyes became distant as she checked in with her Captain. Apparently satisfied, she settled herself in position. Maia thought that she looked like some strange Goddess with her woman's body, cat's head and black-spotted arms and paws. She didn't seem to have a *tutela*, unlike Maia's tiny thundercloud, which was spinning at her left shoulder as if watching proceedings. Maybe her whole body stood in lieu of it? From what she'd heard, *Dragon* and *Gryphon* didn't have one either.

"Our orders are to follow the coast and anchor off the mouth of the Dee," *Leopard* informed her. "Raven will meet us there and I'll be picking up a consignment of those new weapons you had. You know, the ones that can get through the Fae defences."

She tactfully didn't mention the fate of the *Regina*, but the implication was there. Maia had the feeling that the Ship was itching to try one out for herself, though naturally not on her sister Ships. The Fae vessels would make good targets.

"I still don't see why I'm coming with you," she said.

Leopard huffed, a strangely primitive sound and Maia wondered where she was from originally. Perhaps she'd grown up seeing leopards in the flesh, in which case she was from Africa or Hind.

"You're not staying aboard me," the Ship told her. "You're going on land. Raven will explain further when we meet him. He's coming with the weapons."

Raven? It had been a while since they communicated and she'd rightly assumed that he was busy, though she'd suspected she'd see him again before too long. He'd hinted as much the last time she'd seen him.

"I can't see what use I'll be on land."

Leopard closed her eyes briefly and Maia got a sense of amusement from the feline.

"Who knows what that old terror's got up his sleeve? I can guarantee it'll be interesting. Where he goes, trouble follows! I suggest you take it easy and let me do all the work until we get to the estuary in a few hours. At least we have a fair wind. I'm just waiting for a couple more passengers, then we'll be off. The sooner we arrive the better it will be, so pray to Zephyrus to get us there faster!"

And not only Zephyrus, Maia thought. The wind had already swung in their favour, impeding any that might seek to stop them. Unfortunately, they weren't the only ones who would benefit from a west wind.

III

It was mid-morning and Julia was sick of walking.

It was obvious to her after the first few miles that the popular view of Mages was a load of absolute rubbish. She'd envisioned whizzing through magical portals or speeding above the countryside on a pegasus, not this incessant trudging along rough lanes that were barely more than sheep tracks.

Their guide strode on ahead, occasionally pausing as if listening for something, but Julia suspected it was really so she could catch up. Milo was doing the best he could to cheer her, though there was only so much he could do to break the journey. She'd already insisted that he stop calling her Highness in case he inadvertently let her status slip and, to be honest, she quite liked being treated as nobody special for the first time in her life. Apart from having to walk, that was.

They were deliberately avoiding inhabited areas and this made the going harder. Intermittent showers of rain had already started to penetrate her clothing and she prayed for some sunshine to warm her up a bit.

After several hours, Emrys called a halt in the shelter of a small copse of trees to rest and eat, though she could tell that he was impatient to be off again.

"Do you know where we're going?" she muttered to Milo.

"Not a clue," he said cheerfully. "Just enjoy the journey."

"Can you find out how long we'll be?"

He laughed. "I'm afraid to ask."

So that was that. One thing was apparent. They were moving through a flat land with bleak hills to the left and mountains ahead.

"Do you think we'll skirt the Lake Country?" She'd been taught geography by her tutor, so had a rough idea of where they were.

Milo sucked his teeth.

"I don't think so. Let me have a word with him."

Emrys was standing guard at the edge of the copse, the brown of his cloak merging seamlessly into the trunks of the trees. Milo joined him and the two men had a whispered conversation. Julia strained her ears but to her annoyance couldn't make out what they were saying. In the end, she gave up and began munching on the bread, cheese and strips of dried meat in her pack while listening to the drips fall from the leaves above. Everything was soggy, including her.

A thought suddenly popped into her head, like a little ray of cheer. She was a Mage, wasn't she? Surely there must be a spell to keep the rain off, or at least dry her clothes. It was a good bet that Milo would know it. He returned shortly, hunkering down next to her. He did look drier than she was.

"It's not far, but there will be some ascents. He's decided to take us over the tops, rather than on the lower route, as they're less travelled."

That didn't sound good.

"I need you to teach me a warming spell," she said. "If I get soaked through and catch a chill, you might not end up with a princess on your side at all!"

She fixed him with a glare that always worked on the palace servants. He sighed.

"All right! But don't run too much Potentia through it, or we'll have to put out the flames."

Her spirits rose. This sounded promising! It had been ages since she'd been taught anything new. There had never been any time or opportunity lately.

Milo's expression became serious.

"Firstly, still your mind. Drive out any discomfort or worries about our destination. Centre yourself."

Julia calmed her breathing and retreated inwards, as Raven had taught her. It was a bad idea to go into spell working with turbulent thoughts.

"Now, picture something that represents heat and warmth to you – nothing too big and I would recommend against anything with a naked flame."

What would she choose? No fires and definitely not the sun. An image came to her of the little charcoal braziers that were used throughout the palace in winter, gently radiating heat in the corners of the rooms to supplement the underfloor hypocaust heating. Maybe a tiny one to start with? She drew a picture of one in her mind, the coals gently smouldering in their pierced metal box. How many times had she warmed her hands on one?

"What have you picked?"

Milo's voice came from far away as she concentrated on the image.

"A charcoal brazier."

"Good choice. Now imagine you're moving up to it and feeling the warmth spreading outwards from it, drying your clothes."

She did as she was bid, feeling the change almost immediately.

"That's it. Now put the image to the back of your thoughts and hold it there. Open your eyes."

Julia obeyed, to see wisps of steam rising from her sodden cloak. It was working!

"Hold it!" Milo warned her. "Don't lose focus. You have to be able to keep it in mind while carrying on in the real world."

It was like balancing a tray as you walked and holding a conversation at the same time, she decided. Your body adjusted automatically, certain muscles taking the load as the rest of you simply carried on chatting or whatever. That these were magical muscles shouldn't make any difference.

"I think I've got it," she announced, after a few wobbles.

Milo gave her a look of approval.

"Well done, though if you get distracted it will shut down. You'll need more practise in maintaining it for longer periods."

"Like you can."

This time, he laughed, his eyes crinkling at the corners. "I've had a lot of practice! An Agent's life involves being out in all weathers, so I mastered it pretty sharpish."

Emrys's deep voice cut in, sounding as though he was next to them instead of several feet away.

"The lesson is finished?"

Julia, caught by surprise, had to grab at her spell before it dissipated.

"Yes," Milo answered.

"Right then. Let's get moving. I want to reach our destination by nightfall."

So, they weren't going too far after all. Was it too much to hope that there'd be a hot bath and a meal waiting for them?

Milo hefted his bundle on to his back, but not before she had caught sight of a rusty object protruding from the bottom of it. What was he doing carrying around an old piece of metal?

"What's that sticking out of your pack?"

He glanced at her, then swung his load around to inspect it.

"Oh, just something I picked up."

The two of them stared at it for a while, before he tucked it back inside his blanket. Julia shrugged and got to her feet.

"Off we go," she said. "Back on our mysterious journey."

Milo grunted. "It's all good fun, isn't it?"

Their way led them steadily upwards. The rain had stopped and there was a fresh breeze blowing from the south promising warmer days to come as spring turned into summer. They'd have more light day by day, but whether that was a good thing or not, Julia didn't know. It was easier to go about secret business hidden by darkness and there was more chance of meeting travellers on the road at this time of year.

"Watch where you put your feet," Milo told her as they reached the moorland path. "You don't want to turn your ankle on a stone."

They had to go single file now as the track wound its way between swathes of heather, the new green leaves showing above last year's old growth. The breeze blew tendrils of hair loose to tickle her face, and she wished she'd been able to cut it short in reality instead of maintaining the illusion. It was too warm to keep her hood up now the rain had abated. She took the time to admire the view of the mountains, the highest she'd seen though she knew that the ones further north were even higher. Her spirits lifted as they went, as if they were striding across the top of the world. Below them were valleys dotted with sheep and the odd farmhouse or small settlement with smoke curling up from stone chimneys. Overhead, birds sang, their song rising and falling. She could just make out tiny dots in the sky.

"What are they?"

"Skylarks," Milo said, shading his face with his hand as he followed her gaze. "They nest on the ground at this time of year."

"They sound so free."

"I've always liked them," he admitted. "The curlews too. I don't suppose you've ever had much chance to go birdwatching?"

"I've not seen the ones around here," she said. "It's mostly been garden birds, water fowl and the hawks in the mews."

"And owls?" he asked over his shoulder.

She rolled her eyes at him.

"Very funny."

It wasn't long before the path began to descend from the high places, dropping down into a wooded area beside a stream, its cheerful babble accompanying them as they went. Julia was glad that the track had levelled off now and widened, even if it meant that it was more travelled. Sure enough, they began to pass people on the way, getting some curious looks and greetings though everyone seemed too preoccupied to stop.

"Is it me, or do they seem worried?" Milo asked Emrys.

"Something's up, all right," Emrys, replied, his face darkening.

At last, an old man carrying a load of firewood stopped them.

"Good day to you, friends! Have you come from the north?" He seemed eager for news.

"We have," Milo replied.

"Have you heard the rumours? Villages along the coast have been attacked, and it isn't Northmen."

Milo shook his head.

"Our Priest got word from one of his friends." The villager lowered his voice. "Sounds like Fae."

Emrys and Milo exchanged glances. It had only been a matter of time before the enemy acted.

"There was nothing happening at Luguvallium," Emrys replied. "We're on our way south, but if it's true you must take precautions. Gather the people and get your hands on as much iron as you can. Petition your local deities too. You might have to move quickly."

The authority in his voice was unmistakeable and the man nodded at every point.

"Aye. We have long memories around here. We're hoping the King will bring Excalibur and lead the legions himself," the man added, hopefully.

"Don't count on it," Milo said. He refused to give them false hope. "Marcus is a usurper and the sword's fake. You must look after each other."

Emrys shot him a piercing look and the villager's face paled. "You're sure?"

"Oh, I'm sure all right. It's all a Fae glamour. The Sword's still stuck in the Londin Basilica and Marcus is in league with the enemy."

So much for secrecy. The man regarded them warily, then he relaxed.

"You must have been sent from the Gods to warn us." His eye lingered on Emrys, as if sensing that the man was more than he seemed. "Thank you, friends. All respect to the Gods! In truth, I don't know what the world's coming to. First the King dies, then this! Well, I wish you good fortune in your travels. Take care, son."

He gave Julia a sad smile and she nodded.

"May the Gods smile on you too," Milo said. "Who are the main ones around here?"

"We Carvetti people pray to Lug and Cocidius Silvanus. Also, the Huntress."

"Then we'll petition them too."

They parted company, the old man grumbling quietly to himself as he hurried onwards to his village.

"Cocidius of the Woods," Emrys mused. "It makes sense for the Deer People to favour him."

"I've not heard of him, only of the one allied to Mars that they worship in the army," Milo said.

"He's been blended with an old woodland God, the oldest of the Britannic deities. That one has many names." Julia thought that the Mage knew more than he was saying. "You've warned them and that will have to suffice. We leave the path here, as it goes into the village and we don't want that. We'll be cutting across fields from now on."

True to his word, he led them off at a tangent. Julia followed the men as they pushed through hedges and scrambled over ditches, an occasional curse coming from Milo as his pack snagged on grasping twigs. She was just about to demand a halt, when they emerged into a level space, a natural bowl surrounded and enclosed by guardian hills. At the centre was a ring of irregularly shaped stones, some small, some larger, all ancient and weathered by the centuries. As they drew nearer, she felt a tingling in the air and a strong aura of active Potentia.

"Now I see," Milo muttered. "Very clever."

Julia walked over to the nearest stone, reaching out to touch the roughened, lichen-spotted surface.

Milo moved close to her.

"Can you feel it?" he asked.

"It's remarkable," she replied, running her fingers over a crack. "How old are they?"

"That answer's lost to us," Milo said. "Some say these circles were made long before people even knew how to smelt metal. They built using the bones of the land and marked their sacred places with these. You've heard of the Great Stones? These are a much smaller version. I've seen others, dotted all over the country."

"It's old magic," she said.

"Ancient indeed, but not as old as the forest magic of the Heart of Albion. This was made by human hands."

"Is that why it feels more familiar and less..." she struggled to find the word.

"Forbidding?"

Julia frowned. "I don't know. It's as if the stones are saying, 'Look, your ancestors were here and changed the landscape'. Trees, well, they just grow."

"I agree. Some Mages have more of an affinity with them than others. Perhaps it's in the blood."

Her attention turned to Emrys, who was moving slowly around the perimeter.

"What's he doing?"

Milo squinted over at the old man.

"I think he's looking for something."

Suddenly, the air changed, becoming heavier and more charged, as if something dormant had been released and set in motion. She could sense subtle vibrations begin to ripple through the earth.

"I would guess he's found it," she observed. "Earth magic."

Emrys beckoned them over.

"I'm opening a portal," he said without preamble. "When I tell you, step through it."

Julia's eyes widened. He wasn't going to draw a circle? She felt Milo tense beside her.

"To where?" he asked.

"Straight to the Heart of Albion. When we arrive, say nothing, do you understand? I'll do the talking."

"I thought it wasn't safe," Milo objected.

Emrys shrugged.

"It's where we need to be. Safety is relative at the moment and this way is best. We won't be killed on sight, if that's what you mean."

Milo opened his mouth to object, to no avail. The Mage strode into the centre of the circle and raised his arms. Instantly, a purple line appeared, hanging in mid-air. Seemingly satisfied. Emrys drew his hands together, then apart in one swift motion. The line widened, becoming a portal filled with an iridescent shimmer, as if spread with a film of oil.

"Now!" he commanded, the strain of holding it open evident in his voice.

Before she knew what was happening, Milo grabbed her hand, dragging her into the circle and through the portal.

*

Caniculus walked briskly through Segedunum, noting the impressive array of shops and thriving businesses lining the broad streets. The northern city was doing well, prospering from the flow of trade that poured in from the rest of the Empire and beyond. It was a far cry from the remote border port that had existed a thousand years before, hugging Hadrian's Wall at the far reaches of Roman rule.

This was the most optimistic he'd felt since leaving Londin in haste several days before, working his way up the Great North Road. He'd eked out his resources by taking advantage of the mild spring weather by camping out, or dossing down in empty farm buildings. After about forty miles, he'd been confident enough to hitch rides on wagons and had ridden most of the rest of the way. Everything seemed normal, except that because of his direction of travel he'd frequently been pumped for information about the latest events in the capital. The death of one king and the accession of an unexpected candidate had set tongues wagging, though most believed Marcus was the rightful ruler.

"It stands to reason," one fellow had told him as they rolled along in a cart hauling fleeces. "Julia can't inherit being female, and her Uncle's out at sea and old to boot. It would have come to Marcus eventually, right?"

If he hadn't witnessed Marcus's actions with his own eyes, Caniculus would have agreed with him. Instead, he had to bite his lip and nod politely. He was glad to hop off when the road forked and watch his host trundle off towards Lindum, and not only because the smell of the unwashed wool was making him feel nauseous. Several lifts later he'd reached Eboracum, where he'd managed to offload some of the little items he'd snaffled from the palace, no questions asked. His former life as an Agent meant he knew places that law-abiding people had never heard of. Consequently, with his coin purse full and the rest tucked secretly about his person, he'd kept on travelling, keeping his ears open, through the farmland to the north and heading for the Wall.

He'd considered getting a boat and escaping to the Continent, but decided to keep that as a last resort as he was close enough to a harbour if he really needed to make a run for it. He picked

Segedunum as it was a busy place where his accent wouldn't be noticed too much. He could have tried to fool the locals, but he was never as good at it as Milo was. His friend could pass for anyone from just about anywhere. He spared him a prayer as he hunted for some accommodation, then added one for himself. As a traveller, Mercury was the obvious choice and he knew that both he and Milo needed all the help they could get.

The *mansio* was by the river. It seemed clean enough and relatively inexpensive, with a large enough turnover so that his comings and goings wouldn't be remarked on. He hadn't used it before, so if anyone was still looking for him it wouldn't be down as one of his usual haunts. Caniculus had to admit to himself that he was looking forward to sleeping in a bed instead of on cargo or the ground.

The owner was a stocky fellow with a cheerful face and a bushy black beard that made him look like a Northman. Perhaps he was, Caniculus thought. There were enough of them about. He certainly looked like he could handle himself in a fight.

"I'd like a room, please. Single, if you've got one."

Caniculus had no inclination to share. The last thing he wanted was for some light-fingered roommate going through his pack in the middle of the night.

"You're in luck, sir. We have one left. Will you be staying long?"

Caniculus thought for a moment.

"Not sure. It might take me a while to conclude my business. I'll pay for three days, then let you know, if that's all right?"

The *mansio* keeper beamed at him. "No problem, sir. If you're wanting meals as well, you can pay now, or as you go. I'm Knut, by the way. Just ask for me if you need anything."

Caniculus decided on the latter. It would be cheaper to grab food from a stall and save money. He didn't know how long this would have to last. Knut was a Northern name, so he'd been right about one thing, though the man had a local accent. Probably mixed heritage.

"Business good, then?" Knut asked.

It was the usual polite enquiry. Caniculus made a see-sawing motion with his hand.

"Could be better, but you never know."

His host grunted.

"It could always be better. At least the threat of war is averted, though I've heard there's some trouble with raiders to the west. Not Northmen," he hastened to add. "I'm named for my uncle, as my Dad was from Norvegia originally. Mam's a Briton."

An older woman with a scarf tied around her greying hair looked up from where she was cleaning a table and called over.

"You gossiping again, lad?"

"Who, me? No, Mam."

His mother snorted and resumed her task.

"Who's doing the damage, then?" Caniculus asked, with a sinking feeling that he already knew. Knut grimaced.

"There are some wild tales that they've come over from Hibernia."

"By the Gods, I hope not," Caniculus replied.

"If they have, they'll be sent packing once the King hears about it," Knut said with confidence. "He's got Excalibur, so they'll get their arses kicked right back into the sea."

It was sad to see how much faith the ordinary people had in the monarch. Marcus had not only broken that covenant, but smashed it and jumped on the pieces.

"That's right."

There was no point in saying what he knew. All he could hope for was that there wouldn't be too many casualties.

He took the key, attached to a wooden tag with *Riverside Mansio* burned on to it in large letters along with the number nine, and followed the directions to his room. Once there, he threw his pack on the floor, took off his coat and boots and flopped down on the metal-framed bed, noting with relief that the mattress didn't feel too lumpy. The place seemed clean enough, so he hoped that he didn't wake up covered in bites. Despite the noise drifting in through the partially-open window, he was asleep before he knew it.

It was early evening when he woke, hungry and needing to use the latrine. He poured some water from a ewer into a basin and splashed his face, then tramped off downstairs, shutting the window and carefully locking the door behind him. While attending to business, he reflected on the fact that he was still in possession of the Helmet of Invisibility. Part of him was glad that he still had an advantage, while the rest of him was concerned that it hadn't been reclaimed. It wasn't that he particularly wanted to run into any more Gods, but it would have been quite literally a weight off his shoulders. As it was, he could hardly drop it off at the nearest temple with a note.

Caniculus slipped out with the key, not trusting it to any of the *mansio* staff. If anyone said anything he'd simply claim that he'd forgotten and that was that. Once in the streets, he headed off to find food and a bath, in that order. There were plenty of such establishments catering for travellers, so he picked one, perching on a stool at the counter while he made his selection. The smell of the flatbread topped with meat and melted cheese made his mouth water, so he ordered a portion of that and a jug of the local ale to wash it down.

He kept both eyes open for any suspicious activity while he waited, but after a while he concluded that he was the only one that appeared shady. It was reassuring to see that everyone was intent on their own business and the atmosphere was calm. He caught snatches of talk, mostly about trade, and tossed a coin to a newspaper boy in exchange for a fresh copy of the local scandal sheet. In his experience, the important news usually consisted of someone's lost cow, but this time the headline caught his attention.

MYSTERY ATTACKS.

Underneath, in smaller letters. WEST COAST RAIDED. VILLAGES BURNED.

This had to be what Knut was talking about. The boy's calls encouraged others to hastily grab copies. Soon, the chatter of the food stall grew more strident as people digested the information.

"I tell you, it is not the Alliance!" A large, fair-haired man banged on the table for emphasis. "If we were at war, my Ship would tell me!"

"I bet it's pirates," another said. "Let Admiral Pendragon go and sort them out, now he's made up with his son."

That was met with general agreement. Caniculus finished his meal, then got up, leaving the paper on the table.

"You want that?" someone asked.

"Please, take it," he replied, making his way out on to the street again. It was time to take a bath while he could, then think about his next move.

IV

It was less than a day's sailing along the coast before Maia caught sight of the mouth of the estuary, guarded by a peninsula to the north side and rolling hills to the south. There was a good amount of commercial traffic moving up and downstream, but they quickly made way as the *Leopard* approached.

<I've been given the order to anchor here,> the Ship informed Maia.

It made sense. Nobody wanted to be trapped upriver. Sometimes there were defences, such as chains that would stop a larger vessel from moving inland in order to protect the populace from raids. There had been plenty of those during the war with the Northmen and some of the old precautions could still be useable. There had been no indication that Marcus knew of *Leopard*'s whereabouts, but it was better to be cautious. It was perhaps too much to hope for that the sudden purge had thrown the Government Agents into disarray, furthermore, there would be plenty of folk happy to make extra coin for passing on information.

It wasn't long before the rattle of the anchor chains reverberated around the vessel. Sails furled, the *Leopard* bobbed at anchor, mindful of the tides. There would perhaps have to be adjustments made later and Maia wished she could access the maps that were stowed below. She had never been to this area before and the information would come in very useful to her later, tucked away in her strange memory.

Part of her chafed at her immobility, the rest baulked at what lay ahead. She hadn't set foot on land for many months and never as a Shipbody. She could move under her own power but barely above walking pace, so they would have to rig something up to transport her effectively. She hoped it wouldn't be a wagon. A carriage would be better, but was probably impractical. Also, she doubted they would be using the main roads. Maybe some sort of litter would work? She could recline, like a high-born lady.

Of course, by birth she was a high-born lady. The brief taste of luxury she'd known had been ruined by Echidna's attack, and the rest of it had all been an illusion. Since then, she hadn't had time to spit before another crisis hove into view. Had there ever been a start to a career like hers? She thought not. Even the *Emerald*'s kraken attack, horrible as it was, couldn't compete.

Leo's mental call jolted her back to the present.

<We're nearly ready.>

In contrast, he sounded optimistic. It was all a new adventure for him, she supposed, though as a sea Captain he would be in an unfamiliar situation as well. Maia pulled herself out of her self-pitying mood. They would face whatever the Gods had in store for them as a team, united in purpose.

<What's the plan?>

<We'll take a boat ashore tonight and meet up with Raven. He's going to move us inland, whilst the *Leopard* will take delivery of the new weapons and return to the fleet.>

<Where are they being made?>

Maia knew from her studies that the seams of coal running in the north-west meant that there were factories of all sorts springing up, mainly woollen or cotton mills and ironworks. It stood to reason that there would be one specialising in the manufacture of armaments, presumably working in secret.

<No idea,> he replied. <But if I was to hazard a guess, I'd say in the Mamucium area, possibly by Salixford. It's become more industrialised lately.>

<It's not very close, then?>

<No, but they'll probably come by river, then overland a short distance.>

He broke off and she could tell that he was talking to Amphicles. She gazed across the rail, noting how her hostess dwarfed the other craft. In one way it was a shame that it was the month of her birth, as the nights were short and they would have to move quickly to minimise the risk of being observed.

Maia, the reason she had her name. It was still how she thought of herself and now another year had gone by. She would never know the exact day, but the staff at the Portus Foundling Home had estimated that she'd only been a couple of weeks old when she'd been left there, so Maia it was. One fact she could know, she was now twenty years old. It was twenty years since her mother had held her. Twenty years since her father's death. Such a short length of time for a Ship, but the whole of her life.

Ships didn't tend to mark birthdays but she would remember, if only to honour her father's memory. Maybe one day she would be chatting to a new Ship, as *Diadem* had spoken to her and remembering back when she was here, in this place, about to venture into the unknown.

If she survived. There was always the possibility that Marcus would win and have her chopped up into kindling. Then she would sleep until death took her mortal remains.

<There, it's all sorted. I expect you'll be glad to see Raven again,> Leo Sent.

He paused. The link worked both ways.

<What can I do to help you?>

His concern was evident.

<Oh, I'm just in a mood, that's all,> she answered. <I just realised that I'm now twenty years old.>

<You've had a birthday?> She felt his realisation. <Oh, that's why you were called Maia.>

<That's right, but Ships don't celebrate birthdays, do they?>

She felt him smile as he corrected her.

<*Old* Ships don't. They can't be bothered, but you haven't had enough of them yet. Right!> His tone turned business-like.

What was he planning? Maia wished she hadn't mentioned it. This could get embarrassing very quickly.

<It doesn't matter,> she said quickly.

<Too late.>

She rolled her eyes, knowing that anything she said now wouldn't change his mind. She checked her internal clock, noting that it was barely four hours to sunset. That wouldn't give him enough time to do anything ridiculous, surely?

She settled in to prepare, watching as the crew went about their duties. Captain Boduogenus had assigned tasks to keep the men busy, plus it was accepted practice when anchored to do a number of tasks that were more difficult when at sea. From all the rushing around, Maia decided that he'd ordered a spruce-up, as the vessel was being scrubbed to within an inch of her life. Below, her gunners were doing dry runs and marines were being drilled on the quarterdeck, practising loading and reloading over and over again, even though it was already automatic. Some of the cannon crews had new members, so it was essential that everyone knew his place, moving in the orderly dance of war. In the heat of battle, training would be what they would rely on to get them through.

A minute later, *Leopard*'s Captain appeared on deck as if conjured by some arcane spell and made his way over to her. His sea-dark eyes met hers.

There was a sadness there, but also a knowing. They were bound by their otherness in the world of mortals.

"*Tempest.*"

She returned his salute.

"Captain."

He stood next to her, so close that they were nearly touching. His lips formed words for her ears alone.

"I imagine you have questions."

Did she?

"Not really. You are what you are. I presume others know?"

He snorted quietly.

"Not many. My Ship, my Priest, Pendragon and Raven. Some people from my youth."

"I'm not surprised Raven knows."

He smiled, "Yes, he does tend to know more than everyone else."

I wonder if you know as much about him. It humbled her to think that she had seen something of the Master Mage that nobody else had in many hundreds of years.

"You can rely on my discretion," she murmured.

"Thank you."

The urge to tell him more of her origins was strong. He clearly had divine blood, perhaps from some sea-nymph or Mer-Lord, but did that justify putting him in danger? Jupiter had been very clear on the matter, but she decided to be daring.

"You have your advantages, just as I have mine."

She saw him take a breath, as if in confirmation.

"I thought so. Do you know that few Ships ever alter their form, let alone adapt with such readiness? Which element do you command?"

She nearly laughed out loud. "Command? None, but I do petition the spirits of the air in the hope I will be heard."

"I knew you weren't water, but I heard that the King of the Ocean favours you. Do you happen to be a Ship by divine decree?"

This was more dangerous territory.

"I obey the Gods, especially the Thunderer."

His eyes widened as he stared at the horizon. They were both being careful not to name names.

"As must we all, and your devotion and obedience have been noted. You will be moving beyond my family's sphere, but you will have other protectors. I foresee that help will come to you when you truly need it. Don't be afraid."

He turned to her, and she saw the sparkle deep in his pupils, like gold coins falling through water. A tremor rippled through her Shipbody and she knew that someone else was speaking through him, even as she had been used by Nemesis.

"I thank you, Mighty One," she whispered. For a few seconds time itself seemed to stop, suspended, before a sudden sea breeze caught Boduogenus's hat and sent it tumbling across the deck. Suddenly, everything was normal again. The Captain blinked, as if he had been asleep, before running his hands over his black hair which she could now see was sprinkled with silver. A shout went up as several crewmen scrambled after the errant item, though nobody dared laugh at a superior's discomfort.

Maia scanned the rigging immediately to see if she could catch a glimpse of the culprit. There was nothing there, but someone had decided to intervene. The Gods were playing some elemental game among themselves that she was unaware of.

A gangly sailor with a shock of bright red hair snatched it before it flew over the side. He presented it to his Captain, proud to be the rescuer. Boduogenus took it with a wry smile.

"Well done, Frontius! You've saved me a trip to the outfitters, though I must confess it wouldn't have been happening any time soon."

The little joke got a ripple of appreciation from his men.

"Aye, sir."

Frontius returned to scrubbing the deck, getting pats on the back from his mates. Their soapy hands left wet patches on his shirt, which they thought hilarious.

Leopard was amused too.

<Good job it didn't go over the rail. It's his favourite and they cost the earth these days.>

The deck pooled and rose as she formed next to Maia, her emerald eyes gleaming.

<Bod told me you'd seen him in the water. He seems to think you're hiding something as well.>

<Bod?> Maia bit her lip. It didn't seem appropriate for the grave and dignified Captain. *Leopard* shrugged.

<I've known him since he was a boy, so I've the right. Well?>

<He has good instincts, but I can't say anything,> Maia hedged.

Leopard sniffed, her nose wrinkling. <He does. I knew you were different. First, Neptune appears in person, then you get the Admiral, not to mention that you knew what *Regina* was planning. Then there was the Potentia you shoved into the shields. I'm glad you're on our side!>

Maia didn't know how to answer her.

Leopard's eyes narrowed in a feline smile, then she addressed her Captain.

"All's ready, sir."

"Excellent! Let's make a start, shall we?

Maia looked from one to the other. "Sir?" she ventured, puzzled.

Boduogenus made an innocent face. "Your birthday party."

Maia felt her jaw drop.

<Leo!>

<What?> His tone was all innocence.

<What have you done?>

Maia realised that every face on the vessel was plastered with a huge grin, including Big Ajax and Hyacinthus, who were hovering waiting for her reaction. Even the usually imperturbable Osric's lips were twitching.

"It's not the time," she objected.

"Nonsense!" Boduogenus said. "We need a celebration after all the sadness, and what better reason is there than the special day for one of our own?"

He raised his hat.

"Three cheers for *Tempest* on her birthday!"

The answering huzzahs startled the seabirds into adding their raucous cries.

"All crew not on watch are given leave to make merry," the Captain continued, "though we'll have to go easy on the rations for now."

It was a subtle reminder that they were still technically at war, but the men rapidly cleared a space for dancing and a makeshift Ship's band. Soon, several were dancing a jig whilst the others clapped, slapped their knees and sang along, not always with the approved lyrics.

Maia joined in, remembering the happy evenings in The Anchor. This time she wouldn't have to clean up any messes or get her backside slapped by over-enthusiastic patrons. It was a brief respite from the horrors.

"See," Leo's voice sounded in her ear. "I do have some good ideas."

She turned to him, laughing. "For once, I agree with you!"

Cheers heralded the arrival of a stretcher being man-handled up the ladder. The figure strapped to it waved a hand, more like an Emperor than a lowly sailor. Maia was delighted to see Teg's beaming face as he was carried into the circle.

"All right, Shipmates! You'll have to do the dancin' without me fer a bit! Carry on!"

A chorus of rude remarks were hurled in his general direction, to which he responded with a grin that nearly swallowed up his face. His party piece was well received with cheers, and he continued to wave majestically as he was carried over to her.

"Teg!" she cried. "I feared the worst when I couldn't see you."

The little sailor looked smug.

"Nah, ma'am, it 'ud take more than that ter see me off. Shame about the lads, though."

She nodded.

"They won't be forgotten."

His wrinkled face grew thoughtful.

"Aye, an' they're out of this mess. They tell me you're goin' ashore? 'Tain't no place fer a Ship, beggin' your pardon, ma'am."

"It does seem strange," she admitted, "but they must have a use for me."

"Gods know what that is," he agreed. "I'd come with you, but I'll 'ave to learn to 'op first!"

The sagging blanket over his missing leg was all too obvious.

"I wish you could as well."

"Still, once I'm better they'll give me a peg leg. Then I can do some kickin'!"

She had to smile. He was irrepressible, despite all he had suffered.

"I'm famous too!" he announced, proudly.

Maia was mystified. "Are you?"

"Oh aye, ma'am. The King's monkey's called after me, you know!"

He puffed out his chest as much as he could from his supine position.

Maia did her best not to splutter.

"That's quite an honour," she managed. Next to her, Leo was going red trying not to laugh.

"Aye. The King comes up and says to me, 'Well, Teg, the Princess Julia 'as called her beloved monkey after you.' 'Oh, Your Majesty,' says I, 'that is most kind of 'er Royal 'ighness.' And now Little Teg is with 'im all the time!"

"That's wonderful!" Maia said, meaning every word.

"A great honour indeed," Leo interjected. "Now, don't overdo it. You must rest and get well."

"Aye sir! I'll be back to me duties in no time!"

He snapped off a salute and grinned so widely his nose disappeared, to general cheering, before being carted off surrounded by his friends.

"The man's a legend," Leo told her and she had to agree. Teg would be cared for and found work. Ship's cooks had often been injured in the line of duty, though whether she would trust him in the galley was another matter. It had been kind of Pendragon to speak to an ordinary seaman and make sure that Julia's decision hadn't caused offence. Cei would make an excellent king, even though he hated the idea.

<Patience to Tempest! What's this I hear about a birthday?>

Maia groaned to herself.

<Does the entire fleet know?>

<Oh yes.> Her friend's amusement rippled through the link. <Prepare yourself!>

Abruptly, the link was filled with Ships chorusing the birthday song. Maia hadn't heard it since the Foundling Home. She pulled a face at Leo.

"They're all singing to me!"

"Good! Let's join in!"

As the Ships finished, a signal was given and the men started the song again, bawling it out with great delight. Maia bowed in token of her appreciation.

"I think we'll make it a new tradition aboard the *Tempest*," Leo declared. "Ship's Birthday Celebrations!"

Nearby, *Leopard* rolled her eyes.

<Thank you, sisters,> Maia Sent. <I'll have words with my Captain later. He's decided to make it an annual event.>

She could hear the sniggering across the miles.

<Hey, *Leopard*!> *Jasper* called cheekily. <Shall we do the same for you?>

It seemed that the little Ship was back to her normal irreverent self.

<Only if you promise never to sing again, you tone-deaf minx!>

<Bloody cheek!>

<You said it!>

It was all good-hearted and lightened the atmosphere.

<I wonder if Longships can sing,> Jasper replied, undaunted. She began to warble a tune. <Oh, my lovely kitty…>

<Piss off!>

"Ship banter," Maia explained to Leo. "It's good to hear it again."

He blew out a breath. "Absolutely. Thank the Gods that we're united once more."

They both knew that certain Ships hadn't re-joined the link, but the odds of being fired on by their own had decreased significantly. *Justicia* was skulking about somewhere, and as for *Regina*, who knew where she'd ended up? Maia couldn't honestly find it in herself to care too much.

The light slowly faded and a light rain began to fall. Most of the sailors were undeterred, but the fiddle player objected to the damp on his instrument so they adjourned below to the gun decks leaving Maia, *Leopard* and the watch on deck. The Ship hadn't lit her lamps yet, leaving blurry-edged shapes in the gathering gloom through which men moved with purpose.

Respectful hands rigged Maia for travel once more and *Leopard* lowered her boat. The Ship and her Captain came over to say their farewells to Leo and those of her crew who were accompanying her. Boduogenus seemed unaware of the message he'd given her and she wasn't going to enlighten him. The Gods moved as they would, seen or unseen.

"May Fortuna watch over you, my friend."

Boduogenus gripped Leo's forearm in the salutation of equals, then pulled him in for a clap on the back.

"And may the Gods grant you a fair wind and a calm sea," Leo replied. "My Ship and crew thank you for your hospitality."

"Farewell, *Tempest*," *Leopard* said. "May you return to us triumphant!"

"Success to you also, sister."

<Give us as much information as you're allowed,> the big cat's voice growled softly in her mind. <We all want to know what's happening.>

<So do I,> Maia replied, with a wry edge. <So far, nobody's saying anything. I had thought *Patience* was coming with me.>

<No, she'll get her new vessel as soon as it's adapted, as will *Farsight*. *Unicorn*'s still under repair. Give my regards to Raven when you see him!>

<I will,> she promised.

Then it was time for her to be swung up into the air again and lowered into the boat. She could see the shadowy outlines of her men following her over the side and hoped that they weren't being observed. She had the suspicion that her new slimmed-down crew had been hand-picked, but for what reasons she couldn't fathom. She naturally had her Captain and Amphicles, her Adept, Hawthorn, Danuco, Hyacinthus, Big Ajax, Vestinus her carpenter, plus Musca and his number one gun crew of six men including Monkey. She wasn't surprised that the faithful Victor was accompanying his master, as no Captain could be expected to be without his servant. Osric and four marines completed the party of twenty. It seemed a small crew after the many she was used to.

<Is this everyone?> she Sent to Leo.

<No. *Leopard*'s sending another boat with four more marines as escort.>

<We'll be quite a sizeable party, then?>

Twenty-four seemed a lot for a group expected to move unseen and she would have to add Raven to that number as well. Still, she wasn't going to turn down heavily-armed men, as they would need all the protection they could muster.

It was interesting that Vestinus had been included as well. A carpenter's knowledge of timber was always vital for a Ship and she had long suspected that he was much more than a simple joiner of planks. There was a trade Mystery there that none but initiates would be privy to. She could see his stocky figure as he stepped carefully to seat himself next to Hyacinthus. The boat rocked a little more as Big Ajax boarded, then steadied as he found his place. It hadn't escaped Maia's notice that he and Hyacinthus were her two most experienced crewmen. Presumably she'd be assigned more when they got to wherever they were going.

Once they were all aboard, Maia Sent to *Leopard* and the boat began to move silently towards the southern shore. A few scattered lights flickered in the darkness, though there were none immediately before them so they weren't heading for a settlement. Maia could sense the moving water beneath her. The sensation was muffled, as if she was feeling a familiar object through heavy cloth, and her depth perception felt skewed. There was none of the sensitivity she had come to rely on when in her own vessel. She pushed the unease aside to concentrate on the way ahead.

The men were silent, each in their own thoughts, though she could tell that Leo was watching for something.

<There!> he told her. <See that?>

She had indeed, a brief glow as if from a concealed lantern.

<That'll be Raven.>

He sounded confident and with good reason. The Master Mage's voice entered their private link with the flash of red she always associated with him. It was interesting that he was contacting her, for once.

<Greetings, Maia!>

She experienced a rush of relief at hearing his voice, despite her annoyance at his caginess during their last meeting.

<Greetings, Raven!>

She tried to sound collected, but had the suspicion that she'd already given herself away. <We're heading towards your position now.>

<Excellent! Inform Leo that all is ready.>

She did as she was bid, feeling Leo's relief echoing hers. There was so much that could go wrong and they were heading into enemy territory.

<Thank you. You can contact *Leopard*, but maintain link silence. I don't want any Ship chatter from now on,> Leo told her.

<Aye, sir.>

So, she couldn't even contact her sisters until she got the word. This was unusual, but not unexpected. She consoled herself that she would have more to tell them when she was permitted to resume communications.

They were almost at the shore now, a level expanse of mud, fringed with grasses.

<This is where we get dirty,> Leo grumbled quietly.

<Just don't drop me,> she answered.

<We'll do our best.>

Four marines, aided by her crewmen, hauled the boat out of the shallows until she could feel its keel grinding on the land. The marines immediately took up defensive postures, muskets at the ready and alert for any sign of trouble.

"It's not too bad, sir," Hyacinthus reported. "Only ankle-deep, but watch where you put your feet."

The rest of her crew disembarked, leaving her alone.

<Maia, tell them I'm approaching. I've no desire to be shot.>

<Leo, Raven's here.>

She heard the whisper in the darkness and Osric's acknowledgement. A muffled conversation ensued, then it was time for her to be brought ashore. This was the moment she'd been dreading. It was one thing to end up on another Ship, but to be taken on land without official naval sanction was another matter. There would be no specially prepared Admiralty berth waiting for her here.

"Steady now, lads." Amphicles had taken charge. "We'll have to carry you to the wagon, ma'am."

Maia resigned herself to being lugged about. So, it would be a wagon.

"Here, ma'am, put your arms around our shoulders and we'll carry you in a chair lift." Hyacinthus said.

It wouldn't be the first time he'd dragged her off to parts unknown. She wondered if the irony wasn't lost on him too.

Big Ajax and two of the strongest marines joined him to transport her ashore. She could hear their feet squelching in the mud, though strangely enough the odour of rotting weed was largely absent. Come to think of it, as a Ship she hadn't much use for smells and none at all for taste. It was more noticeable now that she was back on land for the first time in her Shipbody. Yet another thing she would have to adjust to.

A grey blob ahead of them resolved itself into the form of the ancient Mage. A horse's quiet snicker told her the position of a large hay wagon and soon, not without a little grunting and muttered instructions from Hyacinthus, she was aboard and sitting awkwardly on the straw covered floor, her own deck planks wedged under her backside as an anchoring point. It was hardly dignified but she was past caring. The sooner they could set off, the better.

A pile of crates to her left had to be the weapons, ready to be delivered to the Fleet. There was a sizeable amount, and it gave her satisfaction to think of the damage they would wreak on the Fae vessels. They were already being loaded as the rasping sound of another boat being beached told them that the rest of the men had arrived. As soon as one boat was full, she was ordered to signal *Leopard*, then again when the other one was filled. All the men had to do was push the boats out and the Ship would do the rest.

<Thank you, *Leopard*,> Maia Sent. <I'm under orders not to contact anyone from now on.>

<You're welcome, *Tempest*. I'll tell the others. May the Gods smile on you!>

A rustle of robes, and Raven was next to her, followed in short order by Leo, Danuco, Amphicles and the others. A quiet clicking and the wagon set off with its escort. It would be slow but steady progress.

"Are you alright?" Raven whispered to her.

She bit back a sarcastic reply.

"I'm fine."

"I've sent Musca and his crew ahead," Leo informed her. "The fewer we are, the better."

"Who's driving?" she asked.

She was facing the rear of the cart. It was probably possible to extend her neck and see ahead, but she feared the effect would look too grotesque.

"Hyacinthus, with Big Ajax next to him. Would you believe he grew up on a farm?"

She stifled a laugh. "What, Hyacinthus? I can't see him ploughing a furrow."

"Well, he did. Ran away to sea at twelve."

"If you wouldn't mind keeping it down," Raven said crossly. "We are supposed to be hiding."

<We'll have to chat like this instead,> Leo Sent, unabashed.

<Some secret operation, surrounded by armed guards,> Maia replied.

<Not for long, apparently. We just have to make it to a nearby villa owned by one of Pendragon's friends and supporters, then Raven's going to portal us to where we need to be.>

<And then I'll get my new vessel?>

He paused before answering.

<Apparently. I don't know any more details. Raven's only told me what I need to know, in case we're captured. Likewise, you can deny any knowledge of his intentions.>

<Then we'd better not get captured.>

<Exactly.>

Maia glanced across at her Priest. His eyes were closed, though how he could sleep with the bone-jarring bumps and jolts of the unmade road they were moving along was beyond her. Leo shifted on the straw to find a more comfortable position and she was glad that the rigidity of her Shipbody meant that she would suffer no aches and pains. The unyielding wood was both a blessing and a curse in their situation.

<Try to get some rest,> she told her Captain. <The Gods only know when you'll get the chance again.>

Leo twisted in place, piling up a little more straw behind him.

<Knowing my luck, this will be full of fleas.>

She ignored his grumblings, listening as his thoughts quietened and he fell into a doze. It would do him good.

She opened the link to Raven.

<How long will it take us to get to this villa?>

For a second, she thought he wouldn't reply.

<We'll be there just before dawn, all being well.>

She thought he sounded stressed, as well he might. It was unlikely that Marcus had his men watching this far out, but you could never tell. She closed their link and let him be, concentrating instead on the sound of the horses' hooves and the creaking of the wheels as they moved inexorably into the darkness.

*

"Sire, Sire. Wake up. There is news."

The urgent whisper penetrated Marcus's dreams. He tried to ignore it, attempting to sink back into the welcome arms of

Morpheus. The God of Sleep had been begrudging of his favours of late.

"Sire! You must wake up! This cannot wait."

Still half-asleep, he put a face to the voice. Kite. Damn it, couldn't the man leave him alone for more than a few hours? He needed his sleep!"

"Go 'way."

"Sire!"

There was nothing for it. The God had fled, banished by the insistence of his Prime Mage. At that moment, Marcus could have cheerfully run the man through. He groaned and rubbed his eyes before propping himself up on one elbow.

"If this isn't worth it, I'll have you chopped into little pieces and fed to my lions."

"It is, Sire."

"Spit it out, then."

"We've had word that Antonia Drusilla, wife of the late Senator Rufus, has landed on the south coast near Dubris with a force of mercenaries. It seems she is intent on avenging her husband's death."

A chill that had nothing to do with the temperature settled over Marcus like a pall.

"She's what?"

"Her father, Gnaeus Clodius Drusus is the wealthiest man in Roma, Sire. He's obviously had no qualms about providing her with funds to assist her in her quest. The rumours are that the Emperor has sent troops also, though whether these are legionaries or auxiliaries isn't yet known. He won't want to act in an overt fashion while you are recognised as king so they won't be raising any standards."

"Gods below! How many legions do we have in the area?"

Kite's painted face swam into focus as Marcus snapped fully awake.

"We currently have one garrisoned here in Londin, with two more within a few day's striking distance. The others were sent to quell the ports and prevent your father from landing a force of his own."

Damn his father and damn Drusilla too. He'd thought that slitting her husband's throat would have silenced opposition from that quarter, but apparently he'd been mistaken. He cudgelled his befogged brain for a response.

"Withdraw the legions from the ports and get them there as soon as possible. The enemy forces won't be going anywhere in the next couple of days at least until they've secured their supply lines. It's one thing to raise an army, another to feed them. I want hourly reports."

"Should I send the Second Legion down to meet them?"

"What, and leave Londin unprotected? Gods, no!"

Kite might be a powerful Mage, but it was clear that he wasn't an expert in the arts of battlefield deployment.

"Leave me and send in Macro."

Macro was the one he needed now. Kite was good for liaising with his new allies and arranging his upcoming marriage, but military strategy was best left to his generals.

"Immediately, Sire."

Kite bowed and left. Marcus sat up, calling for his personal slaves. There would be no more sleep for him this night.

Damn it all to Hades!

*

The twelve hooded figures stood in a circle, lit only by the flickering of lamps and a central fire that burned with an eerie blue-green intensity that seemed not of the mortal world. It cast the painted statues of the Gods with a glow that seemed to jump from one to another, as if the marble had suddenly come to life. Above them, columns rose to the ceiling of the temple anteroom to disappear into the gloom of the plaster ceiling.

Aquila chanted with the rest, his bulky figure clad in white, until the ritual was completed and the conclave could begin.

"Brothers and sisters," he intoned. "Welcome, and thank you for attending at short notice."

The figures bowed, their silence encouraging him to continue.

"As you know, mighty Jupiter is angered by the arrests of Priests and the challenge to himself and his family. I have called you at this late hour because there have been further developments. My agents have informed me that a force led by the Lady Antonia Drusilla has landed to the south, intent on deposing the Usurper. Whether they have any chance of success is uncertain. I call upon the High Priest of Mars to give us his insights."

A voice issued from a tall figure opposite from where Aquila was standing.

"The God is active and delights in this turn of events. He is gearing up for battle, as should we. He has been ordered to lend his strength to our army."

There were nods and murmurings from the others, probably of relief. Mars was unstable at the best of times, and only his father's iron hand kept him in check.

"Athena Sulis Minerva also offers her aid." Her Priestess's voice rang out in the chamber. "The murder of Senator Rufus will be avenged!"

Aquila raised an eyebrow. Using all three names showed that the fearsome Goddess meant business.

"The Lady Juno favours Pendragon and his supporters."

This was his old friend, Vibia Laelia, High Priestess here in Londinium and senior in her temple. It seemed that the Goddess hadn't forgotten Cei Pendragon and those close to him.

Aquila cast his mind back to the unfortunate incident with the Captain and his rogue Ship. It had been Diana's doing, of that he was sure, but her subsequent meddling had led to a severe punishment. Jupiter didn't release Nemesis lightly. Nothing had been said and the Huntress's Priestesses had remained tight-lipped on the entire matter, but the rumour was that she'd been forced into the guise of a mortal by her father. It was a dire punishment indeed, rarely enacted since Apollo and Poseidon had been forced to build the walls of Troy all those years ago. Pretending to be a mortal was one thing – Mercury did it all the time – but being compelled to behave as one was quite a different matter.

He'd heard that the result of the ill-fated union of Aura and her mortal husband was now a Ship herself. The frightened girl he'd met had been translated into something largely beyond his comprehension. *That* magic was beyond his bailiwick, for which he was very grateful. The rites at the Temple of Zeus in faraway Dodona, where the rest of the Empire ships got their talking oak boughs, were far more straightforward. He'd never really got to grips with the strange fusion of ancient myth and earth magic that held sway in these isles.

Naturally, Juno would delight in cheering on anyone who annoyed her husband, though she tended to be more tactful about it these days. The Goddess of Marriage had certainly pleaded the girl's case, though secretly Aquila thought it harsh that Maia Abella been forbidden all contact with her mother. Juno had probably had something to do with her being made a Royal, too. There was no end to the Queen of Heaven's machinations when she put her mind to it, and it boded ill for Marcus that she supported Jupiter for once.

The other Priests and Priestesses gave their reports one by one. That of Mercury's High Priest was interesting.

"He's very busy. Unlike some, he's been in on this from the start."

There were a few mutters at that. Mercury's Priests tended to get the good gossip first.

"The Lord Apollo is currently in the east," his Priest pointed out, "but will obey his father. His bow is ready if required."

Now that was interesting. Apollo's arrows brought pestilence wherever they landed. It could be at his own whim, or, more often, on Jupiter's orders. It was an unsettling thought.

"What of the Huntress?" Aquila asked. Jealousy was an evil guide and often led an aspect of that particular deity down dark paths.

"She obeys the will of Jupiter and supports the Princess Julia."

The Priestess's voice was harsh. Aquila bet that she hadn't slept much in recent weeks trying to keep up with her errant mistress's antics. Still it was good that Diana was back within the Olympian fold, though where she was now was anybody's guess.

"So, all are agreed that Cei Pendragon's claim must be supported?" Aquila asked as the last Priest finished speaking. Bacchus hadn't had much to say on the subject, loath to leave warmer climes.

"Don't be too hasty, Priest of Jupiter."

The cracked voice could only belong to Junia Elin, the ancient Priestess of Ceres. He stifled a sigh. Trust the Earth Mother to have more to say on this matter. She was the closest to the old religion of Britannia and probably regarded the rest of them as upstarts.

"The Sword of Kingship will decide, as it always has. Nothing is guaranteed."

"So, you mean that Pendragon will have to get to the Basilica and pull it out?" Gwynn, Vulcan's representative asked. He'd just remarked that his God was 'working flat out', but declined to give further details. "I'd like to see him try that. The whole place stinks of Fae magic."

"Well, perhaps the Smith could devise something to rid us of it?" Aphrodite's Priestess snapped. Her Lady had been noticeably absent lately and Aquila surmised that she was feeling a little left out. It was also a chance to have a dig at her husband, Vulcan. There'd been bad blood between them for a couple of millennia now, ever since she'd been caught *in flagrante delicto* with Mars.

"Now then, let's not bicker amongst ourselves," Aquila interjected. Honestly, sometimes he thought they all identified too closely with their assigned deities. "I'm sure everyone's doing what they can to help put Britannia back on course again."

"We need to be rid of these Fae as quickly as possible." Neptune's Priest sounded upset. "*You* haven't seen the bodies in the water, or those thrice-damned vessels heading this way. They've already started enslaving our people along the coast."

"You're right," Aquila agreed. "They must be stopped. The problem is that the legions are being recalled, or have been ordered to take no action. The local militia are doing the best they can and have ordered the population into the fortified towns, but no-one knows how long they can hold out."

"I expect the Usurper will gather his forces and march down to meet Drusilla and her army. He won't want them to become established and pick the battleground."

The High Priest of the God of War knew what he was talking about.

"We must continue to work together."

The Priest of Pluto, God of the Underworld, had a light voice for one with such a dreaded master. "My God welcomes all, but supports Olympus in this matter. Fae rule benefits none of us here."

A murmur of support flowed around the circle.

"Then it's decided," the High Priest stated. "We offer aid to the Lady Drusilla and her troops and petition the Gods for direct aid. They're already outraged, so it shouldn't take too much to encourage them to act, if they will it. Maybe the Priests of Mars can encourage dissent among the legions. We can also petition Mithras and the Egyptian Gods to ally themselves with us."

Nods reinforced this belief.

"What of the Britannic Powers?" Gwynn asked.

It was a tricky question. Some were worshipped jointly, allied with the Olympians and sharing the benefits. Others were more local and an unknown quantity.

"Who knows?" Aquila replied. "It's possible that most won't care who rules mortals. Some are so old that they barely register millennia, never mind years and months. Others may even welcome the return to barbarity and human sacrifice. Do what you can to keep them sweet in ways best known to yourselves. In the meantime," he continued, "I believe we are all in danger. Marcus means to eradicate us, so take steps to protect yourself. Use Mages where you can. Many opposed to the regime have already gone to ground and I know some of you are sheltering them in your temples."

There seemed little more to be said. A few more words were exchanged, then Aquila closed the meeting.

As the fire died out the figures around him winked out one by one leaving him alone under the eyes of the Gods.

V

Julia had no time to prepare herself.

The transition through the strange portal was cold and clinging, sucking at her flesh as if she were being pulled through a sheet of aspic. It could only have lasted a couple of seconds, but it felt much longer until she emerged with an audible pop into sudden darkness. She could feel a firmness beneath her feet and dampness in the air, but nothing was visible. Milo released his grip and she instantly ran her hands over her face, expecting to find some sticky remnants clinging to her skin, but there was nothing. The unpleasant sensations slowly faded, even as she heard movement in the blackness.

Julia opened her mouth to shout, just as a little ball of light appeared to reveal Milo's face.

"There, we're in."

His voice echoed strangely off a rugged stone wall, all fissures and sharp edges, and she could see in the dim glow that they were in a cave. It was impossible to see how big it was, but she guessed it was quite large.

A purple glow flickered at the edge of her vision and Emrys materialised. He turned immediately to close the portal, taking his time to make sure it was properly secured before looking them over.

"I see you're both intact. Excellent!"

Julia hoped he was joking. Given the choice, she wouldn't use that method again, however convenient.

"Where are we?" she asked.

"In the borderlands between what is, what was and what might be."

She'd heard of such things, liminal spaces where the boundaries between worlds were thin. Crossing them was never recommended because of the dangers; it was all too easy for overconfident Mages to be lost forever. There were enough tales of them in stories of bold heroes and wandering princesses discovering strange lands. She'd loved reading them when she was younger but it was an unsettling thought that she was now in one. It confirmed her assessment of Emrys's skill that he'd got all three of them through safely.

"I've heard of these caves."

Milo's whisper bounced off the rocky ceiling, then faded into the lightless depths. "Our distant ancestors used them for rituals."

"Not only our ancestors," Emrys said. "They are still relevant, though their origins go too far back for anyone to remember. The people that adapted and decorated these caves were here long before our Gods took their current forms. I've brought us into one of the deepest parts of this system. We'll have to make our way out carefully, so keep close. There are dangers but wonders too and you'll have the privilege of seeing things few living eyes have."

Julia was desperate to ask how he knew his way around, but held her tongue. Was he also a Priest of the Mother, that he was privy to such things? Not to be outdone, she formed her own light, a sphere of white and purple hovering six feet ahead and low, so as not to destroy her night vision.

"Use your Mage sight," Milo told her. "Concentrate and it will come to you, then you don't have to rely on the spell."

She'd noticed that Emrys hadn't made a light of his own and reckoned that was what he was using. Milo must have created his for her benefit if he had it too. She would need to keep her wits about her, as the floor was uneven and the ceiling seemed to get lower ahead. Julia had never been afraid of confined spaces, but was less than thrilled to be in the bowels of the earth. She kept her eyes on Emrys's back as they made their way onward. If there were any obstacles, he would have to navigate them first and he was much taller than she was.

They picked their way through one room-like structure after another, until Emrys stopped.

"Look," he said. She tore her eyes from his coat and followed his pointing finger.

The animals were running along a lengthy stretch of wall. Horses, stags, huge bulls, their outlines defined in red, orange and brown paint, the skill of the artists evident in their taut muscles and life-like appearance. She moved closer for a better look, resisting the urge to touch.

"Who painted them?"

"Our ancestors, a very long time ago. Before writing as we know it.

"Why?" She asked, awestruck.

"We can only guess. Perhaps to remember what was important. To entreat the Mother to make the animals fertile, so they could be hunted and eaten. As a sign that people were here. I do know that the ancients thought that everything came from the womb of the Mother, and that is deeper still. Nobody goes there now, but I have and there were many bones, both human and animal."

"A place of life and death," Milo said, his voice solemn. "There must have been many rituals here."

"Yes, but now they are lost to time, which takes everything in the end. Still, they left something of themselves behind for their descendants."

"They're amazing," Julia breathed.

He seemed pleased. "Aren't they just? I suppose I'm a sort of guardian now. Some have been lost to rock falls and the ones near the entrance are weathered until only scratches remain, yet these still speak to us. And that's not all. We were talking of the people. Come."

He led them onwards in silence for a few minutes before halting once more.

"Here they are. Say hello to your ancestors."

Julia had expected faces, or at the least figures. Instead, there were handprints. Big ones, small ones, all outlined in the same colours, up high and some lower, as if made by children.

"It looks like they're waving to us."

"Defying the millennia," Emrys agreed. "That's what they're saying. 'Greetings! We were here, in this place'. Messages from a time we can't even imagine now." He sighed. "So much time. I wonder what we will leave to our descendants. Paper burns and stone can be shattered, but these are eternal."

Julia reached out, choosing a print that seemed the same size as hers. She placed her hand over it, careful not to smudge the colour, feeling the rough texture of the limestone against her palm and fingertips. How long had it been since another person had done the same?

"Hello, ancestor," she whispered. "I know you were here. My respect to you."

Tears welled in her eyes as, for one second the past seemed to fall away, connecting her to someone she could never know but who lived on in her blood and bones. She shuddered at the memory.

"You feel it too," Milo said. "They were here, and they were us."

"Even ordinary mortals feel the power here," Emrys told them. "But we aren't ordinary mortals."

Julia noticed Milo flinch at that. Was it because he wasn't actually a Mage, though he could do some magic? Why hadn't he been trained, or sent to become a Priest? There was much about her companion she didn't understand and hadn't asked, being too wrapped up in her own woes. She would have to rectify that as soon as they were out of here. It didn't feel right to involve Emrys in the conversation and it would be important to pick her moment carefully.

She turned away from the handprints with reluctance, as if she were bidding farewell to family. It didn't feel right to leave them alone in the dark, though down here they would be safe. Their bodies had returned to the Earth Mother, while something of their spirits remained.

"Wonders indeed," she said. "But where are the dangers?"

"They're the usual. Rock falls. Slippery surfaces. Sudden floods. Maybe other things. As I said, this is a magical space and the barriers between worlds are thin here. Sometimes creatures from elsewhere find their way in."

She swallowed. His tone had been light, but serious nonetheless.

"Have you ever seen anything?"

He nodded. "Aye, and fought them too. Have you never wondered where many of the great monsters of myth originated? A very old friend of mine met one, to his great cost."

"What happened?"

Emrys shook his head.

"That's his story to tell. So far as I know, he's only ever told it to two people, and I am one of them. I shouldn't have mentioned it. My wits must be wandering."

"I hope not," Milo said. "We're relying on you to get us out of here."

Emrys snorted, the sudden noise making her jump a little. "It's this place. I'll be better once we reach the light."

Julia blinked. For a split second his eyes looked more animal than human and the branching shadows of antlers loomed on the jagged ceiling above his head. A shiver ran up her back. What was he, exactly? Then it was gone and he was simply a tired old man.

"Let's go," Milo said.

Had he noticed anything, or were her eyes playing tricks on her? Julia decided she was better off not knowing and followed Emrys's dark figure onwards towards the surface.

It took a few more hours of careful steps and the occasional crawl through low tunnels before the cave system widened. Much to Julia's relief nothing leapt at them out of the dark though Milo pointed out some interesting spiders and rock formations. It was part terrifying adventure and part scholarly expedition, but she felt privileged that she had been granted a glimpse into this secret place. If it wasn't for what awaited them, she would have thoroughly enjoyed herself.

They made brief stops to eat and drink, but just as the air became fresher Emrys came to a halt, settling himself down on a convenient rock ledge.

"We'll stop here for now as I don't want us to turn up tired. We'll need to be sharp in the hours ahead, so I suggest that you make yourselves as comfortable as possible and get some sleep. We'll go in at dawn."

"What's the plan?" Milo asked.

"You'll be under my protection, though I think there'll be no trouble as far as you're concerned, *Milo*. If anything, there might be too much enthusiasm at your arrival."

Julia frowned. So, Milo was a pseudonym? What was going on?

"Will I be in danger?" she said.

Emrys sniffed.

"You're female and royal, so I don't think so. I just need to make sure that you're not used as part of Ceridwen's agenda."

"Ceridwen?"

"The High Priestess of the Mother. She rules here, but I fear she might have been compromised."

The thought that such an important figure might support her cousin was a horrifying one. Why would Ceridwen do that? Then she realised.

"She knows about the Fae. Does she seriously want them to triumph?"

"Not so much that," Emrys replied, "but for the old ways to return. Year by year, people are forgetting the past. You've seen the factories, the new ways of doing things. All those inventions and machines. Some think things are going too far."

"Change happens," Julia objected. "If not, we'd still be drawing pictures on cave walls and following the herds. She can't stop progress."

"That's the problem. She thinks she can."

"And we're to do what? Why have we come here to the stronghold of the enemy?"

Emrys was silent for a few moments.

"Because there's no other way. There are other Powers here and we must ask their aid."

"Here?" Julia said in disbelief. It seemed that the old Mage had led them straight into the lion's mouth instead of to their allies. She'd have been better off anywhere else.

"I should be rallying troops against my cousin," she snapped, "not walking into the heart of the conspiracy!"

"She's right. It's not safe for her here."

Julia was glad that Milo was finally taking her part. Perhaps the two of them could persuade him that this was sheer folly.

"She needs to be here, as do you."

It was obvious that nothing they could say would make him change his mind, besides which they had already come too far.

Emrys ended the conversation by leaning back and throwing a fold of his cloak over his face. Milo threw up his hands and followed suit, leaving Julia staring at the wall. She fancied that she could detect traces of something there, a lump that could be a shoulder, an indentation that might be an eye, but there was no colour. Now her imagination was playing tricks.

She gave in to the inevitable and tried to make herself comfortable on the hard stone, propped against the wall. She'd close her eyes for a minute or two.

When she awoke, Emrys was gone and Milo was sitting chewing some dried meat. She blinked, realising that she could make out more of his face in a dim light filtering in from the entrance. So, they hadn't been far from it at all. He offered her the water.

"Good morning."

She drank, feeling stiff and not a little chilly.

"Where's Emrys?"

"Gone scouting. I think we'll be making our way outside soon, but he wanted to get the lie of the land first."

Julia regarded him for a moment. His hair was tousled and he needed a shave. She probably didn't look much better.

"Why will they be pleased to see you?"

Milo chewed for a few moments, then swallowed.

"I was born here. Ceridwen's my mother. She'll be delighted I've returned, even though it was she who sent me away."

It was all she could do not to gasp. He was the High Priestess's son?

"Why did she send you away? Shouldn't you be a Priest, or a Mage? Not an Agent."

"It's a long story."

He saw her mouth open and held up a hand.

"Alright! It's not that long. I was taken away as a small boy to be educated among the Mages, but for some reason they didn't let me stay. I ended up abandoned in a foundling home, though I later discovered that Raven had been keeping an eye on me. He taught me bits and pieces, but being an Agent seemed the best option. It's been an interesting life."

"You make it sound like it's over."

He shrugged.

"It probably is. The Gods alone know what's coming."

"Why didn't they bring you back here if they didn't want you? You're certainly good enough to be a Mage."

He gave her a wry smile.

"Thank you. I don't know. One minute I was an apprentice, the next I was out. Eight years old. No family, no friends. I blamed Raven for years, but he was all I had left until I made a new life for myself."

"And you haven't seen your mother since…"

"I was four when she told me I had to go."

He spoke evenly, but she knew that it must have broken his heart. Not one, but two childhood rejections didn't bear thinking about. She couldn't think of anything to say, unable to imagine what he must be feeling.

"The Gods play with us, don't forget that." He pointed his bit of dried meat at her. "They must be very amused by my sorry tale. Still, it could be worse."

"We could be dead."

He grinned. "True."

They froze as a figure obscured the light.

"It's me."

Emrys approached, crouching down so that his head was on a level with theirs. Milo spoke first.

"What's happening?"

"Nothing much that I could see, and that's a worry. There was smoke from the houses, but nobody going about everyday business. It's all too quiet."

"Do you think the Fae have already arrived?"

He shook his head. "There's no sign of them, but I would wager it won't be long until they do. We have to stop them before they're entrenched."

Julia almost laughed. "Stop them? Us? How?"

He shot her a look, his eyes unfathomable.

"That is why we're here."

Now it was Milo's turn to object.

"And what can the three of us do to stop an army?"

Emrys corrected him. "Not an army. A small party at most. They're bringing Marcus's new bride here before they take her to Londinium to be married."

"Ugh! He's marrying a Fae?" Julia was horrified.

"She's not Fae. Étain has lived with them for many years, but she's still human. An enslaved puppet, to be sure, but able to be recognised as queen."

Milo grabbed Emrys's arm, his voice urgent.

"Étain, you said? Not... the one who was lost?"

Emrys nodded.

"Yes. I'm sorry, but it's not only you who's come back to their beginning. The price of Ceridwen's support is that her daughter will be returned to her as Queen of Britannia and they never have to be parted again."

"Your sister?" Julia was aghast.

"Half-sister," Milo corrected her. "We've never met. Étain's much older than me and went to be a Ship. She failed her trials and that was the last anyone heard of her. The Fae must have found her wandering between worlds."

"Indeed. Now she has returned. I know it must be hard for you, Milo, but you have a part to play in this. The Gods have prepared you for this moment."

"Have they?" Disbelief, shock and anger warred on the Agent's features. "They must be pleased with themselves. I haven't a clue what to do!"

"All will be made clear."

"That's nice to know. I'm as much of a game piece as Étain, aren't I? What of the Princess?"

"She will have her role too."

"Excuse me." Julia got up and retreated further back into the cave for some privacy. She'd thought it was a straightforward case of fighting her cousin, but suddenly it was turning into something else and she wasn't sure how to react. As she crouched, trying not to soak her boots, she wondered about Emrys' strategy. 'Stop Marcus' had become 'stop the Fae' and she had no idea how to do either.

When she'd finished, she hovered in the darkness for a minute, resisting the temptation to crawl back into the cave and wait until it was all over, like some hibernating animal. She could hear the two men talking but decided not to join them immediately. Wanting to see the paintings one last time, she raised a tiny Magelight and let it hover, marvelling over the colours on the uneven surface and hunting for any more signs left by the ancestors.

Abruptly, there was movement to the left of her. Something was moving over the wall. For a few seconds she thought it was an insect, or one of the cave spiders about its business, until a horned head and two forelegs broke on to the surface, to be followed by the rest of the body as the huge bull charged across her vision. It was followed by a herd of galloping horses, their manes strangely stiff and tails streaming behind them, then a mighty stag that leapt into view. She saw why a second later. A stick figure was running after them with spear raised, aided by a pack of hounds, their bodies low as they chased their quarry.

The figure threw its spear straight into the flank of the stag. Its legs buckled as it crashed to the ground, antlered head dipping and mouth opening in silent agony. The dogs were on it in a second, preventing its rising again and the figure stood over it, arm raised in victory before bending down and dipping its fingers into the blood that was pouring in a red stream from the stag's wound.

Julia blinked frantically, feeling the Potentia swirling about her as the scene came to its grisly conclusion. Then the figure straightened and walked out of the wall towards her, gaining definition and clarity as it changed from a flat picture to something more human-shaped.

This Huntress was dark skinned, with long, black hair tied back from a broad forehead. A necklace of bones hung around her neck and her clothes were of deer hide, sewn with animal gut. Reddish patterns marked her cheeks, and piercing golden eyes met Julia's dark ones with an intent gaze. She broke into a smile that was both unnerving and familiar.

Julia dipped her head in awe. This had to be a very early aspect of Diana. There were no Greek or Roman trappings here, save the savagery of the hunt. That never changed.

The Goddess drew close to her and a musky, earthy smell rose from her body and clothes. Julia raised her head and the Goddess nodded, as if satisfied at what she saw. Shivers ran up Julia's spine as calloused fingers drew a line of warm, wet blood across her forehead and down each cheek. The sharp, coppery tang of freshly-spilled blood filled her nostrils and she swallowed convulsively. There were no words. She was now consecrated, marked by the Goddess, and it was all she could do to remain upright under the weight of that ancient stare.

Julia closed her eyes, feeling the rush of energy coursing through her veins, as if she were holding a lightning bolt. Potentia surged through her, connecting her to the Earth itself.

When she opened them, the Goddess had gone and she could still hear Milo and Emrys talking. It felt as though hardly any time had passed at all, as if she had experienced a waking dream for a few seconds. The conversation stopped abruptly.

"Princess?"

It was Milo. "Have you finished back there? We have to go."

Still in a daze, Julia stumbled towards the light and her destiny.

*

The wagon rumbled on through the night. The only sounds were the wheels on the rough road, the distant bark of a fox and the odd snore from her exhausted men. Maia had moved to support Leo as he slumped over in his sleep, as she didn't want him to wake with a stiff neck. It wasn't as if her Shipbody could provide the comfort that flesh could, but it was better than having his head lolling at an awkward angle. She looked down at his face, much younger-looking now that it was relaxed in sleep, and reflected on the eventful time they'd already had together. They hadn't had much chance for normal naval service and she suspected that his injuries from the Siren attack were still paining him, though he made no complaint. Their first few months had been an ordeal for them both.

Her thoughts drifted to King Artorius. Had it simply been a joke to match her up with her cousin, or had he had some deeper reason? It seemed beyond coincidence, but anyone wishing to know would have to summon his shade from the Land of the

Dead. It was tempting to think that maybe a God had whispered in his ear.

A few hours in, there was a quiet 'whoa' from Hyacinthus as he made way for Big Ajax to take the reins. The old sailor climbed down and found a place in the back, taking the space vacated by Osric, who went to keep Big Ajax company. It wasn't long before he was snoring along with the rest.

The movement lulled Maia too. Staying still wasn't natural for a Ship, despite the fact that she had seen her first ones ashore at the Portus Naval Headquarters. She knew that they moved around as they wished, but the mechanics of how a building was made to be like a vessel were as yet beyond her. Maybe she was about to find out, as they were heading inland? Unless she was to be given a vessel that could navigate a river, she was leaving the sea for a while. She quietly cursed Raven, with his cryptic comments! This was important and he should have given her more information.

It wasn't long before the early pre-dawn light began to appear, telling all that Helios's chariot would soon appear over the horizon. The first blackbird had started its call when Leo stirred then opened bleary eyes.

<Good morning, Captain!>

He struggled to focus for a second, then smiled up at her.

<Good morning to you too. What a pleasant surprise. I'm not used to being cuddled by my Ship.>

<You were rolling about a bit,> she told him, adjusting her arms to allow him to sit up. He rubbed his eyes and yawned.

<Well, we'd better start as usual, with your report.>

<We're on land, heading for the Gods know where. Big Ajax is driving, with Osric next to him. Oh, and Hyacinthus snores.>

This was confirmed by a loud grunt from the back of the wagon, followed by a few mutterings as his companions began to wake in their turn.

Leo looked back at him and raised an eyebrow.

<It didn't disturb me.>

<No, you were flat out.>

<So, what's next, I wonder? Ah, our Mage is awake. Time for me to ask him a few questions.>

Raven was sitting opposite them, milky eyes fixed on the sky. Maia thought he'd slept, but wasn't sure.

"Good morning, Raven," Leo began.

"Captain."

"Report, please."

"Aye, Captain. If you look ahead of us, you will see a large building set back a little way from the road, surrounded by outbuildings. It's an old villa belonging to someone friendly to our cause. Most of his family have temporarily vacated it, but he's agreed to help."

"So we're staying there?" Leo sounded as puzzled as she was.

"No. I'll be creating a portal to take us elsewhere. In the meantime, food will be laid on and we can all clean ourselves up a bit." His head turned to Maia. "Except our Ship, naturally. You'll be going through first, Maia, with your Captain, Vestinus and a couple of the men. Osric and the marines will remain until the last minute to guard against incursions. I take it you've seen nothing unusual on the way?"

"No. It's all been fairly quiet."

Another snore from Hyacinthus made Raven's mouth twitch.

"Hmm. He sounds like a badger with a head cold."

Leo bit his lip to stop himself from laughing. They'd been talking quietly enough, but it had roused Amphicles. Maia thought her new second-in-command looked better than he had. Some colour had returned to his face, so the rest must have done him good.

"Orders, sir?"

Leo raised himself up and leaned over the side of the wagon.

"We'll be stopping at that old villa ahead of us."

Amphicles joined him, staring ahead. "I see it. Good. I'll be glad to get out of this wagon." He picked a piece of straw out of his hair and made an attempt to brush himself down. "I fear we all look like scarecrows, sir."

"No matter," Leo said, his eyes fixed on their destination. Maia, placed awkwardly on the remnants of her deck planks, was quietly galled that she would have to rely on their observations.

"I wonder if Musca and his crew have already arrived," she said.

"Yes," Raven replied. "They were able to move faster across country than we could. They're resting now, but we'll see them shortly."

So, he was in communication with someone in the villa. It made sense and was probably the reason he seemed a little distracted. Maia quelled the momentary stab of irritation she was beginning to feel on a regular basis. Raven was doing her job now, whilst she was stuck here blind and deaf, dependent on others. She made up her mind to try walking more. She'd seen other Ships do it, notably the *Diadem* during her installation ceremony, and it hadn't been too long since she had been in her human body. She'd already had enough of being carried around like some pampered empress.

Shortly, the wagon changed direction, veering off to the right and Maia got her first view of the villa. It had seen better days, with plaster flaking off the external walls and cracked roof tiles. One outbuilding had crumbled completely into a heap of stone, with timbers protruding from the heap like old bones. It must have fallen on hard times for some reason. It was certainly nothing like the opulence she'd seen at Senator Rufus's villa, or even the dream one she'd inhabited. This was more of a working farm.

They passed through large wooden gates and clattered over cobbles into a substantial central yard. Several men and a couple of women, farmworkers by the look of their rough tunics and muddy boots, rushed out to unhitch the horses. An elderly couple, slightly better dressed, approached the wagon. The man leant on the woman and Maia noticed that he shuffled rather than walked. They both appeared to be in their sixties or seventies, wrapped in cloaks over heavy woollen clothing despite the mildness of the weather.

By the time they had reached the wagon, everyone save Maia had already climbed out and were standing, picking off bits of straw and brushing themselves down. Raven greeted their hosts first, a smile on his withered features.

"Hail to you, Gaius Taurus Iucundus, and to you also, Carssouna! We thank you for your hospitality. Now, permit me to make the introductions."

Maia could hear her Captain and officers being introduced and she came to a decision. She swung her lower body aside, reaching down to retrieve her scraps of vessel. She didn't know what would happen if she left them behind, so didn't want to risk it. Then she raised herself up, holding on to the side of the wagon for leverage and concentrated on forming legs and feet beneath her skirts. It stood to reason that she could change on land just as she had done in the sea. Looking down, she could see wooden toes peeping out. Apart from the colour, they looked like hers. She gave them a wiggle, smiling to herself as they responded. Good. Now to move herself.

The floor of the wagon creaked as she walked towards the tailgate, brushing aside straw with her feet. Maybe it would be better if she had shoes? A thought was all it took and there they were, formed to look like the fashionable ones she had seen wealthy ladies wearing and ornamented with shiny buckles. She debated on making them red but changed her mind as navy blue looked better. Simultaneously, she shortened her skirts as well to move more freely. Pleased with herself, she climbed down from the tailgate until her new feet were touching the cobbles.

"*Tempest!*"

Leo's exclamation made her turn to the group.

"Captain. Please introduce me to our hosts."

The startled look on his face made her want to giggle. Did he think she would just sit there and wait for somebody to notice her?

"Er, Gaius Taurus Iucundus, may I present my Ship, *Tempest*."

Maia walked carefully over to them and inclined her head. "I'm honoured, sir, ma'am."

Iucundus bowed. His brown eyes were sharp under bushy eyebrows and she got the impression that he didn't miss much.

"No, ma'am," his voice was strong, despite his infirmity. "It is we who are honoured. Welcome and thrice welcome to my poor house! This is my wife, Carssouna."

Carssouna smiled at her shyly, her blue eyes huge as she gazed at one of the legendary Ships of Britannia. Maia smiled back, for the first time wishing that she looked more human instead of showing the forbidding mask she'd adopted. Perhaps it wasn't too late to change, or maybe it would frighten them even more. She'd forgotten that she was now a creature of half-mythical status, having become used to being regarded as a normal part of a vessel.

"We won't impose on you for long, sir," Raven interrupted. "I trust you found me a place to set up a portal?"

"We have, Master Mage," Iucundus replied. "I'm too old to fight against the Usurper, but I'm glad I can help in other ways."

"Your aid will not be forgotten," Leo assured him. "We shall tell His Majesty."

"May the Gods aid and protect him," Iucundus replied.

"Now, Master Iucundus, you have been standing for long enough," Raven said. "You go inside and leave the rest to us."

Carssouna nodded to them and gently led her husband away back to the main building.

Victor had gone on ahead and now returned with news.

"The food's laid out ready, gentlemen," he told them. "You've time for a quick wash first. I'm to take you to the bathing suite."

"Good," Leo said. "I could eat a kraken on toast. Lead on!"

The group made their way towards main entrance of the villa and through into a large atrium. It looked better on the inside, though the frescoes were faded and some of the tesserae on the mosaic floor had been replaced over the years. After the first few steps, Maia got used to her new limbs. It was almost the same as human movement, but called for a little more effort on her part. She had to be slower and set her feet down more deliberately, but it was much better than being lugged around. She continued to carry her vessel's wood under one arm, but was starting to wonder whether she really needed it.

Her Captain and officers ushered away by Victor, leaving her with Raven and the rest of the men. She was conscious that the old Mage had been observing her closely in the strange way he had.

<You've adapted well,> he remarked.

<I prefer to shift for myself,> she answered tartly. <I saw *Diadem* and others do it, so I knew I could too.>

<Good for you, though I think Leo was a little surprised.>

She Sent him a mental chuckle through the link.

<It's nice to remind him that he doesn't know everything.>

<Getting one up on your Captain, eh?"

<Of course!>

They shared the amusement before she broached the subject of her vessel.

<Do I need these?> She waved the splintered shards in his direction.

Raven looked thoughtful.

<What do you think?>

<I did at first,> she admitted, <but now they feel like an encumbrance. My vessel's gone and that's that.>

<True. Still, I'd hang on to them if I were you, or maybe pass them on to Vestinus to keep them for you. I suspect your carpenter will find a use for them.>

She was immediately excited.

<For my new vessel?>

<Yes. They'll need to be incorporated into the structure. It's nice to have some continuity.>

Maia's spirits rose. So, she was getting a new vessel!

<What's it like?>

The ancient Mage hesitated.

<Different.>

She cast him a look of disgust.

<Are you honestly not going to tell me *anything*? Even now?>

She knew he was feeling smug, but beneath that was an undercurrent of something else as if he was feeling unsettled about their destination.

To her annoyance, Raven ended their conversation as everyone moved into an adjoining room, where basins of water, soap and towels had been placed and tables set up with food and drink. The men availed themselves of the amenities with alacrity.

"*Tempest*, please follow me to the *triclinium*," Raven said. She would join her officers and Priest, as they would not be expected to eat with the ordinary crewmen and marines.

Satisfied that everyone would be well fed, Maia followed him back into the atrium and through into the dining room, taking up position next to the wall.

After a while her officers returned, looking fresher. Leo settled down on a couch with Amphicles, while the others took up position on the remaining two. Victor hurried to serve them, but after everyone had washed their hands, Leo waved him away.

"See to yourself, Victor. We can make do here. I'll call you if we need you."

Victor bowed and hurried off, but not without casting an eye over the arrangements to check all was to his liking.

"Our hosts are generous," Leo said, helping himself. "Can they afford this?"

"They insisted on breaking into their stores," Raven said. He had accepted a glass of wine from Amphicles, but didn't seem inclined to eat. "As to the danger, Iucundus just shrugged and said, 'what more can they do to us? I'll just say that my sons were bound to follow my orders as *paterfamilias*.' He's had some bad harvests lately and then his livestock got a murrain. It's been hard for them these past years, even with their children and grandchildren doing all they can. Still, he remains faithful to the Gods and his King."

"And I hope they'll reward him," Leo replied. "Which Gods does he favour, Danuco?"

They had passed the household shrine and would pay their respects later.

"Jupiter, Ceres and Proserpina."

It was usual that the Thunderer, the Earth Mother and her daughter would be worshipped by farmers, who relied on them to bestow a good harvest. Unfortunately, it appeared that in this case their prayers hadn't been answered as they might have wished.

"Let's hope their luck changes," Amphicles ventured.

"Indeed," Danuco said. "I will attempt to intercede for them. Their current actions should bring them favour."

The Priest seemed subdued, as if aware that he hadn't been able to give them a lot of information lately. Maia wondered how he communicated with his fellows. She knew that Mages used speechstones; perhaps clerics had their own version? Danuco had certainly been staring into space a lot in the past few days.

Raven emptied his wine glass and stood, leaning on his staff.

"I'll go and prepare. You'll have about an hour and a half by my reckoning before everything's set for your departure."

Leo nodded. "I'll need to meet with Musca first. We'll be ready."

Maia stared around the room, trying not to think about how all the food tasted. She was tempted to go for a walk, but had no idea of the protocols for a Ship without a vessel. Hopefully, Raven wouldn't take too long setting up the portal and they could be out of here quickly. She dreaded to think what would happen to Iucundus and Carssouna if Marcus found out they'd sheltered his enemies, despite the old man's bravado.

Her eye fell on Osric, who was tucking into his food with a will.

"I hope there's a bath house where we're going," Amphicles said.

"Who knows?" Hawthorn sounded resigned.

"Raven's not said anything then, sir?" Osric asked, in between bites.

"Not a word," Leo answered.

The marine snorted. "He's an old fox, that one. More tricks up his sleeve than anyone's a right to."

"That's true enough," his Captain grinned. "Good job he's with us."

Osric raised his eyebrows and helped himself to another slice of ham.

"I've some news," Danuco said. All eyes turned to the Priest in anticipation. The Gods had been quiet enough lately, so much so that Maia had dared wonder if they had decided to leave mortals to it and be merely spectators. It didn't help when her Priest had refused to comment.

"The Gods are gathering their forces and will act on our behalf. The High Priest of Jupiter, Aquila, is rallying support to assist the Lady Drusilla, who has arrived at Dubris with an army of mercenaries and others." He sounded like he was reading from a news sheet. "Many Priests have been arrested and some have been killed by Marcus, angering their respective deities. There is also a large Fae fleet setting sail from Hibernia to bolster Marcus's legions."

"Does Raven know this?" Leo asked.

"Yes. He's just been informed through Mage channels."

"And Pendragon?"

"The *Imperatrix*'s Priest will know. There has been a conclave and it has been determined that the Olympians are united against the threat."

"About time," Osric muttered, then looked abashed.

Danuco raised an eyebrow. "You know they do as they will." Maia wondered how she and her crew fitted into all of this. Would one more Ship make a difference, even if she did get a new vessel? She remembered her meeting with Jupiter's High Priest and the one who had spoken through him, his gold-flecked eyes boring into hers as he issued the deadly warning. The echo of the terror she'd felt still remained, even now.

The officers didn't linger over their meal. Maia followed her Captain outside, but not before she caught Osric filling his pockets with any food that could keep. She hoped that there would be enough left for the household. It would not do for them to behave like a herd of rampaging boars, gobbling up everything in sight.

"Do you think you'll starve, Osric?"

The Captain of Marines shrugged.

"Got to take what we can, when we can, ma'am."

She had to suppress a smile. She'd have done exactly the same as a servant, stuffing everything she could get her hands on inside her clothes for later, especially if it was sweet.

"Do leave them something, won't you."

He saluted, pockets bulging, and strode off to see to his men. She would have to have a word with Leo, and possibly Raven, but she didn't want to disturb the latter in the middle of delicate work.

She stepped through to the atrium, where she found her Captain in discussions with Musca. They broke off, saluting as she approached, though she thought her Chief Gunner looked startled.

"Hello, Musca."

"Neptune protect us! I thought you were one of the Gods for a moment, ma'am!"

"No," she laughed. "Just a Ship without a vessel and feeling well out of my depth."

He looked her up and down. "Don't know about that, ma'am. You seem to be pretty sprightly on two legs an' all."

"It's not long since that was what I had."

He sucked his teeth.

"That's true enough. Older Ships would have more trouble. They can barely move on land."

"We must all adapt, Musca."

The grizzled old sailor didn't look happy. "Aye, ma'am, but to what? I take it we'll get another vessel, sir?"

He looked hopefully at his Captain.

"I expect we will. Are the lads ready to go?"

"Just give the word, sir."

"Excellent. We'll be going through in as big a group as the portal can take. Dismissed."

They exchanged salutes, then Musca left them, leaving Leo and Maia alone.

"I'm worried that we're going to leave the family short of food," she said.

"Ha! Everyone's been stuffing themselves, have they?"

"And taking extra too."

He frowned. "I'll give orders to Mr Amphicles and Osric."

"Osric's already filled his pockets."

Leo rolled his eyes. "Yes, I noticed that he was making the most of things. It's normal when you don't know where your next meal's coming from."

Maia decided not to point out that she knew that. He already felt badly about her former position in life and she didn't want to remind him again.

"Any word from Raven?"

"Not yet."

"There's the household shrine. I'm going to tell Danuco to hold the service now. That will stop anyone getting up to mischief while we wait and I can address everyone at once."

He looked around him, a slight frown on his face.

"Blast it! There's never anyone around when you need them. I'll go and find where Amphicles has got to. Wait here."

He marched off, boots ringing on the mosaic. Maia shifted her burden and examined the wooden shrine. It looked ordinary enough, with doors that could be opened to display the statuettes of the Gods, both major and those of the household. There would be regular offerings to both, though lately it seemed that the family's pleas had fallen on deaf ears.

A woman entered from the room they had just left. She appeared youthful, wrapped in a dark cloak of fine wool. She had to be a daughter or daughter-in-law.

Maia greeted her.

"Good day, Lady."

The woman walked up to her, smiling and Maia suddenly became aware that all the background sounds in the villa had ceased. Voices were stilled and even the dust motes in the air seemed to hang suspended. The woman had dark hair bound back with a golden fillet and elaborate earrings swung at her neck. They were jewelled peacock feathers. Maia froze. She knew the signs by now.

"Greeting to you, Gemma Valeria, latterly *Tempest*."

The Goddess's voice was light and pleasant. Maia bowed.

"Lady Juno."

The Queen of Heaven raised an eyebrow.

"Yes, I thought you would see my earrings. I like to give hints. Sometimes."

That meant they must have met before, but even with her prodigious memory Maia had no clue.

"Oh, you never guessed," Juno said. "We Gods like our disguises, and pretending to be someone you know is even more amusing. Still, I am here to tell you that I am your protector and a friend of your mother. It was I who turned Jupiter's wrath from you, though I fear I was too late to help your father. My stepdaughter's enmity ran deep."

"All because my mother left her?"

"Yes. The Huntress has always demanded unswerving adoration, but she has been taught a lesson she won't forget in a hurry." Juno's smile grew wider. "She has other distractions now and will not bother you again."

That was good to hear.

"Still, I wanted you to know that you have the support of Heaven. You have kept your side of the bargain you made with my husband and must continue to do so."

"I thank you, Lady."

Maia was still puzzled. Juno didn't turn up out of nowhere for no reason. The Queen of Olympus laughed, her earrings shimmering in the light.

"When we need to, we act. Your mother is still forbidden to communicate with you, but your sister isn't. She will act as a go-between, as you will be needing her aid over the next few days. Call upon her and she will come, as will Cymopoleia, though I warn you that she is a creature of last resort. Both have been sanctioned by my husband to act in your interests. As to the rest –"

The Goddess drew closer, her dark eyes sparkling.

"– I was curious. Farewell, Child of the Air."

Then Juno was gone and Maia was back in the world again.

The sounds of many feet dragged her back to her current situation as her men filed in, taking up positions around the atrium in an orderly fashion. It was a familiar sight, if not in the usual place. Danuco and her officers appeared next, with Iucundus, Carssouna and members of their household. The space was soon full, with a few extra faces peering from doorways at the back.

<I think that's just about everyone, except those few tending the animals, and Raven.> Leo Sent. <Let's make our appeal to the Gods, shall we?>

<Aye, sir.>

She kept her tone light, knowing that she wouldn't be able to tell him about her latest visitation, even as she tried to work out who Juno had impersonated in the past. It wouldn't have been the evil Blandina that was for sure. There had been something motherly about her. Maybe one of the women who had cared for her at the Home? Perhaps she would never know.

Maia turned her attention to the ceremony. As it was indoors, only token offerings would be made on the little altar. Sure enough, there were some flowers, bread and the obligatory incense. She could see Carssouna and Iucundus now, ready to present them to Danuco. The Priest covered his head with a fold of his robe, opened the doors to the shrine and began the invocation. The usual bronze statuettes of Jupiter, Ceres and Proserpina stood in the centre, surrounded by figures made of plaited corn representing the harvest and a couple of vaguely human-looking wooden figures that looked so ancient she couldn't tell what they were. They had to be local or family protectors, the ancient Britannic Gods of the Land sharing space with the Olympians as was the custom in many houses.

The rituals proceeded in the time-honoured way, with the offerings placed reverently before the Gods. Maia let the familiar words wash over her. However, just as Danuco finished, the doors blew open and a gust of perfumed air swirled around the atrium. Leo made a grab for his hat as the breeze darted about the pillars, fluttering robes and tousling hair. Maia eagerly searched for a clue. Was this her sister? There was nothing to be seen, but that didn't mean that Pearl wasn't present. Instead, she had the sudden sensation of arms encircling her Shipbody and a head resting on her shoulder. At the same time, Leo exclaimed aloud, his hand moving to touch his cheek and a look of wonder on his face.

"All hail the Spirits of the Air!" Danuco cried. His wide eyes and expression of rapture told that he was fulfilling his role as a bridge between the mortal and immortal. "The Gods favour us! Jupiter himself favours us!"

A flash of light lit up the doorway, followed a couple of seconds later by a sky-shaking rumble. Hands went to amulets and lips moved in silent prayer. Some raised their eyes and arms to heaven in mute worship as the King of the Gods spoke.

Maia found herself enveloped in warm cocoon that funnelled around her in joyous spirals. She sent forth a prayer of her own.

<Greetings, Mother!>

For a second the breeze seemed to hover before her, then with a final blast it exited the way it had come.

The final echoes of thunder died away, leaving a shocked congregation. Leo looked stunned, Danuco still appeared ecstatic and Iucundus was quietly crying, overcome by events. Then everyone started talking at once.

Raven's amplified voice boomed around the atrium, cutting through the noise.

"Quickly, get Master Iucundus to a seat. Calm down, everyone! Danuco, I'm sure you can finish proceedings appropriately. Osric, take everyone out and get them ready to leave."

Nobody argued with the Master Mage. Carssouna tried to get her husband to rest, but the old man insisted on being left before the shrine.

"I need to commune with my ancestors," he said, tears running down his cheeks. "Truly we have been blessed by Jove himself! We must arrange a proper sacrifice."

Iucundus's watery eyes fixed on Maia. "You are favoured too, Lady. The Goddess of the Air came to you. I saw her." For a moment his eyes were far away. "I have always seen things others couldn't, you know."

His gaze fell on Leo. "She kissed you!"

Leo blushed. "Erm, yes, she did. I felt it. I don't know why."

"Who knows why?" Carssouna said, despite Leo's embarrassment. "Perhaps she just fancied a handsome Captain?"

Maia knew why. Apart from the colour of his eyes, hazel instead of blue Leo was the image of her dead father. Captain Lucius Valerius Vero was gone forever, but Captain Tiberius Valerius Severianus Leo was very much alive and the temptation had been too great. Maia could only hope that the contact had brought her mother comfort in her enduring grief. Maybe one day she could tell him.

Leo pulled himself together. "Yes, well. Raven, thank you for your intervention. Report, please."

"All is prepared, sir. I suggest that I bring *Tempest* and yourself through first, then Mr Amphicles, Danuco, Hawthorn and the crew in several groups. All in all, it should take less than an hour."

"Very well." Leo turned to his second-in-command. "Mr Amphicles, I'll leave that to you to arrange. See you later. *Tempest*, let's go."

As they followed Raven to the portal, he whispered in her mind. <Did the Goddess speak to you?>

Maia nearly asked which one, but replied as she knew she must.

<No, but I felt her around me.>

<Why do I get the impression that you know more than you're saying?>

She glanced over at him as he matched his pace to hers.

<Because I do, but I can't tell.>

He narrowed his eyes. <Not even for your Captain?>

<Sorry.>

He chewed that over for a minute as they entered the villa's main reception room. Faded hangings warmed the walls and carved furniture had been pushed back against the walls, leaving the centre of the floor bare.

<What can you tell me?>

She thought quickly.

<It was Aura, Goddess of the Dawn Breeze. She's mother to our friendly Tempestas.>

Leo shot her a startled look.

<The one that told us of Artorius's death?>

<The same. The Tempestas can help us and relay messages, so we'll probably be seeing a lot more of her.>

<That's good.>

<Yes.>

She sensed the questions he was desperate to ask bubbling under the surface of his thoughts.

<And why would she help us?>

<Jupiter's orders.>

They had reached the perimeter of the portal now. The markings on the patterned floor glowed as if they'd been drawn in purple light. Raven was gesturing and muttering, causing them to increase in brightness.

Leo's eyes widened. <You'll tell me what you can? I'm not happy that you're keeping so many secrets from me.>

She looked him full in the face.

<I'm not happy about it either, but I do what I must.>

He took a deep breath.

<You never told me what happened to your mother, did you?>

She was saved from answering by Raven.

"Enter the circle, please."

It only took three steps, then the magic whisked them away.

VI

It made a change to have some time to himself, Caniculus decided. He'd slept late and woken to a leisurely breakfast which he'd eaten in the common room among the other patrons. Everyone was intent on their own business so nobody bothered him, which was how he liked it. All in all, it was more enjoyable than having to be on constant alert for new orders.

His plan was to head into the centre of Segedunum and make a few enquiries. His stay at Knut's *mansio* was pleasant enough, though he knew that it was only a temporary solution to his present woes. In the meantime, he was eking out his money and hoping to come across paid work at some point that would tide him over. He couldn't see himself returning south any time soon, not with all the unrest, nor did he want to dwell on the punishments given out to rogue Agents. There would be no public execution. Questioning under torture, then a knife in the ribs and an unsanctified grave would be all he could expect.

He nodded to Knut as he left to wander through the city. He knew Milo had been in this area, but it was somewhere he'd never been before. He told himself it would make a change to be somewhere new, even if he couldn't understand the local dialect very well. The Latin pronunciation was interesting and he found his ear adapting as he went. There were folk from all over the Empire mingling with the locals and bringing goods to be distributed all over the north of Britannia and beyond, even into Caledonia.

Maybe he should take a risk and contact his friend? He told himself that it would be good to have more intelligence and it seemed that poor old Milo was in the thick of things. He activated his charmed speechstone.

<Dog to Ferret.>

He could tell that the device was working, but there was no reply, even after several tries. A coldness settled in his guts. He probed the linkage, trying to get more answers. It seemed fine, but blocked somehow. Perhaps his friend was under orders not to reply to anyone, even him? He tried to shake off the unease, promising himself that he would try again later, and continued on his way towards the mouth of the river.

The port was thronged with a variety of vessels, mostly merchantmen. He couldn't see any Ships though he looked long and hard. There were a couple of Northerners with their outlandish spirits sitting at the prow. One appeared to be a bear, the other some kind of serpent. Probably Marcus had ordered any Ships that weren't with Pendragon back to one of the southern ports, so he could keep his eye on them.

Sweating workers were unloading everything from the ubiquitous amphorae containing olive oil, wine and fish sauce to bales of cloth and sacks of spices, assisted by an impressive number of cranes. All was noise and industry. One part of the port seemed to be solely for loading huge amounts of coal to be sent to the factories down south. He'd heard that there were rich seams of the stuff up here and demand was growing everywhere, especially in Londin. His mother was always complaining that the air was getting worse as more and more chimneys went up.

Caniculus's thoughts turned to his family. Marcus was spending money like water, so they'd be working all hours. Maybe when this was all over, he could persuade his Ma and Pa to retire to the country? The thought consoled him. It was always good to have an end goal in the midst of uncertainty.

He wandered around, admiring the wide streets lined with shops and noting the many statues to the Emperor Hadrian, who had given his name to the great wall that ended at Segedunum and the old Pons Aelius, or Hadrian's Bridge, over the River Tinea to the west. Eventually, he came upon the Forum. It was lined with all the usual administrative buildings and temples, built on the same pattern as every other major settlement in the Roman Empire. Save for the climate, he could have been anywhere from Africa to the Eastern deserts to New Roma, far away over the ocean. In the midst of it, a crowd of people caught his eye and he hurried up to hear the midday news.

The City Crier had taken his place on the podium in the Forum. The portly man in his official robes was the main source of information for those who couldn't read, or for anything that was too new for the presses to have published. It looked like something was up. He was clutching a scroll and looking worried, gesturing to the crowd to gather round. When he was satisfied that he had a large enough audience, he unrolled the scroll with a dramatic flick and adopted a theatrical position.

"Citizens of the Empire! I, Gaius Cottius Florentinus, have the honour of bringing you the latest news, on behalf of the noble City of Segedunum!"

He paused for effect before continuing slowly.

"This day, it is reported that a large force of mercenaries has landed on the southern shore of Britannia! They are challenging King Marcus's reign and making false and malicious accusations against him!"

Exclamations of shock burst from the crowd.

"What are they saying?" One fellow yelled.

Florentinus fixed the man with a look of disapproval.

"They are saying that he ordered the assassination of King Artorius and the murder of Senator Madoc Britannicus Rufus! They claim he is a usurper and that he has a fake Excalibur!"

Caniculus gaped. For this to be announced it must mean that someone, somewhere had proof. There was no way the City Council could get away with this under normal circumstances. Movement to his right caused him and others to turn, only to see a large group of Priests standing on the steps of the Temple of Jupiter. Their appearance caused alarm bells to ring and, by the murmur of the crowd, he wasn't the only one. If this wasn't a sign, he didn't know what was.

"The mercenaries are led by the Lady Antonia Drusilla, wife of the late Senator. She claims to have witnessed her husband's death at the hands of Naevius Sutorius Macro, Chief of the Royal Guards!"

The murmuring grew to a roar. Caniculus took his eyes from the Crier and began to watch the crowd instead. It wouldn't take much for everything to turn ugly. Florentinus, having worked up sufficient interest, was gesturing for calm.

"Good people! Have no fear! Marcus is even now gathering his legions to meet them. Surely the Gods will uphold the virtuous and see that the enemies of Britannia are ground into the dust!"

That was a double-edged statement all right. Florentinus waved his scroll.

"In more news, to the west –"

But Caniculus was no longer listening. The last moments of the Senator's life replayed with vivid intensity in his head, and a sudden, overwhelming hatred for Marcus and Macro washed over him, momentarily blotting out his vision. Rufus would be proud of his wife, returning to avenge her husband like a Fury from the ancient stories. Hopefully she would help to dispatch the evil pair to Tartarus in short order, legions or no legions.

As his sight cleared, he could see that people were already making their way to the adjoining temples to hear what the Gods were saying. Caniculus had no doubt that they would be given confirmation that the rumours were true, despite the Crier's lukewarm protestation of loyalty. Segedunum might be several hundred miles away from the action, but everything was interconnected and the ripples of disturbance would be felt even at this distance. Maybe it was time to leave, but to where? South didn't seem like an option and the west was under threat. If the worst came to the worst he could go north, but the thought of living in Caledonia didn't hold much appeal for him, even if they weren't all painted, hairy-arsed barbarians these days. Anywhere north of the Tinea gave him the jitters.

His stomach grumbled, reminding him that it was several hours since he had last eaten. Everything would look better with some food and a few drinks inside him, so he loped off to find a suitable watering hole. He'd tried to avoid going to the same ones twice, just in case he was still being hunted, but by the sounds of things the Agency would have more to worry about, so he returned to one he'd found had passable food and great ale.

The Blue Monkey was quite crowded for early afternoon, steadily filling with dock workers on their lunch breaks and sailors from several merchantmen that had just made port. Caniculus ordered at the bar, then managed by some miracle to bag a seat. He sat with his back to the panelled wall, sipping his ale and watching what was going on. Even though he was no longer working as an Agent, some habits were too ingrained to break. The talk was of the invasion, both to the south and the west.

"Maybe it's the same people," a fair-haired man said, a German by his accent. "That would make sense, to hit from two sides at once."

"From what I hear, it's Fae to the west and Marcus is in league with them," his companion, a young acolyte told him. The latter leaned closer and Caniculus had to strain to hear what he was saying. "The temples are in a right tizzy. The Gods aren't happy with Marcus and the senior Priests are saying the rumours are true. Jupiter himself has spoken."

"Really?" His companion looked sceptical.

"Believe me. There's some serious stuff going to kick off any time now." The acolyte took a hasty swallow of his drink. "I'm just a lowly dogsbody and even I can see that."

"He's right, you know."

Caniculus jumped. He'd been so intent on eavesdropping that he hadn't noticed the young man sliding into a seat next to him, one which he could have sworn hadn't been there a moment before. The cheerful face beneath a shock of black, curly hair was familiar, though the last time he'd seen it had been at a crossroads far away at twilight. The curse slipped into his mind before he could stop it.

Merda!

Mercury burst out laughing. "Indeed, my hangdog friend. That just about sums everything up. Have another drink."

Caniculus looked into his mostly empty beer mug to see it slowly filling.

"Lord," he said, his mouth dry. He flicked his eyes quickly from left to right, but the God seemed to be alone this time.

Mercury leaned back in his seat and crossed his ankles.

"So, you've travelled far since our last meeting. Can't say I blame you."

"I've still got the helmet. Do you want it back? I can go and get it immediately."

Caniculus was all too aware he was blabbering.

Mercury waved a hand. "Not necessary, besides, you might need it. I've another job for you."

Caniculus clamped down on his thoughts. Though Mercury gave off nowhere near the dangerous emanations he'd felt from Mars, it was wise to be respectful.

"At your service, Lord."

"Excellent! You're to return to Londin and retrieve something that's been buried for a very long time."

"May I ask what, Lord?"

Mercury's eyes twinkled.

"Actually, I'm merely the messenger, acting on behalf of other Gods. They're a lot older than I am and I don't mind telling you that they give me the creeps." He shuddered. "This is their purview, so I'm just doing what I'm told. Mostly. There's always time for a quick drink."

A mug of beer appeared in the God's hand and he raised it in salute.

Caniculus looked at him in horror.

"Oh, you're Britannic, so it might not be so bad for you. Me, I'm a recent import and find all this a bit much. Lug's alright with it all, but as we've already met it's easier for us to talk like this."

The ancient God was often worshipped alongside Mercury, so perhaps they were aspects of the same deity. Religious studies had never been Caniculus's strongest subject. Mercury grimaced.

"Sorry, it's complicated. All I meant was that I'm not the only one involved, so you may get instructions from other quarters as well."

"Whereabouts in Londin do you want me to go, Lord?"

"The Old Fort," Mercury replied. "You see why you might need the helmet? When you get there, hang around and await further instructions. I suppose it will take you a few days to travel south."

"We can't all move like the wind, Lord."

Mercury was amused. "True. I'd lend you my sandals if I could, but I need them myself. Don't worry, you'll have the usual protections, but I'd get a move on if I were you."

Caniculus opened his mouth, but the God forestalled him.

"In the morning. Eat, drink and be merry first. You'll need this." He dropped a leather purse on the table and Caniculus heard the clink of coin. "This will see you right."

There was nothing for it. He scooped the full purse off the table, secreting it beneath his cloak.

"Yes, Lord."

"Don't sound so glum! At least you won't meet the Fae."

Caniculus's Agent instincts took over before he could help it.

"So it is them invading to the west then?"

For once, the God's cheerful smile faded.

"Yes. The ones at sea must be stopped. The few that landed have been dealt with. My half-sister does so love a hunt." Then he brightened. "Hooray for the Ships of Britannia!"

"My friend Milo's aboard a Ship." Caniculus blurted out. "Are they going into battle? I can't get in touch with him."

Mercury gave him an arch look.

"Actually, he's no longer at sea, but I can't say any more, other than he's well and where he's supposed to be, so don't panic. Talking of being at sea, I'd get aboard a boat to Londin if I were you."

A boat? He didn't like the sound of that.

"I could hire a carriage, Lord."

Mercury sucked his teeth.

"I wouldn't. The roads are going to be *very* busy. Never mind! Now, drink up, there's a good fellow!"

Caniculus felt the knot inside his stomach that had loosened at the news of Milo's safety tighten up again. He obligingly took a swig from his mug and smacked his lips appreciatively. Now that was good ale! He opened his mouth to thank the God, but Mercury had departed as quickly as he had come.

"Well, thanks anyway," he muttered. He fully intended to make the most of his last night, so eat, drink and be merry it was. Then it would be time to sleep, settle up with Knut and go to book passage on the best vessel he could find.

He'd worry about the rest later. If he got through the sea voyage in one piece. He hated sailing with a passion.

*

It was after noon and dark clouds were bubbling up over the horizon when the fleet sighted the *Leopard* making her way from the east. The link came alive immediately with greetings and demands for news.

They were answered with the usual abruptness.

<Give me a minute, you lot!>

The Ship was having to force her way against a freshening wind, putting a great deal of her Potentia into keeping her vessel moving the way she wanted it to.

<You've a full load on, girl,> *Diadem* remarked.

<Oh yes!> *Leopard* sounded satisfied with that, if nothing else. <I swapped one load for another, though I can tell you this one's heavier. There'll be goodies for all.>

That was met by murmurings.

<We'll need them,> *Imperatrix* said. <It doesn't look like our regular armaments will have much effect on the enemy.>

<True,> *Blossom* chipped in. <But we all saw what one of them can do. I take it they're those fish things?>

<Torpedoes.>

Leopard clearly relished the word.

Briseis, anchored in the remains of her vessel, spotted her ploughing through the rising seas. *Leopard* could be forced to tack at this rate and that would slow her progress considerably.

<They're all well and good, but we need our Mages back,> *Unicorn* complained. She was undergoing repairs, but it was doubtful whether she'd be fit to do more than support the others. What she needed was a dry dock and plenty of attention, not a hasty jury-rig in the middle of the ocean.

That was true. Without their Mages they'd have little defensive capabilities. Ships could raise a shield, but it took a combination of both theirs and their Mages' abilities to maintain it for long.

<I still don't understand why our cannons didn't do for the Fae,> *Dragon* said.

She and the other Ships had been fully welcomed back into the fold and, as far as everyone was concerned, their previous opposition had been forgiven. The only one to fire a shot in anger had been the *Regina*, and she was still nowhere to be found. The *Justicia* had turned up in Portus claiming the need for repairs, and was keeping very quiet.

<They must have upgraded their spells,> *Vanguard* said gloomily. <Let's hope they don't all have the same defences, or we're in trouble.>

Unicorn refused to be consoled.

<There's not much I can do, the state I'm in.>

Briseis bit her tongue. Snapping at her sisters wouldn't help, though *Unicorn*'s constant whining was beginning to get on everyone's nerves.

<Oh for Neptune's sake, *Unicorn*! At least you still have a vessel!>

Farsight had woken and had no such qualms.

<Sorry.>

Hopefully, that would shut her up for a while. Everyone's nerves were stretched to breaking and the inaction wasn't helping.

"Ah, *Patience*. I see *Leopard*'s returning. There's more good news as well."

Fabillus had come on deck. He saluted Drustan, who was on watch, then came to stand next to his Ship.

"Good news?"

"Yes. They've rigged the *Seashell* to take you."

Briseis felt her spirits rise.

"How will it work?"

"We're fortunate enough to still have Sandpiper. He's recovered enough to assist you with the bonding process. It will take quite a lot of Potentia, as the vessel wasn't built with the channels your old vessel had. It will feel awkward at first, but it's better than nothing."

"It most certainly is!" She smiled at him. "I'm looking forward to it."

"Good for you! So am I," he confided. "Not that everyone aboard the *Imperatrix* hasn't been more than kind, but we need some independence again."

She nodded. "When will it happen?"

"We're going to bring the vessel alongside and transport you across within the hour. *Farsight* will get the *Mallard.*"

"We both kept our Captains, thank the Gods." She gazed at Fabillus fondly. He was unflappable and that was what she needed at the moment. They were indeed well-suited and the thought of losing him so soon into their partnership was an unbearable one.

He saluted her. "It is my honour to serve, ma'am!"

Imperatrix glided over to them, her expression one of approval.

"Captain Fabillus, *Patience*. The *Seashell* is ready for you to board."

Fabillus raised his hat to her. "My thanks, *Imperatrix*. You have been a most gracious hostess."

The Ship was pleased. "Only too happy to help."

"It won't take long," he said. "There's not much to transport over."

"I hope the crew of the *Seashell* won't mind," *Patience* said.

Imperatrix looked surprised. "Not at all, my dear! They fought valiantly against the serpents, but lost a few men in the process. Their commander will be only too glad to surrender his vessel to your protection."

"I've served with Lucius Tetius Micianus in the past," Fabillus told them. "He's a sound officer and an expert sailor, which is why he was given charge of an inanimate. I'll appoint him as sailing master."

"I've heard of him," *Imperatrix* said.

She seemed about to add more, but stopped herself. They'd have to have a chat later, Briseis thought. There was obviously something else, but it might be a Ship matter and not for her Captain's ears. If there was any gossip about her new sailing master, she wanted to know it.

"We'll take our leave then."

Fabillus and Briseis saluted *Imperatrix*, who returned it before sinking into the deck, probably on her way to report back to Pendragon.

"It won't be easy for Tetius Micianus," she said. "He's used to being in charge, then along we come."

Fabillus frowned. "Yes. We'll have to be considerate. I hope he'll get his command back before long. He'll still be a senior officer, but under my orders."

"So he'll be the same rank as Drustan?"

"Yes. Hopefully we can all work together amicably."

Her regular lieutenant, Julius Botrio Tegwyn was doing well, but still in no state to return to his post. Briseis knew that she was lucky to still have her Mage and Priest as well. Awstinus had made it off the wreck, saved, she suspected, by the grace of the God he served, mighty Neptune himself. Her Adept, Woodbine, hadn't been so lucky. Trapped beneath decks, he'd refused to leave his patients and died for it. The loss was still raw.

"Well, here goes."

"Admiral on deck!"

The shout brought both of them to attention as Pendragon strode over, followed by Captain Cornelius. His dark eyes regarded them both as they saluted.

"So, you're to get a new vessel, *Patience*. I imagine the other Ships will have lots of advice for you, but I recommend you talk to *Blossom*. She's done this before and, as you know, is the best placed to teach you how to settle in quickly."

"Thank you, Admiral. I will."

She was very tempted to find out whether he had any news of *Tempest*, but then decided that it wasn't her place to ask. She could only hope that she would find out more before too long.

"Excellent. We'll be in communication again soon."

A final salute, and he returned below.

Cornelius and her Captain gripped forearms.

"I'm glad you're getting your own vessel again," Cornelius said. "Be sure to put Tetius Micianus to good use."

They exchanged a look and Briseis was immediately suspicious. What was it about this Micianus that she needed to know? Reluctantly, she put the question to one side. She had other, more pressing concerns now. The first thing on the list was to find out how her other bereaved sister was doing.

<*Farsight?* Are you ready to get your vessel?>

<Yes, I suppose so.> The Ship sounded less than thrilled.

<Aren't you looking forward to it?>

101

<It's going to take a lot of effort. To tell the truth, I was enjoying the nap.>

<Oh, you! It won't be so bad. Have you done this before?>

<Once, but that was into a properly prepared vessel. I think this is going to be unpleasant.>

Farsight was determined to sulk her way through the whole experience.

<How's Durus?>

<Oh, he's fine. He keeps giving me little talks about how everything's going to be wonderful. I lost half my crew!>

The Ship sounded on the verge of tears. Briseis sighed. First *Unicorn*, and now *Farsight*, who was usually a very steady Ship. People sometimes forgot that they weren't machines. They might have bodies made of wood, but that didn't make them furniture. However much the Admirals protested that they knew their Ships, Briseis suspected that the men didn't have a clue. From what her sisters had told her, Pendragon seemed to be the only one who understood anything about them at all. He certainly seemed fond of *Tempest*, much to *Imperatrix*'s chagrin.

<Look, it will be fine. *Blossom*'s going to guide us through it and I'll be with you too. Listen! *Patience* to *Blossom*!>

<Hello, girls! I hear you're getting new vessels.>

<Yes. We were wondering how it works,> Briseis replied, with as much cheerfulness as she could muster.

<Well, I have transferred to an inanimate before, though only the once, thank the Gods.>

<Oh no!> *Farsight* was near panic. <Was it so horrible?>

<*Farsight*! Calm yourself! You're starting to sound like *Emerald* and she managed it after the kraken attack.>

The older Ship wasn't going to put up with hysteria and Briseis was thankful that she had her mentor to back her up. She felt the tension in the link subside.

<Sorry, *Blossom*.>

<It's not that bad, but harder than if you were being transferred to a specially consecrated vessel. I'm sure the Priests will do what they can, plus the carpenters will use some of your old vessel to anchor you. Think of it as a new and useful skill.>

Briseis tried to remember how old *Farsight* was. She must have had a pretty uneventful career to date to be so rattled.

Maybe she hadn't fought in the wars with the Northern Alliance? There were plenty of vessels who were sent off on long trade or exploration missions. Perhaps it was simply the shock of her loss that was causing the Ship to be uncertain. She made a mental note to ask *Blossom* about her later, if she could remember with everything that was happening. It was a pity she couldn't ask Maia. She never forgot anything.

<*Patience*, stand ready. We're transferring you now.>

Fabillus sounded as though he was announcing the day's rota, his features calm as he surveyed his new vessel. The *Seashell* was a little smaller than her old vessel, but that was no surprise. The *Mallard* was a little larger, but *Farsight* had seniority so that made sense. The inanimate had drawn up alongside and was secured to *Imperatrix* by stout ropes to keep it as stable as possible. Briseis's officers and crew would be able to climb down rope ladders and on to her deck. Across the water, she could see that *Diadem* was guiding proceedings for *Mallard*, so she and *Farsight* would be transferring together.

<Right, ladies.> *Blossom* was all business. <You'll be taken across whilst your bases are dismantled and incorporated into your new vessel at strategic locations. These will be your first points of reference, as you'll be drawn to them. From these, you must push your awareness outwards, as if you're stretching out and feeling every part of the vessel. This is the bit that takes Potentia, so work it as hard as you can. It'll keep trying to snap back into your Shipbody, but you mustn't let it. Are you ready? You can do this!>

<Yes, *Blossom*,> they chorused in unison.

<Good! Remember, everyone will be watching. You must bear yourself with dignity.>

Briseis felt that was aimed more at *Farsight* than her, but agreed meekly. She was glad that the seas were calm, as doing this in a storm would have been nigh impossible. Surely that was a good sign that they had the favour of Neptune. The thought cheered her. Her first allegiance was to the Lord of the Sea now, but for many generations her family had spent their lives serving Apollo. She sent a prayer to him now, hoping that he hadn't forgotten Briseis Apollonia, the little girl who'd run about the temple sanctuary and fed his sacred snake. The familiar litany was a comfort and calmed her mind as she prepared for this next step.

Ships' carpenters were surrounding her now, talking earnestly among themselves as they prepared the tools of their trade. Her own was lost in the sea with so many of his fellows, but a few had survived, including *Imperatrix*'s, and all were time-served masters of their craft.

"Ma'am," he saluted. "We're going to raise you up and remove the remains of your former vessel, ready to fix them into your new home."

"Thank you, Master…?"

"Quercus, ma'am, named for the oak tree like my father and grandfather before me, all the way back to the *Britannia* herself. Or so my family says."

He was of medium height and stocky, with a bushy brown beard that covered a broad chest and seemed as strong and sturdy as his namesake. A different sort of Potentia radiated from him, one of skill and knowledge, and Briseis felt safe in his hands. Her old carpenter, Phrixus, had been good, but this man was at another level. She felt an instant connection and wished that she could persuade him to join her crew, but she didn't think that Pendragon would allow it.

"I know you'll do an excellent job, Master Quercus."

He beamed at her, teeth glinting white through the beard.

"We'll all do our best, ma'am. Right then. Are you ready?"

She nodded. "Proceed."

"If you would just step on to this platform."

The men had rigged up a floating base that she could reach easily. Briseis braced herself to leave behind all that was left of her former vessel.

<*Blossom*! It feels like I have to detach all over again!>

<You are. You're leaving your first ever vessel. Believe me, it's harder when it's complete but worn-out because you're so attached to the old one with all its memories. There's not much to hang on to here, girl. Do it quickly and get it over with.>

She obeyed, feeling the sense of loss, as if she were stepping into a void instead of on to another piece of wood. She knew immediately that it wasn't hers. The surface felt slick, like ice and she gripped on to the ropes that suspended it to keep herself from falling off. It was like standing on a swing.

"We've got you ma'am."

The men quickly wrapped her in netting to prevent her from tipping, though she maintained her death grip.

<Fabillus?>

<I'm here.> She looked down to see that he was at the rail. *Imperatrix* was standing on the poop deck with Pendragon and Cornelius as they supervised the operation. Her Captain gave her an encouraging nod.

Beneath her, Quercus and his men were stripping her plinth to its component parts, removing screws and passing the planks to a chain of sailors to be taken over, piece by piece, to the *Seashell.* Even as she watched, the vessel was being ritually prepared by a chanting crowd of Priests who had been ferried over from the other Ships and were informing the Gods of *Patience*'s new situation. The painted boards at the bow and stern were removed, ready for her to call forth her new name and make the vessel her own.

She remembered doing it the first time, at Pendragon's command. Old King Artorius had been too ill to attend. There had been no Royal status for her, a fact that she hadn't minded in the slightest, unlike her old schoolmate, Tullia. Royals had more pressure and responsibility, though her first voyage had been far from easy. She hadn't forgotten that she still owed Neptune a debt for his indulgence of her prayers. Nonetheless, Briseis felt that she'd acquitted herself well and now was the time to prove that she could cope with even the most difficult of circumstances.

Soon, all the wood was gone. Some part of her remained aware of its location as it was hastily blessed, reshaped and hammered into place on the former *Seashell.* The scattered pieces flared in her mind like tiny beacons of light, giving off a warm glow of contact.

<Good. Now for step two,> *Blossom* encouraged. <You should be able to feel the wood entering the fabric of your new vessel.>

<I can,> Briseis answered, hearing *Farsight*'s affirmative.

<It will guide you. As soon as you are placed on the deck, seek them out. Choose your own image that helps you to anchor to them and fix it in your mind.>

An image to anchor herself? Briseis thought hard. Ropes were the obvious ones for a Ship, but, they weren't the only sorts of anchors. She was still pondering when the activity around her increased.

"Ma'am." Quercus had returned from her new vessel, panting slightly from the climb.

"What happens now?"

"We're swinging you over and down to your new deck. Is *Blossom* telling you what to do?"

Briseis smiled at him through the netting.

"She is."

"Good. We can always rely on her. Been training Ships for ages that one, though she insists it's only been about twenty years."

<Take no notice,> *Blossom*'s voice cut in. <I'm too young to have been doing it on and off for ninety years.>. Briseis laughed out loud before she could stop herself.

"Aye, I know she heard me."

"She says ninety."

"Ha! And the rest! It was the *Porpoise* before her. A lovely Ship, she was."

She knew that he was trying to put her at her ease.

"Yes, *Blossom* told me about her."

"She's the best, she is."

<Tell him he's making me blush,> *Blossom* interjected.

Briseis relayed the information and Quercus guffawed. "Good! Tell her I'll be paying her a visit before too long."

"You move around then?"

"Oh aye." His eyes twinkled. "I'm not always stuck on this old besom, you know."

Briseis's eyes widened, but fortunately, *Imperatrix* seemed to be involved in a conversation with Pendragon. Quercus tapped the side of his nose, and she knew it was their secret.

A junior officer came over to the pair of them and saluted.

"Captain Fabillus is boarding the new vessel now, ma'am."

"Thank you." Quercus said. "Here we go, *Patience*. You know what to do when you're aboard?"

"I think so."

He winked at her. "Nothing to it."

At a signal, the deck of the *Imperatrix* tilted slightly beneath her as Briseis was moved slowly through the air and over the heads of the men. Shouts and orders followed as one vessel fell away and another rose to meet her. All around were upturned faces and, for a moment, she wondered if that was how an Emperor might feel, surrounded by admiring crowds.

"Steady as she goes, lads!"

Quercus's stentorian voice urged them to caution, then she was dropped down, further and further to the deck. Briseis braced herself for the impact. Would it feel like a jolt? Would there be an instant bond? What had *Blossom* said? An anchoring image, that was what she needed now, not this feeling of detached weightlessness.

<*Patience*, don't drift now. Hold your course steady. This is your new home, yours and yours alone. Take it! Its bones are your bones! Masts, spars, rigging, sails, rudder and keel. All yours!>

The old Ship's voice kept her on track. The vessel was hers and she would take possession of it.

Her Shipbody touched the deck. Instantly, flares of light burst in her consciousness, like guiding torches lighting her way and welcoming her aboard. Instinctively she reached out, picturing them as smiling faces of family and friends, all those she had known that anchored her to her past and who she was. Some were still alive, others were gone, but she hung on to the memory of them, absorbing the strength of their love to fling herself into the strange, unyielding wood, feeling it soften like melting wax to allow her passage. She forced her way into every nook and cranny of her new vessel, filling it with her Potentia, her sense of self, and the person she was. She wasn't a machine. She was Briseis Apollonia, she was HMS *Patience*, she was a woman and a Ship, separate yet one, together until the Gods decided that it was time for them to part. This was her home now, her vessel, her body, for as long as they decreed.

She felt the muted pulse of the vessel strengthen as it aligned with the flow of Potentia in her Shipbody, a mystical joining. Her awareness expanded. Voices filled her head on every deck, some known, some new. Images followed as the anchoring faces receded to be replaced by real ones in naval uniforms and hats, waistcoats and scarves, leather aprons and flapping trews. Her crew.

"*Patience*, come forth!"

Her Captain's command called her to full control. She snapped to attention, seeing him standing next to her Priest in front of her new altar, where offerings were laid in rows. Her Shipbody flexed as it adapted to its vessel. If she'd wanted, she knew that she could have travelled to any part of it just as she had before.

Fabillus's face relaxed as she saluted, and she saw the smile of approval hovering on his lips.

"His Majesty's Ship *Patience*, reporting for duty, sir!"

"Welcome to your new home, *Patience*."

The crew gave her three lusty cheers, echoed by the *Imperatrix*'s men.

<Well done!>

That was *Blossom*. Congratulations promptly flooded in from the rest of the Fleet and even the distant *Victoria* added her salutations.

<How's *Farsight*?> she asked. The Ship herself answered.

<I'm not doing that again. That was bloody awful!>

<It was hard,> Briseis admitted.

<Hard? It was like headbutting a wall over and over! I feel bruised.>

<But you did it.>

<Ugh. Only just. Inanimates are too much like corpses to me, all cold and clammy!>

Some Ships laughed, whilst others commiserated. She left them to it and glided over to her Captain, joining him at the altar to make her obeisance to the Gods.

"Hail, O Mighty Neptune, Lord of the Seas," she prayed. "Look upon my crew and myself with favour, I beseech you."

Nor have I forgotten the debt I owe you. I stand ready to pay it.

Awstinus was making more offerings, most of which would be either burnt or given to the waves. His face was furrowed in concentration under his hood as he invoked his God. Briseis glanced at him warily, remembering the time when Neptune had spoken through him directly. She had seen her father similarly possessed, and it had been unnerving then too. She was glad she sensed nothing of the sort now as the Priest continued with his devotions.

<How are you feeling?> Fabillus asked. <Ready to go it alone?>

Briseis extended herself along her new vessel's channels of Potentia, the texture of the wood changing as she touched upon the remnants of her former home.

<It feels fine,> she said, knowing that it would be more difficult for a time. She'd just got used to her old vessel, smoothing out the rough edges until everything worked perfectly. This felt like she was wearing second-hand clothes. The fit wasn't quite right yet. She'd have to make adjustments.

<Good! Time to pretty yourself up.>

Of course! She'd forgotten to form her name fore and aft. She gathered her Potentia into a tight focus, one spot at a time, visualising the lettering and working it into reality. Briseis debated whether she should change the colour, but in the end decided that she would keep it in gold with a blue background, just as she'd had previously. It would be nice to see that some things didn't have to change.

<There she is! Congratulations, *Patience*! You handled that well.>

So, Pendragon approved. It was a relief for both her and her Captain that the transfer had gone smoothly.

<*Imperatrix* to *Patience*. Don't cast off yet. We have deliveries!>

The Royal sounded excited.

<I can't wait!>

<Here you are, ladies!> *Leopard* was broadcasting to all. <Torpedoes for everybody, plus a few other little surprises for those thrice-damned Fae swine, may the Gods rot 'em!>

<Do you know what they are?> *Jasper* sounded eager to get her hands on them.

<They explode.>

<And?>

<They blow stuff up.>

Everyone laughed, even *Jasper*.

<That's good enough for me!> the little Ship declared, Sending mental images of explosions down the link. <Boom! We'll finish them all off!>

<Yes, yes,> *Diadem* said. <Don't get carried away. We have to get past their magic first, and there aren't many of us with Mages.>

<*Victoria* to the Fleet!>

There were startled exclamations. The Flagship had been silent of late, stuck in port and not wishing to compromise herself or her sick crew. Things must have changed.

<This is *Imperatrix*! What's happening, *Victoria*?>

<I'm approaching your position now.>

Everyone was dumbstruck. Surely this wasn't possible?

<Look out, here I come, and I'm not alone! Brace yourselves!>

A couple of miles out to sea, a bright purple dot appeared, swelling in size until it resembled another sun and nearly as bright. Briseis strained to see it more clearly, just as a bowsprit broke through, followed by the rest of the Flagship in full sail. Gasps in the link told her that the others were witnessing it too. *Victoria* was as good as her word. Briseis counted ten other Ships following her through the gigantic portal, one after the other. Fabillus had a telescope to his eye.

<Blood and sand! I can see *Naiad*, *Atlanta*, *Scorpion*, *Diamond*, *Fortress* – how have they done this?>

Briseis didn't have a clue. She had never seen anything like it and neither had anyone else, judging from the cries of amazement from every quarter.

Greetings were exchanged and there were many joyful reunions from Ships who hadn't seen each other for a while, in some cases for many years.

<I bring Mages!> *Victoria* announced. <Lots of Mages!>

Cheers erupted from throats as the great Ships closed the distance. The air vibrated with the sheer amount of power it contained, like a balloon about to burst under pressure. Just because she couldn't see the Gods didn't mean they weren't there. Surely it had taken more than mortal Potentia to manage this feat?

Once all the Ships were through, the portal shrank, dwindling to a dot until it disappeared and the sky was clear once more.

<That made my hair stand on end.>

Fabillus had taken off his Captain's hat and was busy smoothing down his ruffled locks. Others of her crew were doing the same, or were busy rubbing their arms with looks of discomfort on their faces. The atmosphere was still charged, though Briseis was largely immune to the strange effects.

<Has she brought our Ship Mages back?> she wondered. She had been fortunate to keep Sandpiper, but many had been seized and removed.

<Let's hope so, but any Mages will do. I take it that she's liberated them from Marcus's tender care. Either way, it's a blessing.>

In more ways than one.

<Welcome, sisters.>

Was it Briseis's imagination, or did *Imperatrix* sound a little put out at the *Victoria*'s abrupt arrival? She wondered whether Pendragon would transfer over immediately or later. Either way, there would be sparks. She would never have guessed how jealous Ships could be for their Captains' and Admirals' attention. There seemed to be more than a few who would jostle to be noticed by Pendragon.

As the weapons were distributed and crates swung aboard, she soon found that she had too much on her mind to worry about such things. The mechanisms that had been hurriedly put into place were stiff and awkward. It took all her skill to keep them working, and she urged her men to apply liberal amounts of grease. The old *Seashell* hadn't been constructed to contain a Ship and her special demands, though the structure was doing its best. She could tell that it had been a well-loved vessel, as something of the care and attention it had received lingered in its fabric. Maybe even inanimates had a spirit within, created from the people who served and travelled in them down the years.

Fabillus and Drustan were engaged in conversation with Tetius Micianus. She adjusted her hearing and listened in whilst keeping one eye on the crates that were being stowed in her hold.

"…not able to take too much strain immediately," the *Seashell*'s former commander was saying. "She has to go carefully."

He didn't sound pleased to have her aboard, and Briseis's instincts sounded a warning.

"I'm sure *Patience* has the experience to know when her equipment's at breaking point," her Captain was saying. Micianus didn't look convinced. His blue eyes were startling above his reddened cheeks, the skin veined and roughened after years of being in all weathers at sea.

"She's young," he said. So, he wasn't afraid to speak his mind. "We can't afford anything to fail. I know my vessel."

Fabillus nodded. "I understand, Commander Micianus. Please liaise with *Patience* and give her the benefit of your experience."

<See how he likes that!> Fabillus whispered in her mind. <There's a reason he was assigned an inanimate. If he gives you any problems at all, let me know and we can be rid of him.>

<Wonderful! It's not as if I don't have enough to do.>

<You'll cope. If he starts spouting rubbish, give him one of your looks.>

She was puzzled. <What do you mean?>

He laughed. <You know, like when you're so *very* disappointed with people.>

<It's not my fault that I was brought up properly!>

She sighed to herself as Micianus made a beeline for her position. It was going to be a long day.

VII

Milo stood in the mouth of the cave, feeling as if he'd been kicked in the stomach.

He'd long ago given up any hope of ever returning to the place of his birth, or even of seeing his mother again. To tell the truth, he couldn't even remember what she looked like, apart from her long dark hair and the colour of the robes she always wore. He'd buried that part of him in the past, hoping it would stay there among all the other detritus of his life, like an abandoned heap of unnecessary junk that had once had purpose but was now too much to carry.

Despite his arguments, there was nothing he could say to persuade the old Mage that his course of action was foolish at best, disastrous at worst. Emrys was fixed on his goal, as immovable as one of the ancient stones that dotted the landscape and twice as unyielding.

"What are you expecting us to do?" he demanded. "Ambush the Fae from the shadows? Slip poison into their food? There's no other way of stopping them that I can see."

The old man's eyes were shadowed under his brows.

"I told you that all will be made clear."

"It's clear that we're walking into a pit of vipers! What's to stop Ceridwen from handing Julia over to her cousin as a bridal gift?"

"She has value, and so will be safe."

Milo blew out an exasperated breath. Had he been wrong to trust Raven's assessment of this man? He knew nothing about him. For all they knew, Emrys could have been working with the Fae all along.

Emrys put his hand on Milo's shoulder.

"I can tell what you're thinking, and I assure you that I'm not working with the Fae. I've fought them before. I know their ways, their strengths and weaknesses and how this place can affect them and other things. I swear before all the Gods that I am your friend."

His voice trembled with emotion, but Milo refused to give way.

"What's your interest in all of this?"

"My interest? Britannia and her people are my interest and always have been, for longer than you can know."

He paused and sighed.

"I had thought that my time was over, but I can see now that my duty is not easily put aside. I have yet more tasks to complete before my oath is fulfilled."

"Oath? To whom?"

Emrys sniffed.

"You wouldn't believe me if I told you."

For a moment, Milo was reminded of Raven. The two Mages shared a certain world-weariness, as well as a fondness for cryptic pronouncements.

"Do you know Raven well?"

Emrys thought.

"Let's just say that I've known him a long, long time. We have certain traits in common, though from different causes. I like to think that I'm not as cantankerous."

Milo raised an eyebrow.

"Really! I'm the soul of reason, I am."

Right, so that was why he was leading them into the last place they should be at the moment.

"I'll take your word for it," he said at last, rubbing his hands over his face. He could do with a nice long bath and a good meal, but there was no chance of that here. The only path was out of this cave. He gathered up his pack, hefting it onto his shoulder.

What was keeping Julia? She must have finished her ablutions by now.

"Princess," he called. "Have you finished back there? We have to go."

Light footfalls announced Julia's return. Reassured, he turned to follow Emrys.

"Gods below! Are you injured?"

The Mage brushed past him. Milo dropped his pack and rushed over to the Princess's side. The streaks on her face looked black in the half-light.

"Did you fall?" Emrys demanded.

Julia's eyes were wide, as if she was seeing beyond the cave into another time and place.

"It was the Huntress. She came out of the wall."

Her words were slurred and Milo's first thought was that she'd somehow been attacked and drugged. Emrys took her by the shoulders, guiding her to a rock ledge jutting out from the wall.

"Here, sit down." He sniffed at her face, then raised his head, staring into the depths of the cave, like a hunting dog searching for a scent. "Oh, subtle, subtle."

"What's happened to her?" Milo was devastated. Julia was in his care, but he'd been so busy arguing that he'd let his guard slip.

"She's been marked. The Mother has appeared in her aspect of the Huntress."

Emrys's voice was full of wonder. "I never sensed her presence. This is ancient, female magic from the dawn of human time and not for us. This changes everything."

"She's been claimed by the Goddess?"

Emrys nodded. "They won't dare touch her now."

"Does that mean she'll have to stay here as a Priestess?"

Emrys straightened up.

"Not necessarily. I knew she would be safe here for a while, but now all bets are off. She's coming into power in her own right, and the Fates laugh at my plans once more. It's obvious to anyone with any knowledge that she has a special destiny and this will protect her, especially here." For an instant he looked troubled, then his face cleared. "Come on. We've no reason to wait any longer and the sun is rising. Let's go and find out what's happening, shall we?"

He sounded almost casual, as if they were going on a stroll to visit a friend's house instead of walking into the most magically charged place in the whole of Britannia. Milo couldn't fathom him out. All he could do was keep Julia as safe as he could, even at the cost of his own life.

His suspicions that the old man was a mind reader were confirmed when Emrys gave him a nod of approval. He picked up his pack once more and between them they managed to get Julia to stand. She still seemed in a dream, but colour had returned to her face.

"Should we clean her off?" he asked.

"Oh no! We want your mother to see this. It'll give her pause."

They began to pick their way out of the cave. The light had intensified, though the sun was still hidden behind trees and it was only now that Milo noticed the riot of birdsong that was greeting the new day. He breathed in the freshness of the dawn and the scents of the forest. As he did so, it triggered memories from his childhood he thought were long gone. He hadn't spent much time among trees in his adult life, preferring the city, but now it was all coming back. He shook his head to clear it and concentrated on the job in hand. It was where he was in the present that was important, not what had happened long ago.

Julia seemed to be returning to herself as they emerged on to a slope dotted with trees, above which rocky limestone crags loomed. They were heading east, down into a flatter area though he couldn't see much because of the thick vegetation. Some long-buried part of him remembered that there was a path through to a clearing, and that was where the houses were.

As Emrys had said, there was a smell of smoke, but otherwise no sign of human activity. Even the birds seemed to have quietened and the leaves hung still with no breeze to make them dance.

Milo felt the hairs rise on the back of his neck as they reached the houses. The thatched roundhouses were as he remembered them, clustered around the larger central meeting hall where he had played whilst his mother spun or worked on her loom. It just looked smaller, that was all. What had seemed a vast acreage was a small space compared to the Great Forest that surrounded it, as if threatening to engulf the settlement in an unstoppable green wave.

Emrys motioned them to stay back, continuing on towards the meeting hall. Milo halted, making sure that Julia was close enough for him to shield her if necessary, and checked his pistols. He'd loaded them in the cave whilst Emrys was off scouting. Magic was all well and good, but two shots could make the difference between life and death. Furthermore, he wasn't sure how his magical abilities would hold up in this uncanny, haunted place. Even now the space between his shoulder blades itched, as if unfriendly eyes were watching from the shadows of the trees.

The Mage had only taken a few steps, when a female figure emerged from the building. Something about the outline caused Milo's heart to beat faster. She was dressed in a simple green and brown robe, her long hair falling loose and crowned with a wreath of leaves. She approached them without fear, walking steadily across the grassy path and he could see the familiar blue tattoos winding their way over her neck, cheeks and brow. A sharp smell of crushed herbs made his nose tingle, triggering more memories. He'd walked that path before, and still did so sometimes in his dreams.

Emrys stopped, waiting for her to reach him. She finally halted several feet away, regarding them with calm eyes.

"Ceridwen, High Priestess of the Mother, we greet you in this sacred place."

He bowed and she nodded.

"Emrys. I see you are not alone. What business do you have…?"

She trailed off as she saw Milo and he saw her stiffen. A look of disbelief, then hope crossed her face.

"It cannot be! Is it?"

Ceridwen ignored Emrys and Julia, her attention solely on Milo. He felt as though he'd suddenly grown roots, unable to move as the Priestess focused on him, all else forgotten.

"Have you come back to me, my son?"

Her voice cracked and broke. He could only stand numbly as she came to him, recognising her voice, if not her face. Her hair – now *that* he knew. He had used to brush it for her, laughing at

117

how the black and white alternated at the roots. Were there more white streaks there now, or was it the same as it had been? To his adult eyes, she only looked to be in her fifties, but he knew she was much, much older, her lifespan extended by the Goddess.

Her dark eyes locked on to his as he breathed in her scent and the memories rushed in.

"Mam."

His tongue felt stiff and clumsy in his mouth.

A radiant smile lit up Ceridwen's face.

"My son! You have returned!"

She threw her arms around him, burying her head in his shoulder and he staggered under her weight. Her hug was quick before she released him and framed his face with her hands.

"The Mother be praised! She has brought you back to me, at this of all times!"

Milo was unable to share in her joy. How could she be pleased to see him, this woman who had sent him away? She'd turned her back on him without a second thought, abandoning him to the cold charity of strangers.

He saw her understanding a second before she dropped her hands and stepped back.

"You must hate me." The smile died and her eyes filled with tears.

"I don't know you. I suppose you had a reason for what you did."

He forced the words out, part of him hoping that they would hurt. Lying awake in the dormitory of the Foundling Home night after night, he'd often thought of what he would say if they ever met. It had taken years to put the memory of her aside.

Her mouth worked soundlessly, then she took a deep breath.

"I did, my son. Believe me, it was hard and never what I wanted."

"The Mages threw me out. I was sent to a foundling home and grew up there. Did you know that?"

Her expression told him all he needed to know.

She shook her head. "It was not my choice."

He regarded her stonily. She was nothing to him now, and the sooner she realised that, the better it would be for her. He had his own life now, and it didn't include her. So, it had been a professional decision. Had he treated Seren any better, or any of the others he'd deceived in the course of his life as an Agent?

He gave her a nod. "All part of the job, then."

His conception must have been a duty too. If he'd been born out of love, she would have fought tooth and nail to keep him. Maybe he'd been a mistake, or even born to order? The thought chilled him, but he was experienced enough to know how these things worked. Maybe his unknown father hadn't wanted him, or had died? Maybe she didn't even know who had fathered him. As far as he could remember, she'd never mentioned the man.

Ceridwen looked stricken.

"I did what the Mother asked of me."

So, he was right after all. That clarified things. The demands of the Gods could not be denied or evaded. It was just his bad luck to have been caught in one of their schemes, one which had failed, judging from his life so far. He was yet another discarded game piece. It was hard not to think of what they'd planned for him, but he shoved the thought aside with the ruthlessness of long training. It wasn't important now.

"I'm glad that's cleared up," he said, dismissing the subject.

Ceridwen wilted momentarily, but managed to collect herself after a couple of moments, as if finally realising that there were others there. Now she straightened and lifted her head, her eyes falling on the Princess.

"Great Goddess," she breathed. "You are marked!"

Julia was as poised as if she was attending a formal function. Her face gave away nothing, though it couldn't have been an easy scene for anyone to witness. As a royal child she would have been trained from birth to be emotionally reserved, so, as Milo expected, she chose to ignore it completely. Emrys stepped in.

"This is Her Royal Highness, the Princess Julia Victoria Pendragon, daughter of Prince Julius and sister of the late King."

If Julia had expected a curtsey from the High Priestess, none was forthcoming. The older woman advanced on her, fixing her with a penetrating gaze.

"The Huntress has marked you as her own, Child of the Land," she said, her eyes sparkling with purpose. "You are welcome here in the Heart of Albion."

119

"I thank you, High Priestess Ceridwen," Julia replied. "I trust that your welcome also extends to my companions."

Ceridwen's mouth twitched.

"Emrys I know of old. He comes and goes as he pleases. My son is more than welcome. Come, you must be hungry after your journey."

They trooped after her past the smaller huts and towards the large central roundhouse. Inside, it was dark, smelling of woodsmoke and earth, and Milo's eyes took a moment to adjust. A firepit with benches around it was in the middle, with various work areas arranged around the circumference. There were looms with skeins of dyed wool hanging nearby on racks, ready for skilled hands to weave them into cloth and sacks of fleece that would be carded before being spun. He couldn't see any spinning wheels, only some primitive drop spindles. Perhaps they had nothing better to do than to spend a lot of time producing thread the old way, slowly and inefficiently. Naturally, they wouldn't have any of the new water or steam-powered machines here. It looked like somewhere the ancient Britons would have recognised instantly, as if the Romans had never come to these shores. But wasn't that what she wanted, to take them back over a thousand years? But it wasn't only spinning wheels that were lacking. The place was deserted.

"Where are the others?" Emrys clearly had the same thought.

Ceridwen gestured to bowls of water, soap and towels that were laid on a bench.

"They are worshipping in the Sacred Grove. Please, wash. There is food."

A cauldron hung over the fire. He could see it contained a mixture of grains and fruits, standard breakfast fare, together with some bread and cheese on a table to the side.

Alarm bells went off in Milo's head. It could be dangerous to eat anything in this place and he glanced at Emrys for guidance.

"We thank you for your offer of food," Emrys answered.

He went to the nearest bowl and began to wash his hands and face. Milo and Julia copied his example, whilst Ceridwen ladled out the porridge into four bowls, then seated herself on a deerskin-covered bench and waited for them to finish.

Milo gave his hands and face a good scrub. It was no substitute for a real bath, but it would do. The soap smelt of lavender and he pushed away yet another memory. The linen towel was rough, but adequate. He looked at the scummy water left in the bowl and tried not to think how filthy the rest of him was.

There was a splash as Emrys dunked his head. Water overflowed the sides of the bowl, pooling on the rush-strewn floor, but Ceridwen didn't seem to mind. Rivulets streamed from his beard and down his robes as he lifted his head, before enveloping it in linen. Julia was more restrained, but he could see she was scrubbing at her face, trying to get every last trace of blood off. She applied the towel vigorously, then looked around for somewhere to sit. Milo patted the bench next to him and she scurried over.

For a moment he thought it was a trick of the light, but when he peered more closely he could see the looping blue patterns over her cheek and brow, similar to his mother's but with subtle differences. Hers looked less like flowers and leaves. He could see a stag running across her forehead and what looked like a bear's head peering from her hairline at the temple. He looked away quickly before she noticed him staring. The last thing he wanted to do was frighten her, even as he tried to work out the ramifications of the Goddess's act.

He leaned over and picked up a steaming bowl, feeling the curved smoothness of the wood against his fingers and the heat that seeped through it. The porridge smelt good, but he waited until Emrys started eating. The old Mage ate with enthusiasm, shovelling it down as if he hadn't had food for a month. Milo took a spoon, as did Julia, scooping out the thick mess and blowing on it before tasting it. To his surprise, it was good. Julia looked as though she had her doubts but, after giving it a sniff, began eating with a will.

The silence stretched out, the only noise the crackle of the flames and the scraping of spoons on wood. He helped himself to some of the bread, heavy with seeds, spreading the soft crumbly cheese on top. It was all delicious, satisfying some part of him that imported olives and shop-bought bread never could. He tried to ignore the insistent voice at the back of his mind that told him he was home at last. This hadn't been his home for over thirty years, and never would be.

It was only when they were all eating that Ceridwen joined them in breaking their fast. When they'd finished, she gathered their bowls and stacked them to one side.

"Have you all had enough?"

"Yes, thank you," Julia said.

Milo, wondering whether he should ask a question, caught Emrys's eye first. The Mage's almost imperceptible head shake told him that he'd been right to be silent. Instead, he and Emrys both thanked Ceridwen, before she rose.

"Please forgive me for leaving you, but I must see to the arrangements for welcoming more guests."

Her gaze lingered on Milo, as if she wanted to say more.

"And who are they, may I ask?" Emrys asked.

"Emissaries from overseas. They are bringing King Marcus's new bride here to sanctify her before she travels on to London to be married."

"And who is she?"

Emrys wasn't giving away the fact that they already knew.

Ceridwen paused, considering.

"All will be revealed when they get here and we can celebrate the renewal of old ways together. Your arrival here is a sign from the Goddess!"

Her smile was full of joy and Milo felt his insides churn. Emrys was right. She had to be mad. Thank the Gods she couldn't read minds. He hid his disgust behind a blandly interested expression.

"We will await their coming," Emrys replied.

As soon as Ceridwen had disappeared, he beckoned them in close.

"I was hoping to leave before now, but we're too late. The gateway has opened and the Fae approach."

Julia went pale and Milo swore silently to himself.

"What now?" he asked. He hated being in Emrys's hands instead of making his own way as he always had. How could he make decisions without information? Had he led the Princess into a trap? Ceridwen seemed in awe of her, but there was no guarantee that the Fae would be. As a scion of the line of Artorius

Pendragon, she would be at best a hostage and at worst a plaything to be corrupted.

"We wait," Emrys said shortly. Milo opened his mouth to protest, but the old Mage raised a hand. "There's nothing else for it, but I assure you that we won't stay long."

His eyes unfocused momentarily. "The Land won't be denied, and the time is nearly come."

"What time?" Julia's voice was harsh, her mouth set. "What have you done, bringing us here? Are you a traitor, or simply insane?"

Emrys smiled.

"A traitor? Oh no. Never that. Insane? Probably." He chuckled. "It's been a long time since anyone asked me that question, and he used exactly the same tone of voice." He paused. "I wish he were here now. I miss him still."

"Who?" she asked, but he was already moving.

"Come. We must be ready to meet them. Now, listen. Try not to look at them directly. Take nothing that's offered. Make no promises. Let me do the talking and don't rise to anything that might be said. Understood?"

Julia stood, quietly fuming. Milo sympathised, but Emrys hadn't finished.

"Leave your packs here. I'll hide them. You don't want Fae poking about in your things, do you?"

It seemed an odd thing to say, but they obediently piled their meagre possessions into a corner, where Emrys covered them with a couple of deer skins. A few muttered words, and they were hidden, appearing to melt into the wall.

"We can retrieve them later," he said. "Now, are you ready to greet the 'emissaries'?"

"Not in the least," Julia said, her tone acid.

"Well that's too bad."

Milo cast another look at where his pack lay. He felt oddly reluctant to leave it for some reason, but was reassured by its presence. He shook himself. This day was getting stranger by the second.

They felt the shift in the air as soon as they left the building. It wasn't quite a breeze or even a scent, but had the feeling of both, as if they were approaching a cliff path that led down to the sea. Even the trees rustled in anticipation, leaves and branches dancing to greet the visitors, or maybe to welcome them back. Despite himself, a sense of joy swept over him and his heart leapt.

They came through the trees, gliding in procession, their clear voices chanting just inside the range of human hearing. Milo swallowed. He hadn't expected them to be beautiful.

Floating rather than walking, the Fae crossed into the open space and formed themselves into a group around a central figure. There was something almost tree-like about their angular limbs that their flowing robes couldn't hide. What he could glimpse of their faces showed over-large eyes, more like cats or owls than humans, vestigial noses and thin lips above pointed chins. Jewels, set in elaborate workings of gold, gleamed on brows, wrists and fingers. Fae smiths were noted for their cunning, though of course they never worked in iron. Milo closed his eyes for a few seconds to dispel any illusion, aided by the insistent ringing in his ears as his amulet sounded its strident warning. He silenced it quickly, worried that it would overheat or that they would sense its presence and take it from him.

His eyes snapped open at the sound of Ceridwen's voice, speaking what he presumed to be words of welcome in their own tongue. The fluid vowels and trills were more like birdsong than human speech, but she seemed proficient enough. He felt Julia shiver beside him, but she had enough sense to stay quiet. Still, he felt horribly exposed.

His mother was speaking to the taller Fae, presumably their leader, before another party stepped forward. In their midst was a shorter figure in a silvery gown. Black hair cascaded over her shoulders, crowned with a wreath of oak leaves. This had to be his half-sister, Étain. The two women embraced, before Ceridwen took her daughter by the hand.

Milo was instantly aware of the scrutiny as the Fae's attention turned to them. It was only then that he became aware that Emrys had disappeared. He didn't dare turn and look for their guide, clinging to the faint hope that the old Mage was planning something from a place of concealment and not offering them up like Saturnalia treats for the feast.

124

Ceridwen approached, leading the woman, who seemed hardly more than a girl. She moved with the uncanny fluidity of her companions, a slight smile hovering on her lips. Milo felt a chill run up his back. Whatever she was, she was no longer fully human.

"Look, my son! Here is your sister, Étain, returned to us!

His mother's smile was radiant with triumph. Milo took refuge in formality, bowing slightly and responding in Britannic.

"Greetings to you, sister."

He dared risk a quick look at her face, noting the wide eyes with pupils shrunk to tiny dots. The serene and somewhat vacant smile was unsettling, like those worn on the faces of people under the influence of eastern drugs.

"My brother." Her accent was strange, the emphases in the wrong places. He had to remind himself that she was in reality an old woman in human years, preserved by the arts of the Fae like a dried flower or an experiment kept in a jar. The depth of his revulsion took him by surprise.

"See how glad she is to see you," Ceridwen said. Milo doubted that. Étain didn't look like she had a grasp on anything, and he sensed a vacancy about her that he didn't like.

"And this is your betrothed's cousin, the Princess Julia."

Milo sensed Julia stiffen.

"Princess. We shall be good friends."

Again, that uncanny speech. Julia inclined her head, but remained silent. It didn't seem to bother either their hostess or Étain, but the latter stepped forward, raising her hand towards Julia's cheek.

Julia jerked her head away instinctively, and Étain's smile slipped.

"She won't hurt you. She's just curious," Ceridwen said, guiding her daughter away. The Priestess spoke to Étain soothingly, the rising and falling notes reminding Milo of a blackbird at dawn.

"Greetings to you both."

One of the Fae, dressed in shimmering greens, approached from the group. Remembering Emrys's warnings, Milo focused on his mouth but it was Julia who answered.

"Greetings to you also."

125

As the highest ranking person here, she had taken it upon herself to respond. He looked sideways at her, hoping that her eyes weren't meeting the Fae's glance. Like him, they appeared to be slightly lowered and he breathed a little easier.

"We are well met in this place, lady and look forward to our future relationship with your people."

So that's what they were calling it. Milo forced himself to keep his face straight.

"As am I, Lord."

Julia was being every inch the gracious Royal. It seemed that he wasn't expected to say anything, for which he was immensely grateful. The urge to knife the bastard was making his hand itch. Fortunately, the Fae merely inclined his head and glided back to the rest of his party.

It appeared that some unspoken agreement had been reached. The Fae host melted back into the forest like a retreating mist, though the echo of their song lingered for a while. It was only when they were gone that Julia shuddered, like a plough horse after a hard day's work.

"Ugh!" she whispered, rubbing her hands. "Can we leave now? And where in Tartarus is that bloody Emrys?"

"Not yet," he said, his lips barely moving. "We have to allay their suspicions. He'll be planning something, I'm sure of it."

A flash of movement by one of the smaller houses caught Milo's attention. It could have been a squirrel, but no, it was Emrys. Just for a moment he'd seen the old man slipping past the wall. He must have had his own reasons for hiding so abruptly, though presumably Ceridwen would tell her friends of his presence.

He pulled at Julia's sleeve to get her moving. His legs felt like lead, as if he'd been literally rooted to the spot. There was no sign of Emrys now.

Ceridwen led them back into the Great Hall. She seated Étain by the fire, then busied herself adding fresh wood and coaxing it to a merry blaze. The girl didn't move, staring at the flames as if she had no will of her own. Milo felt some strength return to him, now that they were beyond the Fae's immediate presence.

"So, Mother, what now?"

Ceridwen paused, a blanket in one hand.

"You fulfil your destiny, my son."

She draped it around Étain's unresponsive shoulders.

Milo gritted his teeth. "And that is what? I thought I was of no use. Wasn't that why you sent me away?"

Ceridwen pursed her lips, as if in pain.

"I thought... I was told... There was a prophecy, but it turned out to be mistaken, or probably misinterpreted."

Milo stared at her in disbelief. "You're joking. You gave me up because of a damned prophecy?"

"You were supposed to be a great Mage," she replied, not meeting his eyes. "Then it was discovered that you had only moderate abilities."

"Was that why they sent me to the Foundling Home? I could have still trained!"

The old bitterness threatened to rise up and overwhelm him, but he forced it back.

"There was another prophecy. This one foretold disaster if you stayed where you were."

"Two prophecies? I didn't realise I was so important."

"But you are!"

She seated herself beside him and took his hands. He could feel the callouses on her fingers from years of manual work, but he couldn't bring himself to look at her. Instead, he took refuge in sarcasm.

"Really? How wonderful."

She squeezed his fingers. "More so now than ever. You are of my blood. There have been no more prophecies, but I want you with me now for reasons that will soon be plain."

"Tell me now!" he demanded, glaring at her. "I've had enough of secrecy!"

She shook her head.

"The time is not right. Marcus has failed, but he still has his uses."

He scowled at her. What wasn't she telling him?

"He's been acclaimed King."

She laughed then, throwing her head back. "The Sword of Kingship makes a King of the Land, and it has abandoned him. He tried to remove it and failed, forcing him to put on an empty show for the people. His deception is exposed, his plans are destroyed. He must fight or die. He makes a convenient and temporary figurehead, nothing more."

"Then Cei is King."

She shrugged. "Maybe, maybe not. It won't matter soon. The new King will rule a changed land bound to the old ways, and the land will be as it was. No foreign gods, no hideous machines. No more trees destroyed for fuel, no more polluting smoke. The land will be cleansed!"

Her eyes shone with the fervour of fanaticism and Milo knew that there was no reasoning with that. He'd seen that look before, on the face of the spy, Morgan. Ceridwen would never be persuaded from the path she'd chosen.

"Then who will Étain marry?"

"Why, the new King, of course, whoever that may be."

Secrets danced in her eyes, and Milo had the urge to pry them out, with force if necessary. As if sensing his anger, Ceridwen rose.

"Stay here. Rest. Eat. I have much to do."

"When will the Priestesses return?" Julia asked.

"When they have finished their devotions."

Ceridwen bestowed another beatific smile on them all and departed.

Milo watched her go. When he was sure his mother had left, he stood.

"She's done something to them," he said, in Latin. If his sister understood, she gave no sign.

"I agree. Not all would have been happy with her decision."

A shadow fell across the entrance and they both jumped.

"It's me. Come on. Grab your things."

Emrys had returned. They didn't need to be told twice. Étain didn't react, still staring unblinkingly into the flames. Milo would have saved her if he could, but a look from Emrys stopped him.

"There's nothing you can do for her now. I'm sorry."

"She would have been better as a Ship."

Emrys sighed. "Yes, but that was not her fate. Maybe she lacked something even then that caused her to fail? Not all are successful. Now she is as they have made her over the years."

128

If Milo had needed another excuse to hate the Fae, he had one now. His sister was merely a shell, twisted to their purposes, and his heart broke for her.

Their belongings shimmered into view and it was the matter of a moment to collect them and hasten out of the hut. The sun was higher now, its rays slanting down into the clearing and promising a warm day to come.

"They don't like the midday sun," Emrys said, jerking his head in the direction the Fae had left. "They are crepuscular creatures. Dawn and twilight are when they are at their strongest. This gives us some time."

He was already hurrying them away, towards the shadows of the trees.

"Where are we going?" Milo could tell that Julia was at the limits of her patience.

Emrys flashed her a grin. "To make mischief. To upset their plans. To give them an added welcome they weren't expecting. Onward, into the Heart of Albion!"

Milo's spirits rose. This was more like it! Maybe there he would get the answers he needed.

VIII

The first thing Maia saw as she emerged from the portal was that they appeared to be in some large, dusty warehouse or storage area. Wooden crates towered over them, stacked everywhere against the brick walls. Above them, grimy windows allowed a wan light to creep in to pool where they were standing, as if it were reluctant to enter the place. She wasn't surprised. The first time she'd ever used a portal she'd ended up in another store room, albeit one that was a lot smaller. It seemed to be a habit of Raven's to sneak about using back rooms and out-of-the-way places.

The second thing was the noise. It was beyond loud, seeming to penetrate the building from everywhere at once. Maia winced, reducing her sensitivity instantly and glaring at the Master Mage. He could have warned her. A Ship could sense a butterfly landing on her rail, so this unexpected aural onslaught had almost overwhelmed her.

Where on earth were they?

She wasn't alone in her discomfort. Leo was frowning too as the pounding, banging and hissing of great engines reverberated through the air.

Purple lines glowed under their feet, then dimmed as Raven decreased the power with a word and gesture.

"Over here!"

The shout caught her attention, and Maia saw that a man was standing over to one side, holding a bundle under one arm. His robes were covered with dirt and looked like they hadn't been washed in weeks, but the enormous grin and bushy eyebrow lifted her spirits immediately.

"Heron!"

Blossom's Mage beckoned them both to follow. Raven waved them off, staying to bring the others through, so they left him to it and walked over to where Heron was standing. He was delighted to see them, wiping his hand on his robe before taking Leo's though it didn't seem to make much difference to its state. The Mage shook out the bundle to reveal a floor length cloak made from thick wool. He mimed for Maia to put it on and draw up the hood. She complied, the action feeling both familiar and alien at the same time. In truth, she'd thought she'd never have to wear clothes ever again. The texture of the material felt strange against her wooden fingers, but she swung it around her shoulders and felt it settle, pulling the hood well over her head to hide her face. Heron promptly hurried them to a side door, opening it with a flourish.

It was like a scene from Tartarus, though as far as she could see there wasn't any actual torture taking place unless you counted the incredible noise and heat. Leo coughed, his eyes already watering. Maia could detect the smell of soot and gases from the molten metal that was being poured into moulds by half-naked, grimacing men, barely visible under layers of dirt. Steam hissed in angry clouds from machines that pounded the metal like a hundred furious hydras, adding to the cacophony. Her Captain was already starting to sweat, but Heron moved on towards where a rectangle of bright light revealed the exit. It was a small wicket door set into a larger one, and she stepped through the space gingerly, feeling cobbles under her feet. Heron closed the door behind them, shutting out some of the noise. Leo wiped his face with a handkerchief, leaving black streaks on the white linen and Maia wondered whether she was similarly covered. She'd never heard of Ships needing a bath.

"Delighted to see you both!" Heron was beside himself. "This is a great day! Hello, Maia. I bet you never thought you'd be here, eh?"

She had to smile at him.

"Hello, Heron. I'm glad you're safe. Now, could you please tell us where here is?"

He looked confused for a second, then their situation dawned on him.

"Oh, yes of course. Didn't Raven tell you anything?"

"Not a thing."

Leo shook his head in confirmation.

"Oh, well," Heron rolled his eyes. "You know what that old bird's like." He spread his arms in a grand gesture. "Welcome to Mamucium, home of manufacturing in the North!"

The cobbled yard they were standing in was full of people hurrying about on various tasks. Horse-drawn carts vied with chugging steam engines to pull bales, crates and large objects covered in thick cloth hither and thither. It was only slightly less frantic than what they had seen inside. To their right, huge wooden gates reinforced with iron bands stood open, allowing a constant stream of traffic in and out.

Maia stared, fascinated. She'd seen factories in Portus, but had never been in one. Overseer Varus had sold her and the other children in the Foundling Home to be indentured servants instead of factory workers. On the face of it, living in a grand house had been a better position, until she'd been sent to serve Marcia Blandina. She'd have taken any amount of dirt and noise over that.

"Can you tell us what in Hades we're doing here?" Leo demanded. He wasn't wearing his uniform, so he could have been taken for any gentleman visiting the manufactory. As for her, she was just a woman in a cloak, her Shipbody hidden by its voluminous folds.

"Let's get somewhere more private and I'll tell you. Oh, and there are some people who want to meet you as well."

He hustled them across the yard and up some stairs into what appeared to be the factory offices. The door led to a corridor, off which were polished wooded doors with painted plaques affixed to their shiny surfaces. They passed several, including Accounts, Salaries, Advertising and others, before Heron paused at a pair of double doors at the end. Beside it was a button, which he pressed. After a couple of seconds, a rushing, clanking noise started from behind the carved panels. Leo looked at the Mage apprehensively.

Suddenly, the doors slid open.

"In we go!"

"What on earth's this?" Leo was dubious. Behind the doors was a small room, big enough for maybe six people. Maia balked at going inside the confined space, taking a step backwards.

Heron trotted inside and turned to face them.

"It's called an elevator. In short, it's a small, mobile room that moves up and down, powered by hydraulics. Clever, eh? They're being installed in lots of buildings now. It'll save us all climbing more stairs."

Maia wasn't thrilled, but went inside, trying not to clench her fists too tightly.

There was a picture on the wall, so Maia focused on that, ready to grab both men if something should go wrong. It showed cows drinking from a stream, with heather-clad hills in the background. She nearly laughed out loud. It couldn't be further from this place, or maybe that was the idea?

The doors slid shut and she felt the elevator rise for a few seconds before coming to a halt. Heron pressed another button and the doors slid open again, to reveal another corridor, richly carpeted and lined with more pictures. This had to be where the executives of the company worked, as it was unlikely that ordinary employees would be allowed up here.

"That was fun!" Leo said.

Maia almost sniffed. Men and their gadgets. He'd probably want one on her new vessel, to save him climbing the ladders. She could hear the command now. "*Tempest*! Ready the elevator!" She pulled a face at him when he wasn't looking.

They were heading for the door at the end. Larger than the rest, and made of a dark, exotic wood, it had a brass plaque instead of a painted one.

Company Chairman.

So, she would get to meet the owner. Maybe then she would finally learn what they were doing here, as she hadn't seen anything much to do with Ships unless they were forging cannon amid the smoke and noise.

Heron knocked, and a man's voice within bade them enter.

The large room was hushed, lined with bookcases and dominated by an imposing desk. To one side was a large bronze statue, showing Vulcan at his forge, muscles straining as he hammered at what looked like a shield, maybe that of Achilles? Now that did make sense.

The sunlight streamed in behind it through a stained glass window, casting rainbow colours on to the red carpet and making it difficult to see the occupant of the opulent leather chair. He stood as they entered, coming around the desk to greet them so that his face was revealed. Maia knew who he was immediately. The last time she'd seen this man was when he was standing with Pendragon in Portus, watching the *Diadem* transfer to her new vessel.

Her infallible memory supplied his name. She also noticed the ring on his finger, one only given to Knights of the Roman Empire. The man had bought himself a title.

"Greetings to you, *Tempest,* Captain!" He bowed low. Of course, he was a Portus lad. He would have had awe and respect for Ships drummed into him from an early age. Heron didn't make a move, so Maia decided to step in to make the introductions.

"Captain, may I present Julius Epolonius Cardo of Portus, *Eques* of the Empire. Sir Cardo, this is my Captain, Lucius Valerius Severianus Leo."

"I'm honoured that you remember me, ma'am." His pleased reaction seemed genuine. "Captain Valerius Leo! Welcome to my factory! Please, have a seat while I ring for refreshments."

Leo bowed back.

"Thank you, Sir Cardo. My Ship and I appreciate your hospitality in these uncertain times."

Heron excused himself and hurried off, leaving a trail of soot behind. Cardo regarded his stained carpet and laughed.

"He's a rum one, ain't he? Brilliant mind though."

He went over to a speaking tube on the wall and blew down it. A tinny voice echoed through the device. Cardo started to give his orders.

It was time for Maia and her Captain to quickly compare notes.

<Leo, what do you know about him?>

<He's the son of a freedman, built up the family manufacturing business and has more money than Pluto. Didn't he free his workers?>

x

<Yes. Now he charges them rent and sells them food and stuff from his shops, plus he has their political support should he ever want it. I'm not sure how I feel about that.>

<It's an astute move. Surely it's better to be a free worker than an enslaved one?>

<True. He can't keep them against their will, but they still rely on him for a roof over their head and food in their bellies. I didn't know he owned factories this far north.>

<Nor did I. And he's a knight, too. Someone's gone up in the world.>

Their rapid exchange ceased when Cardo pulled another chair from the wall and offered to Maia, who declined with thanks. He took it himself, brushing aside his coat tails and crossing one stockinged leg over another, showing off gold-embroidered garters. Shrewd brown eyes in a round face met hers and it was those that gave him away. It would be all too easy to dismiss this unassuming man until you got to be on the receiving end of his business practices. She wouldn't make the mistake of underestimating him, as many of his competitors had done to their cost.

"You must be wondering why you're here, so far from the sea," he began, addressing them both.

"We don't know," Leo admitted, "but we presume it's to get Tempest a new vessel."

Cardo grinned, his eyes dancing.

"Spot on, Captain! It's just not the sort you're used to. Sorry about the secrecy, but we couldn't risk this leaking. That toad Marcus has spies everywhere, though not as many as he thinks. The last one of his we caught ended up being sent to the banks of the Styx in short order, though we stuck a copper coin in his gob at the last minute to get him across. I'm not *that* cruel."

"May I ask why you don't support him? He appears to have Excalibur."

Cardo shot him a look.

"*Appears* is the right word. I have it on good authority that that bauble he's carting about is straight out the forge. He forced a friend of mine to make it, then had him killed. I owe the swine a death."

For a second, Maia thought he was going to spit on the carpet.

135

"Added to that, the Gods have condemned him out of their own mouths. The Priests are up in arms – those that haven't been arrested or murdered – and then we've got the Old Enemy returning to take us all back to the barbarous past. That do you?"

"Absolutely," Leo agreed. Maia could see that he was slightly taken aback by the man's directness. "I couldn't have put it better myself. You can add to that the deaths of Royal Navy personnel and the destruction of three Ships' vessels, plus several inanimates. You know he ordered the murders of King Artorius and Senator Rufus, too?"

Cardo's face darkened. "I heard that the King's body bled when Marcus touched it, and Macro murdered Rufus. It's definitely true, then?"

"Yes. There was a witness."

"Dear Gods! There's not much he isn't guilty of, is there? You know Lady Drusilla's landed at Dubris? She's being advised by old Favonius, you know, the Spymaster. Marcus is gathering his legions to march on them, but there's trouble in the ranks, so he might have a job on his hands to round them all up."

He was being remarkably frank with the pair of them, but then again, the situation warranted it. A knock at the door heralded a liveried servant bringing in refreshments.

"Here we go. Put it down there, Celsius, then you can leave," Cardo ordered. "Thank you."

Celsius bowed and left. Maia was impressed. She didn't know how he treated his servants, but thanking them was a good sign.

"Right then, Captain." Cardo fetched the table himself and set the tray on it. He was a man who was used to shifting for himself. "Chai, or something a little stronger?"

"Chai would be fine, thank you."

Celsius filled two cups of the thinnest eggshell porcelain, so delicate that she could see the level of the liquid through its translucency. Leo accepted the saucer and added a slice of lemon.

"Cake?"

Her Captain accepted a generous piece of that, too. Maia gazed at it longingly. It was a long time since she'd sneaked the cold dregs from cups after tea parties, savouring the taste on her tongue and wishing it had been hot. As for the cake – she'd taken it where she could.

"Forgive me, ma'am, but I understand you don't eat or drink."

"No, I don't anymore."

He made a sympathetic face at her wistful tone. "That must be hard. My wife loves nothing better than to have chai and cake in the afternoon. Same here!"

He laughed and slapped his stomach. "She's trying to put me on rations, but that only works at home. Whoever insists on the rights of the *paterfamilias* clearly hasn't met a Britannic woman with a goal in life."

They joined in his little joke, then Cardo grew serious again. He brushed himself down, heedless of the crumbs and leaned back in his chair.

"Like I said, Mamucium's nowhere near the sea. There's talk of building a canal to join it to the river system, but that'll have to wait. We've been developing an experimental prototype here that we think will come in handy. Well, I say we, but it's mostly the Mage Artificers, plus some very *special* advisors."

He raised his eyes to the heavens, then nodded at the statue of Vulcan.

"I told you they're against Marcus, right? Anyway, Admiral Pendragon reckons you'd do well operating this prototype. I don't know all the details, but he says you're not like the other Ships."

Maia was even more confused now.

"I'm the youngest," she said. "Perhaps he thought I'd adapt better?"

Cardo sucked his teeth. "Maybe, or maybe it's something else. Who knows? He wouldn't, or couldn't tell me, but I'm not going to argue. If this works, it'll give us a massive advantage. If not…" He shrugged. "You're no worse off and we'll get you another vessel somehow. How does that sound?"

"It sounds fair," she said.

Cardo turned to Leo.

"Captain?"

"I concur, but I'd like to know more about this 'experimental vessel'."

Cardo rubbed his hands. "And you will. Though I warn you, you might wish you'd gone for something stronger than chai!"

The chai party over, they returned the way they'd come, with Cardo expounding on the novelty of the elevator.

"I can just about grasp how it works," he said, "but my strength's in working out how to make a profit out of it. Every tall building in the country will want one, mark my words, and I've got the patent. Hydraulics and steam power – that's where the future lies. Take my advice, Captain and put any spare money you have into the new railways."

"I've heard they're going to be starting up soon," Leo said, "though there's some opposition."

Cardo snorted. "There's always opposition when change comes calling. People are happy enough when it saves them time and money, not so happy when we have to demolish their houses to run the lines through. That's the price of progress, I'm afraid. It's not as if they won't be well compensated."

Maia listened in. She'd seen the road engines, but they were slow and cumbersome and many still preferred horses. Running them on rails seemed a better option.

"Will they go faster than the road engines?" she asked Cardo.

"They certainly will! There's talk of twenty miles an hour once they really get going."

She was impressed despite herself. It would have been interesting to ride on one, but Ships stayed at sea or anchored to a building. Her current situation was, as far as she knew, largely unprecedented. A Ship walking around like a human woman was a sight many wouldn't have credited, though Cardo was too polite to say so.

They were soon back in the yard, where a carriage was waiting.

"It's a bit of a way off," Cardo explained. He and Leo climbed aboard, then helped Maia up. She was becoming more and more used to having legs again, so much so that part of her wondered whether being attached to a vessel had all been a dream. Or maybe this was? It was all a little disorientating but she quelled her discomfort, eager to see what Cardo had in store for them.

The factory site was huge, more like a small town in itself and seemed to be split into different departments. Cardo pointed out

138

what each building was for as they bounced along. Maia was glad when the cobbles gave way to a smoother, paved surface.

<It's like a tall brick labyrinth,> Leo observed. <It's a good job he knows where he's going.>

<I would say that he knows everything about his properties.>

They turned down yet another roadway. The many-storied buildings closed off the light, while above them chimneys reached into the sky, belching out smoke. The air felt dull and greasy, loaded with the waste of a thousand fires. The hurrying workers were leached of colour as if the dust had settled into their very pores, infusing their bodies and clothes with a pall of soot and Maia found herself longing for the open vistas and freshness of the sea.

The road ended in a high brick wall with another set of gates inset, but this time they were closed. The driver hopped down and pulled at a chain to one side. A bell sounded from somewhere within and a hatch opened in the gate. After a short conversation, the right hand gate slowly opened just enough to allow them passage, swinging closed behind them.

A detachment of marines was waiting for them.

"Osric!" Maia exclaimed, brightening up at the sight of the company.

"We can't have our Ship going unescorted, can we?" Cardo said with a grin.

Ahead of them, a high wall blocked the way and another set of gates. There were armed guards as well, dressed in Cardo's livery and carrying muskets. Their host had not been exaggerating when he'd stressed the need for secrecy. The marines saluted, then marched beside the cart as they continued along the wall to yet another gate. This time it swung open as they approached and they went through into the complex proper.

She would have sworn it was a Shipyard. There were piles of lumber, ropes, sailcloth and, in the near distance, something that looked like the hull of a vessel, but oddly shaped and curving upwards more than it should, so that the top was seemingly enclosed. Also, no Ship would want to have gun ports below the water line. And where was the copper- bottoming? As they drew closer, she could see that the flanks were clad with riveted sheets of silvery metal. The prow and stern were there as normal, but

139

there were no masts. Instead, a scaffold of struts made out of the same metal reached up from the deck, looking like the ribs of a giant cetacean. Enclosed within them was an enormous bag of material.

Maia couldn't tear her eyes away from the incredible machine. It had a keel and a rudder, but what were the things mounted on each side? They looked like they were meant to spin.

<What in the name of all the Gods is that?> Leo demanded.

<I think it's my new vessel,> she said, feeling her excitement mounting.

<Are they going to sail it down the rivers?>

<The gun ports would flood.>

They exchanged looks of mutual incomprehension.

"Let's go and see it, shall we?" Cardo was enjoying himself. Maia got down from the carriage, hoping that it was the last time she'd have to be jounced about. It was tiring having to rely on other means of transport.

Osric marched over to Leo.

"Captain!"

They exchanged salutes. From the look on the marine's face, he wasn't any the wiser as to what this thing was either. As Osric was making his report, she heard a shout.

"Maia!"

A man was climbing down from the vessel, his Mage robe tucked into his belt to keep it out of the way. He jumped down on to the ground and waved madly at her. She waved back.

"Robin!"

He jogged over and came to a halt, panting slightly.

"They said it would be you! I'm so glad!" Then his face fell. "I mean, I'm sorry for the loss of your vessel and crew."

"It could have been worse," she said. "The *Regina* could have finished us all off, one by one if it hadn't been for the new weapon."

He blushed, accentuating his birthmark. "We didn't know whether it would be effective or not, but it's led to more improvements. Well, what do you think?"

She didn't know what to say.

"It's…remarkable. What is it?"

Cardo guffawed.

"I'd like to know the answer to that question as well," Leo said. "Hello, Robin."

Robin blinked, belatedly realising who was with her.

"Captain Valerius, sir. Good to see you. And you too, Sir Cardo."

"How's my genius, then?" Cardo asked.

"Erm...,"

"I'm teasing you, lad. How's the vessel?"

"Very good, sir. We've tested as much as we can and it's all working. The Chief Artificer and Heron are waiting for *Tempest* to board so they can integrate her into the systems."

Maia wished she could pinch herself.

"It feels like I'm dreaming," she confessed.

"Not a dream, ma'am," Cardo assured her. "Behold, your new vessel. You will be the world's first AirShip!"

"Gods preserve us," one of the marines muttered. Maia had to agree.

An AirShip. The vessel was built to fly. And who better to power it than the Child of Aura, niece of Cymopoleia and sister of Pearl? Her hand flew to her mouth. This had to be what Pendragon and Raven had been planning.

"I hope I can learn to operate it quickly," she said. "I know there isn't much time."

"I'm sure you'll soon pick it up," Robin encouraged. "I know you have a great memory and Potentia to spare, so it won't be a p - problem."

He was so excited that she could hear the ghost of the stammer creeping into his voice. He'd come such a long way from the shy boy she'd first met, hiding his face and afraid to open his mouth in company.

"I hope not."

"We'll be starting right now," Cardo interjected. "Let's get you aboard, ma'am, so you can see for yourself. Our Chief Artificer would like to meet you."

"I wish I had my uniform," Leo said, tugging at his borrowed coat. "I feel somewhat underdressed."

"Don't you worry about that," Cardo told him cheerfully. "You'll be getting a new uniform soon enough. I got your measurements sent over from Magonius. Nothing but the best for our new AirShip Captain!"

The party marched over to where the vessel towered over them. Maia raised her head, marvelling at the alien spider web structure of struts and metal cables, so different to the spars and ropes she was used to. Its flanks shone silver in the sun, like sunlight on clouds and she wondered whether it would make it more difficult to spot from the ground. Now she was closer, she could see that it was resting on a wheeled undercarriage and hatches of various sizes were scattered on its belly. All the better to drop things on her enemies' heads.

A doorway was cut into the side, linked to the dock by an inclined ramp.

"Good. I won't have to be hoisted into it," Maia said to Robin.

"We've made some improvements on the regular Ship design," he agreed. "The main consideration is tolerances to air pressure and weather, not water, though it can float for a short time if it has to."

"Seriously?" Maia was cheered to think it could sail again.

"You might have to ditch into the sea. It wouldn't be any good if it didn't float, at least for a while."

"Oh, I see. I'll just have to stay aloft."

"Cheer up," Leo whispered to her. "It's going to be great fun!"

She glared at him. It was his favourite word of the day, but not the one she would have chosen.

"More work for me," she grumped.

"Oh, come on. There's not been anything like this since the *Britannia* took to the water. Imagine how she must have felt, as the only Ship. She wouldn't even have had anybody else to talk to."

"Just like me at the moment, then." It irked Maia that she couldn't link with her sisters. It was rare for a Ship to be incommunicado for long periods.

<Don't sulk!> he Sent. <We've got to be on our best behaviour. Think of the damage we can cause. I bet the other Ships will be jealous.>

<I bet they won't!>

142

She had to admit it would be quite amusing to see their reactions. Maia couldn't wait to tell them – that was if she managed to get the thing off the ground. Its hull was only about a third of the length of her previous vessel, so she'd have a slimmed–down crew. She did a mental calculation. Of course, Pendragon had already given her about the right number of men, though she could see that they might need some more marines, gunners and perhaps a few specialists. This Chief Artificer, for one.

A welcome party stood ready to meet them as they stepped into the body of the vessel. Raven and Heron were there, the latter beaming at her, together with another man dressed in workman's clothes with a leather apron over the top and wearing thick gloves. He was quite short, with curly brown hair and a beard. He reminded her of Quercus, though his skin was olive as if his ancestors were from the Mediterranean area. His muscles bulged under his shirt, indicating that he was used to hard labour.

"Welcome," he said. From his accent, she thought that he was Greek. "I am the Chief Artificer."

Introductions were promptly made. When it was her turn to greet him, he looked into her eyes and she knew that she was being assessed.

"I'm glad I finally have the pleasure of meeting you, ma'am," he said. "My parents have spoken to me about you."

"I'm honoured, sir," she replied, puzzled. "Have I met your parents?"

Perhaps they'd been at one of the civic receptions she'd attended before her installation, or even at Senator Rufus's villa? Without knowing his name, her memory was no help.

"You had a chat with my mother just the other day, and my father spoke to you a few years ago."

Was he being deliberately cryptic? Then it dawned on her. He didn't have the heavy presence that rest of his family carried with them, but there was something in his eyes she recognised.

Here we go again. I bet he walks with a limp.

Cardo bustled over. "Shall we do the tour, ma'am, gentlemen?"

Vulcan winked at her, then took up position at the head of the party. He did have a limp. Maia instantly opened her private link to Raven.

<Hello, Raven.>

<Maia. What do you think of your new vessel?>

<I haven't seen it all yet. It seems a bit daunting.>

<Really? I'd have thought you of all people would be well-suited to it.>

<Our *Chief Artificer* seems nice,> she remarked.

<So, you've worked out who he is?>

<He told me as much. As he said, his mother dropped in for a little chat when we were at Iucundus's villa.>

She sensed his surprise.

<Juno spoke to you? Directly?>

<In person. She supports me and pleaded my case with her husband.>

For once, the ancient Mage was temporarily lost for words.

<Well, you do mingle with the mighty. Yes, I know he's Vulcan, but he's in mortal disguise so nobody else knows.>

<Another secret to keep?>

<Another secret,> he confirmed. <You're getting to be almost as good at keeping them as I am.>

<Through necessity,> she admitted. <What else haven't you been telling me?>

He sighed.

<Ah, my dear, there's a long, long list. Now, concentrate on the workings. You need to familiarise yourself with everything, and we don't want to keep the God waiting.>

A thought struck her.

<So, as an AirShip, which God is my patron?>

<Hmm. Definitely Vulcan, but I'd throw in Jupiter, Juno and the Winds as well. Plus there's your family, but we'll worry about that later. Now, concentrate!>

She broke the link and listened to Vulcan. The insides of the vessel could have been any small craft, except much of the wood had been replaced with metal.

"This is the lightest metal we have. It's derived from aluminem, the stuff we've been using for centuries for tanning and dyeing. It's imported from Chin, and I tell you, they're

144

charging a pretty penny for it. Unfortunately, we don't seem to have much in the Empire. There have been promising results in our southern overseas coloniae, but the operation to obtain it there won't be ready for a few years yet."

"What's it called?" Leo asked, rubbing his hand over the nearest surface.

"Aluminium. It's better than iron and doesn't rust, though it does oxidise in the air. We've developed a special coating for it."

"How does it fly?" Maia asked.

"You saw the bag inside the struts? It's made of three separate compartments that are filled with hot air and a new gas we've extracted. It seems the best option at the moment. We tried another gas, but that had the propensity to explode at the smallest spark. The hot air will allow for vertical movement, thanks to your Potentia, *Tempest*, and the new gas provides extra lift. The propellers either side direct it right and left. The rudder at the back keeps you straight, as is normal for a Ship."

It was nice to know that something was familiar. Nothing else was. The God continued.

"Naturally, you'll have to get used to moving in three dimensions instead of two, regulating altitude and so forth."

"This will call for new tactics," Leo said, a glint in his eye. Vulcan smiled.

"It will. Maybe you'll write the book, eh Captain?"

She could tell that Leo was desperate to try it out. She could only hope that her crew would feel the same.

"How will the transfer work?" she asked.

"Your carpenter has already incorporated a little of your previous vessel, *Tempest*. Can you sense it?"

She frowned, then shook her head.

"No. I can't. It's as if something's blocking me."

Everyone looked anxious. If she couldn't make the connection, there would be no AirShip.

"It must be the metal," Vulcan muttered, stroking his beard. "Maybe you'll be able to when we show you where it is, or we might have to incorporate more. I've got to think of the weight, you see. Normally, Ships can tell straightaway where their wood is. Keep trying."

She nodded obediently, reaching out to see if she could anchor herself anywhere. This craft didn't feel like a vessel at all. Instead of being an organic structure, it gave off a more rigid atmosphere, though not as cold as iron. She could feel her awareness sliding off it, as if it were drenched in oil and she was scrabbling at the surface in vain.

Wait. There was something. A tiny gap in the unyielding hardness, like a little handhold she could grip. Maia cast about her, searching for another. Yes, there it was, then another. She triangulated the points and found that they'd been set equidistant around the craft. It had two decks – an upper, command deck, with tiny officer's quarters, guns and, strangely enough, the magazine. That made sense if attacks were coming from the ground, she supposed. The living space for the crew was next to the guns as usual, while the lower deck was for storage, with some smaller gun ports and hatches.

At the prow, there was an open platform from which it would be possible to view their way ahead. Maia immediately decided that this would be where she would station herself. It wasn't a quarterdeck, but she would have a sense of freedom that the enclosed space wouldn't give her. Despite having visuals everywhere on her vessel, she still preferred for her Shipbody to be outside.

Everything was becoming clearer in her mind as she probed. She didn't know whether she'd be able to move about this vessel as she had her other one, but she wouldn't be deaf and blind. Furthermore, the decks were wooden, so that should help in some respect.

She was so busy examining everything that she didn't fully register her surroundings until they came to the mechanisms. They ran through the craft from top to bottom and would enable her to control the hot air and gas system, the propellers and the rudder. She could also open the hatches when necessary.

Maia smiled to herself. Why, it appeared simpler than a seagoing vessel!

Raven's voice slid into her head.

<I know what you're thinking. Don't get cocky. It appears easier, but most of the skill lies in understanding wind and weather conditions. You don't want to get knocked out of the sky

because you misjudged an air current. This is unknown territory, and we wouldn't have rushed you into it if the situation wasn't so dire.>

<Will I be able to make a difference? I've had no training and the *Scientia* is untested.>

<Our Ships have already failed against the new Fae defences once. We're hoping that this will even the balance.>

She didn't like the sound of that.

<When am I going to be installed?>

<Today. Danuco's on his way, as is another Priestess to give you her blessing. This has got to work.>

She felt her heart sink.

<No pressure then.>

He patted her hand.

<Do your best.>

Maia looked at Leo's rapt face. He'd already fallen in love with his new command.

"Now, then, Master Mage, what are you saying to frighten my AirShip?"

Vulcan's face appeared at her shoulder. Raven twitched.

"I was saying, sir, that she shouldn't be over-confident. There'll be much to learn and she must do it quickly."

"That's true. It's fortuitous that she has a perfect memory as I'm going to be loading her with a great deal of information. Don't worry, *Tempest*, you can do this. I'm not the only Artificer who'll be assisting." She could see the God smiling at her in the gloom. "Wait until you meet my sister. She's itching to play with this new toy."

His sister? She didn't dare ask which one.

"We're just waiting for your Priest, then we'll go ahead. In the meantime, I've some more things you should know. Ready for some technicalities?"

Maia nodded. She hadn't spent years at the Portus Academy to be daunted by more training. This was just another type of craft, and one she wouldn't be left alone to operate.

After all, she had Gods by her side.

IX

The port of Tinea was not dissimilar to the ones he was used to on the Thamesis, packed with all sorts of water craft even at this early hour. Caniculus wrinkled his nose at the smells of smoke, tar, old rope, fish and rotting seaweed that permeated the air. They created a miasmic stench that was only alleviated by the morning breeze that tugged at his hat and coat tails.

He offered up a prayer to its Goddess, thanking her for the relief as he strode along the cobbled dockside, trying not to get in anybody's way. Overhead, cranes swung cargo back and forth, loading and unloading vessels from all corners of the Empire, and men and women shouted at each other in every tongue under the sun. There was even a boat from Chin, its strange construction marking it out from its fellows. Nothing, including the threat of war, stopped the wheels of commerce.

He'd left the Riverside *mansio* and its genial host, following Mercury's orders to try and secure passage south on the first craft he could that looked like it would take paying passengers and get him as near as possible to Londin in one piece.

At last, his destination came into view. The booking office handled all passenger transactions, issuing tickets and making sure that the correct taxes were paid. You could take your chances asking on the quay, but this was the safest option. Caniculus was doing this under duress, and he was going to make sure that the vessel was as comfortable as possible.

A bell jangled merrily over the door as he entered and he took his place in the queue behind a red-faced merchant and a woman with two sulky adolescent boys in tow. To one side was a board with upcoming departures chalked on it. This would make things easier, so he checked to see if there was anything that would suit. There. The *Insula Vectis* was due to leave with the tide in a couple of hours, docking at the mouth of Thamesis Estuary before continuing on its way to Gaul. Now he had to hope that there was a berth for him. It would be easy enough to get into Londin from there.

The merchant was going to Massilia in the Mediterranean and the woman northwards. He waited patiently for them to buy their tickets, quietly wishing that he could join the merchant on his trip to the Mediterranean. He'd been to the Continent once with friends, on a holiday to Lutetia which had turned out to be more of a drinking party. He'd always wanted to go further afield, but never had. It wasn't the thought of visiting foreign places that put him off – everyone spoke Latin – but the sea crossing. He could get sick on a child's fairground ride. Despite this, Massilia seemed very attractive at the moment.

"Yes, sir?"

It was his turn at last.

"Good morning. Do you have a first class berth on the *Insula Vectis* please? Just as far as the Thamesis."

The clerk consulted his ledger.

"Let me see, sir." He thumbed to the correct page. "Here we are. The *Insula Vectis*. I don't think…" He trailed off, one eyebrow raised. "You're in luck, sir! I thought it was fully booked, but it seems we had a cancellation earlier today."

Of course you had, Caniculus thought, though with his luck it would be third class just above the bilge pumps.

"One first class berth it is, but you'll have to be quick. It's departing shortly."

"That's not a problem, I'm in a hurry anyway," he said. "Are meals included?"

"No, sir. That's extra."

"I probably won't be able to manage to eat much anyway," he said. The clerk was sympathetic.

"Lollia the herbalist's the person you need to see, sir. She mixes up a remedy for seasickness that will help. Her stall's next to Nehalennia's altar, just down from here. Best in the town and no fancy Adept prices."

Caniculus thanked the clerk, thinking that Lollia was probably his sister, and paid with the money Mercury had given him. It was like the God to have given him just enough, with a little left over for food. Still, with what he was going to face, money would probably be the least of his worries.

He left the office, heading in the direction the clerk had indicated. On the way, he picked up a bunch of flowers to lay on the altar to Nehalennia, the Goddess who protected those crossing the Germanic Ocean. Sure enough, the stall was right next door, in prime position to take advantage of anxious passengers. The altar was crowded, but he added his blooms and paid her Priest a couple of coins to intercede for him, though he rather thought that Mercury would see to that. There wouldn't be any point to all this if he was going to end up at the bottom of the sea. Still, it was a wise move to make doubly sure.

Lollia, who was probably the clerk's mother from the resemblance, was happy to sell him some evil-looking concoction in a glass vial, with strict instructions to only take two drops a day.

"Don't take any more," she told him, "or you won't just be seasick. You'll have the other end to worry about as well!"

She cackled at her own joke. Caniculus would have bet his boots she said that to all her customers and found it hilarious every single time. He gave her a polite smile and scooted off to find the *Insula Vectis*, hoping that it wasn't some decrepit old hulk manned by half-wits.

First class. It had to be good, didn't it? Maybe he'd have a bit of luxury before the perils of Londin.

*

Two days later, Caniculus staggered ashore, having redefined his definition of luxury. His only consolation was that he hadn't had to travel third class, which probably included being strapped to the mast and pelted with mouldy bread. The Emperor Caligula's pleasure boat it wasn't, though he'd had a small cabin to himself and a basin to wash in, as well as room service from a steward.

The sea had also behaved itself, which meant he'd been able to keep some food down for once. To his surprise, Lollia's remedy had actually worked. The worst thing had been knowing that there was a lot of water between him and the sea bottom where nasty creatures like kraken lurked, ready to attack without provocation. He didn't know whether to thank Mercury or Nehalennia. Maybe the Goddess had liked his flowers? Whatever, he was going to make offerings to both of them.

He'd kept himself to himself during the voyage, not wanting to strike up acquaintance with any of the other passengers for the sake of security and disembarked first, a privilege granted because of the money he'd spent. He thought it worthwhile to tip a slave to arrange a carriage to get him to Londin. It would be easy enough to vanish, in his case quite literally, when he got there, but until then he would continue on his upper-class way. As long as no-one thought he was worth robbing, he'd be fine. The lad only took a few minutes, his long legs making short work of the task. Soon, Caniculus bid farewell to the sea and was settling down into the comfortably padded seat of a private carriage. It might have been faster to travel by boat, but he'd had enough of water travel for the time being. It also looked like rain.

He stowed his luggage opposite him and tried to get some sleep. It would take at least three hours, with a stop half way, to get to the centre of Londin. He'd asked the driver to head to the Forum. From there, his plan was to slip on the helmet and await further instructions, gathering as much information as he could in the meantime. He hoped he'd get them before he reached the Fort, the oldest part of Londin. It had been rebuilt many centuries ago, after Queen Boudica burned the first one, and still dominated the landscape of the Old City within the Roman Wall.

"I am at your service, Lord Mercury," he muttered to himself, half-expecting the God to turn up in person. Satisfied that he'd get no answer yet, he tipped his hat over his eyes and dozed off to the swaying of the carriage.

It was the increased noise that woke him, as well as the smells of smoke and human habitation seeping in past the leather flaps that covered the windows. Caniculus felt his insides relax. This was where he belonged, not on the heaving waves or some far northern city, but this sprawling, dirty metropolis.

He wished he could check on his family, but he'd already pushed his luck too far in that regard and wouldn't risk them again. He peeked out to see the familiar landmarks coming into view. The eagles on the roof of the Temple of Jupiter gleamed in the evening light, the whole scene framed by the setting sun. The river wasn't visible but he knew it was near, winding its way onwards as it had done since the dawn of time. Its ever-present stink was building as the days waxed towards midsummer. By July it would be nigh on unbearable and people would walk around with their faces covered.

Caniculus reached across to the opposite seat and grabbed his pack, making sure that the helmet was within easy reach. It would be his bad luck to be spotted as soon as he alighted, though he'd given a false name when booking his passage. He'd pay the driver and make a quick getaway.

The carriage rattled into the Forum, taking its place in the rank reserved for licensed vehicles. Caniculus hopped out and passed coins to the driver, plus a reasonable tip. Being over-generous would cause him to be remembered, but the man seemed satisfied enough.

"I'm obliged to you sir," he began, then broke off as loud chants cut through the everyday noise.

"What can you see?" Caniculus asked. The driver had a better view from his perch, added to which he'd already stood up for a better view.

"It's coming from the temples, sir." The man squinted, making the most of the failing light. "Looks like it's some sort of parade."

Caniculus joined him, gazing out over the heads of the crowd that was assembling as Londiners always had an insatiable appetite for free entertainment. His eye was drawn to the looming Basilica. It looked the same as it ever had, with no sign of the unseen sword that was still presumably sticking out of the column. There was nothing he could do about it now, so he switched his attention to the focus of the crowd's interest.

Lines of Priests and Priestesses were leaving their temples, bearing the sacred images of the Gods before them. Caniculus spotted Jupiter, Mars, Juno, Diana, Mercury, Neptune and Apollo in statue form carried on the shoulders of their worshippers. Minerva, Ceres, Isis and Horus soon joined them. It looked like a gathering of Gods, swaying on their ceremonial litters above a sea of heads as they were carried past, one after another.

The crowd fell back to give them room to pass, the hum of voices rising to an angry susurrus that bounced off the buildings.

"It's not time for a festival, is it?" The driver screwed his face up as he tried to make sense of it all.

"No, it's not."

"This spells trouble," the driver announced. "Think I'll get me and the old girl home quick. Can I take you anywhere else, sir?"

"Don't blame you, but no thanks. Safe travels!"

Caniculus jumped down. The driver clicked his tongue at his horse and snapped the reins to direct the mare out of there at a smart pace.

It was worth staying, Caniculus decided. There were now so many people pushing their way into the Forum to see what was happening, nobody would spot him among the masses. He gripped his pack tightly and shouldered his way through.

A gasp from the packed multitude told him that more deities had joined their fellows. Even the soldier God Mithras had emerged from his underground shrine, escorted by his warrior Priests. This was a huge show of unity and made a change from their incessant squabbles. A few were more recent imports and largely unfamiliar to him, maybe Gods from New Roma, or Cuzco, though those deities' worship was curtailed in the Empire where human sacrifice was strictly forbidden. What strange alliances had been made by the Powers that ruled the mortal lands? He looked at the goggle-eyed, fanged idols with a shudder. Still, each to their own.

The various hymns and chants rose in volume as more and more Immortals were represented. Slowly, everyone else grew silent in awed respect, many raising hands in supplication as their favoured God went past. The air of anticipation faded as apprehension grew. This was no happy celebration, more an invocation.

The slanting light of evening vanished, as dark clouds boiled up with supernatural speed, obscuring Helios's friendly orb. Caniculus's hair began to rise as the atmosphere thickened and the tension rose.

"Mighty Jupiter, protect us!" A woman screamed.

It was almost full dark now. The faces around him were shadowed and ghostly, but still no-one moved, waiting to see what the Gods decreed. The procession halted before the Basilica, led by the distinctive shape of Aquila. There was no mistaking Jupiter's High Priest as he mounted the steps and held up his hand.

All sound ceased, a breathless hush descending on the great space. Then Aquila spoke, his voice magically amplified.

"Good people of Britannia! I have been chosen to bring you a message from the Gods. Marcus is not your King. He is a murderer and liar who has falsely claimed the throne, aided by the ancient race of Fae who are even now invading our shores to the west. He seeks to overthrow the rule of Olympus and tear down the temples of the Gods. There will be no tolerance, no law and no civilisation under his bloody hand. Furthermore, he has deceived you all."

Aquila paused for effect, then gestured behind him.

"Behold, the Sword of Kingship!"

A crack of thunder followed his words, shaking the stones of the ancient city and reverberating off the buildings around them. Heads swivelled, following the Priest's pointing hand as the tremors died away, though Caniculus would have sworn that he could still feel the echo rattling his bones.

One intense flash of light and the sword was revealed. It glowed as if self-illuminated, radiating silver beams through the gloom. Jupiter's Potentia had blasted away all traces of the Fae glamour.

Several thousand mouths dropped in unison.

"Jupiter passes judgement!" Aquila's voice rang out, answered by a searing flash as a thunderbolt hurtled from the sky, passing over the Forum like a comet with a fiery tail.

The explosion was the loudest thing Caniculus had ever heard. Then the wailing began in earnest.

He squeezed his way through the massed bodies, desperate to find some space so that he could put on the helmet. He thought that the divine weapon had landed just to the south, somewhere near the river and in the approximate location of the palace. Indeed, a rosy glow was already starting to rise above the rooftops.

A path opened up in front of him and he hurled himself into it. The crowd seemingly couldn't decide whether to stay and watch the spectacle or bolt to safety, but enough people had moved to give Caniculus some breathing space. He ducked into an alley and dragged out the helmet. As usual it felt like it was watching him, but he didn't have time for idle fancies and rammed it onto his head.

Relief swept over him and he leaned back against the crumbling brickwork for a minute to catch his breath. When he peeked out into the Forum, wails and chaos still ruled. He could see the Gods' images being returned to their shrines, followed by straggling lines of anxious worshippers. The one following Jupiter was the longest. Caniculus couldn't remember when the Gods had acted so publicly. He thought there'd been a reported glimpse of some of them at the funeral of Julius, Artorius's father, who had been killed years before in a hunting accident, but there hadn't been anything in Britannia since. This only confirmed to the whole population that the Olympians and their allies were preparing for outright war.

Now he had to find where that thunderbolt had landed and wait for his orders. Caniculus slipped out of the alley and took a less crowded route in the direction of the fire. He was starting to smell it now, as wisps of smoke were being carried by the breeze and saw that he wasn't the only one heading in that direction. He had to swerve and sidestep to avoid any unfortunate collisions. Everyone scattered as a team of horses clattered past pulling a fire engine, its warning bells ringing and the vigiles in their brass helmets and blue uniforms hanging on its side. There would be others too. Fire was an ever-present danger in any polis and the service was well-funded. Caniculus peeled himself off a shop front and followed in its wake as best he could.

As he came out into the open square that fronted the huge ironwork gates, all became clear. The palace was burning. Thick black smoke billowed up, forming a huge column in the sky. Figures were emerging from the smoke, coughing and choking, their faces and clothes stained with soot and smoke. Some lucky ones were clutching bundles of possessions, though most had got out only with the clothes they stood up in. One slave was cradling a silver candlestick, a bewildered look on her face. She'd probably been cleaning it when the bolt struck. Caniculus sidled up to her.

"Listen to me. Go to Aspicius the jeweller on Silver Street. He'll buy it, no questions asked."

The woman jumped, terrified eyes darting around before raising to the heavens.

"Praise the Gods!" she whispered, before shoving the candlestick down her dress and legging it into the shadows. Caniculus grinned. It was better that she had the benefit. Every slave had something put by, if they had any sense.

Buoyed by the satisfaction of a job well done, he dodged through the gawkers and well-meaning helpers to stand just inside the fancy railings. More windows were shattering now as the flames took hold, steadily devouring the entire façade. He could only hope that most of the staff had got out alive, and that Marcus and his loathsome allies had borne the brunt of Jupiter's wrath. Maybe their charred corpses were even now burning merrily under the rubble?

He rooted about in his pack to find something to chew on, and settled down to watch and wait.

*

How they made it to the kitchen entrance, Marcus didn't know. One second he'd been in the throne room hearing reports from the south coast, then the next there was an indescribable noise and the coffered ceiling began to cave in on top of him. If it hadn't been for Kite's quick thinking, he'd have been left as a crushed smear on the marble. The Mage had thrown up a shield and dragged him from his throne. Marcus had lost sight of his guards under the collapsing masonry, but was too busy saving his own skin to worry about anyone else.

156

They'd made for one of the internal passages that riddled the palace, exiting on to a service corridor while around them everything seemed to be screaming, burning or disintegrating, sometimes all at once. He'd pulled his cloak over his face with his free hand, Kite holding on to his other arm with a fierce grip. The only thing protecting them both was the Mage's magic, its sickly green halo tinting the scenes of devastation so that it seemed like they were moving underwater.

It wasn't much better once they emerged. Several fire engines with their attendant vigiles were pumping steady streams of water in through blazing windows, but they might as well have been spitting on it for all the good it was doing. Several lumps lay on the flagstones, covered with blankets, and Marcus averted his eyes.

"Your Majesty!"

He knew that bellow. Macro strode from the smoke like an angry wraith, followed by half a dozen of the palace guards. Kite released Marcus and bent at the waist, gasping for air.

"Get me out of here," Marcus snapped. He didn't know what had happened, but it had to be some kind of attack. Explosive shells maybe, hidden and detonated by one of Favonius's Agents. There would be time enough to ask questions later. For now, his safety should be everyone's priority.

"Yes, Sire. This way. We'll head for the river."

There were horses waiting. Marcus repressed a grumble. He much preferred to travel by carriage, but horseback was quicker and they wouldn't be confined to the wider streets. He heaved himself up into the saddle and galloped off surrounded by his escort.

It was only a short ride to the banks of the Thamesis. River travel was even quicker than horses and there were several royal residences he could choose from, both up and downstream. He fully expected to see the Royal Barge with its liveried oarsmen, but was met by an ordinary ferryboat. This wouldn't do at all.

"Where's my barge?" he demanded.

"Someone's trying to kill you, Sire," Macro replied bluntly. "I think it best not to draw too much attention to ourselves. With your permission."

That was true. The shock must have dislodged his wits.

"Yes, of course. Carry on."

Two guards helped him aboard and he collapsed heavily on to the bench. The whole waterfront was lit up now full darkness had fallen, casting blood-red reflections on to the rippling Thamesis. The oarsmen cast off and the dock receded. Marcus felt the lurch as the current took them. The tide had to be on the ebb as they were heading smoothly away downstream. Opposite him, Macro removed his helmet and wiped his face. Kite stared into nothing, probably reporting in to their friends and allies. Marcus was glad when the shouts and yells faded into the distance and the normal sounds of the city resumed the further they got from the stricken buildings.

It wasn't particularly cold on the water, but he drew his cloak about him as best he could, rubbing at his bruised arm where Kite had seized it.

"What happened?" he asked Macro.

The normally unflappable commander frowned. "It came from the heavens, Sire. I was getting reports of a disturbance in the Forum when –."

He raised a brawny arm and slammed his fist into his palm.

Marcus felt his stomach lurch.

"A thunderbolt?" He couldn't help whispering.

"Seems so, Sire."

And here he was on a small boat in the middle of the river, an easy target for both Gods and mortals.

"That's not all." Kite's harsh voice broke into the horrified silence. "The glamour on the sword is broken and you have been publicly denounced by the Olympians."

Panic threatened to overwhelm Marcus, but he beat it back into a corner by sheer force of will.

"Damn them! There has to be a way of salvaging this."

"The legions won't fight for you now," Macro stated. He'd dropped the Sire, Marcus noticed. The big man shifted uneasily in his seat.

"But we have others who will," Kite interjected. "Our forces stand ready to be transported, by sea and land. We can open a portal and bring them through."

The knot in Marcus's stomach loosened.

"Will that be enough?"

"Against mortals?" Kite sniffed. "I should think so. All we have to do is to stop your father getting his hands on the sword and the Land is officially without a king."

"True. He's still to the west with his precious Ships, and we have enough allies to ensure that he won't be able to reach the Forum."

He could feel himself relaxing a little, his confidence returning. Olympus had taken its shot and missed. He was protected by other Powers now.

"Exactly," Kite agreed. "We'll divert your bride and the nobles of the court to Greenfields. We can make it our base, and this time I'll make sure there are more protections in place. Let the Thunderer rage all he wants. His time here is almost done."

Marcus nodded. His palace at Greenfields was even more luxurious than the old Londinium House, which quite frankly had been draughty and outdated. In his mind's eye he could already see the wonderful new building he'd put in its place. As to the details of troop movements and battle strategy, that was why he had Kite and Macro. They could sort it all out.

He enjoyed being King, and soon he would be King forever. If the Gods had eternal life, why not him?

It wouldn't be long now, and the Fae always kept their promises.

X

<*Blossom* to *Patience*. How's it going?>

Briseis was glad to hear the old Ship's voice through the link but she thought for a second before formulating her reply. If anything, her Captain had been too optimistic about Briseis's effect on her new sailing master. He'd been hovering at her shoulder like a particularly annoying wasp, insisting on constant progress reports. No wonder the man had been assigned an inanimate!

<Hello, Blossom. What would be the penalty if I threw Tetius Micianus overboard?>

There was a second of stunned silence, then *Blossom* guffawed loudly.

<Oh no! I've heard from others he's unbearable. He must be if you're wanting to chuck him over the rail!>

<That would destroy my reputation,> Briseis admitted.

<Or enhance it. What's he done?>

<He's at my shoulder every waking minute. It's '*Patience*, have you adjusted this? Have you done that? No, that's not the best way, you need to do such and such.' And so on, *ad infinitum*!>

<What does your Captain say about it?>

<He's not here, and don't I know it! Micianus has been taking full advantage, strutting about and issuing orders like they were going out of fashion.>

Fabillus and the other Captains had been called to a meeting aboard the *Victoria*. Pendragon hadn't been able to disguise his joy at seeing the Flagship, but was staying aboard the *Imperatrix* for the time being so as not to offend her. It was as if he was trying to juggle several wives at once like some Eastern potentate, all too aware that they might start scrapping over the least slight. Most of the Ships found it secretly funny. *Imperatrix* had largely remained silent, only dropping into the link to make official announcements. It was clear that she was back to her normal self and Briseis was very glad that she was no longer aboard her. *Victoria* was more accommodating, but they all knew that she wouldn't stand for the situation forever. The two Ships were being very polite to each other.

<That shouldn't matter,> *Blossom* told her. <Open your link and tell him that Micianus is being a pain in the backside. He can be transferred.>

<He could go to the *Imperatrix*,> she suggested. <I'd like to see him face off against her!>

<He wouldn't last long there,> *Blossom* agreed. <You shouldn't have to put up with it. You're a Ship and he isn't a Captain. It's your vessel now and he has to lump it. He's only been allowed to stay because he's well-connected. The rumour is that the Navy wanted to throw him out, but his senator father objected and pulled some strings.>

That was probably what the *Imperatrix* had been going to say to her. Unfortunately, it didn't help her situation. If Fabillus had been aboard, she could have retreated to his cabin to get away from the man, but now she had no excuse. Furthermore, due to his years of experience, Drustan was finding it hard to stand up to him.

<Well, I'm not putting up with it any longer,> she informed *Blossom*. <I'm going to tell him straight. He can't treat me like this just because I'm young.>

<You get them sometimes. They either treat us as if we were machines, household slaves, or even, like Micianus, something unnecessary grafted on. I heard Silvius, the *Regina*'s Captain, was like this. Hopefully he's gone for good, but who knows? She might have rescued him.>

They both knew it was a Ship's duty to save her Captain if possible.

<Is there still no word on her?>

It was unsettling not to know the *Regina*'s whereabouts, just as it was not to know how *Tempest* was. It was unnatural for Ships not to talk and share so many details of their lives.

<She's not dead.> *Blossom* was firm. <We always know when one of our kind ceases. You felt it with the *Augusta*, didn't you?>

<Yes. I was in the Med, but I knew.>

The ancient Flagship had cried out and then was gone. Just thinking about it made her want to shudder, Shipbody or no.

<Then *Regina*'s lurking somewhere, biding her time. Think about it. Would you come crawling back asking for a new vessel if you'd just sunk your sister Ship?>

Blossom had a point.

<It would be hard,> Briseis admitted.

<Even when there's been justification, it's never an easy thing.>

Briseis was startled.

<What do you mean? I know about the *Livia*, but have there been others?>

The link went silent.

<One that I know of.> *Blossom*'s voice whispered into her mind. <Went rogue, but that was long ago and the Navy kept it quiet. I don't have the details.>

<Another thing we don't talk about?>

<Yes. Forget I said anything. On the surface, we're all serene, obedient Ships, serving our country and protecting our shores. It's been that way for years, then this comes along.>

Blossom sounded weary all of a sudden and Briseis felt guilty for complaining. After losing her Captain under horrendous circumstances, she had borne his death with dignity. Next to that, the irritating Tetius Micianus was nothing. He wouldn't be the last incompatible officer she would have to deal with, so it was best that she devise a strategy here and now.

<I'm sure it will all return to normal soon,> she consoled her sister. <This, like Micianus, is just a temporary inconvenience. Once the Gods have dealt with Marcus, we'll be back to our normal sailings in no time, just you see!>

<Oh, may the Gods bless you, *Patience*!> *Blossom* Sent. <I knew from the moment we met that you would make an excellent

162

Ship. You're just the sort we need at the moment. Of course you're right. We might even have it in our hearts to forgive *Regina* when she turns up, as long as she's suitably contrite. Now, as to Micianus –,>

<Don't you worry about him,> Briseis said firmly. <I'm going to have to learn how to sort these things out for myself. I think we'll have a private chat.>

<That's an excellent idea.>

Blossom sounded more like her old self and Briseis knew she'd done the right thing. The old Ship had enough responsibility as it was, supporting her sisters and calming everyone down. The least she could do was to support her as much as she could. Speaking of which, she could see the man himself approaching her with a determined look on his face.

<Here he is now,> she said. <I'll report back later!>

<You do that,> *Blossom* replied. <And don't take any nonsense!>

"There you are, *Patience.*" Micianus's brusque tones were an unwelcome interruption. "I'd like a word."

She gave him her best smile.

"Excellent, Tetius Micianus! I was thinking the same thing. Shall we retire to your quarters?"

She saw doubt flicker in his pale blue eyes, before he answered.

"Very well."

She sank into the deck immediately, leaving him standing. It wasn't as easy as it had been on her old vessel. Then it had been like moving through silken water; here it was more like pushing her way through viscous oil. It took longer than she would have liked but she still beat him to his cabin and emerged to settle herself on the bulkhead.

Naturally, Micianus had had to give up his commander's cabin in favour of Fabillus as rank dictated, so this one was smaller but still adequate. It had none of the luxuries of Ship accommodation, but he'd done his best to display his wealth. The desk and chair were richly carved, more so than the utilitarian furniture most Captains had, and the bed was hung with expensive cloth. A silver wine jug and goblets were set on a small, inlaid table and there was an elaborate sea-chest, bound in brass that had been polished to a high gloss. Even the customary personal shrine was better than ones commonly found at sea.

Next to it, in a gold frame, was a portrait of a stern, aristocratic-looking man wearing a toga with a purple stripe. A senator, then. It was common for younger sons to enter the services, so Micianus probably hadn't had a choice in the matter. The elder Tetius must have been disappointed that his son hadn't made Captain, but with his offspring's attitude to Ships she wasn't surprised he'd been sidelined.

Briseis had had just enough time to take all this in, when the door slid open and Micianus entered, removing his hat which he placed carefully on a trunk. It was a nice hat too, though it had obviously seen some wear. It was only then that he turned to face her. He didn't show it, but she guessed that he wasn't comfortable with her being here, though the day cabin had been out of the question. She didn't give him the chance to speak first.

"Thank you for agreeing to meet with me, Tetius Micianus. I think there are some things that we need to discuss."

When he straightened his back and stuck out his jaw, she knew she'd have a battle on her hands.

"There are indeed, *Patience*. I am concerned that you're pushing this vessel beyond her limits. She isn't fully-rigged for Ship operations, and with your inexperience you aren't aware of the tolerances."

So that was how he wanted to play it. It was interesting that he referred to the vessel as 'she' as well. Inanimates were regarded with fondness, but assuming they had personalities was unusual. It was time for one of her 'looks' as her Captain had so charmingly put it.

"Please don't confuse my years of service with inexperience, Commander," she said. "I am a fully-trained Ship of the Royal Navy, and as such qualified to operate *any* vessel that is allocated to me, large or small. As to tolerances, I am aware of every plank, nail, rope and scrap of canvas. They speak to me and, should they become overburdened, I'll know it, just as you know when your body reaches its limit."

She intensified her gaze, watching a flush of red creep up from beneath his collar.

"Furthermore I am given to understand that you have many years of experience in the Navy. I have to confess that I'm astounded that you aren't aware of these facts, even though you haven't served aboard a Ship lately. I would also prefer that you don't call my expertise into question in front of my crew."

His whole face was red now. To his credit, he'd given her time to speak, but that was all she'd give him. He swallowed.

"As we are speaking candidly, ma'am, I'm going to tell you a few home truths. I don't want you on my vessel. The *Seashell* was perfectly capable as she was, crewed by men and under the control of men. I don't agree that we need Ships at all. We've developed direct communication methods and our Mages can handle the Potentia side of things."

He became more animated as he warmed to his pet subject.

"As to power, the new steam engines will soon be able to end our reliance on sails. It was fine when we couldn't do things for ourselves, but you're rapidly becoming obsolete. Perhaps it's time you started thinking about a new career."

Briseis couldn't help it. She burst out laughing and applauded, her wooden hands clacking loudly in the confined space.

"Oh, you're too good, Tetius Micianus! As for a new career, have you ever considered working in a factory? You're obviously wasted at sea!"

His mouth dropped open. He'd probably hoped to upset her, or provoke a frantic denial. Instead, her mirth had wrong-footed him.

"You know so little of Ships," Briseis continued, when she'd managed to get herself under control, "that you've also forgotten that I'm able to speak to my Captain at any time. As per his command, this entire conversation will be relayed to him. I'll leave him to decide what to do with you. After all, Captains order, Ships obey!"

She swept back into the bulkhead with an air of satisfaction. She hadn't been intending to tell Fabillus anything, but now the man had shown his true colours, it had been her pleasure. Hopefully he'd be transferred immediately to somewhere he could be watched. He'd been useful to the Service so far, but after this he'd be lucky to command a tugboat on the Thamesis.

She opened up her private link to Fabillus, resisting the temptation to spread the gossip around the Fleet. That would do for the man and she wasn't prepared to completely destroy his career.

<*Patience*? Everything all right?>

<I've just had a word with Tetius Micianus. I'd had enough of him correcting me in front of everyone and I thought I could clear the air.>

He was interested immediately.

<And?>

<Apparently, the *Seashell* was fine as 'she' was and Ships are soon going to be 'obsolete'.>

Fabillus was amazed and outraged in equal measure.

<He actually said this to you directly?>

<He did indeed. I laughed in his face.>

<Any other Ship would have punched him through the bulkhead.>

<Oh blast! I never thought of that,> she said, with mock dismay.

<Of course you didn't, my lovely Ship. You're far too sensible.> He sighed. <Have you spread this around?>

<To my sisters? No, though I think they should be warned.>

<I think most of them already know,> he answered grimly. <This was his last chance to restore his standing and get a Ship of his own, but he's comprehensively blown that now. There was talk of giving him the *Blossom*.>

<She's had a lucky escape.>

<You mean he has! Our lovely flower is even-tempered, but she wouldn't have stood for him spouting such rubbish. I applaud your self-control.>

<He didn't like me laughing at him. Oh here he is coming on deck now. He's keeping away from me.>

Micianus wasn't even looking in her direction.

<The man's a fool, shielded by privilege,> Fabillus agreed. <I'll have a word with the Admiral and see what he says, but I hope he hasn't got much to pack.>

<He may be right about some things,> she said. <There are changes coming and fewer candidates.>

<I don't care if he is,> Fabillus objected. <He's an ass, and disrespectful to boot. How dare he talk to you that way? He's finished, believe me.>

<It will be a relief to see him gone,> she admitted, <but what of his crew?>

She still had many of the old *Seashell*'s hands aboard.

<They can follow their Commander to Hades, if they so desire.>

Ooh, he was so angry. Briseis quite liked seeing this side of her Captain. A little thought surfaced.

It won't harm your reputation to be rid of him either.

Content that she was doing the Fleet a favour, she settled into her duties and waited for Fabillus's return.

It wasn't long before she had orders to send out her boat to pick him up from the *Victoria*. To her surprise, the Flagship herself came through the link.

<*Victoria* to *Patience*.>

<Greetings, *Victoria*! It's good to see you with us again.>

The Ship was as gracious as ever.

<Thank the Gods, you mean! I know they intend to thwart the Usurper at every opportunity, but even so, sailing through that portal was quite an experience. Now, I've just heard what happened with you and that idiot Micianus – and no, I haven't told anyone else. This is between you and me. Pendragon doesn't want any political repercussions, though why he's worrying about them at a time like this I don't know. He's going to be recalled to the *Imperatrix*, so that the Admiral can tear a strip off him, then he's going to be put on the smallest inanimate we've got, and not as Commander either. He'll be out of your hair and none of us will need to worry about him ever again. To be honest, it's better than he deserves.>

The Ship sounded satisfied.

<He thinks vessels will be fitted with communication devices and steam engines, so they won't need us.>

Victoria snorted.

<In his dreams! These New Men think all the world's problems can be solved by machines! Still, I'm always up for new devices, especially weaponry. Have you got your new torpedoes yet?>

<Not yet, but there's a consignment heading my way.>
They were being unloaded from the *Leopard* and distributed very carefully.
<Excellent! And well done with Micianus. I hear you showed great restraint.>
Briseis chuckled. <Sort of.>
Her sister joined in. Really, she was the most approachable of the Royals, bar *Tempest*, of course.
<Ready to give him his marching orders? Oh, I'm being told to send a boat for him now. The Admiral is *not* pleased!>
<Thank you, *Victoria*.>
<You're most welcome, *Patience*!>
As she signed off, Briseis couldn't help but wonder what was happening to her friend. Surely she would have her new vessel by now? She gazed at the horizon, hoping for another portal to open and a Ship to come sailing through, but the choppy sea gave away no secrets.

Oh well, she'd find out soon enough. Now to the happy task of saying goodbye to her obnoxious sailing master for good.

*

Boots clattered on the deck as the loading of the vessel, soon to be the new *Tempest*, was intensified ahead of her all-important installation. Maia did her best to block out the commotion and shouted orders to concentrate on the Chief Artificer's instructions. It was crucial that she learned as much as she could in the short time she had available to her.

She was relieved her initial thoughts had been right. Operating her new vessel wouldn't be vastly different in principle to the one she'd had formerly. If anything, there was less to juggle. Gone were the complicated rigging mechanisms, replaced by regulators for the air and gas, plus a heating system that she had to keep charged with her Potentia. Likewise, the rudder was the same as usual, though instead of making adjustments to sails she had her propellers to give her speed.

The real challenge was the spatial awareness.

"You can't think of your heading as a flat plane anymore," Vulcan told her.

They were meeting on the observation platform. There was none of the space she had been accustomed to on her previous vessel, no day room and no proper cabins for the officers, more of a little cubby space for each. Despite it being minute compared to his previous quarters, Leo had been enthralled with every detail. He was getting a briefing of his own with Heron and Robin down among the machinery, so Maia had some time to herself with the disguised God.

"You'll be manoeuvring in three dimensions," Vulcan continued, "so you must master the lifting mechanisms and account for wind currents and temperature, all of which will affect you on a minute-to-minute basis."

"I'm used to taking constant weather readings," she agreed, "though learning how to use them to my advantage in this situation is another matter."

"It will come with experience," he agreed. "There will be test flights, so you can get a feel for everything."

She grimaced. "Yes, but if I make a small mistake at sea I'm unlikely to sink, whereas in the air I won't have as much leeway, will I?"

He blew out a breath. "True. Your Potentia will help and you won't be going too high at first, for obvious reasons. We'll give you time to adjust to your mechanisms, then we'll start with a little rise and fall, plus anchoring. That will cover the basics."

He was sounding more confident than she felt.

"When will I be installed?"

He tilted his head, listening to something she couldn't hear.

"As soon as my sister arrives. She's due any minute, then we can proceed. She's taken a great interest in all of this, besides which she has a vested interest in seeing the Usurper dealt with. Preferably with extreme violence."

For one moment, Maia had the terrible feeling that it was her old enemy that was on her way. Hadn't she been told that the Huntress was busy elsewhere? What would she do if the Goddess turned up, large as life?

He picked up on her worry instantly.

"Don't worry, you haven't met before. Here she is. Come, I'll introduce you."

That was a blessing. Maia relaxed a little and it was obvious to her when the tall, cloaked figure entered the cabin that it wasn't Diana. It was only when the Goddess threw back her hood and fixed Maia with a pair of sparkling grey eyes that the Ship recognised her face. She'd seen it on enough statues down the years.

"Greetings to you, *Tempest*!"

Maia bowed. "Hail to you, mighty Minerva."

The statue in the Portus temple wasn't a bad likeness, but there was no mistaking the Lady's commanding air. Maia took a moment to admire the fine weave of her robe. She'd probably made it herself.

Minerva nodded, as if divining her thought.

"So, are you ready to take to the air?"

"It came as a surprise to me, Lady," she admitted, "but times change and we must change along with them."

Minerva quirked an eyebrow, and Maia was aware of her intense scrutiny.

"Indeed. I suggested to my father that you should be the one to try out this new invention. The loss of your vessel merely compounded his decision."

Now that was interesting. If she hadn't been sunk, would she have been transferred anyway? It made her feel a tiny bit better, though she would have willingly donated her vessel to her friend.

"I obey the will of the Gods," she replied. It was the safest thing to say.

Minerva smiled. It made her look more human.

"Then we'll proceed. I will be attending, but only my brother and you will be aware of my presence."

"And what of the Master Mage?" Vulcan rumbled.

She gave him a stern look.

"He won't see me if I don't want him to, despite his...*abilities*."

She almost sounded disapproving, perhaps because of his strangeness. Raven had told her that even the Olympians couldn't account for his longevity, and Maia had the feeling that they didn't like something they couldn't control or explain. As the Goddess of Wisdom, it was probably something that irritated Minerva most of all. It made a change that Maia would know something he didn't and it served him right for keeping so much from her. Maybe one day she'd be able to tell him.

"The day isn't getting any younger," Vulcan pointed out, "and I'd like her to be operational by nightfall."

The Gods exchanged a glance.

"I agree she'll need to be ready as soon as possible," Minerva said. "The war isn't coming, it's already here."

Maia stared at her in dismay. Battle strategy was Athena Minerva's speciality, and she was always at her father's side through all the Immortals' conflicts. If the Goddess was foretelling a clash of arms, it was a foolish person who didn't listen and take heed.

"Aye, I've seen Drusilla's forces to the south. They're making their preparations," Vulcan said. "I take it you're supporting them?"

Minerva's grey eyes flashed.

"Macro slew my faithful worshipper in cold blood, on Marcus Pendragon's orders. This slight must be avenged! His shade cries to me from the land beyond death, and I have promised his widow that justice will be served. In this, I am acting in my aspect as Pallas Athena and it is by this name you may address me."

Maia echoed her vehemence wholeheartedly. Senator Rufus and Lady Drusilla had been kindness itself when she had been a guest under their roof. It wasn't their fault that the Huntress and Echidna, the Mother of Monsters, her deadly ally, had wreaked death and destruction on their Saturnalia celebrations. Then Rufus himself had been murdered in cold blood. Maia would do everything she could to help put Marcus where he deserved to be – in Tartarus, or whatever dark place the Gods devised as punishment.

"I hope you can keep that promise," Vulcan said. "There are other forces at work and nothing is certain. The Fates keep their counsel to themselves."

He glanced at Maia. "But enough of this! It is for us Olympians to worry about, eh? We must all play our part."

He gave Maia a reassuring smile. She smiled back, trying not to think about the strangeness of everything. Here she stood, listening to two Gods discussing an imminent war, just before she was going to learn how to fly. She almost laughed at the absurdity of it all.

"Your Captain will have finished his meeting now," Vulcan said. "Let's get him here, together with that Priest of yours, so we can get the ball rolling. Is there anything you'd like to know?"

"What's the new gas called?" Maia asked. She couldn't keep on calling it 'that lighter-than-air stuff'.

"We've called it helium after Helios, as it rises into his domain." Vulcan grinned. "He's quite pleased, though he pointed out that his chariot doesn't need it to fly!"

Athena rolled her eyes.

"Joking aside," he continued," it's good stuff. I daresay we'll improve on the design in the next one, but this will do for now."

"You have all the technical specifications?" Athena asked Maia.

"I have, Lady." Maia was glad of her memory. She wouldn't need to refer to the manual, unlike her crew, as it was all safely stored away. Now she would just have to work out what most of it meant.

The Gods left her to see to the preparations, while she and her new, slimmed-down crew assembled on the main deck. Leo arrived soon afterwards, wearing a fancy new uniform. Instead of naval anchors, wings embroidered in gold thread stood out against the sky blue of his sleeves. He paraded before them all like a self-assured cockerel. She couldn't help but notice the flash of envy on Amphicles' face, but knowing Sir Cardo, there were probably new uniforms on the way for all the men. It looked so fine, she debated whether to change her appearance to match, though she wasn't going to tell Leo just yet.

<Well, what do you think?>

<I think Sir Cardo has a flashy taste in uniforms.>

<I think he has excellent taste. Furthermore, I'm to be a Sky Captain!>

<Not a Sky Admiral?> she riposted.

<Give it time.>

Their faces betrayed nothing of the laughter they shared as Vulcan appeared, leading a small procession. Maia was pleased to see that Raven, Heron and Robin were present, as was Danuco and Vestinus, her carpenter, who she knew had been working

172

diligently throughout the vessel to place the remnants of her old home in strategic places. She wondered whether her Priest knew who the Chief Artificer really was. Danuco gave him a courteous nod, which told her nothing, while the Goddess seemed to fade into the background, unnoticed as she had said.

Still, Maia couldn't help wondering whether the Thunderer himself was using his Priest's eyes, as he had done through Aquila in Londinium. It was an unsettling thought, though she knew that she'd been under scrutiny ever since that day in the temple. It was rare for Ships to be assigned someone who served Jupiter and not his brother, Neptune, and there had been more than one comment in the past.

Acolytes, who also appeared to be Artificers, came forth and set up a small altar against a bulkhead, bolting it securely to the deck in the naval manner. Danuco performed the sacrifice of two unblemished white doves to appease the winds and spirits of the air, reddening the pristine stone with their blood to please the Gods. As they were in an enclosed space, the ritual burning would be done outside, but it was essential that the Powers got their just dues.

Was it her imagination, or did the air move a little? She could see the Gods' eyes tracking something nobody else could see. Vulcan caught her watching and gave her an infinitesimal nod in confirmation. Her mother was here. Visible only to immortals, she had come to see her daughter installed and shortly to partake of the smoke of sacrifice. Maia felt her heart fill with an emotion she could never express out loud.

Mother! I send you my love!

The tiniest of breezes caressed her wooden cheek, then it was gone.

The gust that blew in through an open port was anything but subtle. It danced about the deck, ruffling robes and hair in equal measure before spiralling over the altar to suck up droplets of blood. These gave it more substance, forming a suggestion of a face and flowing hair, the torso and limbs insubstantial beneath it as Pearl helped herself to the offering.

"Greetings!"

The faint voice was audible to all, bolstered by the energy of the sacrifice.

"Hail, O Spirit of the Air!" Danuco intoned. "Bless this vessel and her guiding *anima*! Grant her your aid and speed her passage safely through your realms!"

Her crew, impressed, muttered prayers and charms of their own, individual appeals to the guiding deity.

"Hello, sister," Pearl whispered in her ear. *"This is exciting! You'll be able to fly with me!"*

<Hello, Pearl,> she Sent privately. <I think I'll need any help you can give.>

<*I will be near, as will Mother,*> her sister promised. <*Jupiter himself has given the order.*>

She darted away, insubstantial once more, and the Mages stepped forward. All three conferred quietly, then Heron came over.

"Well, *Tempest*! Are you ready?"

She looked into his eager eyes and answered with a show of confidence.

"I stand ready to serve the Gods and Britannia."

He winked at her. "Then I'll go and take up position by the devices. As soon as you're installed we can start the trials." He rubbed his hands, his mind already occupied with his engines and the tests they would need to perform. "Come on, Robin! Let's go!"

He scooted off, oblivious to everything else.

"You'll be fine, *Tempest*, Captain," Robin said, before nodding to Vulcan and disappearing after his mentor. Leo's mouth twitched.

<Nothing changes there,> he observed privately as heads turned to watch their retreating backs. <I wonder where Sobek is? He could be the first flying crocodile.>

<Somehow I don't think he'd like that,> Maia said, though she wouldn't refuse him a berth.

Now it was Raven's turn. This part of the ceremony was nothing to do with the Roman Gods, calling instead upon the ancient magic and traditions of Britannia.

The Mother's Oak suddenly appeared in Maia's mind, its spreading branches arching protectively over the Sacred Grove where Ships' mortal bodies lay and where their Shipbodies were returned at the end. One day, hers would join them, the inert log

174

that had housed her soul for so many years her only grave marker. But for now the pulse within was strong, her linked Potentia amplified by root, sap and leaf. She drew on it as Raven chanted, anchoring herself to this new vessel through the wood, extending herself along unfamiliar channels as blood through veins, all supported by the blessings of the Mother.

For a timeless moment it felt as though she was back in the earth of the Grove, swaddled in roots and the leaves of ten thousand summers, deep in the darkness and silence of an eternal peace.

A burst of light and sound wrenched her up and away.

"*Tempest*! Come forth!"

Raven's face swam into focus. She'd had to go back to move forward.

Maia wriggled mentally, sending tendrils of herself deep into the strange new wood like questing rootlets. Channels took her senses to every corner of the structure, even into the metal, which tasted hot and sharp, like the smell of a new stove or freshly-soldered tin. Her awareness raced up and into the struts, touching the huge bags of gas, then down on to each deck, over the piles of armaments and thence to her machines, sorting every cog, gear and lever.

It was all hers, from bow to stern, propeller to rudder, struts to gun port. The tethering ropes were a hindrance. She longed to cast them off and rise.

"*Tempest*! Report for duty!"

She fixed her Mage and Captain with a steady eye.

"This is *Tempest*. Installation complete!"

She didn't care if she was grinning at them like a madwoman.

"Well done!"

If anything, Vulcan looked crazier than she did. The crew gave three cheers and Maia raised her arm in triumph.

HMAS *Tempest* would soon be ready for duty.

*

The messenger arrived late afternoon.

Two hippocampi appeared, bursting upwards in a froth of white water, powerful fluked tails thrashing as they galloped over the waves at speed. Behind them was an ornate chariot, embellished with gold over a coralline structure. Cei was alerted immediately. The Ships' initial alarm at the unexpected appearance was amended to one of greetings as the Mer-Lord pulled up alongside the *Victoria*, controlling his vigorous beasts with an expert hand.

Cei was already on deck, telescope to his eye.

"I recognise him," he told his officers. "Damn it! Of course, he thinks I'm aboard the *Victoria*. *Imperatrix*, tell Captain Vitalianus to update him on our situation."

He immediately reproached himself for showing irritation. It wasn't the *Imperatrix*'s fault that he wasn't aboard his Flagship, but her increasing possessiveness of him would have to be dealt with. If only the *Diadem* had seniority! She was far easier to get along with. He made a mental note. If they ever got out of this mess alive, he would post *Imperatrix* on an extended mission to the New World, or maybe to Chin. Meanwhile, he would have to see what news Neptune was sending.

As expected, the Mer-Lord made short work of the distance to the *Imperatrix*, bounding aboard in the spectacular fashion of his kind, as much a reminder that this was his territory as a show of strength. Cei had already lined up the crew to give him a suitable greeting and strode forward to meet his old friend.

"Lord Nerites! My sincere apologies for the diversion."

The Mer-Lord flashed him a smile, teeth white against his dark grey skin. Droplets of water trickled from the long braid down his back and tracked their way down his muscular frame, halted only by the elaborate bracelets that marked him out as marine royalty. His uncle, Proteus, was second only to Neptune himself and, it was rumoured, far older than the Olympian. Even the God listened when he spoke on behalf of his people, so Nerites' presence here was no mere courtesy call.

"Admiral. Or should I call you King? I understand that the honour is not yet official."

"Admiral is more than sufficient, my Lord, as the Sword of Kingship has not yet conferred the right on anyone."

And definitely not my son, despite all his tricks.

A flash of sympathy showed in Nerites' dark eyes. "It is of that I must speak, at the God's command."

Formal bows were exchanged and Cei led Nerites down to his private quarters. There was one thing left to do before they could start. Cei opened up a private channel to the *Leopard*.

<Madam, inform your Captain that Lord Nerites is aboard.>

<Already done, Admiral,> was the swift reply. <He's on his way.>

He broke off the Sending and opened another channel, this time to *Imperatrix*.

<*Imperatrix*, prepare for another visitor. When he arrives, send him to me.>

<Acknowledged, sir.>

He could tell that she was still in a snit about his previous comment. He would have to watch what he said, but if he ordered her not to listen in, that would cause even more trouble.

Nerites followed him in and glanced around.

"Still not many luxuries, eh Cei?" He draped himself elegantly on a wooden chair as if it were the most splendid throne. "A little hard, but at least I won't dampen the soft furnishings."

Cei laughed. "What soft furnishings? There's the bed, I suppose."

Nerites raised an eyebrow. "Even that doesn't look very comfortable." He broke off, head tilted as he sniffed the air. "Here's my son now. I hope he's proving useful."

"He most certainly is, as you know full well," Cei answered. He dragged a chair for himself out from behind his desk as another Mer-Lord entered. The similarity between them was striking, as if they were brothers.

"Admiral. Sorry for dripping all over the planks."

It was an old joke.

"It's what I expect these days, Marinus."

He watched as the two Mers embraced, careful not to use the Captain's real name. The existence of a powerful shape-shifter in the Britannic Royal Navy was only tolerated because of the secrecy, much like *Tempest*'s origins.

"It's good to see you, son," Nerites said. "You seem well, if a little tired."

"Things have been a little hectic lately, what with the Fae stirring up the *Beisht Kione Dhoo.*"

Nerites' face darkened. "Yes. There was little we could do in that regard, but Manannen's serpents have been appeased for now. They suffered too, and for that we wish to revenge ourselves on the instigators."

So, the People of the Sea had had no hand in it. The Fae had made yet another enemy by meddling where they shouldn't. Perhaps Manannan himself had been unaware of the use to which his creatures had been put. It was true that many of them had been hurt, even killed.

"We had no choice but to defend ourselves," Cei stated. "If they were forced to attack against their natures, we will make what reparation we can."

Nerites and Marinus shared a look.

"Don't blame yourself. Some of them were probably willing participants, seeing you as easy pickings. They've been disabused of that, so you shouldn't have any further trouble from them for a while."

Cei nodded. "I suppose they've forgotten about the fight with Merlin."

Marinus looked to his father. "Merlin?"

"Oh yes, he had dealings with them in centuries past. I suppose he's dead now?"

Cei spread his hands.

"Who knows? There were rumours that he wasn't entirely human on his father's side, so he could still be around. If he is, we could do with his help now."

"Definitely," Marinus agreed. Pendragon noticed that he was still standing to attention. He might be able to change shape, but naval training was not so easily disguised. "I hope Artorius the Great and his Companions come charging to the rescue as well, but I don't think that's going to happen."

Cei took a deep breath. "I suppose not. It's up to us now."

"Speaking of which," Nerites said. He'd resumed his pose, the delicate webbing of his hands fanning over the arms of the chair. "I have news. The Fae are crossing in a fleet, from Hibernia to the west coast of Mona. You may have enough time to stop them before they make landfall."

The urge to swear loudly was strong, but he hadn't spent the whole of his life mastering his emotions to disgrace himself before an ally. His control had already slipped once today. Marinus uttered an oath instead.

"Father, you should have led with that!"

Nerites raised an eyebrow. "I wanted to get the pleasantries over with first and spend a little more time in your company. I know there's a need for haste, but they've only just set off. We have watchers off the coast. I have to warn you, they're loaded with magic."

"And we have new weapons," Cei said. He felt his face harden. "I pray to the Gods that they will be enough."

But Nerites hadn't finished.

"I'm sorry to be the bearer of bad news, but I've been told that they're attacking on land as well. They're working on opening a portal to the south of Londinium to bring troops through."

Cei's heart sank to his boots. They were being attacked on two fronts – three if you counted the minor incursion to harry the north. The legions that had been sent there as soon as Marcus's deception was uncovered would be on their way now. He'd have to get word to them immediately and turn them around before it was too late. Even with Drusilla's extra forces, he would have a job on his hands to stop them. No wonder they'd targeted the Priests and Mages to deplete him. Too many had died.

"Admiral, are you all right?"

A hand gripped his elbow and he realised that he was standing, swaying a little. How had he lost time?

"Here, sit down, sir. Should I call an Adept?" Marinus's voice penetrated the shock.

He forced himself to take deep breaths until his wits returned.

"No, no. It was just… unwelcome news. *Imperatrix*, say nothing, I'm fine."

How long had Marcus been planning this? A year? Five? Ten? He'd done everything he could for his only child, or thought he had. His duties had meant that he was rarely home, and the distance between himself and Severina hadn't helped. She had been chosen for him and enjoyed her position as princess, but that was all. They'd both done what was required of them, then separated with relief on both sides. Marcus had been left in the middle, trained as a royal prince, and had been expected to follow his father into the army or navy. He'd baulked at both, but Cei had hoped he'd step up in time.

Where had he gone wrong?

As far as he knew, Severina had remained at their country estates, throwing parties and entertaining her string of lovers with little thought of political power. He supposed he could be grateful for that. She hadn't openly supported her son, but he'd heard nothing from her either. She was probably waiting to see who would emerge victorious and then claim her position as either Queen or Mother of the King. He couldn't find it in himself to blame her.

A glass was thrust into his hand and he drank, barely aware of the brandy as it burned its way down. The warmth did help him and he gestured for another.

"I am truly sorry, my friend."

Nerites' voice was soft. Cei raised his head to look into the depths of the Mer-Lord's eyes.

"I wish I was as lucky with my son as you are with yours. Truly, Marinus, you are more of a son to me than he ever was."

Just like Sabrinus had been.

The grief was a dagger in his heart, and every hour twisted it a little deeper. Was this the end of the Pendragons? Even if he were to ascend to the throne, Severina was long past child-bearing age, and he couldn't bear the thought of being forced into another marriage. His family had never been numerous and now everything rested with his niece. Raven assured him that Julia was safe, deep in the Heart of Albion and facing her own trials, whatever they may be. He still had hopes of a suitable marriage for her, but unless he was victorious and she fell pregnant he could see no hope for them or Britannia. Without a clear successor there would be war as each petty lord tried to claim the throne, and he doubted that the Emperor would be able to intervene.

He collected his thoughts, taking refuge in formality.

"I give you my thanks, Lord Nerites, and to you also, Lord Marinus. I will address the fleet and direct them to engage the Fae. As for myself, I must leave my position here and take up the mantle of Commander of the Britannic Legions. My next battle will be fought on land."

"I will do what I can," Marinus said instantly. "I may be able to cause a distraction or two."

Cei smiled at him. He had seen first-hand what Marinus's distractions were like.

"A dragon will come in very handy."

As to his own role, he had no choice. To save Britannia and unite the land, he would have to kill his son.

*

Briseis and her sisters watched as the Mer-Lord's chariot went first to one Ship, then another. Pendragon wouldn't be best pleased that the emissary had had to be diverted, but by rights he should have already left for the *Victoria*.

<Hah, this will speed up the process,> *Blossom* Sent to a few of them, quietly so that the Royal wouldn't hear. <Get ready for the old dame to throw a cog when he does. She still thinks she should be the Flagship!>

<Not with her snotty attitude,> *Dragon* agreed. <Has anyone got a better view of things? *Patience*, is that your boat?>

<Yes. Tetius Micianus is leaving me. What a shame, too bad.>

There were a few snorts and I 'told you so' from *Persistence*, who had wormed her way into the conversation.

<Knew even you wouldn't stand 'im fer long. What did he do?>

Briseis could sense more ears tuning in, so she decided to be diplomatic.

<He's just not suited to being aboard a Ship. I think he'll be better commanding an inanimate, like before.>

She could tell that the others knew they weren't hearing the whole story, but it was more than his life was worth to say what he'd actually said.

<You stood him longer than anyone else,> *Blossom* said. <Goodbye, and good riddance!>

Briseis couldn't find it in her heart to forgive the man. She did feel a certain amount of pity for him, even though he had been his own worst enemy. He could have continued in his career with no-one the wiser, but he had well and truly scuppered that.

Commanding an inanimate was usually a stepping stone to a Ship, to demonstrate knowledge of the sea and its ways and not an end in itself. There was no helping some people, she reflected. As to his motivation, who could tell? Even if he was proved partially right in the end, Ships could command forces that a mere piece of floating wood couldn't. That was why they were the envy of the rest of the Empire.

She shrugged mentally and dismissed him from her thoughts. *Imperatrix* could have him with pleasure, and, from what she knew of that Royal, she'd delight in tormenting him. It was Micianus's bad luck that Pendragon had chosen to stay aboard her for the time being, though everyone knew he'd transfer back to the *Victoria* as soon as he could.

Her new vessel was still rough around the edges, but it was getting a little easier to operate. Of course, riding at anchor wasn't the same as facing the open ocean, but it had given her a breather to become accustomed to the new systems. She cast an eye over her crew, pleased at the way they had shaken down after the recent horrors and wondered how *Tempest* was doing.

Had they given her an inanimate, too? It was strange that they'd had no word as to her progress. There were mutterings in the link about secret plans, and theories as to what they consisted of, but there was nothing definite. Those that might know were remaining close-mouthed, which was exasperating for the gossipy Ships. Nor was there much news from the mainland. Everyone knew that a land battle was imminent, but there wasn't much they could do about it from here. The Fleet's main concern now was to see what the Fae would do next.

<The Mer-Lord's boarding!> *Dragon* announced.

Her red and gold Shipbody, the largest in the Fleet, was hanging high off her mainmast like a banner to get a good vantage point. <Did you see him jump? Just like *Imperatrix* not to be giving us any details, the snooty cow!>

Briseis strained to see as much detail as possible, glad that she had a direct line of sight. Some of the more distant Ships were already demanding to know what was going on.

<He asked for the Admiral,> *Victoria* broadcast, opening up the conversation. <I've had to say that he's on *Imperatrix*.> It

182

was the first time she'd sounded put out. <Be prepared, ladies. I don't think this is a courtesy call.>

<He looks senior,> *Diadem* said.

<Good looking, too!> *Jasper* chipped in. <He can visit me if he wants!>

There were a few giggles and grumbles at her levity, before *Imperatrix* joined the link. She obviously couldn't resist the opportunity to show that she was in the thick of events.

<I'm making arrangements for his arrival. The King is ready to greet him.> She paused for a moment. <He says his name is Nerites, son of Nereus. I think he's met with Pendragon before now, as they seem to know each other. And I heard what you called me, *Dragon*!>

That was interesting. Briseis supposed that the Admiral had met quite a few of the Mer-Lords in his time and it made sense that Neptune would send somebody familiar. She could see him more clearly now as he guided his chariot away from the *Victoria*. His smooth skin was the usual dark grey of the Mer People, more like a dolphin than a human, and well-muscled. She could see why *Jasper* was taken with him. Nereus was the brother of Proteus, so he was Mer royalty. The Admiral had friends in high places to warrant such a visit.

<Summat's up,> *Persistence* insisted. Nobody disagreed with her.

<If he's been sent by Neptune, it will be news of great importance,> *Imperatrix* announced.

<That's what I said, yer daft brush.>

Imperatrix's indignation was immediate.

<You can just shut up, *Persistence*! We're not interested in your stupid comments! Or yours, *Dragon*! You'd better be quiet after backing Marcus!>

<Ladies!> *Victoria* was not amused. <We are Ships, not brawling fishwives!>

It was a good job no-one could hear most of Ships' conversations, Briseis thought. Brawling fishwives had nothing on most of them. *Swiftsure* and *Persistence* were already happily swapping ribald comments about lusty Mer-folk, encouraged by *Jasper*, who had bounced back from her disgrace and seemed likely to turn the pair of Harridans into a trio very soon. She sighed to herself at the knowledge that *Imperatrix* and *Dragon* would be at loggerheads for a while now, as both Ships had stubborn streaks a mile wide.

<Another Mer-Lord has come aboard!> *Imperatrix* told them. She sounded puzzled. <Nerites is greeting him. It's his son, apparently. They look alike.>

<Must have been in the area,> *Dragon* said. <You can bet that we're being watched.>

That made sense.

<Is he gorgeous too?>

Jasper was irrepressible.

<We could 'ave one each!> *Swiftsure* cackled.

<He could bring his friends!>

The laughter broke the tension.

<*If* I may get a word in edgeways,> *Imperatrix* continued, <Lord Nerites is delivering his message and – Gods protect us! The Fae fleet has been sighted. They're heading for Mona!>

The chatter ceased as Pendragon broke into the link.

<All Ships! The noble Lord Nerites has informed me that a large Fae fleet is making its way across the Hibernian Ocean towards Mona. Your task is to stop them. At the same time, a portal is opening to the south of Londinium and the land invasion has begun. The force to the north was but a diversion.

<It is time to fight for our lands and for the freedom of the mortal realms against our Ancient Enemy. We must show them that we are not cattle to be traded, or playthings for their amusement. We will win or die.

<It is my greatest regret that I must leave you now and lead the Britannic Legions in battle, not on the ocean as would be my wish, but on land. Captain Vitalianus of the *Victoria* is now appointed Lord High Admiral in my stead. Obey him as you would me. May the Gods watch over you!>

<You have our duty and obedience, Your Majesty.> *Victoria*'s voice was sombre. <May the Gods grant you a swift victory!>

One by one, the Ships echoed her words, knowing that they would always have his heart. Even when he was far away, the sea would always call to him by day and night. It was yet another reason to despise his treacherous son.

Nobody would come out of this unscathed. In the meantime, orders were flying thick and fast as the Fleet prepared to leave. Briseis went about her preparations automatically, taking the strain of the new vessel and resigned to whatever the Gods had in store for her.

<Lord Apollo,> she prayed quietly. <Do not forget me, your former servant. Bring me light in the darkness and hope from despair.>

She offered up a prayer on *Tempest*'s behalf as well. Something told her that Maia needed it.

*

The first day had its challenges. Maia remained tethered, but after a couple of false starts managed to power up the systems to heat the air and get it under control. The first time she pumped in too much and nearly blew it all, which made Vulcan curse like an army veteran.

"Jupiter's beard, girl! You'll blow us up before you start! Go easy on it. A bit at a time!"

She hastily reduced the flow to a trickle, wondering where the extra Potentia had come from. Perhaps Raven had been right when he said that she'd grow into it, but the King of the Gods' words returned to haunt her.

She'll have as much Potentia as I say she'll have.

It could be all his doing.

It took an effort, but she did her best to quash any doubts, concentrating on not endangering her crew and vessel. The equipment was sensitive and too much was as bad as too little. It would be the same for the steering, so she had to try not to over-compensate. Vulcan calmed down by the afternoon, though Raven seemed distracted and left her mid-morning, claiming 'urgent business'.

There was definitely something in the air besides her. The trials were finally finished for the day and the crew went for some much needed food and rest, though being near the end of Junius it was still light. Robin joined her on the observation platform, munching on a meat pasty.

"Hello, Maia! Well done for today."

185

He looked happy enough, not caring that his face and robe were covered in grease stains.

She snorted. "Hardly! I nearly wrecked everything."

He shrugged. "There were bound to be teething problems. You sorted it out in the end."

"I thought –" she nearly said Vulcan, but stopped herself in time, "– the Chief was going to have a fit."

Robin laughed, spraying bits of pastry, "Yes, he was rather cross, wasn't he? He's calmed down now. The next thing will be the propulsion systems, but I can't see you having any trouble with those."

"I can operate the ascent, the descent, the propulsion and steering," she said. "It's doing them all at once that's the tricky part."

"You'll have time to get used to them."

"Not as much as I'd like." She stared up at the sky. "It's nice to have this space to be outside. Ships aren't meant to be confined for too long."

Robin looked over the rail and pulled a face.

"I don't know how I'll feel about floating way up in the air. Heron has a good head for heights, but I get dizzy standing on a ladder."

"I'll have to hang on to you, then."

He looked dubious. "I could rig up securing ropes. The hope is that the elevation will be such that large guns can't be brought to bear on you. The worst thing will be battle spells, which is why we've put every bit of fireproofing and shielding into your vessel as we can, both scientific and magical."

Maia had to repress a shudder. The memory of her injuries was still strong, and coupled with a Ship's vulnerability, it was an unpleasant combination. Belatedly, Robin realised what he'd said.

"Oh, Maia, I'm sorry. It must still trouble you. All that and you lost your vessel as well."

He put a tentative hand on her arm and she covered it with her own.

"It's fine, really." She'd have to get over her fears. "I'm sure you've covered everything. If the worst comes to the worst, I can make a controlled landing on our enemies' heads!"

He smiled. "We'll splat them!" He blew a raspberry to emphasise his point, making her giggle.

"They won't see us coming. I might do it anyway, then lift off again. I could bounce around flattening all of them."

Robin burst out laughing, miming their enemies being squashed and she couldn't help joining in, as if they were still a couple of rowdy children in the playground and not people about to head off to war.

Dragging footsteps interrupted their mirth and they were forced to compose themselves quickly. Vulcan's head appeared through the hatch, his brow furrowed. For a second she thought she'd done something wrong, but he caught her worried expression and shook his head.

"No, it's not you – for once! I'm sorry to have to tell you that the Fae are using the energy in the earth to fuel a sort of giant land portal, which is heavily guarded. We can't risk using you there yet. The fleet are moving to meet the Fae at sea off Mona and Pendragon's gathering the legions to join Drusilla's troops. We can only hope that they'll get there in time before the attack."

Robin blanched. But Maia met his eyes evenly.

"What are my orders?"

He sighed. "There's no time to waste. You're going to be deployed immediately, ready or not and it's been decided that you're going to help your sisters first. With any luck we can bomb those bastards to the depths of the ocean, eh?"

"They won't see me coming," she agreed, with more confidence than she felt.

"That's the spirit! Now, back to the preparations. Time to test the props, but remember…"

Maia sighed. "Go easy on the Potentia."

This time, she couldn't afford to make any mistakes.

XI

Milo followed Emrys out of the settlement, his eyes hardly registering where the old man was leading them. His thoughts were strangely muted, and he found it hard to grasp that he'd just met his mother again after so long apart. So much had been familiar, but at the same time alien, and he finally realised that his dreams of a happy reunion had been the desperate wishes of an abandoned child. There would be no good end to their relationship, tenuous though it was.

"How are you?"

Julia was walking close by, her whisper barely audible. He blinked rapidly, forcing himself away from the past.

"Numb more than anything. I don't know what to make of it all."

"It'll take time. I had a strange relationship with my mother too."

He flicked his eyes sideways. She was staring ahead, a determined look on her face.

"You were royal. I was just a bastard of the grove. I still don't understand what happened to me."

"You made your own way in the world," she told him, "despite everything they could throw at you. Remember that."

He nodded. He supposed it was something he could be proud of.

They were among the trees now, following a path that seemed little more than a deer trail and crowded by thick undergrowth from which huge trunks rose at intervals. Branches with leaves in summer fullness blocked out the sky, shivering and muttering in the slight breeze. It felt like a massive green temple, filled with unseen eyes watching and waiting. Milo could feel the hairs prickling up his arms and the back of his neck, as if thousands of tiny pins were being secretly jabbed into his skin. A slow pulse beat through his boot soles, throbbing upwards through the roots and vegetation and he could feel his grasp of time slipping away, as if they'd already entered the Eternal Lands.

The way narrowed, forcing them into single file, Julia in the middle. This made talking harder, but as Emrys forced the pace they found that they needed their breath for walking. Milo couldn't see that far ahead, but suddenly the ground began to slope away, forcing them both to watch their footing so as not to trip over projecting roots. Slowly, the hint of an open space began to appear through the trees and the track widened, until they could walk side by side again.

"I can see water ahead," Julia said.

She was right. They had come to the shores of a broad lake, with hills like guardian beasts rearing dark heads in the distance. Before them was a rough wooden jetty, the water rippling around its piles. A rowing boat was moored alongside.

"Seems like we're going on a boat trip," Milo said, squinting across to a small, heavily wooded island in the distance. He couldn't remember ever being in this place before. It seemed to him that they'd left the Heart of Albion behind, or maybe it was much bigger than he'd thought it was.

"You are correct," Emrys said, his gaze fixed on the water.

Satisfied by whatever he was sensing, he set off along the jetty, boots thudding on the planks. Julia shrugged and followed him. Milo faced back the way they'd come, checking for any pursuit. He could have sworn that they were being watched, the sensation intensifying as he stood there. But if the woods were occupied, whoever or whatever it was gave no sign.

After a few seconds, he gave in to the inevitable and stepped after Julia. Emrys was already helping her into the boat. From the look on the Princess's face, Milo thought she was remembering their last sojourn in a similar craft, but at least this time they weren't in the middle of the open ocean. His palms still ached from the blisters. The small boat rocked as he got in and he gripped the side to steady himself. Julia was searching around her, her forehead wrinkling in puzzlement.

"Where are the oars?"

That was what had been bothering him. How were they going to get across?

"We shan't be needing them," Emrys told her. Once they were both settled, he raised a hand and the boat set off smoothly across the lake.

"We're going to the island, then?" Julia asked.

"Yes. There's someone you need to meet, Milo."

"Who's that? Come on Emrys! I've had enough hints from Ceridwen. Apparently I'm important to her schemes. Tell me!"

Emrys blinked. "You're important to all our schemes, but it's only just become apparent we've been on a wild goose chase for many years. I doubted myself and others, cursed the Gods and the Fates for leading me astray and it's only now that I can see the truth. Even I was misled. That's what comes of believing you're infallible."

Milo took a deep breath.

"Out with it. What did you get wrong?"

Emrys snorted. "Everything! Some prophecies are only meant to be understood at the proper time and not when we will them to be."

"Who made these prophecies?" Julia asked.

Emrys nodded at Milo. "His mother. If it helps you any, she never wanted to give you up, though as a male you would have gone anyway. Perhaps to the Priesthood."

"But she sent me to be a Mage."

"It seemed the right thing to do. It was the prophecy, you see. A great Mage was to be born, one who would save Britannia from her foes."

Milo gaped at him. "And you thought that was me?"

"We did."

"So where is this Mage then? I presume he's about somewhere."

Emrys's mouth quirked. "I sincerely hope so. It's one of the reasons we've come here. The person we're going to meet might know where he is."

"But why was I just abandoned?" Milo insisted. "I could have become a regular Mage!"

Emrys shook his head slowly. "That was the other prophecy. You had to be sent on your way, fatherless, without clan or family, to discover the world for yourself. It had to be done, or Britannia would cease to exist as we knew it, swallowed up by the Shadowlands once more."

Milo couldn't believe what he was hearing. None of it made the slightest sense. Perhaps they were in the company of a madman, after all. He was an Agent, and prided himself on being a good one. He'd sacrificed much for his country, but as to saving it, that was ridiculous.

"I think you're talking a load of bol…"

The boat's keel juddered as it grounded on the pebbly soil of the lakeshore.

"Here we are!" Emrys said. "Out you get. We don't want to keep our hostess waiting."

Bedraggled as she was, Julia raised herself to her full height and looked down her nose at him.

"And who might that be?"

Emrys was unruffled.

"The Goddess of this place. The Fae hold no sway here. Can't you feel the difference?"

It was true. Milo could hear birdsong and the island had a much more welcoming feel than the place they had just left. Emrys strode off towards the trees, leaving Julia with her mouth open to ask another question.

"I can't believe it! He's doing it again!"

Milo was amused, despite himself.

"Let's go and meet this Goddess then. I'm just glad we're away from the Fae and my mad mother."

"Not to mention your half-sister. There was something not right there."

"I don't suppose you'd be quite sane if you'd spent decades with that lot."

"I think you're right. She gave me the shivers. Well, they all did, come to that. When do you suppose this Great Mage is going to turn up?"

Milo grunted. "He'd better get a move on, but personally I'm not holding my breath. Come on, let's get this over with."

They trudged up the shoreline.

"I wish we could stop," Julia announced to nobody in particular. She removed her coat and draped it over her arm. "My uncle must be worried about me. I should be with him, especially with everything that's happened. I'm all he's got."

Milo shot her a sympathetic look. He had no idea what Cei Pendragon would think of his niece now. "Maybe you could petition the Goddess?"

"Anything's worth a try."

The island was bigger than it first appeared. Milo reckoned they'd been walking for about a quarter of a mile before they saw the little temple. It looked like any he might see in a country place, standing in its own grove and dedicated to the local deity. Built of local stone and crudely ornamented, it looked nothing special, but a familiar prickling up his spine told him that this place housed an ancient power. Emrys was standing on the worn steps in the shadow of the columns, waiting for them.

"There's definitely something in there," Julia whispered.

"I know. Didn't you believe Emrys?" Milo said.

"I don't know what to believe any more," she replied.

He shrugged and saw her bridle. Good. If she was annoyed, it might make her less afraid. He had to take it on trust that this Goddess was friendly.

They left the shadows of the trees and stepped into the sunlight. Milo closed his eyes for a moment, tilting his head up to the skies. The warmth on his face was comforting after the dampness of the previous days, making him more reluctant to enter the darkness of the shrine.

"Do you think we'll have to offer something?" Julia was saying. It snapped him out of the moment.

"Do you have anything left?"

She gave him an arch look.

"I might have. The odd trinket or two."

"Well, that should stand us in good stead, if she's like every other deity in the cosmos. Get them ready."

Julia obliged, rummaging inside her tunic. He wasn't going to ask where she'd concealed her treasures, but her forethought was paying off. Her hand re-emerged, clutching a diamond bracelet.

"Ready."

He nodded, and they mounted the steps to meet Emrys. Julia showed him the bracelet.

"Think she'll like this?"

His mouth quirked under his moustache. "I wouldn't worry about that if I were you. There are more important matters to discuss. Put it away for the moment."

She did so, looking surprised, as was Milo. He'd never heard of a God turning down gifts. They could always offer it to her later, if needed.

Emrys led the way into the sanctum, which was little more than a small antechamber leading to a central shrine. Its walls were painted in various shades of blue that were cool and restful after the rising heat of the grove. The bright colours belied the weatherworn exterior, which made him think that there must have been later renovations. In the centre, an irregularly-shaped pool of water was open to the sky, throwing dappled reflections all around. Moss and ferns grew around its edges, softening them and making it more a natural place that seemed older than the structure around it. So, the Goddess was a water nymph. Several altars were ranged against the walls, symbols of past devotion erected in thanks or hope of favour.

The largest stood proudly in a place of honour, the red letters standing out against the white-painted stone. Something told Milo it was the oldest one there, but what really caught his attention was the skull sitting on top of it, crowned with a golden circlet.

TO THE GODDESS COVENTINA
ARTORIUS PENDRAGON SET THIS UP
WILLINGLY AND DESERVEDLY FULFILLING HIS VOW

"Is that who I think it is?"

He stepped forward to examine it more closely.

"It is. Arthur, King of the Britons. Or *Dux Bellorum*, as he was officially."

Emrys's voice was soft and full of memories.

193

"Why is his skull here?" Julia demanded. She'd moved up beside Milo and was staring at the remains of her ancestor in horrified fascination. "He should have had a decent burial!"

"He still watches over the land, to keep faith with the Goddess and his people. This is his place and it is right he should be here."

"But what has that got to do with us?" Milo asked.

Emrys was silent, his gaze fixed on the crowned skull. At last, he closed his eyes.

"She approaches."

He heard Julia's gasp as the water rippled and the Goddess emerged.

She was naked and ageless, her body glowing in the sunlight that poured into her sanctuary. Blue-white hair cascaded to her feet, revealing her divine origin as she hovered above the surface of the water. Emrys bowed deeply. Milo and Julia fell to their knees, acknowledging the Goddess in her temple.

"Praise to you, Coventina, Queen of the West, Lady of the Waters and source of knowledge! Pour out wisdom from your cups. Let us taste the sweet streams and be divinely supplied!"

The Mage's deep voice echoed around the shrine. Coventina smiled.

"Emrys! It has been many years since you visited me."

"Too long, Lady, but the time has come at last. See who I bring to you!"

The Goddess turned to him and Milo fell into the depths of her sapphire gaze.

Coventina's eyes stripped him bare layer by layer, every emotion, every path he had taken, every choice he had ever made. He was examined piece by piece, dissected and his bones picked clean. Nothing could be hidden. Here, truly, was the guiding star of his fate and he knew now from whence the prophecies had come.

No Olympian she. This was an ancient Goddess, worshipped in Britannia for centuries as Coventina, Sulis, Sabrina, the Lady of springs, lakes, rivers and wells. She was also the Guardian of the portal to the Lands of the Dead. He trembled violently as the Goddess raised him up and took him in her arms.

"At last, Gwydre, son of Artorius!"

He couldn't move, couldn't think. It was the name his mother had given him at birth, though he never used it.

Gwydre, Prince of the Britons. It had to be a joke.

*

The stone flagged floor was hard under Julia's knees, but the discomfort was nothing. She couldn't look away as Coventina glided over the surface of her pool and embraced Milo. He shook as if he were possessed. If she could have moved, she would have tried to help him, but she was frozen in place.

Then the Goddess spoke.

Coventina's words had the weight of decree, of a prophecy coming to pass. He had a royal name and lineage. Suddenly, things began to click into place, one after the other as the connections became clear. The woman at the omnibus stop had spoken the truth when she'd thought Julia his son.

He looks like you.

She did look like him, like all the Pendragons. Gwydre had been the son of Artorius the Great, King of the Britons, whose skull was resting on the altar in tribute to his guiding deity. The only Arthur that Coventina could be referring to was her grandfather, Artorius, the Old King. He must have gone to the Heart of Albion and met Ceridwen for this purpose. Now it all made sense.

Milo was her uncle, half-brother to Cei and of the Royal Bloodline. But why had he been hidden?

Because Marcus would have had him killed, like he did my brother.

That was one possibility. Her mind raced to find others, even as the Goddess spoke again.

"Have you brought it?"

Milo – she couldn't think of him as Gwydre yet – looked dazed.

"It, Lady?"

Emrys presented him with his battered pack as Coventina let him slip gently to the mossy floor and waited.

"You've been carrying it for a long time," the Mage said.

Milo frowned, then his face cleared and he laughed. Julia watched in bemusement as he tugged at the fastenings, pulling forth a rusty length of metal. Pitted and twisted, it looked nothing more than a length of old iron until she saw the remains of a hilt, still wrapped in gold, the only part of it that hadn't perished.

"I never knew why I kept this useless old thing." Milo said, dreamily. "I found it in a bog in Kernow. There were headless dogs all over the place."

He held it out and Coventina took it.

"And from death, it shall be revived," she intoned, bending her head over the ravaged weapon.

The air around the rusted blade began to shimmer as the Goddess of healing and renewal summoned her power. Coventina's form dissolved, becoming a glittering fountain of light and energy, so bright that Julia had to shield her eyes from the sudden radiance. A sound like a thunderous waterfall swept over her, elemental in its power, and some part of her welcomed it, reaching out as if to seize part of it for herself, absorbing the wellspring of Potentia until she was full to bursting.

Time ceased to matter. She was a conduit for the energy that ran through her veins, opening her, remaking her even as the sword was remade, the waters of the land flowing into her, pouring in knowledge unbound by the ordered march of centuries. She saw a man kneeling before the Goddess, and knew it was her ancestor, the first Artorius, accepting his sword. Next to him was a young man, stocky and square-faced with black hair and the piercing eyes of a falcon. He turned to her and took her hand. She heard his words through the dream, knowing that they would alter her very existence.

"Will you accept my burden and defend Britannia?"

She knew what she had to do.

"I will."

"Then take it."

She opened her mind to him and, in that moment, the person she had been ceased to exist.

*

Milo felt his palms touch something smooth, then the light vanished leaving him blinded. His vision returned slowly, after-images dancing until his sight cleared allowing him to see what it was he held.

The scabbard and baldric were made of dark green leather, embossed with curling patterns that wound in and out like intertwined branches. It was longer than it had been, in a more modern style than the rusted old gladius he'd pulled from the muck, though hints of it remained in the shape of the hilt and the gold work on the pommel. He raised his head, but Coventina was gone. The age-browned skull resting on its altar seemed to regard him, approval in its empty sockets. Milo tore his eyes away from it to see Emrys crouched on the floor next to a prone Julia. Mindful of his duty, he staggered over to them.

"Is she all right?"

His voice was more of a croak. Emrys remained bending over her, his hand on her wrist.

"She'll be fine, eventually. Give her time."

He looked up at Milo, who was shocked to see how much the old man had aged. It was as if the vitality had been leeched from him, leaving a withered husk behind. His eyes were more deeply set and the cheekbones more prominent, stretched over grey skin like that of a corpse.

"What happened?"

"All is renewed. You have the sword you call Excalibur and you must use its power to attack the Fae."

Milo couldn't believe what he was hearing.

"But Excalibur's in Londin, stuck in the Basilica!"

Emrys's hoarse chuckle echoed off the walls.

"No, no. That's the Sword of Kingship, the one Arthur pulled from the stone, giving him the right to rule. There were two swords, though most have forgotten it. Caledfwlch, now known as Excalibur, was given to Artorius by the Lady of the Waters and was returned when it was no longer needed. It's not fully of this realm, see? Now it's needed again and you must wield it."

Milo gulped.

"Does this mean I'm the King?"

"Haven't you been listening?" That was more the Emrys he'd come to know. "The Sword of Kingship will decide and I must warn you that nothing is certain. It may choose Cei. Listen. You must leave this place now. Julia knows the way, though I must warn you that I bequeathed her my power, as was foretold, so she won't be entirely the person you have come to know. She, too, has her own destiny."

Milo examined her with a professional eye. Her breathing was deep, as if she slept soundly.

"She looks the same."

Emrys grinned. "She'll look how she wants to now, as do I. I didn't start off like this, but it became expected and I got used to it. Besides, it stopped too many questions."

He doubled over coughing, as if in pain.

"You need help," Milo insisted, but the Mage shook his head.

"No, Gwydre. My time on this plane is over. Too many centuries have passed since I was a young man, helping another take the throne. I have laid this burden down at last. It is all gone to her now."

He jerked his head at the sleeping woman.

"She accepted. Now I must go. Farewell, and good luck!"

Milo cried out in shock as Emrys's body collapsed in on itself, shrinking into his clothes which collapsed into a heap on the floor. Underneath, something rustled, writhing under the heavy cloth and struggling to be free. Before he could back away a feathered head emerged, eyes bright and sharp beak parted. Uttering a sharp chittering cry, the little falcon spread its wings and shot out of the sanctuary. His eyes followed it until it dwindled into a tiny dot then disappeared from view above the trees.

Milo knew that wherever Emrys had gone, he would not return to the mortal realm again. Merlin had been here all along, but his work was done and Julia was his successor. The prophecy had been correct, but it hadn't been aimed at him.

He slumped down beside the sleeping woman, listening to her gentle breathing. Above them both, Arthur the Great's skull regarded his descendants with its enigmatic stare. Milo was suddenly thirsty, but didn't dare drink from the sacred pool. He leaned over to peer into its depths, wondering if he would see the Goddess gazing up at him. Instead he could see the golden glint of other offerings, plus a shadowy suggestion of yet more skulls.

He shivered and drew back hastily. Were they human sacrifices from ages past? Like most people brought up as a citizen of the Roman Empire, he had an abhorrence of the practice. Animals, yes. People, no.

He turned back to his companion, a wave of sadness engulfing him. It was possible that this would be the last bit of peace Julia would ever know. The fate of Britannia lay in both their hands now.

Excalibur rested, quiet in its scabbard. He drew it forth, admiring the play of sunlight along its blade, his eye drawn to the intricate patterns. Holding it at arm's length proved its perfect balance, as if it had been made for him. A sort of contentment rose from it, yet beneath that was an awareness of purpose and readiness for battle. Milo sheathed it again, unwilling to examine it further and quietly cursed his fate. Could he have escaped this moment, or was all pre-destined? He should have left for the New Continent as he'd once planned to do; maybe then he wouldn't have ended up here.

The light in the shrine intensified as Coventina rose again from the water. Milo hauled himself to his feet and bowed. Beside him, Julia stirred.

"Good, she wakes." The Goddess said, her voice rippling through the sanctuary. "It will take time to fully assimilate the power she has been given, but she has enough for now."

"So she's the new Merlin?" Milo asked.

Coventina shook her head, her locks flowing like weed in a brook.

"There was only one Merlin."

He was about to question her further when Julia sat up, blinking. Then her gaze sharpened and she nodded.

"I understand now."

Milo observed her as she stood in one fluid motion. It was true that she had changed, but he couldn't have said how. Perhaps it was a different air about her. The hesitant, uncertain Princess was gone, replaced with someone who knew what she was about.

"Greetings to you, Owl." Coventina inclined her head, a faint smile on her lips. "Are you ready to take up your duties?"

Julia's eyes unfocused a she sought something within.

"I am."

She sounded much as usual, but Milo wasn't fooled.

"Then you must do as Merlin directed and leave here. Go to join Cei Pendragon and his forces, where they prepare to meet the Old Race in battle."

Again there was a delay, as if Julia was hearing something he couldn't.

"I will do so, after I restore balance to the Grove of the Mother. I ask for your blessing, Lady."

"You have it, both of you."

Coventina stretched out her hand and Milo saw a tiny flow of sparkling motes pass through the air, setting on Julia's forehead. The tiniest of sensations told him that they had come to him also and his nerves tingled with the thrill of untapped Potentia.

They bowed, and then the Goddess descended once more, leaving the surface of the pool still and unbroken.

Milo didn't know what to do. Julia stood, eyes closed, swaying slightly in place and he had no desire to disturb her. Privately he wished himself a few thousand miles away. He cast one final glance at the skull, relieved that it hadn't shown any inclination to move or speak of its own accord, picked up his pack and exited, trotting down the steps into the glade. It seemed the best idea to wait for Julia outside.

He sat down on the grass and rummaged in his pack for his water bottle. It was almost full, so he uncorked it and drank his fill, relishing the coolness and the sun on his face. If the Goddess's words were anything to go by, it would be a long time before either of them had a chance to relax. Julia's comment about the Grove of the Mother worried him. He assumed that they'd be leaving for the south immediately, but there was clearly something else on her agenda. Surely she didn't mean to take on the Fae host single-handed? A worm of worry was already starting to gnaw at him when Julia emerged from the temple.

Wordlessly he offered her his water bottle and she drank, though she didn't seat herself. Her dark eyes had a different focus now.

"We must return to the Grove," she said.

"Is that wise?" He was hesitant to challenge her but he had to know her reasoning.

"I have business there. All is not well. You remember that Ceridwen told us that the Priestesses were away worshipping?"

His stomach clenched.

"I take it she lied?"

"She did. They are captive and only we can free them. Tell me." Her gaze raked him. "Do you have any loyalty to your mother and her schemes?"

He stood and faced her, meeting her direct gaze with his own. Tiny golden flecks danced in the depths of her pupils.

"None. She may have given birth to me, but she's as mad as a sack full of rats. I must oppose her, though I don't know how."

Julia raised both eyebrows, then dipped her chin towards the sword.

"I think you have more power than you realise, Uncle."

He gasped before he could stop himself. It still hadn't sunk in. There were two Pendragons here, and one bore Excalibur.

"Still, we are only two and they are many."

Julia bared her teeth in a feral grin.

"Not as many as there were. Some have gone ahead and I'm sure we can deal with what's left, though I fear it will be hard on you."

Milo swallowed. "If I must choose, then I choose you, Lady. Niece," he added. "And your father, of course."

Cei Pendragon is my half-brother. Gods preserve us!

She took his hand.

"We are blood. We are family. We will save Britannia."

He gripped her cool fingers and wished he had a quarter of her confidence.

"What now?"

"Follow me."

She strode off, and, after a moment, he slung his pack over his shoulder and made his way after her. It seemed that Julia hadn't only inherited Emrys's powers, but his attitude as well. The marked change in her personality alarmed him. Part of him wished that she would revert to herself at some point, but not until they'd dealt with their enemies. Only the weight of Excalibur provided comfort now in this strange new reality.

It wasn't long before they were back at the forest's edge, looking into the clearing. Milo suspected that Julia had used some sort of magic to get them back so quickly from the temple. Each seemed to exist in a bubble, or possibly interlinked lands that could only be traversed by initiates.

He longed to engage her in conversation about her new state, but she seemed totally preoccupied with the task at hand. Wryly, he could see the original Merlin being like this with his Artorius. Did it annoy the old King as much as it did him? It was hard for someone used to making his own decisions to be so reliant on the skills of another, but he bit his lip and put up with it for now. There might be a time when she would need him again. Surely the old Julia hadn't been completely superseded by this new version? Emrys had told him that she would need time.

They crouched in the undergrowth, watching. There was no sign of the Fae, but smoke was rising from the Great Hall, presumably where Ceridwen and Étain were. Something told Milo that more time had passed than he'd thought. The sun seemed higher, as if days, not hours had slipped by while they were at Coventina's temple.

"There are only four of them left as escort," Julia whispered, never taking her eyes from the view. "We must act to dispose of them."

"How?"

"Stealth. Don't draw the sword, they'll detect it. It is not always a subtle weapon and its time has not yet come. This is knife work."

Milo's hand moved automatically to his right hip. He had a concealed dagger in his boot as well, but the knife was better for slitting throats. The sword would be a nuisance though if he was creeping about.

"Should I leave the sword hidden?"

"No. Take it off and sling it across your back."

"But the baldric won't –"

"It will adjust itself. It's magical, remember?"

How could he forget?

He did as she told him and felt the leather re-shape itself. It felt more comfortable that way, even if its intelligence was slightly unnerving. He couldn't wait any longer.

"How are you?" he demanded. "This change you've undergone. Are you the same person I knew, or are you something else now?"

"Oh, I'm still Julia, sort of," she replied, almost absently, "but there are a lot of other things going on in here as well. Tons of information I have to deal with, plus some new senses. Don't worry about it. I could still do with a hot bath and a good dinner."

The reference made him smile, but not without regret. Any naivety she'd possessed had been stripped from her when she accepted Emrys's offer.

"I just wanted to know," he said.

"Of course you did. Right. I think I should cast a concealment spell on us so we can sneak about."

"That's more my style," he admitted. "I take it it's throat-slitting time?"

"Absolutely. They'll be camped out under the trees waiting for orders."

"How do you know?"

"The Goddess told me, plus I can sort of smell them."

That was strange. He changed the subject. "We've been gone a while, haven't we?"

"Yes and no. Time has its own laws here but Ceridwen hasn't sent her daughter off yet after so long apart."

"Why doesn't she go to Londin with her?"

Julia pursed her lips. "She's bound to the Mother's Grove. Her power, even her name, is granted by the Mother, but she's abused it. The Mother has withdrawn her favour."

Milo thought for a moment.

"Is she the one we call Ceres?"

Julia laughed quietly.

"She has as many names and faces as there are peoples, but yes. We Pendragons officially worship her as Ceres. The Greeks call her Demeter, the Aegyptians, Isis. The Northmen have their Frigg and Freyja. She is our Mother, and she is older than time. Coventina, too, is part of the pantheon. All are aspects and she presents herself in her own way. Now, are you any happier?"

"It's a relief to know she's with us, but aren't the Fae her children too?"

"They are, but this is no longer their place. It is that and the faithlessness of her Priestess that distresses her. We must tread carefully."

He watched the smoke curl lazily from the thatched roof of the hall as he mulled over her words.

"But I was led to Excalibur for a reason."

"Oh yes, Gwydre Pendragon."

He grimaced. "I'd rather be Milo, Government Agent."

"Maybe you can be both, as I am both princess and Mage. Time to put your training to good use."

She bowed her head, concentrating. Milo felt the weight of a cloak settle about them, as if they'd been draped with translucent fabric, muting the colours of the leaves and grass. It was far better than he could have done himself and he had to admire her enhanced skill. At her gesture, they left the protective cover of the trees, making their way over to the other side of the clearing by threading their way past the huts. Everything looked abandoned, as if no-one had been there for many days and Milo frowned to himself. What had happened to the women and children who should have been here, busy about their daily tasks? Was that why the Mother was angry?

He pushed the worry aside for now. There was killing to do.

The Fae hadn't gone far. There were four of them, lounging around a fire above which a carcass hung on a spit. The smell of roast pork filled Milo's nostrils and his mouth watered. It had been too long since he'd had a proper meal. One Fae checked it, then drew a slim bronze dagger to cut a slice. So they didn't eat their meat raw. He'd always been told that they were more like animals, but the sophistication of their clothing and weapons belied that fact. Only their unsettling appearance screamed at him that they were far from human.

Four were too many. Ideally, they would need to lure one away. Julia grabbed his arm and pointed to herself.

I'll distract them, she mouthed.

Dropping her own portion of glamour she headed off at a tangent. After a few seconds, he heard her crashing about in the bushes.

The Fae started like deer, heads up and noses in the air. They muttered among themselves, their voices muted trills, before two of them went to investigate. That evened the odds somewhat, but Milo still wasn't sure he could take on two of them by himself. He was debating whether to make his move, when there were two shrill cries from the trees and the sound of bodies falling.

The remaining Fae exchanged looks, then set off after their fellows, moving cautiously. Protected by his glamour, Milo chased after them as silently as he could, catching up to the rearmost as he entered the trees. A quick jerk on the Fae's hair brought the creature's throat within reach. One practised swipe and he was holding a dead weight. The other one had already disappeared into the shadows. Mio was about to throw his knife, when roots erupted from the ground, twining about the Fae's limbs and pinning it in place. Julia stepped out from behind a trunk.

"I think you'd better finish her off," she said.

Milo got to work. The blood was paler than a human's and there wasn't as much of it, but otherwise the technique was the same.

"I thought they'd be harder to kill," he said.

"We caught these off-guard," Julia remarked, "and without any of their Mages or magical creatures. It won't always be this easy."

He sniffed. "A pity."

She waved a hand and the roots retreated back underground, dragging the corpse with it. A rustling noise made him turn to see that the other one he'd killed was being dealt with in the same manner. He didn't ask what Julia had done to hers, as he suspected he wouldn't have liked the answer.

"Was that the first time you've killed anything?"

She nodded and he was relieved to see that she looked slightly sick, as if the original Julia was showing instead of this new, augmented version he wasn't quite comfortable with.

"Yes. It wasn't pleasant, but it was necessary. I suppose you've had to do it before."

"Occasionally. I am a spy, after all, and there always people who don't want you sniffing around, be they smugglers, pirates or foreign agents."

She winced. "That's how it is. Well, we'd better go and find out what's happened to everyone. I take it there should be a lot more people here?"

"Yes. From what I remember, there was a whole community of Priestesses, their servants and children. My mother's got some explaining to do."

They found Ceridwen in the Great Hall, stirring a pot over the fire. Étain looked as if she hadn't moved from the last time they had seen her, still staring glassy-eyed into the distance, as if unable to function independently without the presence of her Fae masters. Maybe it was the shock of returning after so many years but it was still unnatural, as if the woman had been robbed of some vital essence that had made her human. Whatever, it was a glimpse into one possible future and raised the stakes of their mission. Milo knew the Fae wouldn't hesitate to do to everyone what they'd done to her.

His mother straightened up and smiled as they entered. She could have been any ordinary housewife tending to her family, not the High Priestess of the most important Goddess in the land. It was suddenly clearer to him. Repeated contact with the Fae on her daughter's behalf had affected her too, stripping away the independence and resilience she'd once had. It must have been so gradual that she hadn't noticed as they'd dug their barbs into her a little further each time, until everything had become normalised and she was completely under their sway.

A tingle down his spine reminded him of his burden, as if Excalibur were agreeing with him. The thought that the weapon might be able to communicate with him, even on a basic level, turned him cold. It wasn't only the Fae who could work subtle magic.

"There you are, my son. I wondered where you'd got to. Where did that old goat take you?"

She looked past them, looking for Emrys's tall figure.

"We went to worship the Goddess," Julia said.

"Good. You are already sanctified and of royal blood, so you can take up your duties here immediately. Emrys knows that I will need a successor soon. It's why he brought you here."

"What about me?" Milo said.

Her face broke into a smile. "Why, you will kill Marcus and take the throne, of course, with Étain at your side!"

He almost choked.

"But that's up to the Sword of Kingship!"

"Which will approve you."

"How can you be so sure? It might choose Cei."

She shrugged. "Then we'll work with that, and you'll be the heir. Whatever happens, your path is laid out."

Milo concentrated on his breathing, using all his training to remain calm and give her no hint of his true feelings. The Furies be damned. Mother or no mother, he wanted to draw the sword and run her through where she stood.

"But where are the other Priestesses?" Julia asked, her voice light, as if she had just achieved her heart's desire.

"I will take you to them," Ceridwen replied. "They'll need a little persuasion to accept the new way of things. I fear that they fail to fully understand the wonderful opportunity we've been given to put everything back to rights."

She tutted to herself, as if she'd found that her bread had gone stale, or the milk had turned.

"I'm sure we can explain things," Julia said. Milo braced himself for Ceridwen's angry response to the delicate layering of suggestion that threaded her words, but his mother seemed oblivious.

"Oh yes. We'll go now. Come, Étain. It will do you good to have a walk."

She fussed around her daughter, fastening a cloak more firmly around the unresponsive shoulders. Étain stood, and Milo was reminded of an automaton he'd seen at a fair once. He went to her and took her hand.

"How are you Étain?"

Her gold-rimmed eyes moved to his, as if in a dream.

"I'm fine. It's good to be back with Mother."

"There, you heard it for yourself. She's still adjusting to this realm," Ceridwen said. "She'll be more herself soon."

Milo doubted that very much. His mother lifted the pot off the fire and set it to one side.

"We'll all eat when we get back," she said.

He couldn't tell what she'd been cooking, but there was an edge to the aroma rising from the stew that made his nose twitch. He wouldn't have wanted to eat what she'd prepared, that was for sure. A look from Julia told him that she'd noticed it too.

Outside, it was a glorious summer's day. Étain shivered as she moved into the sun and pulled the hood of her cloak over her head to protect herself. Ceridwen took her by the arm, and the little party walked out of the clearing and along a broad path. Milo could see a hill in the distance and, sure enough, they began to climb, aided by an occasional flight of steps set into the hillside. He fell back to whisper to Julia.

"This is the way to the hill of stones. It's one of the few things I remember. They must be there."

Julia's eyes flicked to him, but she gave no other sign. The change in her was becoming more pronounced as if she was possessed, but by who or what he couldn't guess. He felt more and more out of his depth as they ascended. He was already soaked in sweat by the time they reached the top.

The summit of the hill rose from its surrounding trees, covered only by grass, wildflowers and a rough ring of stones that crowned it like so many crooked teeth. Ceridwen, guiding Étain, made her way up to and through it without hesitation, stopping in the middle and waiting for them to catch up.

As he got nearer, he could see irregular lumps in the grass. Bits of coloured cloth showed through twisted strands of bindweed and honeysuckle, the latter's cloying scent heavy in the still air. He ran over to one, dropping to his knees and tearing at the woody stems.

"It's all right, they're not dead." Ceridwen called. "I can wake them."

Milo gritted his teeth. No wonder the Mother was angry.

"Then do so," he answered.

"Not yet."

Julia had joined her in the circle, her features impassive as she saw what Ceridwen had done. The atmosphere began to grow heavy and a shadow seemed to fall over the sun, though Milo couldn't see any clouds in the brilliant blue of the sky. His mother sensed it too. She paused before stepping towards Julia, like a worshipper in the presence of an angry God.

The tattoos stood out sharply against Julia's pale skin and now there seemed to be more of them, coiling around her features. Milo blinked. Were they moving? Quietly, he stayed low and began to back out of the circle. He couldn't help these women, and whatever was about to happen didn't involve him. All his Agent's instincts were screaming at him to get out of there fast and he wasn't going to argue.

The pungent smell of crushed grass and herbs rose around him as he retreated, and he could sense the heat of the earth, as if he were moving over a living skin rather than simple soil and plants. He passed between two tall sentinels, their rough, lichen-spotted surfaces marking the boundary he had to cross. As he did so, he felt a tension in the air snap, as if he'd broken through invisible threads that reconnected as soon as he was done. It wasn't until he'd moved several body lengths down the hill that he halted, wanting to see what would happen.

Julia's voice was low and full of Potentia.

"You have offended the Goddess by attacking her worshippers. You have broken your sacred promise to preserve this place and its people."

Ceridwen drew herself up to face her, her lip twisted in scorn.

"I see you now, you and your borrowed mantle! You think to trick me."

"There are no tricks here, Ceridwen, formerly High Priestess of the Heart of Albion. You have broken your compact with Britannia and her peoples that was forged in ages past. Now you must pay."

"The compact was a lie!" Ceridwen screamed. "The land is corrupted, its people enslaved! The old ways are gone!"

Julia nodded.

"Yes. The old ways are gone. There are new ways now, and this is how it must be. You cannot fight fate or turn back time, however much you might wish to."

"The Fae can restore it!"

"No. They can't. All is illusion. That's what they deal in, which is good according to their lights, but their ways are not of this land and they must depart. In time, they will vanish altogether into the twilight realms and trouble mortals no more."

A slow smile spread across Ceridwen's face.

"Tell that to the army which is attacking even now. They have spells and weapons that are proof against cold iron. Did you think them idle all these centuries? They want what is rightfully theirs and are prepared to fight for it. Your cause is doomed before it starts! Now, Emrys, release the Princess from her bondage before I do it myself."

"Oh." Julia drew out the word. "You think I'm Emrys? It's true that I have some of his memories and his skills, but I assure you I'm not Merlin. I am the Princess Julia Victoria Pendragon and I am also Owl, granted power by the Goddess herself to lead the Mages of Britannia. And I have had enough of you and your delusions!"

The earth rippled and heaved, as if a great underground beast shifted in its sleep. Milo threw himself flat, desperately covering his head with his arms. The spell crashed over him like an avalanche but the energy of Excalibur pulsed at his back, deflecting it away and into the trees that groaned and cracked at its passage.

Then, all was quiet. Milo's heartbeat throbbed loudly in his ears as he panted in short gasps, unwilling to look up and see the devastation that had surely been wrought by the blast. It was the women's voices that roused him from his stupor, several of them, all talking at once like a flock of startled birds.

Far from being flattened, the hilltop looked much as it had done. The Priestesses were sitting up, some gathering their children to their breasts as they tried to work out what had happened.

"Ladies!"

Julia assumed command of the situation. "Your unlawful bondage is ended, by order of the Mother herself. The perpetrator has been punished and one of you will be called to take her place as High Priestess. Return to your houses and your lives. Continue your worship. The Mother will make her wishes plain to you."

She spun, leaving the bemused women to tend to their families and each other and strode down the hill to Milo.

"Our work here is done."

He stared up into amber eyes, seeing for a brief instant the spirit of what she had become. It took him a few moments, but he staggered to his feet.

"Where are Ceridwen and Étain?"

An exclamation from one of the Priestesses made him look to where she was pointing. There, at the edge of the circle were two rough stones where none had stood before, one leaning into the other as if trying to shield it. There was no covering of lichen or softening moss, just edges and curves suggesting a shoulder here, a draped knee there. Here they would stand forever, open to wind and weather and mute testament to the power of the Earth Mother. He could only hope that they had in some way become part of her and, in their own time, be granted forgiveness.

Milo bowed his head, filled with a swirling mix of emotion he couldn't name. Relief and sadness certainly, but also the sense that this had been destined. Nothing and no-one could part mother and daughter now.

A hand touched his shoulder and he spun around. The woman was youngish, with a pleasant face and long reddish-brown hair. A small boy clutched at her skirts, whilst behind her a girl stood watching, her brown eyes wary.

"I am Arianrhod," the Priestess said. "Don't be afraid, Gwydre. You are favoured by the Mother, not only because of what you carry, but because of your faithfulness to her servant."

Her eyes darted sideways to where Julia was standing. Milo knew immediately who the next High Priestess would be, and he bowed deeply.

"I am at your service, Lady."

She smiled at him and he sensed the power swirling around her, settling on her shoulders like a mantle.

"Please be kind to your children," he added. "Promise me you won't abandon them, as my mother did me."

Arianrhod nodded gravely. Tiny green lights shimmered in the depths of her pupils.

"That was ill-done." The boy whimpered and she bent, taking him in her arms and lifting him on her hip. "You have my word."

The other women and children joined her, standing as one. Slowly, they all smiled and Milo felt their strength unfurl, like petals welcoming the morning sun.

"Go now and fight for the land," Arianrhod commanded.

He bowed again, just as another silent explosion of Potentia sucked him backwards, away into the dark.

XII

Caniculus woke early, after a few hours of snatched sleep. He'd opted for tucking himself into the corner of two walls for the night, all the better to observe the comings and goings at the palace, but had dozed off when nothing much was happening. The Londin Vigiles had done their best to try and contain the fire, managing to save surrounding buildings, but the old Royal Residence was largely reduced to smouldering ruins.

The stench of burning still hung heavy in the air, lingering on everything in the vicinity. He stretched his cramped limbs and shook out his cloak, thinking that he was getting too old for sleeping against a wall, even though the night had been temperate. It was promising to be a hot day, though he had the feeling that the early summer sunshine wouldn't last long. There was a heaviness in the air that set his teeth on edge and made him even jumpier than he was already. He'd spent many a night out in the open, but not while wearing a helmet and he wanted to get the thing off as soon as possible.

The grounds were crawling with a few polismen and workers trying to salvage things from the rubble – but not Marcus's guards. That was interesting and he wondered where the Usurper had crawled off to. It was too much to hope that he'd suffered a direct hit. Caniculus sidled over to a couple of polis lounging against a fire-blackened column and listened in.

"– won't find anything in this lot," a burly, pock-marked fellow said to his comrade. Soot-streaked, stubbled chins and reddened eyes told him they'd been up all night. The other, a veteran by his grey hairs, cast a jaded eye over the toiling slaves. "You're right there! This place is well and truly flattened." He fingered his winged phallus amulet superstitiously. "Can't say I'm surprised."

The first one hawked and spat to clear his throat.

"Bloody smoke. All that's left is a pile of ash and a few corpses we'll have to dig out when it all cools down."

"Got to watch them." The veteran replied, jerking his head at the diggers. "They'll nick anything they can."

His companion snorted. "Aye, and so will we. Molten metal's the thing to look for, right? Marcus won't miss it." He straightened up and raised his voice. "Oi! Don't try and move that! It'll all come down!"

The older man rolled his eyes. "Stupid arsehole. Nearly had another corpse there. So, what now?"

"Look on the bright side, Agrius. We could be facing a horde of Fae. I'll stick to guard duty, thank you very much and leave the heroics to our brave boys in the legions."

They exchanged knowing looks.

Caniculus felt his spirits lift a little. It seemed that the legions had switched allegiance away from Marcus now that the sword was revealed. That had to be good.

"A bloody portal on the South Downs," Aulus said. "Who'd have thought it? I don't know if we can hold them and I don't want to be here if they win. I've told my missus to get ready to run for it."

"What, to the Continent? You'll be lucky. There won't be any boats left. From what I hear, most of Britannia's getting out already. This is crap like you wouldn't believe."

Caniculus almost choked inside his helmet. A chill swept through him at the thought of the Ancient Enemy coming over in force.

The pair seemed chatty enough, so Caniculus decided to take a risk. He darted out of sight and removed his helmet. He needed to ask more direct questions and presumably these polismen had been briefed. But first he would need to bring offerings.

An opportunistic trader had set up his pie stall just outside the grounds. He quickly bought three, then replaced the helmet when no one was looking. A quick trot through the gates and he was back in the palace grounds. It was fortunate that there was space around the building, or half of Londin would have gone up in flames. The fact that he was already inside meant that he shouldn't be questioned.

Caniculus dodged behind a half-ruined wall and took off the helmet, shoving it in his pack before smoothing his hair and breaking into a brisk stride. He hoped they wouldn't notice his crumpled clothes and grubby face.

"Good morning, lads. You alright?"

His tone made the polismen straighten instinctively.

"Gaius Crispus, Public Health." He flashed one of the fake badges he kept for such an occasion. "It's a mess, isn't it?"

Their wariness dissipated as he identified himself as a Londin official.

"Too right it is, mate," Agrius agreed. "I was just saying to Cimarus here that it'll take some sorting."

Caniculus sucked his teeth. "It will. I've heard there are casualties, but not much else. Hardly any information's come down and I've been running about like a blue-arsed fly all night. Oh, I grabbed these on the way in, as I bet you've not had time for breakfast either."

He saw their eyes light up as he proffered the pies. The waft of hot pastry made a pleasant change from the stink.

"That's very kind of you, mate," Cimarus said, as Aulus also mumbled thanks. They wasted no time in cramming their mouths as full as possible.

Caniculus let them eat in peace for a minute. They weren't of the best quality, but they'd do for hungry men.

"I take it Marcus got out?" he said at last.

He was angling shamelessly, but his ploy worked.

"That bastard? Oh yes. Jupiter missed, alas! He's holed up at Greenfields, as nice as you please."

Agrius spat again, this time to show his opinion of Marcus and all his cronies.

"Let's hope the Thunderer has more in his arsenal, eh lads?" Caniculus agreed. "Fancy him having a fake sword!"

"And now it's clear that Marcus had King Artorius topped," Cimarus added, not to be outdone. "I hope the Furies drag him to

Tartarus screaming, with Cerberus having a go at him on the way down."

All three of them paused to reflect on the pleasing image.

"What's this about a portal?" Caniculus asked.

"We got word in the night." Agrius looked grim. "That's how they've got here so quick. There's going to be an almighty battle." He tapped the side of his nose. "That's on the quiet, you understand. We don't want to cause a panic."

"Good Gods!" Caniculus didn't have to pretend to be appalled. "Have the troops mustered?"

"They're trying to get as many down here as they can," Cimarus said, as Agrius finished off his pie in two huge bites. "Bloody Marcus sent a load to mess about up north, didn't he? Now they've got to get back fast. Between you and me, mate, it isn't looking good."

"Where's Pendragon?"

"Oh, yeah. Him drowning was another lie, thank Mithras. The rumours are that he's on his way. I suppose he's the true King now."

"If he pulls out Excalibur," Agrius reminded them.

"If he doesn't, we're neck deep in the manure pile," Cimarus said glumly. "He has to be the King. There's nobody else now, unless you count the Princess."

There was another period of contemplation.

"So, what do you think Marcus will do?" Caniculus asked. "They say he's been in league with the Fae all along."

Even he was impressed with the torrent of curses.

"Wouldn't surprise me, knowing what we do now," Agrius said, when he'd finished. "He'll have Greenfields defended, but it won't save him if the people rise up."

"My bet is he'll go to join his new friends," Cimarus added, disgust written large on his grimy features. Caniculus finished off his pie.

"Well, I'd better be getting on. I have to make a tally of this and that, you know how it is. They want this report yesterday."

All three nodded at the predictability of bureaucrats.

"Good luck with that," Aulus said. "And if you have a family here, I'd start packing, just in case."

Caniculus saw his own fear reflected in their eyes.

215

"May Fortuna smile on us all," he answered.

He hurried away, mimicking the walk of the perpetually harassed from long practice and considered his options. Should he risk contacting his family? Knowing his mother, she'd have had the information long before him. He was so deep in thought that he nearly ran into a workman pushing a wheelbarrow full of rubble.

"Watch where you're going! Wouldn't want you to fall down a hole, would we?"

The voice was familiar. Caniculus froze on the spot.

"It's a pretty pass, isn't it? Ready for the battle?"

The relish in the man's voice turned him cold. He turned slowly.

"Lord Mars."

It was the eyes that frightened him most, though the huge grin came a close second. When he was a boy, his father had ordered a tiger, brought all the way from Hind to star in the arena. He'd stood in front of the cage as it was brought in, and had never forgotten the fierce rage on the beast's face, knowing that only a few metal bars stood between him and certain death.

He shoved the memory back, all too aware of the God's power.

"My father has ordered that I speak to you, before I gird myself for the field." He glanced down at his rough clothes. "Needs must, I suppose. Now, listen. Mercury sent you here for a reason."

Caniculus locked his knees to stop them from shaking. This tiger was also caged, but he had the feeling that the door would soon be opened and he'd rather not be around when it was. He was no soldier, though he could handle himself in a fight if he had to. He was better at skulking about.

Mars stretched his back and flexed his muscles. They were impressive.

"You're to stay in Londin. You have two tasks. Come back to the palace when the embers have cooled because you need to find something buried here. But first you must go and get the Sceptre of Britannia from the strong room in the old *Castra*. Got that?"

Caniculus felt the blood rush from his head.

"The Sceptre?" he croaked.

216

"That's right. Britannia has need of it and you're going to take it. Don't faint!"

The command was like a dash of cold water to the face. Caniculus blinked.

"I obey, O Mighty One."

"As you should." The terrible smile vanished. "You mustn't fail, or the consequences will be dire. Do you understand? The helmet will aid you. Oh, and you'll need this."

A small wooden box appeared in the God's hand. It was covered in marks that Caniculus couldn't read. He took it carefully.

"Open it only when you need to and hold your breath when you do. Now, I must go. You know how it is. Armies to lead, things to kill." The God's eyes gleamed in anticipation.

Caniculus swallowed. "Yes, Lord."

"And don't hang about."

"Yes, Lord."

He blinked. The wheelbarrow remained, but the Lord of War had gone. Caniculus took a deep breath and stared at the box. His hands were clammy, so he took time to wipe them on his cloak before stashing the God's gift in a secret pocket.

The Sceptre of Britannia. One of the most magical and treasured items in the whole kingdom, locked away under guard in the old Fort of Londinium. Even Marcus hadn't dared be seen with it, such was its power. And he was being ordered to steal it. *Merda!*

There was nothing for it but to obey the God's command.

If anyone had told him a few months ago that he would be meeting up with Gods on a regular basis, he would have laughed in their faces. It seemed now that his life had turned into some sort of improbable story, like the tales of old peddled about by hawkers on street corners. Come to think of it, everything had become strange and unpredictable lately. A bit of adventure was all very well, but you could have too much of a good thing. He missed the days when the worst he could expect was a beating by some thugs on a night raid, and right now he'd have given his eye teeth to be back in the land of predictability, with orders coming from Favonius and not bloody Olympus. It was all getting a bit much.

After some thought, he decided to hole up in an inn not far from the Old Fort, just inside the ancient city walls, and think through his plan for getting his hands on the Sceptre. It wasn't too crowded, and he could have a drink while he decided what to do. The fact that Mars had given him some sort of defence scared him half to death. It stood to reason that the artefact would be guarded and it was a pity that the God hadn't told him what to look out for. He probably viewed the whole thing as entertainment, like a star turn in the Games.

Let's see how Caniculus copes with this challenge, Ladies and gentlemen! Will he manage to accomplish his task before he's torn to pieces? Place your bets now!

Once safely seated in a back room, he took another swig of beer and wondered whether Jason had felt this way when he saw the Golden Fleece was guarded by a dragon. Perhaps whatever was in the box was the equivalent of Medea's magic potion? It was an encouraging thought, but he couldn't count on it. The Gods helped those who helped themselves and were not always known for their charity. He could almost feel an invisible audience taking their seats for the next scene.

The beer was almost gone and he was rapidly running out of options. He reviewed what he knew about the Old Fort for the umpteenth time.

Big, high-walled and full of soldiers. The official residence of the Imperial Governor in Britannia, successive post holders preferred a newer and far more comfortable town house, so its function was mostly as a barracks. Legions were moved in and out on a regular basis so they couldn't get comfortable, or up to mischief. As the Empire's influence had waned so had the Governor's, but he was still an important personage, second only to the Sovereign. It also made sense that items of national significance were kept there, both for security and as bargaining chips for Roma to keep the *Brittunculi* in line.

All this made it nigh on impossible for anyone to get near the strong room. Anyone lacking a magical helmet that is. He forced his racing thoughts to slow. Hadn't he sneaked about often enough, even before he had the power to become invisible? He could slip inside the gatehouse no problem, dodge the guards and make his way to the administrative buildings. Every fort in the

Empire was built along the same lines, so he wouldn't need a map. Usually, the valuables were kept in an underground room in the heart of the Fort, guarded day and night. With any luck, it would be a quick in-and-out job. He might have to knock out a guard and steal the keys, but that was something he'd done more than once.

Get in, grab the sceptre and get out fast. Presumably, the Gods would know when he was done.

He finished his beer and slid out of his seat, wishing desperately that he had time for a visit to the baths but there was no time. Also, Mars's threat had been explicit and he didn't even want to speculate on what would happen to him if he didn't follow the God's orders to the letter.

As he left, the bells for midday started to ring. He'd debated whether to wait until dark, but decided against it. Thieves usually operated at night, and he didn't want to be predictable. With any luck most of the personnel would be lined up waiting for their dinner, so it was a better time than most.

It wasn't long before he was once more peering through the helmet's eye holes and heading off towards the Fort. Its towering walls were impossible to miss. Built a thousand years before, they dwarfed the neighbouring buildings, ancient and impregnable, at least before the importation of gunpowder. Even now it would take some serious cannon fire to breach them. These days, everyone regarded them as more of a symbol than an actual defence, mere relics of more turbulent times.

There were only a couple of guards at the gatehouse, not half as many as he'd been expecting. Caniculus shivered as he passed under its shadow, and not only because of the lack of sunlight. He was treading in the footsteps of Artorius the Great now. Some Agents liaised with the Imperial authorities on a regular basis, but he hadn't been one of them. He knew he wasn't supposed to be sightseeing, but he couldn't help goggling at the impressive buildings that harked back to when the Romans were still foreign interlopers, with a shaky grasp on their new acquisition. That had changed so gradually that nobody thought of it anymore. It felt like they'd always been here now.

Caniculus had been in forts before, but this one was huge. He'd expected it to be swarming with armed soldiers, but it was unnaturally quiet. The red Imperial banners, with their golden eagle above the letters SPQR, hung listlessly in the noon sun. Others proclaimed this to be the temporary home of the Twentieth Valeria Victrix Britannica. Maybe they'd already marched out to join their brothers against the Fae, leaving only a small garrison to protect their rear? He permitted himself to feel a shred of hope. If the place was mostly empty it should make his job easier.

All senses on high alert, he made his way towards the Headquarters Building that held the administrative offices and, with any luck, the strong room. He knew that in most forts it was a poky underground cellar, just large enough for important documents and the legionaries' pay, but in this case it would probably be something more impressive. He would have to rely on luck and the help of the Gods to pull this off.

He slipped silently between the barrack blocks, noting that even his meagre noon-day shadow was invisible. He could hear voices coming from open doors, but it seemed that most were busy inside. Food aromas hung in the air and a couple of slaves passed him, carrying covered trays. Caniculus congratulated himself – meal time had been the right choice. He scooted past, coming face-to-face with the shallow marble steps and columns of the Headquarters. Unlike the rest of the fort, there was more activity here. The doors were guarded by armed legionaries, muskets at rest over their shoulders and their red coats bright as blood. As he observed them, a clerk came hurrying out carrying a leather case, presumably full of important documents. His face was grim as he skipped down the steps and headed over to an adjacent building. Caniculus would have liked to see what his business was, but he made himself move on up the steps, past the watchful guards and into the atrium.

The usual ornamental pool was elaborate, as were the mosaics and frescoes, but he only gave them a cursory glance, searching for anything that might give him a clue as to the whereabouts of the strong room and taking care to keep his steps inaudible. Two more clerks exited from a side door and he craned his neck to see past them before it closed. It looked like a large workroom full of secretaries and cabinets of files. These would be the outer offices for the junior staff and general pen pushers. He needed to get to the inner sanctum. If he had to bet on it, his target would be off the Governor's office. Presumably the Chief Clerk, or even the Governor himself, would have to authorise any entry. A nasty thought struck him. Could it only be opened by magic? After a moment he dismissed the idea. This was an ancient Roman space, for Imperial Agents only. No Britannic Mage would be permitted to go snooping about here. There would be guards and, presumably, a key. The first he could trick, or overpower to get the second. But where was he to start?

Again, it was the guards that gave the location away. They stood like statues before a door with an elaborate architrave. He decided it might as well have had a sign on it shouting 'This way to the Secret Strong Room!' Either that, or the Governor had a very special latrine. Caniculus sniggered to himself as he sidled up as near as he dared. He debated whether to use the old 'I'm an official clerk, let me in' tactic, but these legionaries weren't run-of-the- mill polis like his new friends Agrius and Cimarus. These were highly trained and very suspicious professionals. Magical helmet or no magical helmet, he wasn't going to take the risk of alerting them.

He leaned against a wall, the marble chilly through his cloak, and chewed his lip. There had to be a way. For a moment he considered opening the box, but something told him that this wasn't the time. Instead, he concentrated on examining the door. As he'd surmised, there was a heavy lock in place but neither guard appeared to have a key. He racked his brains, reviewing what he knew of Government protocols.

Right. There would be two keys. Presumably the Governor would have one, if only for symbolic reasons. The other would be held by his Deputy, the one who actually did all the admin work and passed it over for a signature. He would be known by sight, so it wouldn't be possible for Caniculus to impersonate him or pretend he'd been delegated to fetch something from the vault. He had to find the Deputy, Chief Clerk, whatever he was called and obtain the key by fair means or foul. It was tempting to whip off the helmet and demand the key in the name of the Gods, but that would be a last resort.

He was just about to set off on his search when his prayers were answered. A tall, older man with an aquiline nose and a pronounced stoop emerged from a neighbouring door and approached the guards. His arms were full of files, presumably of a sensitive nature if they had to be locked away so securely. He looked like one of the Imperial freedmen who made up most of the civil service, spending their lives hunched over desks as they did the donkey work of the state. The guards stood to attention as he fumbled at a chain around his neck and produced a heavy iron key, inserting it into the lock and turning it with a click.

Caniculus breathed his gratitude heavenwards and glided across to stand behind him, but not so near that the man would feel like someone was breathing down his neck.

It took more than one turn. Some secret mechanism inside ratcheted up and Caniculus could hear the sound of many bolts withdrawing to release the catches.

"Here, Master Meleager, I'll give you a hand."

One of the guards handed his musket to his fellow and pulled the door open with a grunt. What appeared to be ordinary enough from the exterior was several hand spans thick and sheathed in metal.

Caniculus stood on his tiptoes and glimpsed steps leading down into the darkness. Meleager thanked the man, his Greek accent evident. He took a step inside and reached for something on the wall, emerging with a lantern and a pack of vestas, which he used to light a candle. There were no Magelights here. Caniculus thanked the Gods again that the helmet would help him to see and crept after the official, trying not to tread on his heels.

Meleager descended the stairs briskly, his lantern held high. Its light illuminated the neat stone blockwork of the walls, laid centuries ago with mathematical precision by the first builders. Instead of the spiral he'd been expecting, they passed several square landings, going deeper and deeper underground. The air smelled musty, though not as damp as could be expected. Eventually, they came out into a level corridor.

Caniculus surveyed it with dismay. This was no single strong room, but a vault! He counted two rooms to the left, the same to the right and one at the end. The one at the end had a Latin inscription which he couldn't quite make out in the dim light, but he would bet his last coin that this was the door he needed to enter.

Meanwhile, Meleager had approached the first door on the left. Caniculus was expecting more keys, but instead the man spoke in Old Latin.

Open in the name of the Senate and the People of Rome!

So, there was some magic involved. It was surprising, but the place was old enough for Merlin himself to have laid the spell. Maybe he had.

The door opened outwards and the official went inside. The space was quite large and filled with shelves and racks. Boxes, books and scrolls were stacked neatly, each tagged to identify the contents. It didn't seem the place for the Sceptre, so Caniculus left the clerk to it and approached the door at the end. Aided by the helmet, he read the four letter inscription.

CAVE

Beware. Great. This was definitely where the good stuff was. Only the Imperial Bureaucracy knew what was hidden away in here, but he was gambling it included the Sceptre. Now all he had to do was get in and out again in one piece. He pulled out the little box and spoke quietly, copying the phrase he'd heard and hoping that the clerk was busy filing his documents and oblivious to all else.

There were no clicks or bolts this time. The door slid sideways into the wall, leaving a gaping hole. For a moment all was blackness, until he realised that he could see a long space stretching out before him, lined with shelves and lit by a dull purple light. Instantly, a pungent stench hit him in the face and he took a step back, trying not to gag. Caniculus knew what it was immediately. He'd cleaned out enough cages in the past, though this one smelt as if nobody had shovelled anything for the past hundred years. He blinked, trying to breathe through his mouth even as he tried to place the stench.

Definitely not elephant. Reptile? He didn't think so. Not a large lizard or a snake. No, this was big cat, with an edge of something else.

A quiet rustle came from the darkest corner, followed by a clicking, tapping noise, slow and measured. Caniculus was acutely aware that he was in the middle of the doorway and slid sideways, pressing his body up against the frame ready for a rapid retreat.

He hoped that it wasn't a basilisk, or he would be dead for sure. Nothing could withstand a glare from that beast. He held his breath and waited. A soft, questioning caw followed, sounding like a giant parrot more than anything else, and the tapping stopped. A bird, then. As long as it wasn't of the Stymphalian sort that liked the taste of human flesh, he would be fine. He would have sworn it was feline.

Caniculus released the breath he'd been holding, then gasped as a head poked out of a gap between the shelves. He had just enough time to take in the vicious beak and beady yellow eye, before the rest of the creature emerged. The clicking sound he'd heard had been the huge talons on its front feet. Its rear lion paws were silent on the hard floor.

The gryphon cocked its head, making the strange interrogative noise it had earlier. Its muscular lion body merged seamlessly with the feathered head and neck, while the tufted tail swished in anticipation. Huge wings lay flat across its flanks.

Caniculus's first thought was *He thinks I'm here to feed him.* His second was, *What in Hades are they thinking of, keeping an animal here alone in the dark?*

His annoyance almost made him forget the danger he was in. He only remembered seeing gryphons a couple of times, when he was very small. They were too rare to be used in the arena now and his Dad had said that they were for private buyers. How long had the poor thing been locked up down here?

The gryphon seemed puzzled, bobbing its head from side to side, confused that it couldn't see whoever had entered. Then it lifted its head and Caniculus realised that it was sniffing the air. It could smell him! Were its senses enough to guide it? His question was answered a second later when it emitted a deafening shriek and charged.

Caniculus took a deep breath, opened the box and flung the contents in its face.

The beast backed off, choking and Caniculus felt a pang of guilt. He hadn't wanted to kill the creature.

He swung out of the vault, holding his breath for as long as possible, only to hear a shout.

"Hey! What's going on?"

A bobbing light and slapping footsteps confirmed that Meleager had heard the ruckus and come to investigate. His face appeared in the lantern light, eyes wide and mouth open in alarm as he searched in vain for the intruder.

"You can't go in there...oh! Fido! My poor boy!"

The freedman rushed inside and knelt beside the gryphon. The beast was lying on his side, his chest heaving. A black tongue lolled out of the partially open beak. Good, he wasn't dead, just knocked out. Caniculus was opening his mouth to shout a warning, when the official slumped down next to his charge and that was that.

He decided to wait a minute or two, to allow the air to clear as much as it could. So, they'd installed a traditional treasure guardian to patrol the artefacts in here. Caniculus scowled to himself. It was one thing to have it out in the open or even buried, with the gryphon to guard the spot, but to confine the poor creature here underground for years on end was plain cruel. It was another reason he'd left the family business. It was one thing to have trained people kill each other in the games, but it never seemed fair on the animals.

After a while he decided to risk entering, though he still held his breath as he edged past the unconscious bodies. To his amusement they were both gently snoring in concert, though in Fido's case it was more of a whistle. He also noticed that the gryphon's wings had been clipped and its coat looked dull. It had a large bald patch on its breast too, showing stubbled pink skin where it had pulled out its own feathers. If he ever got out of this, he'd be making a complaint.

He had to work quickly now, as there was no telling how long the powder would keep them under. Caniculus scanned the shelves for anything that was sceptre-shaped, or might hold a sceptre. He reckoned it would be a bit longer than his forearm, so he could rule out the tiny boxes and round packets. If he'd had the time, he would have liked to have a good poke about and read the labels as Olympus knew what was down here, hidden from sight. The Romans would have confiscated lots of things from the Britons that they thought dangerous but useful, hanging on to them as leverage, or just put away for everyone's safety. Some of the objects were gold and he was tempted to slip a few of them in his pockets, but he resisted the temptation The Gods might not approve of downright stealing and he could hardly claim them as a perk this time.

Caniculus sighed in frustration. There was just too much stuff here, everything from statues to furniture. This would take forever. Then he felt a gentle pressure turning his head to the left. The helmet was guiding him! He fixed his eyes on the line of sight he'd been granted and walked forward.

The Sceptre had a shelf to itself, as if it was too important to share its space with anything lesser. The little nook was slightly recessed, so easy to miss if he hadn't been prompted. It was thicker than he'd thought, more like a chunky baton just over a foot long, with a gold dragon on top, wings outstretched. It lay on a purple cushion with gold fringing, fit for an Emperor.

Caniculus reached out and picked it up. It looked like it was made of solid gold and was certainly heavy enough. He thrust it into his bag, then picked up the cushion for good measure and stuffed that in as well. It might be possible to sell the bullion fringe later and he could claim that they came as a set. Job done. Now it was time to make a quick exit. On the way out, a pang of conscience made him move Meleager into a more comfortable position, his head resting on Fido's feathered neck. The man had shown some concern for the gryphon after all.

Retreating the way he'd come was the easy part. When he reached the outer door, he knocked, knowing that the guards would open it. Sure enough, it swung outwards and he sprinted through, leaving two perplexed men in his wake. What happened next wasn't up to him, but he expected they'd find the sleepers soon enough. Part of him hoped that Fido would wake first and make a dash for freedom.

The Fort showed more signs of life now that the lunch hour was finishing and people were getting back to work. Caniculus tucked the bag under his arm and reflected on his next move. Time to hole up somewhere safe and wait for instructions.

Heavens knew what the Gods would want him to do next.

*

"One more time, *Tempest*! On my order... now! Full power!"

Maia tried not to sigh as Vulcan bellowed into her ear for the umpteenth time that day. She'd been put through her paces non-stop for hours, but at last it seemed that the God was as satisfied as he was ever going to be.

"We're out of time," he grumbled to Leo, who had joined him in the bowels of the vessel. Her Captain regarded the great engines with awe.

"It's all working well, I presume?"

The Chief Artificer nodded.

"Aye. Now we just need Raven and we can be off. Blast the man! He knows we're out of time."

"He always has his own agenda," Leo stated. "If he's not here promptly, we'll have to leave without him. We have Robin and Heron, so they should be enough."

Vulcan squinted at the younger man, his bushy eyebrows almost interlocking with the force of his disapproval.

"No. We need him. He'll be here, if I have to find him myself and sling him over my shoulder!"

Leo blinked in surprise, but Vulcan simply laughed and stamped off, calling "Come on, young man! Let's get this bird in the air!"

<I can't fathom him at all,> Leo Sent. <He's not scared of anyone, even Raven!>

<He's an engineer aboard his vessel,> she responded. <And King here, just remember that.>

She couldn't afford him to have a confrontation and harm himself through his ignorance. It was another thing she'd have to watch out for.

Leo set off up the ladders, muttering about the madness of Artificers in general, but it was true. They tended to be single-minded and attempted to steamroller anything in their way. Maybe they all took after their God?

Her crew had been drilled exhaustively too. Most had taken their new situations in their stride, but a few were doing their best

227

to pretend that they were still aboard a sailing Ship, not about to take flight over the tree tops. They were looking to her to reassure them that all would be well.

Her marines seemed solid enough. Osric had them cleaning their weapons and equipment, polishing buttons until they shone and generally not giving them a second's free time. Likewise, Musca was giving his gunners a talking to. It would be better if she was present, so she pushed her way up and on to the gun deck. The cannons were smaller and lighter than she was used to, but hopefully would have just as deadly an effect, especially from above. Instead of being horizontal, they were fixed to platforms that could be angled downward, fixed in place with chains to absorb the recoil.

"Yes, they look different, but the effect is the same," Musca explained. "Part of the strain will be taken by the shields our Mages will put up. We've got three, you know, or we will have when Raven gets his arse back here." He rolled his eyes to a few groans. "We'll have more room to adjust as we fire downwards. Otherwise, it's the same. A lighter charge and shot, but plenty of damage. Just don't fall out the bloody hole and you'll be all right. We're setting off shortly, so grab some rations while you can and have a nap. I don't know how much food and sleep we'll be getting once we get going, so make the most of it. Any words, ma'am?"

Maia surveyed the faces before her. Monkey looked especially hopeful.

"Never forget, lads, the Gods are on our side," she said. It was important to keep up morale. "This is new for all of us, but we have been specially chosen to serve. The Fae won't know what's hit them!"

"Three cheers for His Majesty's AirShip *Tempest!*" Musca bellowed.

The confined space made the cheers even louder, just as Leo appeared.

"Indeed! Well done, men. Now, as our Chief Gunner has said, food and rest. We leave in less than two hours."

<With or without Raven.> he added privately.

The men went off to get a hot meal, the last they would see for a while. It was strictly cold rations while they were in flight.

"You need to take your own advice," Maia told him.

"I know. I'm dining with Amphicles, Danuco and the Chief Artificer. It'll be the last time we're on land for a while. I keep wanting to say ashore, but it doesn't sound right."

"A lot of things will change, but we'll get used to them."

He rubbed a hand over his face.

"I reckon I've time for a quick bath and a shave before we go. I'm leaving Musca in charge, so liaise with him. Any problems, I'll return immediately."

"Aye, sir."

He shot off to make his preparations. She watched his retreating back, wishing she could go with him. She hadn't said anything, but she was finding her new vessel more of a confinement than anything. She'd gone from having many decks to a tiny fraction of that and there was less room to roam. She chose to return to the little viewing platform and scanned the skies, hoping for some relief.

A familiar figure came into view below and she could have cheered. Raven was striding along, stick in hand and heading straight for her.

<Hello Raven! Have you got any news?> She couldn't wait to hear what was going on in the world.

The bright red thread shimmered in her mind.

<Hello, Maia! Been behaving yourself?>

<Naturally. I'm a good girl. I bet you haven't.>

<I'm always good, until I'm not. I won't go into specifics, but we're ready to go. Where's your Captain?>

<Having a bath, then dinner.>

There were a few seconds of silence.

<Good Gods! Doesn't he know there's a war on?>

<I've been told we're setting off in about two hours.>

<You'd better tell him to make it one if we're to catch the Fleet.>

Maia relayed Raven's words and got a groan in response.

<So, he's turned up then? This will be the fastest bath in the history of the world.>

She could feel the scrape of the strigil as Victor removed the oil and dirt from his back and pulled away slightly. Sometimes she could get too close and it was important not to overstep

229

boundaries, as she had learned to her cost. She'd not got inside his memories as she had with Raven, *Blossom* and *Augusta*, and hoped she never would.

<As long as you've eaten. I don't want you passing out on me.>

<I'm finishing up now, then I'll eat. You'll just have to fly extra fast, won't you?>

<Just watch me!> she promised, and cut the connection just as Raven appeared next to her.

"The fleet is making good time," he said. "As soon as we're nearer, you'll be able to contact them."

"At last!" she retorted. "Ships aren't meant to be on their own. It's unnatural."

He grunted. "So it is, but you can't tell them about your new vessel yet. Let it be a surprise."

"It'll be a surprise all right," she replied. "Everything's going better than I thought it would, but I have to admit I'm disappointed to only have small cannon."

He pursed his lips. "It's what you do with them that counts. You can also aim spells and missiles from your lower hatch. Don't discount yourself before you've started!"

"I'm not! It's just…I don't know how much I'll be able to accomplish in this state."

"None of us does until we try."

Raven swung around to face her, and she was struck yet again by his shrivelled face and ruined eyes. He of all people knew what it was like to start again.

"True."

They lapsed into silence. Maia didn't feel like making small talk, and the Master Mage's thoughts seemed elsewhere. Was he thinking of the fleet and their destination, or of Pendragon's desperate attempt to rally the legions? Either way, the outcome seemed uncertain. It was time to screw up her courage and make sure her vessel and crew made as much impact as possible.

She began to think about what she would say to her sisters, when she caught up with them again. 'Look up!' would probably be appropriate and she smiled to herself picturing the older Ships' reactions. *Persistence* and *Swiftsure* would be bound to let rip a few choice phrases. Above all, she was desperate to talk to *Blossom* and *Patience* again. They had been close for so long and she missed the bond they shared.

"Oh, I forgot to tell you," Raven said aloud, breaking into her musings. "I've invited aboard a special visitor."

Maia resisted the temptation to roll her eyes.

"Really? Who's that, then. Do I know them?"

Raven placed both his hands on top of his stick and smirked at her. She scowled at him in return. What was the old buzzard up to? She didn't need hangers-on, especially now.

"He's just portalled in. I'll ask him to come and see you, shall I?"

His deliberate obtuseness made her want to knock him over the rail and claim it was an accident. He'd certainly be able to stop himself falling too far, but it would be worth it to wipe the look of glee off his face.

"Whatever you like." She refused to give him the satisfaction of thinking she was bothered.

"Ah, here he is now. You should be able to see him any minute."

Short of Pendragon, she couldn't think of anyone else who would be going into battle with her. 'He' meant it wasn't Julia, which was a pity as they'd got on so well. She also couldn't believe that the Princess would be put in danger aboard what was basically an experimental craft. Instead she sighed loudly enough for him to hear her and folded her arms with an air of being completely put upon. Sure enough, she soon spotted Leo, Danuco, Hawthorn, Amphicles, and the Chief Artificer making their way towards her. She was pleased to see that her Adept had returned, but there was a sixth member of the party, wearing a naval uniform and presumably the 'special visitor'.

Maia magnified her vision to make out his features and froze. Some part of her knew that Leo was hailing her, but she couldn't respond. Her whole world lurched for a moment as everything she thought she knew was turned on its head.

"See, I told you he was special," Raven said.

Emotions surged through Maia – astonishment, disbelief, rage, then finally, understanding.

"You said he was dead!"

Her cry thundered around the factory.

231

"I did, didn't I?" Raven was unperturbed. "You know why. I had to wait until his family was safely smuggled out of the country. I used a bit of glamour on another body to fool poor *Blossom*. Believe me, I'm more afraid of what she'll say to me when she finds out."

Maia realised that her mouth was hanging open and hurriedly shut it. A voice she'd never thought to hear again sounded from below.

"Greetings, *Tempest*! Requesting permission to come aboard."

If she'd still been flesh, she would have been a mess. As it was, she took a moment to gather her scattered wits.

"Welcome back, Captain Plinius!"

Then he was in front of her, smiling. She was aware that Leo, Danuco and Vulcan had joined them, but she only had eyes for her first Captain.

"Hello, *Tempest*."

She saw the tears in his brown eyes and knew that he was struggling to contain his emotions too.

"Captain!" It came out between a sob and a laugh. He took her hands in his own.

"I'm glad to be back and yes, before you ask, *Blossom* knows."

His eyes slid sideways to where Raven was standing and he leaned forward to whisper.

"She's not very happy with a certain person. Can't imagine why."

"Me neither. Where have you been?"

He straightened up, very much the dignified Captain once more.

"Hidden away in a safe house. Believe me, I would rather have been with you all, and I'm sorry for what you had to go through, but I was knocked out by the blast. The next thing I knew, I was elsewhere. Magic, eh? I've been sitting twiddling my thumbs for far too long."

"I offered to get him to Gaul, but he refused." Raven's dry voice interrupted.

"My family are well cared for, and I know my duty," Plinius said, reprovingly. Raven merely nodded.

"We're glad to have you back, Captain," Leo said.

He moved a little closer to Maia and she wondered whether he was just a tiny bit jealous of her reaction. Vulcan was standing to one side observing the mortals with benevolent interest, but now he cut in.

"I'm delighted at this happy reunion, but you have a craft to test! Unfortunately, I am needed elsewhere at this time. Captain Valerius, it's up to you and your Ship now."

"Thank you, sir. It's a shame you can't accompany us. Gentlemen, I suggest we go inside for a moment and get our coats. It's going to be very chilly up here soon. *Tempest*, make preparations."

The salute was automatic, as was the order.

"All hands to stations! All hands to stations!"

Vulcan and her officers promptly departed, Plinius with another smile in her direction, though Raven remained.

"Are you staying with me?" she asked.

The Master Mage sighed.

"I'm sorry, Maia, but I can't accompany you. My place now is with Pendragon as he prepares for battle."

"Oh."

That was an unpleasant surprise. Truly, she'd never imagined that he would leave her. Over the years she'd come to think of him as her special guardian and mentor, always there by her side. He'd even mutilated himself to save her.

"I have to think of Britannia," he said, gently. "If it was my choice, I would stay."

"I understand."

She was a fully armed AirShip, not a lost foundling child. This would be the first of many partings and, she told herself sternly, it wasn't like she wouldn't see him again, whatever came to pass.

"You have two Captains, two Mages and the Gods on your side," he remarked. "You don't need me."

"No, I don't suppose I do."

Even as she said it, she knew it was a lie. Some part of her did need him. Why, she couldn't explain, not even to herself. The bond between them was too strong.

"You can keep me updated through our link."

"Likewise."

She stared down at the scurrying figures moving towards her mooring cables.

"You'd better go then. I'm about to cast off."

"Good luck!"

He paused and, for a second, she thought he was about to add something. It was only when she turned to check that she saw that he had vanished, undetected even by her Ship senses.

"To you, too," she whispered. As always, the irritating old bird had had the last word.

Alone once more, she turned her face skywards, noting the thickening cloud that was creeping over the blue of the summer's day. She had the feeling that there would be more stormy weather to come before long. Hopefully, she wouldn't be on the receiving end.

Her respite was only for a few moments. It was up to her now to charge her engines with Potentia as she had been taught, ready to make her first real flight. Orders flew as her crew rushed to their posts and she prepared to cast off her mooring cables. It felt strange to have the air push around her hull instead of the constant motion of the sea, though she could still sense the pressure of the moving currents as she swayed and bobbed.

Maia scanned her vessel, noting the orderly way her crew went about their business. Having no quarterdeck to stand on, Leo, Amphicles and Plinius had taken up position centrally, where they would have a good view of operations. All were wearing their new uniforms with pride. Musca was checking his guns and the marines were stationed alongside the weapons ports, muskets at the ready. Osric stood within hearing distance of Leo, his face impassive as usual. He'd given no hint of what he thought about his new posting and Maia wasn't going to ask.

Robin and Heron were inspecting the dials and gauges that told them how much Potentia she needed to use, as well as other things such as height and speed. She would have to keep close watch on the helium level and her batteries, to make sure that she wasn't underfeeding or overloading them. Enough air had to be heated without taking them to dangerous altitude. Vulcan had explained that if they went too high, there was a danger of ice and the mechanisms would seize up.

She checked below. Smoke was still rising from the latest of Danuco's sacrifices to Jupiter and she could only hope that the King of the Gods was pleased by their efforts. Having Vulcan and Minerva as their patrons didn't hurt either. She didn't know who or what the Fae worshipped. Perhaps they thought they were the Gods and had no need for protective deities? Whatever, she had to put her faith in the Olympians, as well as any other Powers friendly to the human inhabitants of Britannia. There were certainly enough local Gods who might lend their aid and support. She sent up a few general prayers to any who might be listening and focused her will on her engines, building up the store of Potentia.

As she felt the air in the envelopes above her begin to heat, she addressed Leo.

"Captain, ready to cast off."

A surge of excitement sped through the link.

"Acknowledged, *Tempest*. Order the ground crew to release the cables. We'll ascend to eight hundred feet, heading nor' nor' west."

"Aye, sir! Sending the command to the ground now."

It was impossible to miss the flickers of worry from her crew, so she did her best to sound confident and in control. Gone were her rigging and sails. Instead she had propellers and a dozen other devices to take into consideration. What did it matter that there was no ocean? She would soar on currents of air.

Maia projected her voice to the men below, who promptly rushed to untether her from the huge iron rings embedded in the concrete of her mooring area. This was a well-rehearsed and crucial part of the operation. All had to be done simultaneously or it could damage her vessel. She guided them through it, retaining her mental hold on her mooring ropes so that they wouldn't slip at an inopportune moment and sighing with relief when she felt their hold loosen. Maia drew them in as quickly as she could, feeling them twist and squirm up to her lower deck where they would rest like sleeping snakes until she had need of them again. The sensation was nothing like the slow measured weighing of anchor, though the sudden awareness of freedom was the same. Being tethered could be a comfort, but sometimes she simply wanted to launch herself into the unknown with all its attendant joys and perils.

"Untethering accomplished, Captain. Beginning ascent."

"Very good, *Tempest*. Moving to the observation platform now."

He wasn't going to miss the view. Amphicles and Plinius followed him as she stood ready to relay any orders he might give. Heron had promised to rig up a clear shield of some special glass-like material to keep the worst of the weather from the small space when he had more time, as it would be cold and windy if they went very high.

Everyone else was adjusting to the new situation. Danuco's lips were moving, Robin and Heron were busy checking the machinery and Osric was watching his men for any sign of sickness. She hoped they would have a smooth ride, or they would all need Raven's Magic Drops. Presumably they worked for air travel as well as a sea voyage.

She rose higher, already calculating her course and speed against all the various factors she now had to take into consideration. In some ways this vessel was far more manoeuvrable than her ocean vessel, being able to turn on the spot. Below her, the waving figures dwindled into mere dots as she climbed, constantly referring to the dials until she could get a sense of her new three-dimensional reality. In time she'd be able to rely on them less, but for now they were a necessary aid.

To her relief, the sky had cleared somewhat and there was even a hint of sunlight as the clouds began to break. As if on cue, a little breeze sprang up, pushing her on her desired course.

Mother, is that you?

The pressure on her hull increased a little and she smiled. There were more ways to communicate than mere words and Aura's presence was a blessing, though she had to remind herself not to become complacent. The Fae could work the weather too and had many powerful Mages at their disposal. It was more than possible that their Potentia could eclipse that of one minor Goddess.

She thrust her fears away, concentrating on her tasks and the new routine of charging her engines with measured doses of Potentia.

Slowly at first but with increasing speed, she achieved the designated height, orienting the bow and propelling herself onwards to where her sisters were waiting. Her belly full of weapons and her crew on alert, Maia could only pray that she reached them in time.

XIII

The trip through the portal was uneventful.

Cei had half-expected there to be some sort of delay, but everything went smoothly. He was passed from one set of Mages to another quickly and efficiently, relieved that Raven had given him his tonic against sickness or the welcome parties would have been treated to the sight of a royal prince spewing up his guts every single time. He only hoped that he would have enough of the potion to last through the transition from sea to land, as the nausea always took a few days to subside.

On his arrival it was already early evening, and the sun was beginning to dip toward the horizon. He took a moment to admire the skill that had set him down just before his command post, a large tent with the Pendragon banner rippling above it. Another stood to one side, the painted eagle's outstretched wings seeming to flap in the breeze above symbols of divinity. That was puzzling. Nobody had mentioned the return of the Imperial Governor, and as the man had fled at the first sign of trouble he hadn't really been expecting it, but there was obviously some representative of the Emperor here. It was good that he was lending some support now that Marcus's treachery had been fully exposed. Losing Britannia would be a blow to the Empire, so it made sense that he would finally get involved. Cei wasn't expecting a vast force to come to his aid, but it would be interesting to see who had arrived.

As he'd expected, familiar faces were there to greet him. Some he knew only through brief meetings and by reputation,

238

though the senior general who saluted him was known to all. Titus Aelius Felicio had been *dux* of the Britannic army for several years and had been a friend of his brother, Julius. They'd grown close, even though Felicio wasn't from the upper strata of society, his father having been a freedman. He'd worked his way up through the ranks through merit and Julius had recognised that, taking his part and advising their father to promote the young soldier. Just seeing Felicio made Cei half-expect his brother to appear, clapping them both on the back and demanding to know the day's news.

Damn it Julius! You should have been here!

The bitter grief at his brother's senseless death still had the power to catch him unawares, but now was not the time. Still, he could see the knowledge of it in Felicio's eyes as the man snapped to attention, or was it thinly veiled pity? No, he had to be imagining things; the man was a professional to his core and there was no emotion on that blunt face. Wind and weather had taken its toll on them both, the grey hairs and wrinkles mute testament to lives in service.

"Aelius Felicio, it's good to see you! I trust everything is in order?"

Faded blue eyes met his. "It is, sir. We've assembled everyone we could. Some are still on their way in and I'm glad to say that troops have arrived from the continent with the Lady Drusilla."

Cei nodded.

"Where is the lady now?"

"She insisted on staying with the troops, sir. Her tent's the red one, flying the eagle above the banners of Minerva and Diana."

Cei couldn't hide his surprise. An army camp wasn't the place for an aristocratic lady, even with protections.

"She's here representing the Emperor?"

Felicio's mouth quirked.

"Oh yes. Imperial Governor in all but name. You haven't seen her shock troops yet, sir. She's brought Amazons and Centaurs."

Now that was different. He'd heard of the skilled warriors, naturally, but they worked as mercenaries and usually confined their operations to the east. Looking to where Felicio indicated, he could see the tent surrounded by concentric rings of horses being tended to by their riders. The Amazons wouldn't have come cheap, but from what he knew of her, Drusilla's family had money to spare and vested interests to protect in Britannia. Senator Rufus's family was powerful enough to buy an army, and from what he was seeing, they had.

Speaking of the lady, he could see her approaching him – carried in a litter guarded by two heavily-armed Centaurs of all things – and flanked by Amazons. Just behind her, he could glimpse Favonius the spymaster, though what influence he had left now was debatable. Cei could only hope that he had some Agents left who had survived Marcus's purge.

"Ah, here she is now."

Felicio raised an eyebrow, but refrained from commenting. Cei got the impression that his general shared his views and could only hope that she hadn't been trying to advise him on tactics. The slaves set the litter down in a set of practised movements, then one parted the curtains to allow Drusilla to emerge. She wasn't wearing armour, but a subtle shimmer around her silks told him that she had more potent protections in place, as did he. There had been one too many assassinations lately, and he wouldn't put it past the enemy to try something similar again.

As always, Antonia Drusilla was immaculately dressed, her sharp, patrician features emphasised by skilled application of face paint and her dark eyes rimed with kohl. She could have been a statue of a Goddess in her temple. The only concession she had made to the Britannic climate was the sturdy, yet fashionable pair of boots she was wearing, all the better to negotiate rough ground if she absolutely had to. This was not the time to wear dainty shoes.

The Centaurs shifted their hooves, never taking their eyes from their surroundings. Both were male, heavily bearded and armed with muskets and pistols. The Amazons preferred long *spathas*, or cavalry swords, together with bows and arrows. They disdained black powder weapons as cumbersome and too awkward to use. Legend said Centaurs could shoot out a gnat's eye at forty paces and, seeing them in the flesh for the first time, Cei didn't think it was much of an exaggeration.

240

His observations over in a second, he fixed on Drusilla, as she swept an elegant curtsy.

"Your Highness."

He held out his hand and assisted her to rise.

"Lady Drusilla."

So, she was sticking to rigid protocol, though some still insisted on calling him Sire as if it was a done deal that Excalibur would choose him. Felicio had also been considerate in that matter. He was happy to be addressed as sir or Admiral, and he resolved to make his wishes known. Only the sword had the power to choose the King of the Britons, though the actual pulling out had never been done since Artorius the Great's time. The succession had never been contested. It was only now that it was in deadly earnest.

"Lady Drusilla. It's good to see you again, though the circumstances are not those I would have wished for. My deepest condolences on the death of Senator Rufus. I assure you that I shall do all in my power to avenge him."

Poised as ever, Drusilla inclined her head.

"Thank you, sir. I, too, intend to avenge the murder of my beloved husband. To that end, I have brought the best troops money can buy and cyclops-made cannons. They are at your disposal. If there is anything else that is within my power to accomplish, I will strive to do it."

Her measured words almost led him to miss the flash of rage in her eye that would have done credit to a Fury. This was a woman who would not be swayed one iota from her mission to destroy the one who had betrayed them all. She could have been receiving him into a dinner party rather than standing in the midst of battle lines.

"I give thanks to the Gods that you have brought such aid," he said, feeling as always somewhat provincial next to her Roman speech and manners. "Please, will you dine with me tonight?"

It was only to be expected that he would entertain her. He sensed Felicio's disapproval but they would have enough time to talk tactics before dinner, and starving themselves wouldn't benefit anyone.

"I would be honoured, sir."

"The commanders of your troops are also invited," he added.

It made sense to meet the leaders of the mercenaries, both Centaurs and Amazons and to know something of the people he was fighting alongside. Once again, he wished he was at sea. He knew the strengths of every Captain and Ship, but here he felt like the rawest midshipman on his first assignment. This would give him the opportunity to listen to more experienced heads and eating would mean that he wouldn't have to sit there like a cabbage. It also meant that Drusilla wouldn't be the only woman present, though they would have to make allowances for the Centaurs.

"Most gracious, sir. The seventh hour?"

It was the best time. This wouldn't be an all-night event.

"Excellent. Until then."

She curtseyed once more, then returned to her litter. Favonius was waiting to one side and Cei waved him forward. The Agent looked much as usual, though there was evidence that he had just shaved off a beard, presumably grown as a disguise. A light cloak was draped around his shoulders despite the warmth of the day, all the better to conceal weapons and other devices about his person.

"Master Favonius. I am pleased to see that you escaped unharmed."

The Agent bowed. "The Gods favoured me, Sire, though many of my people were less fortunate. I have a report for you on the current situation."

Cei had expected no less. The man was always prepared, though even he could not have foreseen the calamities that Marcus's treachery had brought upon them all. From what he knew of the man, he probably berated himself about it day and night.

"I'll have it now," he said, wanting to get as much of a grip on the situation as he could in the shortest time possible. "We'll return to the command tent."

Favonius nodded briefly, falling into line behind Cei and his bodyguard. Once in the shade, Cei dismissed the guards and gestured for wine for Felicio, who was sticking to his side like a burr, the Chief Agent and himself.

"That will be all," he told the slave, who exited, leaving the three of them staring into their wine cups. Cei roused himself to propose the toast.

"To Jupiter, Best and Greatest, and to Mars, Lord of Battle! May they grant us a swift victory!"

Felicio took a good swallow and the others made haste to follow his example. Cei thought of sitting, but decided against it. He was used to standing on deck for long periods, and could think better on his feet.

"Sit, please." He waved them to seats. "Believe me, I'm happier standing."

Felicio planted his feet squarely. "Thank you sir, but the same here."

Favonius made no move to sit either, so Cei gave up.

"Very well, gentlemen. I've been told that the auguries are good and a Fae victory is the last thing Olympus wants. Now, Favonius, what have you got for me?"

"A mixed bag, sir."

It was indeed a mixed bag. The carefully-constructed network had been shattered and Agents largely left to their own devices. Cei listened, saving his questions until the end, whilst the furrows in Felicio's forehead deepened.

"So, you're left with a few, many are missing and others are presumed dead?"

"We were infiltrated, sir. Shapeshifting Fae. We are woefully lacking in devices against them, though some have been sourced since."

"What happened to them?" Felicio asked.

Favonius waved a hand.

"Killed as soon as they were exposed, but we don't know how many escaped beforehand. One thing's sure. They have intelligence on our strengths and know how to exploit our weaknesses."

"Yes, well. Maybe we can exploit theirs. We have new technology that can help, especially at sea and the Mage-Artificers are working night and day."

"The reinforcements will help, sir, but how we'll do in a pitched battle is anyone's guess," Favonius said.

Cei fixed the Spymaster with a look that had made veteran Captains quail.

"We have divine aid on our side, trained legions, cavalry, Amazons, Centaurs and presumably anyone who can pick up a pitchfork. Don't turn anyone away. If I have to, I'll fight alongside Clubmen and local militia. What about the Britannic Gods?"

"You'll have to speak to the Priests about them, sir. I have intelligence that Aquila has left Londin to join us, bringing many of his people. There will be prayers to every deity we can think of who has an interest in this, including the native ones, though they're more unpredictable. Some Lesser Fae may aid us. I understand that they have no wish to live under the rule of their more powerful cousins either."

Cei nodded. Many a farmer had a brownie under the same roof, classed along with the household Lares or a guardian dryad in a wood. Springs, ponds and wells had their naiads. Others, such as black dogs and boundary spirits were less friendly, but might defend their territory. He wouldn't like to bet on which would actively help.

"We'll have to presume that many will be neutral," he conceded. As Favonius had said, that was one for the Priests.

He rubbed his eyes, suddenly weary.

"I need to see the deployment, then get ready for this meal."

Felicio, at a loss with talk of Fae and spirits, was only too eager to oblige. They left the tent for the second time and walked a short distance to the highest point from where Cei could have a clearer view. He was pleased to see that defences had been dug around the perimeter and a palisade hastily thrown up, in traditional Roman fashion. To the rear, the artillery were already in position, the huge metal cannons lying quietly on their carriages like dormant beasts ready to awaken at a moment's notice. They dwarfed the ones Ships deployed, their size and weight governed only by the ability to haul them over distance. The crews were camped behind them, stores of powder and shot constantly guarded against sabotage.

"It all seems in order."

Felicio grinned without mirth.

"We're ready for them, sir. Cyclops do good work and these beauties can fire the new exploding shot up to three miles away. Hopefully we'll blow the creatures to pieces even before they get to us."

He spoke with a confidence Cei didn't feel.

"Don't bank on it. They've developed strong shields, resistant to metal projectiles. Even my Ships couldn't smash through them – that's how *Tempest* lost her vessel. We can't rely on them causing any damage."

Felicio was silent for a few moments, though Cei could imagine the curses running through his mind.

"Then we'll smash the ground around them," he answered. "They'll find it harder to move through a shattered field and, at the very least, it will distract them."

Cei's vision blurred. He blinked away the moisture, keeping his face still. He'd be damned if he'd ruin his reputation for stoicism in the face of adversity. That was Felicio all over, always finding the nugget of gold in the dung heap. His general was the perfect counterbalance to his more pessimistic nature. If they got through this, he knew who he wanted at his side and all the useless aristocrats and senators could go to Hades with his boot up their arses.

"Well said, General. We'll give them something to think about, all right, magical shields or no magical shields."

He held out his arm. Surprise swept over Felicio's face, then he grasped it in the greeting of equals.

"You do me too much honour, sir. We haven't won yet!"

Cei smiled at him.

"We will if you have anything to do with it. You're too stubborn to do anything else!"

"Guilty as charged, sir."

Cei gave his forearm a final squeeze before releasing it.

"Now, let's have a look at the rest of the army, shall we?"

They surveyed the camp together, Cei dredging up what he remembered from his schooling on military tactics. He thought ruefully that Caesar's Gallic Wars wouldn't be much help in this situation, but even he could see that they'd camped on the best land available. In the infantry sections, the rows of eight man leather tents had formed a new township stretching a good way into the distance, wreathed in smoke from each *contubernium*'s cooking fires.

The horse lines also seemed to be in good order, though he could have wished there were more of them. Britannic cavalry units were renowned for their speed and manoeuvrability, though how the animals would hold up against a non-human enemy was an unknown factor. Now all they could do was wait for intelligence on the Fae's movements and ready themselves for the inevitable clash.

Felicio took him through the salient points, then they parted company to prepare for the evening. The tent was being reconfigured with an open end to accommodate their Centaur guests, who would eat standing up, and to extend the space so that everyone in a position of authority would have a seat. Cei's private space was blocked off and his servants were waiting with hot water.

He suffered their ministrations, inwardly reviewing everything Felicio had told him. Even he knew that a pitched battle in the open was their best shot. The cavalry could deploy over the ground and move at speed and the artillery could see what they were aiming at. The worst scenario was that there would be a night attack. He wasn't sure whether the Fae could see in the dark, but they certainly preferred twilight. The Gods grant that his scouts would provide warning.

Cei forced his racing mind to calm. This meal was more for diplomacy and morale than anything else, something he was well practised in. Centaurs and Amazons were something new, though he was well acquainted with Master Pholus, the Chief Naval Architect. Somehow he thought that his continental brethren would be different, possibly more warlike. He'd have to keep the Centaurs away from the alcohol. History was full of warnings about their lack of tolerance to wine and spirits and it wouldn't do to have a drunken rampage on his hands and to have to shoot a few. As to Amazons, they could probably drink everyone under the table.

He waved away the scent bottles and hair pomade. Being clean was good enough for him and he was well-used to lacking the luxury of a bath. Ships weren't the most fragrant places and the ever-present stench of hemp, tar and seawater had become the smell of home after so many years. Soil and grass just weren't the same.

His thoughts returned to his fleet. He'd left Teg the monkey in the care of the *Victoria*'s crew and he was already missing him. It wouldn't have been fair to bring the little fellow to a battlefield. His musings were interrupted as a freedman entered and bowed before him.

"The guests are assembling, Highness."

Cei struggled for a second to remember his name.

"Thank you, Luccio."

He'd been so abstracted that he was only now hearing the murmur of voices and the sound of movement beyond the heavy curtaining. Despite his lack of appetite, the smell of the food caused his stomach to rumble. He cursed silently as a gold-embroidered cloak was draped and pinned around his shoulders, elaborate dragon brooches winking at him with tiny ruby eyes. Not for him a simple naval uniform. Here and now he had to look like a king, even though his whole nature revolted against it.

The gold laurel crown was placed on his brow, its weight transforming him into the very image of a royal commander. Legend claimed that it had been worn by Artorius Magnus himself. Cei could only pray that some of his ancestor's luck and courage had remained within it, to rub off on his descendant.

It was time for the play to start. He lifted his chin and strode out to meet his audience.

They were waiting for him, standing respectfully as he took his place at the head of the low table, next to Lady Drusilla. Cei was surprised to see that couches had been procured from somewhere, making the scene even more reminiscent of some ancient time. The nagging feeling that he'd somehow ended up in another person's life threatened to overwhelm him before he forced himself back to the here and now.

All bowed their heads before taking their seats, or, in the Centaur's case, moving up to his high manger. There was only one, whom Cei presumed to be their commander. Drusilla made the introductions, speaking Latin so that all would understand her.

"Prince Cei, may I present Ophion, son of Amychus, leader of the Centaurii."

Like all centaurs Ophion was heavily bearded, with wide-set eyes and skin like leather. His horse part was covered in shaggy hair, more like a stocky mountain pony than a thoroughbred and probably twice as durable. Cei was used to Pholus, but here was a warrior. His torso and flanks bore the scars of battle, earned across the Empire wherever his patrons ordered him to fight. For now, Drusilla was paying and he would remain loyal to their contract. He bowed from the waist respectfully.

"Dioxippe, Xanthe and Laomache, of the tribe of Amazons." The women nodded, their eyes watchful. They too were on the payroll. Cei wished that he had more Britannic troops, but every addition to their forces was welcome and had to be treated with respect, even mercenaries for hire to the highest bidder.

"I bid you all welcome," he said. "Please, begin."

He gestured to the laden table, then helped himself to various dishes. The Centaur plunged his hands into the manger, grabbing handfuls of mashed grain and cramming them into his mouth. He chewed with stolid determination and Cei forced himself not to stare. It was a strange cross between how a human and a horse ate, Ophion's physiognomy being a mixture of both. The Amazons waited for a nod from their leader, Dioxippe, before selecting their favourites. Drusilla opened the conversation.

"I was telling our esteemed warriors about the nature of the foe we face, as far as we understand them," she said.

Cei dipped his bread in the garum sauce. "We don't know as much as we would like," he admitted. Dioxippe shrugged.

"If they can die, we will kill them," she said. Her Latin had a Greek accent, mixed with a trace of something more exotic. It was probably her third language. Her black hair was plaited against her skull and pulled into a braid, though her two companions wore theirs short. They looked to be in their late twenties or thirties and would have been trained in warfare from the age they could pick up a weapon.

"I understand they are magical creatures." Ophion said. His voice had a high edge to it, almost but not quite a whinny, which seemed at odds with his rugged appearance.

"They have certain abilities," Felicio agreed, "though we have battle Mages that can counter their attacks."

There was no doubt in his general's voice and Cei was quick to back him up.

"It has been many years since they tried to take this land and we have a few surprises in store for them."

"We have heard of your new weapons." Dioxippe took a good swig of wine, smacking her lips in appreciation. "Are they also powered by women with Potentia?"

"You mean, are they like our Ships? Some are."

He wasn't going to show his hand too soon, besides which the *Tempest* was on her way to support her sisters. With the Gods' blessing, he could direct her in as backup as soon as the battle at sea was done. Reports were coming in hourly, but as yet they hadn't engaged the enemy fleet. Being hit simultaneously at sea and on land was a blow, but it was what it was.

"Our Potentia comes from the Goddesses," Xanthe said, "especially the Huntress. We will sacrifice to her and the Mother before we fight."

"Yes, it is one of the reasons we are here," Dioxippe added. She leaned forward. "Our Queen had a message in a dream. We are to lend our strength to yours. It is the will of the Gods."

There was total certainty in her voice. Cei felt the hairs prickle on the back of his neck.

"And the pay is good." Ophion's comment brought them all back to earth. The Amazons raised their glasses and even Felicio had to smile.

"The favour of the Gods cannot be bought," the general said. "We have had omens as well. Olympus is ordering us to put down this scourge once and for all."

"That is true," Drusilla said. "And, begging your pardon Prince Cei, the Furies do not look lightly upon murderers."

Cei forced himself to swallow his food past the sudden constriction in his throat. He couldn't afford to show any weakness here, but it took all his self-control to speak evenly.

"My son murdered his cousin the King, your husband the Senator, allied himself with the enemy and is doubtless plotting to kill me too. He deserves everything the Gods have planned for him."

"May his name be forever cursed," Felicio said.

The Amazons busied themselves with eating, all too aware that this was a family tragedy as well as a matter of national importance. Ophion looked down on them all, stuffing his mouth with hay. The sound of his jaws and the flapping of the canvas was the only sound in the tent for several heartbeats.

"The enemy and their allies are doubly damned," Drusilla said at last. "All who fight will be richly rewarded."

"That's what I like to hear!" Dioxippe said briskly. "And all in the service of the Gods."

She grinned around at the company. "It will be a legendary battle. I can't wait!"

A servant refilled their glasses as Cei smiled graciously. He'd already had enough of bloody legends to last several lifetimes and dreaded what the morning would bring.

Damn Marcus, damn the Fae and damn himself if he couldn't put a stop to this before everything fell to ruin.

*

The wind had got up in the night. In the liminal place between sleep and waking, Cei thought himself back aboard the *Augusta*, her canvas snapping around him as she caught a sudden gust. Then his eyes opened to darkness and he remembered.

His beloved Ship was dead and he was in a tent. A couple of pegs must have come loose, as it had been the sound of hammering that had woken him, the dull thunk of wood on wood penetrating his restless dreams. He gazed dully at the striped cloth, his body trying to adjust automatically for the movement of a vessel. Sitting up led to a wave of nausea. Cursing under his breath he reached for the little bottle by his bed and took a gulp, then lay down and waited for the worst to subside.

It wasn't yet dawn, though he had no way of knowing the exact hour. Maybe he would have a little time to himself before the demands of the day overtook him. Last night, the business-like attitude of the foreigners had been impressive. They were no rabble of money-grubbing hirelings but a hardened battle force and Drusilla had been well-advised to choose them. It wasn't that he felt optimistic, more that his pessimism had subsided a little.

"Sir?"

It was Felicio, waiting respectfully on the other side of the curtain. So much for having even a minute to himself. It had to be later than he'd thought.

"I'm awake, Felicio."

"It's a quarter to three, sire. Our scouts have reported a force of approximately five thousand Fae approaching from the west."

So, they were counting on a pre-dawn attack. The longer days weren't favouring the enemy, but waiting for autumn hadn't been an option.

"On foot?"

"Some. Others are riding what could loosely be described as horses. They have four legs anyway and our men didn't want to get any closer to say exactly. They're about five miles away and setting up camp. More are coming from that damned portal, which is why these ones seem to be waiting."

Cei rubbed a hand over his face, feeling the sharp stab of bristles.

"Have we had reinforcements?"

"Some of the Third arrived in the night, but not as many as we'd hoped."

That was unwelcome news.

"I see. Any news on Marcus?"

"As far as we know, he's still holed up in Greenfields."

Disgust rose in Cei's breast, like a bitter taste that would never leave him. His son couldn't even lead his own troops like a commander should. For a second, the thought crossed his mind that his real son could have been stolen away at birth, replaced by a changeling creature beholden to the enemy. There seemed no other way to explain his treachery, both to his family and his people. Oddly enough, the idea comforted him. In some parts of the land, folk still left knives in cradles and hammered horseshoes over doorways. Perhaps they had the right of it and he should have been more superstitious. Anyway, it was too late now. He gathered his wits. Movement around him told him his servants were hovering.

"I see."

"Also, Raven is here."

Now that was better news.

"Excellent! Send him in."

The General's footfalls retreated and Cei resigned himself to the inevitable. The only saving grace he could see was that he was unlikely to meet his cowardly son on the field of battle. He didn't have long to dwell on this thought before Raven appeared.

"Well, Master Mage, how goes the fight? Please, take a seat while I prepare. Bring a chair and refreshments!"

His attendants scuttled to obey, eyeing the wizened figure with barely concealed awe. Raven thanked them and settled himself down, accepting a goblet of wine.

"Our young lady has adapted well, sir. I have high hopes for her efficacy in battle, but only time will tell."

Cei grunted in agreement as his barber lathered his chin.

"Any other news?"

"I found a few stragglers who'd had the wit to conceal themselves from Marcus's purge, both Mages and Adepts. They're in the camp now."

"How many?" Cei earned a sharp look from his barber. "Sorry, Commius."

"I would prefer not to cut you, sir."

"Indeed, my apologies."

"Twelve Adepts and six Mages. I wish there were more, but too many are unaccounted for. And…" he added, before Cei could speak again and jeopardise a layer of skin, "others may yet turn up. Unfortunately, I suspect that Kite has seduced too many with the promise of power and enhanced abilities."

The thought that Britannic Mages would be fighting against their own people sickened him. If they got though this, he'd make an example of them that would be remembered for two thousand years. Such treachery had never happened before, at least not to his knowledge. It had to be something to do with the dilution of immortal blood and the subsequent diminution of Potentia. There were always fools who wanted more and would do anything to get it. Furthermore, using women as Ships had removed their abilities from the population, but it had been a price his ancestors had been willing to pay for the benefits they gained. Moreover, women were much less likely to want to leave their children and forcing them wouldn't have worked. It was the main reason they tried to find their candidates while they were still young.

They both waited for Commius to finish his task. One last scrape and he was clean shaven again. Maybe, if the war continued, he'd grow a beard to save himself the trouble of this daily ritual.

"Thank you Commius. Leave us."

He waited until he was alone with the Master Mage. The old man was picking at some bread and cheese.

"Tell me, where is Julia? Surely she can't stay in the Heart of Albion for long?"

"As I said before, she's fine," Raven assured him. "You know I would never willingly put her in danger. Surely you wouldn't want her here? Believe me, she's better off where she is."

It was something, he supposed. He trusted Raven implicitly, and if the old man said his niece was protected, he'd have to accept it, for now. He had enough to be dealing with. There was another question he had to ask, of equal importance.

"Can you get me to Londin? You know I need to try for Excalibur."

Raven took a few moments to finish his mouthful.

"I can't, sir. Believe me, I have my reasons and they're good ones."

"Then tell me!" Cei's rage and frustration bubbled beneath the surface. "How am I expected to go into battle without it? Even Artorius would have been defeated without its power!"

He kept his voice low, but the sudden change in air pressure told him that Raven had raised a barrier to prevent them being overheard.

"The reason is simple. The sword stuck in the Basilica isn't Excalibur."

Cei's heart plummeted. Were the very foundations of his dynasty a lie? This couldn't be true. Every sovereign since Artorius had worn the damned thing at some point in their lives. It had been a symbol of power and strength in Britannia for hundreds of years. There could only be one explanation.

"You mean it's another fake?" His voice sounded like it was coming from someone else.

"Oh no, it's not a fake. It's the actual sword that Artorius pulled from the stone to claim the kingdom," Raven replied, cheerfully. "But Excalibur – Caledfwlch – was always something

253

else. It was only lent to him and, when he died, it had to be given back."

"Why don't I know this?"

"Because Merlin went to a lot of trouble to ensure that nobody remembered. He told me, of course. I've known him for centuries."

Cei could only stare in disbelief. He was in a legendary tale, after all.

"Gods grant me strength!"

"Indeed. But this has little to do with Olympus."

"So where is Excalibur, then?" Cei demanded, "And why don't I have it?"

"It was never meant for you. It is to be wielded by another and he's on his way. I fear that you're in for a few surprises, Cei Pendragon. The world is not quite what you thought it to be."

"Then I'm not destined to be King?"

He felt a stab of guilt that he was happy at the thought.

Raven shrugged. "That is for the Sword of Kingship to decide, not you or I. Possibly, possibly not. A *dux bellorum* isn't always a king, you know."

"And Merlin? Is he here also?"

If the greatest Mage of all was suddenly to appear, they had a chance. He'd beaten their enemy before and the Fae would remember. His rising hopes foundered when Raven sighed and shook his head.

"No. He has laid down his burden and departed for the Summer Lands. We will see him no more. He has, however, left a successor. A Mage of great power, called Owl. This Mage is accompanying the wielder of Excalibur, but you must say nothing to anyone yet."

Cei took a deep breath.

"Have you anything else, or is that it? Not that I'm ungrateful, but I would have liked to know all this sooner."

Raven pursed his lips. "I didn't know all this myself. It's a recent development."

"You knew about Excalibur!"

The Mage shrugged. "Well, yes, but I don't go around telling everyone state secrets, even you."

254

He cocked his head, listening intently to something Cei couldn't hear.

"And now you must get ready. I'll leave you to your ablutions, and go and supervise the Mages. I want to whip up something nasty to greet our unwanted visitors."

"I suppose you must. Send in my attendants on the way out, will you?"

Raven rose, bowed and left, his spell dissipating with an audible pop.

Still dazed, Cei permitted his attendants to strap on the protective lightweight armour that had been newly-made to his measurements. He could sense the Potentia in it – nothing but the best for him. He'd been told that three Mages had worked on it for hours, though his men would have to protect themselves with standard-issue enchanted gear. Gods, but he wished Excalibur was already here. Who could have claimed it? He couldn't help but hope that whoever it was would take this responsibility from him. Then there was the Sword of Kingship, as Raven had named it. Quite frankly, he would be delighted for a cowherd to pull the thing out if it meant he could return to his Ships.

Dressing done, he marched through the curtain to find breakfast laid out for him. He forced himself to take a few bites of bread and sips of watered wine. It wouldn't do to feel faint, even though his stomach was telling him intermittently that he was on a rolling deck. Still chewing, he waited for his advisers to report back and hoped that his innards wouldn't rebel. Between them and his new-found knowledge, his mind was in a whirl.

It wasn't long before Felicio returned, sombre-faced officers at his side. Talk immediately turned to deployment, tactics and the evacuation of civilians. The Gods alone knew how many had already fallen to the cruel enemy, slaughtered, or worse still, captured. Better broken bodies than broken minds, lost in mazes of the Fae's devising. Another reason to defeat them utterly.

Urgent voices outside led to the admittance of a scout in dun-coloured clothes, dirty and dishevelled from spending days and nights in the field. He snapped to attention before them, the lamplight accentuating the lines of strain on his unshaven face.

"Scout Ramio reporting, Sire. The enemy have settled in the forest just over three miles away."

Cei forced himself to nod impassively. For the moment, they were out of range of the cannon. The artillery would have to wait a while.

"And the portal?"

The scout twitched, as if the memory of what he'd seen was hard to bear.

"Fully open, Sire. There were Fae and other things we couldn't guess at. We only caught a glimpse before we had to run."

"There were more of you?"

"Three, Sire. I'm the only one that made it."

Ramio stared straight ahead, but Cei knew that whatever the man had seen would haunt him for the rest of his days.

"They will be remembered and their families, if they had them, well-compensated, as you will be. You have performed a great service and have my personal thanks. Now get some food into you and rest while you can."

Ramio saluted and left. Cei stared after him for a moment, then came to a decision.

"Gentlemen, I will tour the camp. It seems that there will be no attack for the moment."

It would hearten the men to see him, plus he couldn't stay in this damned tent a moment longer. He knew it was traditional to address the men and he already had some words in mind. If they survived this, some historian would doubtless dress up his speech, adding flowery phrases and sweeping rhetoric worthy of Julius Caesar. He'd be damned if he'd bother. Any battle speech was basically 'kill them before they kill you' and his would be no different.

He exited and waved away the horse that was produced for him. He'd go on foot and look them in the eye as he had always done. A faint glimmer in the east told him that it wouldn't be long before the dawn would appear. For now, torches and lamps would have to light his way.

"Assemble the men while I go for a walk," he told Felicio. The general frowned.

"Is that wise Sire?"

Cei arched a brow at him. "I'll have my bodyguard and I won't have time to go far."

The six hand-picked men had moved up as he spoke, weapons at the ready. He knew that Felicio would only have chosen the best. They didn't have the look of ceremonial soldiers but tough veterans, ready to lay their lives down for their commander. Each had a musket, a pistol and a sword. He nodded to them.

"Let's go."

The ground was damp, but the dew would burn off quickly enough in the summer heat. Although he would have given much for a sea breeze, the future day promised fair and still. Perfect for relaxing by a pool, in solitude, or with friends. Not so much for killing.

As he walked through the camp, legionaries left off their tasks and jumped to attention, standing straight as ramrods. He could greet none by name as their commanders could, but he did his best to project strength and confidence despite the lack of shared experience. His Ships and their crews were far away, facing who knew what dangers as they tried to stop the Fae advancing by sea and every instinct cried out for a report. He couldn't spend time now following their progress, not with the Fae about to advance on their position.

It was but a short circuit of a section of the camp before he had to turn back. The expected dawn attack had not come, maybe because the enemy were still readying their forces. Now they would have to play a waiting game until dusk.

It would be a long wait.

XIV

It was a perfect day for a cruise. The rising sun cast shafts of light on the foaming spray, turning it to jewelled rainbows as HMS *Patience* ploughed her way through the water at full speed. Briseis would have enjoyed the sensation if she hadn't been all too aware of the danger she and her sisters were heading into. Good weather or no, what was waiting for them wouldn't care.

<All Ships, keep formation!>

That was the *Victoria*, relaying orders from Vitalianus, now High Admiral in Pendragon's absence. He was capable enough, though they all missed the sure touch of their former commander. He preferred to delegate to his Ship rather than speaking directly, so it was something they would all have to get used to. She expected that he was probably busy with other matters and coping with his rapid promotion. As to keeping formation, Briseis was doing her best with what she had, but her new vessel didn't have the power of her old one and just couldn't generate as much speed, however much she coaxed it. Some of the rough edges had rubbed away and it no longer felt quite as uncomfortable, but the old *Seashell* still wasn't a patch on her previous housing.

She brushed the irritation away and concentrated on pushing herself to catch up. Her sisters were in a relatively tight grouping, the *Victoria* in the lead, flanked closely by the *Persistence* and *Swiftsure*. The other, larger Ships were shepherding the smaller ones like mother whales with their calves, all on constant alert for any change in sky, wind or water that might give an indication that the enemy was on the horizon. They had rounded the coast of Mona without incident, the dark line of the land to their sinistra side and turned south-west into the open sea.

<*Patience?* Are you managing?>

It was *Blossom*, forging up behind her and clearly concerned.

<I'm having to stretch things a bit,> she admitted, <but I'm fine, honestly. Sandpiper is helping.>

She was fortunate to still have her Mage. Many Ships were still without and most of the inanimates hadn't been able to keep up as it was. They'd have to follow on at their own pace.

<Good.> *Blossom* didn't sound quite convinced. <It won't be for much longer. Did you see the island we passed a few hours ago, off Mona?>

<Yes, I saw it. I don't know much about it.>

<It's the Sacred Isle, a centre of the old Britannic Gods,> *Blossom* explained. <To be honest, some of the stones and burial chambers there are so old nobody really understands what they're about now. Even the names of the Gods are lost. If the Fae make landfall there, they could tap into a lot of Potentia. The Romans did their best to crush the old ways, but something lingers on in that place.>

That didn't sound good.

<Then we have to stop them getting to it.>

<That's the spirit! We can scupper their plans here and give Pendragon a chance to defeat them on land. The poor man must be feeling out of his depth,> she added. <It's hard for a navy man to adjust to land battles. He's had the training and led some coastal skirmishes, but the rest is all theory.>

<If anyone can manage, he can.>

<You're right. He'll –>

<All Ships!>

Their conversation was interrupted by the *Victoria*'s urgent message.

<Eyes ahead, sou' sou' west!>

<It looks like a fog bank,> *Swiftsure* chipped in. <Shouldn't be anything like this this time o' day in these conditions.>

A ripple ran through the link as the implications sank in.

<I've heard that the enemy prefer concealment,> *Victoria* said grimly. <Slacken speed to half. All hands to battle stations!>

259

The preparations had already been made with decks cleared and gear stowed. Briseis opened the link to Fabillus, repeating her orders. He was at her side in an instant, telescope raised.

"It looks like fog alright, but there's something unnatural about it."

He turned to her with a grimace.

"Well, *Patience*, we've done all we can. The new weapons are primed and we're ready with the shields."

"We must pray that the Gods will aid us."

"Indeed. Awstinus is on it now."

A string of orders followed as she ran through her checks one more time. Sandpiper stood ready to augment her defences and the crew obeyed with tight-lipped efficiency. A command prompted her to move to a new position as the Ships formed into line to engage the enemy. At the last moment they would swing and bring their cannons to bear, together with the new weapons as needed. This was standard procedure, though how the Fae would counter this was anyone's guess. They were fighting nothing human here.

All too soon, the great bank of fog blotted out the horizon completely.

<Looks like there's a lot of them if they need that much cover,> *Jasper* muttered.

<More for us to 'ave a go at, then,> *Persistence* answered with relish.

The others, already battered from the serpents and the *Regina*'s attack, said nothing. That one Ship had done enough damage, so what an entire fleet would do didn't bear thinking about. Briseis hoped that she wouldn't be reduced to hand-to-hand fighting, but if she had to, she would. If she had to keep transferring from one vessel to another, so be it. She had sworn long ago to be a faithful servant of the Gods, and now was the time to show that her spirit was strong.

<Sisters! Remember what we're fighting for!>

Surprise rushed through the link. The other Ships weren't used to this new, fierce *Patience*.

<Well said!> The *Victoria* signalled her agreement. <Now, ahead dead slow. We're not to enter the fog if we can help it.>

260

<Aye, let's give 'em a few broadsides from out 'ere!> *Swiftsure* declared.

<They've probably got shields that repel our shot,> *Victoria* warned. <You'll have to deploy the new weapons instead, but be sure of your target! We've only got a limited supply.>

<I know that!>

Briseis tried to pierce the murk with her Shipsenses, but all she could get was the impression of things moving. *Victoria* was right. It would be all too easy to waste ammunition and weapons by firing blindly.

<But if it's moving with them, how will be able to get a range with any accuracy?> *Dragon* demanded, her mental voice tinged with worry. <We're used to being able to see the enemy.>

<I'm relaying that to the Admiral now. Stand by.> *Victoria* answered.

Mutterings rippled through the link.

<Shipsenses blocked, and nothing to see. This isn't good.>

<We should take our chances and fire anyway. If we hit something it might blow holes in this fog.>

<What we'll do is up to our Admiral!> *Blossom* wasn't standing for any nonsense. <You all heard *Victoria*. Stand by!>

It was wise not to be hasty, though Briseis shared her sisters' unease. Maybe their Mages could dispel the unnatural gloom?

Fabillus was squinting ahead. <Any ideas, *Patience*?>

<We're all at a loss, sir.> She hated to admit it, but she was the least experienced of them. <Maybe some of the older Ships will know what to do in this situation?>

<I don't think we've faced this situation, as you put it, before. Monsters, pirates, Northmen, yes. Not this lot.>

Victoria broke into the link once more.

<All Ships! Prepare for intelligence from the *Leopard*!>

What was this? Briseis was momentarily confused before realising that the older Ship must have some resource they didn't know about, perhaps a new device? She'd been quiet for a while, which was unlike her.

<*Leopard* to all Ships. Prepare to receive firing co-ordinates and range!>

<What in the name of the Gods?> *Dragon* couldn't believe her ears. <How can you see anything in this mess?>

<I have my sources. Now trust me and do as you're told!> *Leopard*'s growl was fiercer than usual, forcing *Dragon* to back down hastily.

Briseis's gun crews were already waiting for her instructions. She held her position in the line of battle, Ships before and aft with cannon primed and ready. Marines lined the rails and had already climbed the rigging, ready to fire at the first opportunity. They were as ready as they would ever be. And still there was nothing she could discern.

The orders came through in a rapid stream, directed at each Ship in turn. Briseis quickly triangulated the range and direction, realising that *Victoria* and *Leopard* were each firing upon the same position. The great guns spoke from each, shattering the peace of the dawn, muzzle flashes lighting up the water before veiling the gun ports in sulphurous smoke.

An orange glow appeared through the mist, spreading as something beyond began to burn.

More orders, more cannon fire. Briseis awaited her own turn with trepidation, straining to see anything through the concealing veil as the glow intensified. It seemed that the shot was hitting its mark and she dared to hope that the Fae vessels would be vulnerable after all, despite what they had seen with the *Regina*. Then, vivid green flashes began to overtake the fire, swallowing it up as the Fae began to use their magic. It seemed that some damage had been done, but not enough.

A shrieking roar erupted from the mist, together with glimpses of huge wings shredding the fog into tatters with every beat. For a second it cleared and Briseis could see a writhing, scaly body plummet into the waves. Had they killed a Fae dragon? Surely the creature wasn't on their side? There was another roar, this time from the ocean as a great serpentine head shot out of the depths and latched on the prow of a barely visible Fae vessel. The beast had teeth the length of a man's forearm, and Briseis couldn't help but shudder at the memory of her own mauling.

<He's on our side!> *Leopard* Sent. <Keep firing if you can, but not at him!>

There were hints of other vessels, though the gaps were rapidly closing up again and the orders had stopped coming through. A few Ships were aiming as best they could, but there didn't appear to be any more hits.

<Cease firing!> Vitalianus wasn't going to waste any of their precious resources going in blind. It seemed the source of information had dried up. As the last rumble died away, the ferocious hissing of the sea monster combined with the sounds of splintering wood carried clearly through the fog. Briseis hoped that the creature was destroying as many of the Fae vessels as it could. It made a change to have a monster on their side. For one awful moment, she'd feared that the *Beisht Kione Dhoo* had returned.

Abruptly, the unnatural calmness of the sea was disturbed by giant ripples from the battle which raced outwards, slapping against her hull. The mist parted briefly to show the Fae vessel already mostly submerged. Briseis thought that its fellows might have come to support it, but there was no sign of the others. Indeed, the fog bank had moved, exposing more of the stricken vessel. Its task accomplished, the serpent had disappeared, only to reappear, snapping up struggling figures from the surface of the water. Then it dived once more, its sinuous tail propelling it back into the sea.

<They're moving off!> *Diadem* reported, confirming Briseis's observations.

<Seems they're happy to sacrifice one of their own if it keeps us off their back.> *Blossom* answered. <Cold-hearted creatures, aren't they?>

<They're relying on their cover,> Briseis agreed. *Leopard* interrupted the conversation.

<All Ships! New sighting. Ahead slow and ready your guns!"

So, their unknown informant was back. It had to be something to do with the serpent, though how it – he – could communicate, she couldn't fathom. The *Leopard*, or someone on board her, seemed to have a special connection.

It wasn't long before she got her orders.

<*Patience*! Your turn!>

She relayed the co-ordinates directly to her gun crews, who rushed frantically to adjust for direction and elevation. Everyone braced as they began pounding, the heavy iron shot tearing holes in the mist, to reveal – nothing.

"Damn it to Hades! Where are they?" Fabillus cursed. "We were spot on."

<No hits,> Briseis reported.

<They've picked up speed and spread out!> *Leopard* was enraged. <There's only so much our friendly monster can do, though he's trying his best. We have to keep up with them. *Victoria*?>

<You're right.> The normally unflappable Flagship sounded strained. <They're trying to outrun us and make for landfall.>

A roar rising to a shriek, together with more sharp cracks, came from the distance. Good. The creature had caught another, but there was no way he could deal with them one at a time. They would have to presume that the dragon was dead, knocked out of the sky by enemy spells. Attacking from below was the only way.

<We could still try our torpedoes,> *Jasper* suggested. <It would be better than nothing.>

<Stand by, *Jasper*.> There was a pause. <Sorry, the answer's no. All Ships! Ahead full! We have to keep up with them as best we can!>

Even as she piled on the power, Briseis knew that it would take more than mortal skill to penetrate the Fae's defensive cocoon. What use were cannon and muskets against something they couldn't see? They must have learned from the encounter with the *Regina* and found a way to block Shipsenses. Normally darkness was no obstacle, but this fog had an unearthly quality about it, dulling their abilities and inspiring fear. If it wasn't for the friendly creature, they wouldn't have made any inroads at all.

<Battle report coming in now. Three enemy vessels hit and two destroyed by the creature.> *Victoria* sounded resigned. <There are approximately fifty vessels left.>

<Damn it, I want to use my new weapons!> *Dragon* said. <We can't just keep pace with them. If we fire enough, we're bound to hit something!>

<Not necessarily!> *Victoria* snapped. <Hold your fire!>

Now they were quarrelling among themselves, and from the toing and froing, Briseis had the feeling that their Captains were also divided as to their best course of action. The only good thing was that the Fae had decided not to engage, concentrating on making headway instead. She didn't know whether to feel relieved or insulted.

She pushed on, staring into the unnatural mist, praying for all she was worth for help to come before all was lost.

*

HMAS *Tempest* was making more than good time. Maia found that, once airborne, it was relatively easy to keep on course and she'd never moved so fast in her life. Some of it was business as usual – wind speed and direction being what she was used to – but there were new variables to take into consideration. There might not be rocks and hidden reefs to worry about, but altitude was just as important. As for atmospheric pressure, every seafarer kept one eye on the weather at all times and it had become as natural as breathing had been for her flesh body.

Leo's enthusiasm for his new command was undiminished, though Maia noticed that not a few of her crew still had their doubts. Being enclosed helped, as it was easier to forget that you weren't in a regular Ship. Maia hoped that there wouldn't be problems when the hatches were opened and the men got a good view of the outside.

They had already passed over several towns, their grid patterns and major buildings laid out before her and one thing was obvious: the roads were clogged with traffic as the population evacuated eastwards, carts, carriages, even engines moving slowly and laden with people. Many were walking, carrying what they could in an endless stream, desperate to escape a possible invasion. Her magnified vision showed upturned faces and hands raised in supplication as she glided hundreds of feet above them.

<There are thousands of people below us,> she Sent to Leo. <I hope I'm not frightening them.>

<They probably think we're something from the Gods,> he answered. <It's a shame I'm under orders not to show our colours yet.>

Robin emerged from her engine deck, his robe smeared with grease and a look of concentration on his face. His eyes snapped into focus as he approached her Captain and whispered in his ear.

"The enemy have been sighted, sir. It looks like they're travelling shrouded in fog, so our Ships can't get a good view. There's been some engagement, but little damage."

Maia could hear everything from her spot on the observation platform. Damn the Fae! A Ship relied on her eyes and her talent. If the enemy had found a way to block both, they were in trouble. It also meant that she wouldn't be much use either. How could she fight a foe she couldn't see? Robin had to be getting his information through the Mage network, which irritated her. Why couldn't she contact her sisters directly?

She was pondering these questions when the two men came to join her. She would have liked Plinius to come too, but he had a marked aversion to heights. Still, she could include him in the conversation if permitted to.

"Ideas?" Leo asked. Undeterred by their position, he raised his telescope to get a good view of the landscape.

She thought hard.

"It's just this fog, then. Any magical shields?"

"None anyone's seen, but we have to assume they've prepared some."

Robin frowned. "It's possible that they're concentrating on this veil rather than other defences. It must be taking a lot of their energy to power it. The Fae seem determined to get to land. They'll feel more secure there and we daren't fire on them for fear of hitting the population. From their course, we think they're heading for the Sacred Isle to the west of Mona."

"Where there are massive sources of power," Maia added.

She'd read quite a few books on Britannic geography. The passage on this particular island had been interesting, though the details of the ancient practices had turned her stomach. Perhaps the Fae hoped to awaken whatever might still lie dormant beneath the hallowed earth.

"It's imperative we stop them before they get there, Leo said. "So, any ideas?"

"It would be easier for me to get back in the link and contact my sisters to get more information."

Leo sighed.

"Sorry. You're to be kept a secret for as long as possible."

That was annoying, but true. Hopefully, the Fae wouldn't think to look up. Now, what to do about this fog? The answer came to her like a lightning bolt. For Jupiter's sake, she was a Ship and, furthermore, a Ship with connections.

"We have to clear it," she said. "And what clears fog?"

"Wind or heat." Leo raised an eyebrow. "This isn't ordinary, though."

Maia felt the grin stretch her cheeks.

"Neither am I."

Leo's blue eyes widened as he understood what she was getting at.

"Our friendly Tempestas?"

And the rest, Maia thought. It was time to ask for favours.

"I can't promise anything," she warned.

"Do it. Call on whom you will and beg them for aid." Her Captain's mouth was a determined line. "The Olympians say they're backing us. It's time for them to prove it."

"Aye, sir. We'll need a sacrifice."

Maia thought quickly. She could petition her mother and Pearl, of course, but surely she had to be related to the major Winds as well. There was no harm in trying. Maybe Eurus, the East Wind, could help them?

Even as she began to formulate the prayer and alerted Danuco, another idea crept into her brain. This one took the form of a twisted braid of fur and feathers, rarely used but holding the promise of violence. Would she get a response? That too was worth a shot. She had to try.

"Immediately," Leo was saying, but her attention was already turning inward. Part of her registered that she could see the coast up ahead, the patchwork green of fields and woodlands ending in a flat blue line where the great river snaked out into the Hibernian Ocean. She was moving swiftly with the slight breeze in her favour and, if she wanted to make a difference, she hadn't much time. First, she had to contact her family.

Aura, Goddess of the Dawn Breeze, come to my aid! I ask you to intercede with the Gods of the Air! Eurus, god of the East Wind, lend me your strength!

The answering pulse was so subtle, she almost missed it, a sensation of pressure and movement, unseen by mortal eyes.

Only a Ship with her gifts would have known it was there at all. Then it was gone, but Maia knew she'd been heard.

She reached inside and examined her threads, running them through imaginary fingers as she had become accustomed to doing. Pulsing red for Raven, far away with Pendragon. Vivid pink and shimmering blue for the *Blossom* and *Patience*. The calm green of new leaves for Captain Plinius, restored to her. Then there was the other. Scales, coarse fur and eagle feathers, the pattern of the Longships. She'd been admitted into their company, but had never dared contact them before now. Would they think it presumptuous of her? There was only one way to find out. She mustered her courage and grasped it firmly, concentrating on the different textures, smooth, soft and prickly.

Howling winds, rising seas. Lightning blasts the darkness.

She pushed the image as hard as she could, using the thread as a pathway. Its end stretched off into far places, spooling away from her as if she had cast out a long, long line in the expectation of hooking a fish. Then it connected, latching on and Maia's head was full of images.

Ears alert, nose sniffing the air, swift paws, query? Recognition!

She knew she had found *Wolf of the Waves* instantly, though there were others in the background that weren't as familiar, crowding behind him in a mass of claws, fur, scales and teeth as if to get a better view of the summoner.

<*Tempest*! I hear you! We all hear you.>

Amusement swept through their link.

<Sorry. I didn't know if I could reach you.>

She could almost see his jaws open as he laughed, red tongue lolling.

<Hah! You are loud.>

He paused and she knew he sensed something different about her. This was a wily and ancient entity and it didn't pay to underestimate him. It would be well to remember that he was an agent of a foreign power, for all they had things in common. Maia clamped down on her thoughts, trying to give him only surface impressions.

<Is everything well with you?> she Sent.

Sadness invaded her mind.

<I was attacked by the Fae, as you call them. My vessel was sunk, but,> he added, more cheerfully, <my crew fought bravely and now feast in Valhalla with the Gods!>

Maia reined in her horror. It was one way of looking at things, she supposed. It seemed that resting in peace wasn't something Northmen aspired to. There were no Elysian fields of bliss for them. But what about Julia?

<What of the Princess?>

<I saw her to land. The Gods watch over her. More than that, I do not know.>

Maia felt a knot of anxiety form in her breast. <I pray they will keep her safe. Have you got a new vessel?>

She decided not to mention her own situation.

<I have. It was waiting for me in Norvegia and I claimed it!> He sounded triumphant, as if he'd had to fight for the privilege. <Another wanted it, but I knew it was mine by right! Then I moved with swift magics.>

So, the spirits of Longships weren't just assigned, the strongest got the best vessels. Maia was glad that this wasn't the case with Ships. Still, it was only because of her direct heritage that they'd made her a Royal. She quelled the pang of loss, but not soon enough.

<You also have a new vessel?>

<Yes,> she admitted. <The Fae sunk me too.>

It was best not to mention the *Regina*'s involvement. Heaven alone knew where she was now. Her reticence was fruitless.

<The other big Ship. The Queen. I heard she did it,> he said, the edge of a growl rumbling through their link. He took Maia's silence as assent. <We both have a reason to fight them, yes?>

Now they had come to it.

<About that. The fleet has sighted them off the Sacred Isle. They're moving fast and hiding in a fog bank, so we can't see to aim. Are there any Longships in the area who could assist?>

Eagerness, desire for revenge, paws speeding over waves, battle ready, fierce purpose.

The burst of emotion and images pounded her, one after another, almost too quickly to catch. It seemed that *Wolf of the Waves* would like nothing more than to be revenged on the ones who had killed his crew and destroyed his vessel.

<I and others are patrolling to the north of Mona, keeping watch on the situation,> he told her. <Wait while I ask. I must have consent to join in battle.>

Maia felt his attention turn away and her link gently shunted, as if he'd entered another room and closed the door to prevent eavesdropping. She wasn't sure of the command structure, but he would be contacting whatever passed for the Admiralty in the Northern Alliance. It was interesting that they had been in Britannic waters, but for once, she wasn't objecting to their secret presence. If they survived, she could flag it up later. She felt him return after only a couple of minutes.

<*Tempest*! We will join with you!> He was jubilant. <A victory for this enemy will benefit nobody. Also, they attacked us first, and that cannot be permitted to go unavenged.>

<That's good news!> she managed. <How many of you are there?>

<We are eight, but more will come.>

<We don't have long,> she warned him. <They are only a few hours off the coast. The fleet is shadowing them looking for a weak spot, but the Fae are refusing to engage.>

<Then you will have to force their hand. I will see you soon!>

He was right. They had to try anything to delay them.

She broke the link and returned to her next task, aware that even while she had been talking to *Wolf of the Waves*, she was bearing down on the Fleet's position. Her vantage point was such that she could see the flat outline of Mona ahead and the mountains to the south. It would be a short trip across the island, over the Sacred Isle and then she should be able to see where her sisters were trying to hold off the foe. It was so much faster when there was no need to go around anything.

<Captain. I have news.>

The wary expression on Leo's face cleared as she relayed her conversation with *Wolf of the Waves*.

<So, they were in the area all along, keeping eyes on us? Sneaky pieces of work, aren't they?>

<They do have a habit of turning up when least expected,> she agreed.

<That's something we'll have to look into another time. For now, I'm just glad some of them are near enough to help.>

He broke off to confer with Plinius and Danuco. The latter was washing his hands in a basin, the water already stained with pink. Doves were the logical sacrifice to get the Gods' attention, and the unruly winds were no different. They also didn't take up much room, essential on a vessel such as this. The scent of burnt offerings, drifting up from the observation platform was sure to entice a friendly power closer.

"That's all the major gods and a few of the lesser ones invoked," Danuco said. "The rest is up to our Ship and her contacts."

They exchanged knowing glances. Leo must have told them about Pearl. Leo called to Amphicles.

"Mr Amphicles, your report!"

Her second-in-command looked up from the chart and saluted smartly.

"If we maintain current course and speed, we'll be past Mona and over the Sacred Isle in… fifteen minutes, sir."

Plinius raised an eyebrow.

"I could get used to this mode of transport, as long as I don't have to look down. Do we know how much further the fleet is?"

"They were about twelve miles off the coast, sir, but the distance is shortening."

Leo frowned. "And our speed?"

Amphicles couldn't help but grin. "Around seventy knots, sir."

Plinius muttered an oath "Ye Gods! I didn't know we were moving that fast. It beats twenty-five. *Tempest?*"

She replied from her forward post, not wishing to push her way through the bulkheads into the main body of the vessel to join them. It wasn't as easy to do in this vessel and she wanted to keep an eye on how things were progressing from the outside.

"We're moving at a fair old clip, sir. I am monitoring speed and timings. We should arrive at the Fleet's last reported position in approximately twenty minutes."

She wondered whether it was a sign of things to come that they hadn't asked her first. It was gratifying to see Leo blush as he realised his error. In a way, he was far too taken with the new devices.

<I suppose he's still learning,> she Sent to Plinius, on their private link.

<He certainly is. Machines are all well and good, but without a guiding intelligence they are simply tools to be used. Let Heron fuss over his engines. I know where the real power lies.>

She smiled to herself, remembering the dreadful time when everyone thought he'd been killed. *Blossom* would be so happy to see him. She was attached to Leo – he was her Captain after all, but Plinius had been her first Captain and would always be special.

<We'll have to keep reminding him,> she replied and was rewarded by a smile in return.

Leo's head came up. She'd been careful to shield their communication, but he suspected something was going on. His fellow Captain did his best to look innocent.

"*Tempest*! Keep reporting."

"Aye aye, sir. We're crossing Mona now. Maintaining course."

It wouldn't be long now before she could open the link to her sisters. They were in and out of each other's heads so much and the enforced silence had been an unpleasant form of isolation that she didn't want to experience again. Ships needed other Ships, for who else could truly understand?

It was then that she saw it. Ahead, the calm blue of the sea and sky was blotted out by an ominous silvery mist, dotted with glints, like droplets of melted quicksilver darting through it. This had to be the Fae barrier. It was obvious why her sisters were struggling to see anything. As she sped closer, masts rose above the horizon like a forest of distant spires, festooned with canvas as each paced parallel to the foe like stalking cats. They had formed into a long line, their flanks presented to the mist, ready to fire broadsides as soon as they were able. It was clear to Maia that time was running out. A few more miles and the Fae would be sailing into the large port to the west of the island.

She opened her link to *Wolf of the Waves* and the Longships to check on their status, even as she alerted her crew. Immediately, the vision of a pack flashed into her mind, lean and hungry bodies running as one with a single purpose. Then they caught sight of the prey.

We approach! Warn your sisters!
Maia gasped aloud as she realised that the Ships might not realise that they were allies.
<Leo! I have to have permission to contact the Fleet. The Longships are bearing down on their position and my sisters don't know they're friendly!>
He responded instantly.
<Do it. I'll answer for any consequences. We've been silent long enough.>
Maia opened the link and plunged straight in. It was like coming home.

*

<We can't keep on like this.>
Fabillus and Sandpiper had joined Briseis on deck, faces creased with worry. Over all, Awstinus's voice droned on, running through the list of Gods as he prayed.
<Jupiter, Greatest and Best, hear our plea. Mighty Neptune, hear our plea. Mars, Lord of War…>
She tuned him out, focusing instead on the immediate danger. The debate about the best course of action was still raging over the link, with Ships relaying their Captains' opinions. Some were almost in open revolt that they couldn't just open up with the new weapons, prepared to go down fighting.
"What is Vitalianus waiting for? Is he intending to corral them in the harbour and open fire when we have a better chance of hitting something?"
"It would make sense," her Mage said, "As long as they've evacuated the town."
"It's a desperate strategy. The Fae might have time to get their troops off first, concealed by this barrier." Fabillus's lip twisted in disgust. "I'm starting to side with Cornelius and the others. Maybe we could punch some holes through it, but we won't know unless we try."
"It's proved resistant to everything so far." Sandpiper said. "I fear that, unless the Gods intervene, we'll have to ram into the fog and take our chances."

273

"Neptune's beard! It sounds like a good way to lose another vessel!" Fabillus was not enamoured of this idea and nor was Briseis.

"Can you think of anything else?"

Her Captain rubbed a hand over his face.

"We wait and follow orders. Gods, but I wish Pendragon was here," he muttered, almost absently.

Briseis estimated that they were about five miles off the coast and the distance was shrinking rapidly. There wasn't much time left. Then her senses started screaming at her and she yanked her attention to the north. Vessels, moving fast. Alarm after alarm began to resound around the Fleet, before the *Victoria* burst into the link.

<All Ships! I am informed that eight Longships are approaching from the north with others following on. They have come to aid us. I repeat, they are allies!>

The link was immediately overtaken by a babble of relieved Ships, all talking at once. Briseis could hardly credit it. Northmen? Maybe they felt threatened by the Fae too?

<Makes a bloody change,> *Dragon* announced.

<Aye,> *Swiftsure* answered. <Time was, they'd have stood by and watched us burn.>

The old Ship still held grudges from centuries of enmity.

<Well, I'm glad they're here!> *Emerald* said. <Maybe they can see what we can't?>

Briseis was inclined to agree with her. The Northmen had strange magics, not all of them known to the Empire.

Then, out of the blue, a familiar voice slipped into her head.

<Hello *Patience*! Can you hear me?>

<*Tempest*!>

She was astonished. <Where are you? *How* are you? Have you got a new vessel?>

<I'm fine and yes I have. I'm heading in your direction right now. Oh, and I've brought some friends.>

So, that was how the Longships had found them. Briseis was all too aware of her friend's talent for communication, though she had kept the knowledge to herself. It had certainly come in handy and never more so than at a time like this.

<Thank the Gods! I hope they can see through this unnatural fog. We've smashed a few of the enemy, but not enough. They're completely veiled. We haven't even been able to use our new weapons.>

<So I see. Give me a moment, then we'll see. Incoming!>

Her friend's voice was full of a savage joy, quite at odds with the girl she knew. It seemed that battle had tempered both of them. She scanned the horizon, expecting to see the new HMS *Tempest* sailing towards them at full speed.

<I can't see you anywhere. Are you invisible?>

Her friend laughed.

<No, *Patience*. I'm *elevated*!>

Elevated? Briseis was confused, until a shadow passed overhead, blotting out the sun.

Finally understanding, she looked up.

XV

Caniculus woke early in the morning, safely tucked away in his hidey-hole in one of the least salubrious areas of Londin. He'd slept badly, plagued by dreams of running from something just out of view that he couldn't evade however much he tried, and now he had to face yet more hours stuck in a cheerless room with no company.

He splashed some tepid water on his face, rinsed out his mouth and rooted about for something to eat. There wasn't much. Thoroughly miserable and nagged by guilt, he stretched a little and tried to think positively.

Part of the problem was the boredom. He wasn't used to so much inactivity, at least without any obvious purpose, and just hanging about hoping for divine orders wasn't something in his job description.

As for the guilt, he was loath to admit it, but knowing that his friends were risking their lives against the Fae whilst he was sitting around guarding a lump of gold, however fancy and important, galled him. He knew a number of dirty tricks to disable an opponent. Presumably Fae had their tender parts in the same place too and they would certainly benefit from a good kicking.

He slumped down on the old mattress that served as a bed and chewed on a hangnail. The room, at the back of a grimy tenement, had one small window that led on to the flat roof of an outhouse. It was a good escape route, leading to a filthy, debris-strewn alley, even though the air could get a bit ripe in warm weather. The vaunted new sewers hadn't reached this district and wouldn't for some considerable time to come. The window cost extra, but it was no good having something on the top floor with only one way out.

He'd stashed some food in a secure chest several months ago, together with a store of wine. His only problem was water, but he'd sneaked out after dark and filled jugs at the nearest fountain. No cooking was allowed on the premises, so he'd had to content himself with cold meals. It wasn't worth the risk of showing his face at a food stall or inn.

The only bright spot in the room was the opulent purple cushion. Caniculus decided that the Sceptre wouldn't mind him borrowing it as a pillow, though it seemed incongruous next to the battered table, stool, and scratched chest in the corner. It was the first time Caniculus had slept on velvet, and Imperial purple at that. He resolved that if he ever got rich, he'd order a few just like it.

It was a pleasant enough dream to while away the time, and he was enjoying picturing all the things he would do with a shed full of money when there was a knock at the door.

His heart leapt into his mouth. Drawing a dagger from a forearm sheath, he went to stand against it.

"What do you want?"

"Delivery!"

What in the name of Hades was this?

"I haven't ordered anything. Get lost!"

He thought he heard a chuckle from the other side of the door and braced himself for violence.

"I guarantee you'll want what I've brought."

The voice sounded familiar. Caniculus groped for the memory. Then it came to him and he opened the door.

The curly-haired youth grinned at him and waved a covered dish.

"Well, I am the Messenger of the Gods. Bet you're glad I'm not my half-brother!"

He sighed to himself, partially with relief that Mars hadn't come calling again. Mercury entered the room, winced at the stench from the outhouse and plonked the dish down on the table.

Caniculus eyed him dubiously. This had all the hallmarks of a bribe.

"Not the best of places, is it?" the God remarked. He waved a hand and the stink vanished, to be replaced by something a lot more savoury. Despite his suspicions, Caniculus's mouth began to water.

Mercury's gaze fell on the worn mattress. Lacking a hiding place, Caniculus had stuffed the Sceptre underneath it.

"Oh, good. You did well with that, by the way. No permanent damage and no-one the wiser."

"Thank you, Lord."

Mercury took up position leaning against the wall, arms folded and crossing his legs at the ankles.

"Have a look in the dish."

Caniculus lifted the cover gingerly. The rich aroma of beef stew rose from the plate.

"You'll need some bread with that, I expect," Mercury said. A loaf, freshly-baked, appeared next to it. "Don't stand on ceremony. I expect you're tired of dried meat and Ship's biscuits."

He was, so he sat at the table and began to eat. The stew was hot, tasting just like the one his mother made on special occasions. Truly, the ways of the Gods were miraculous. Mercury watched him, seemingly satisfied.

"Here's the latest news, just for you. The Fae have assembled, there's going to be a big battle and your Ships are in a stand-off near Mona. It's all happening, but don't worry, you can be a part of it too. I expect you want to know how you can help."

Caniculus looked up, a chunk of bread dripping gravy half-way to his mouth. Mercury laughed at his expression.

"Oh, you're so well-named! A little hangdog, methinks. Don't worry, it's nothing too onerous, just a little light digging."

Digging?

"Not grave robbing?" he blurted out before he could stop himself. Mercury looked puzzled, before his face cleared.

"Oh no! I've already done some of that with friend Milo. I wouldn't want to repeat myself – that would be boring. No, you must go to the ruins of the palace, find where the throne room was, and excavate for something we're going to need."

Caniculus swallowed. This must have been what Mars meant. "It might take me some time. There's a lot of rubble and they haven't had time to clear it all yet."

Mercury stuck out his lower lip thoughtfully.

"True. I'll arrange for some help. Big brawny workmen – that's who you'll need, plus a little priestly help, though Aquila will only be there a short while to provide guidance. I can't see him wielding a shovel, can you?"

The God laughed at his own joke. Caniculus laughed and shook his head. Aquila's imposing presence had the authority of the King of Olympus backing him up, so he wouldn't be getting his hands dirty.

"When do you want me to start, Lord?"

"As soon as you've fortified yourself with that stew. I take it it's your favourite?"

"Indeed, Lord. It's delicious."

Mercury beamed at him. "No dormice stuffed with lark's tongues for you, eh? You're a man of simple tastes." He chuckled at Caniculus's expression. "As far as food's concerned, that is. Trust me. You pull this off, and I'll give you a dozen fancy cushions."

"Thank you, Lord."

"Oh, you'll need this."

A spade had appeared in Mercury's hand. It didn't look like anything special, just an ordinary metal one with a wooden handle.

Caniculus wiped up the last of the stew with a piece of bread, resolving to keep the rest of the loaf for later, and took the spade.

"One more thing. I'm afraid I'll need the helmet back now. It's served its purpose, and Hades has a use for it."

Caniculus propped the spade against the table and went to his pack. He lifted out the helmet, not without regret, looking into the empty eyeholes for the last time before handing it over.

"It was an interesting experience," he said.

"Oh come on," Mercury teased. "It was great fun, wasn't it?"

He had to admit it. "Yes."

"Sorry, but you're back to being an ordinary Agent now." He corrected himself "No, I mean a workman, going to clear the palace. Orders from the Temple of Jupiter. Right, that's me done.

Don't hang about. You can leave the Sceptre here. It'll be safe enough under this horrible old thing."

Mercury looked down at the blanket-covered mattress with distaste.

"But what am I looking for?" he asked.

""You'll know it when you see it. It's big, made of metal and would hold an awful lot of stew!"

Mercury burst out laughing and pushed himself away from the wall.

"Good luck, Little Dog! Get digging!"

There was a brief gust of air and the God was gone, leaving Caniculus the possessor of a spade, half a loaf of bread and an empty dish.

It seemed he wouldn't be bored after all, but he was missing the helmet already. It had always felt like he had company when it was in his possession even though it had spooked him at the beginning.

He shrugged to himself and belched loudly. The meal had been good, just what he needed, though it seemed poor recompense for all the running about he'd been doing. No nectar and ambrosia for him. Then again, even that might taste disgusting to anyone who wasn't immortal.

He shouldered the spade and tucked the remains of the loaf inside a bag before leaving. Locking the door behind him, he skipped down the stairs and into the city streets.

The first thing he noticed was that there were less people about and those he did see hurried along, intent on their own business without passing the time of day , strained looks on their faces. It was as if the very air was tainted with fear and uncertainty. He would have liked to investigate further, but Mercury had impressed upon him the urgency of his errand and he didn't dare hang about.

The thick black lettering of a newspaper headline caught his eye, pinned to a board outside a printing shop. FAE INVASION – LATEST NEWS! The door opened and a newsboy darted out, his heavy bag over one shoulder, looking for anyone to sell to.

"Hey, boy. Over here!"

The child's eyes brightened. A quick sale meant one less paper to carry. Caniculus groped in his purse for a couple of coins and dropped them into the waiting palm.

"Thanks, mister!"

The boy gave him the broadsheet and ran off towards the Forum, crying the headline at the top of his lungs. Caniculus saw him make four more sales before he turned the corner. Londiners were eager to hear what was happening – those of them who hadn't already left for the continent or gone to join the fight.

He dodged down a few narrow alleyways that ran perpendicular to the criss-crossing streets, all familiar to him from his earliest days. The back streets of Londin were veritable rat runs, despite the authorities' desire for Roman neatness and order. Hidden doors led to courtyards and through tenement closes, through public gardens and liminal spaces where street people quietly conducted business in the shadows or slept in corners. Caniculus marched through briskly, his spade a sure advertisement of his supposed trade.

He emerged a block away from the remnants of the Palace, slipping out of a small green door set unobtrusively into the wall of a brewer's yard. Only then did he glance at the paper.

It didn't tell him much that he didn't already know. The ports were jammed with the wealthy trying to flee and everyone else was holing up with stockpiled supplies crying to the Gods to save them.

There were shortages of everything. Trade had virtually ceased for, after all, who wanted to risk getting caught up in this? The merchants would be waiting to see what happened, selling their goods nearer to home. In the meantime, Britannia was crippled by uncertainty and portents of doom.

At this rate, he thought, the newspaper would be worth more as lavatory paper, as there were probably shortages of that as well. Quite a few of the shops were shuttered, even though it was the beginning of the day.

The gates to the palace were unmanned. Technically, there wasn't even a king any more now that Marcus had been unmasked. His father hadn't returned to claim Excalibur, so even this compounded the unease. Presumably everything of value had already been removed and the City Polis had been assigned elsewhere. Caniculus trudged through them, just another lowly servitor come to clean up some of the mess as best he could. There wasn't much left. He could still smell the acrid tang of burnt wood, though the rubble had been piled into more orderly heaps. He cudgelled his brain to remember the floor plan, trying to imagine how it had once looked. It was important to work out where the throne room had been. He could see it now, as he had when Marcus and his puppet masters had met, but finding its location was another thing entirely.

He paced out the spaces as best he could, coming finally to a place where broken, blackened columns rose jaggedly into the empty sky like rotted stumps. This was the ceremonial entrance, once set with huge, metal studded doors higher than two men. Now they guarded nothing, no barrier to any who wanted to pass. Caniculus walked between them unchallenged, and stopped.

Aquila was already waiting for him, sitting like Jupiter on his throne in the midst of the wreckage, flanked by two attendants in temple robes.

"Here's our man now!" he boomed.

Caniculus approached him with some apprehension. The Priest had a formidable reputation. Some said that the God spoke through him on a regular basis and no-one ever knew whether they were dealing with the man or the God.

"Lord Aquila."

He bowed respectfully. To one side he could see there was a work gang assembled, armed with a variety of implements and he wondered why it was necessary for him to be there at all. Surely there were enough men to accomplish the task Mercury had set him?

"We have our orders, friend. I have marked the spot where we must start."

Caniculus suppressed a laugh. In the time-honoured tradition the dig site was indeed marked with a large painted cross. As to the 'we', it was clear that Aquila was there in a purely supervisory capacity. A small table was next to his chair, bearing a jug of wine and a plate of figs.

The workmen were already hefting their tools, so Caniculus went to join them.

"Alright, mate?" a brawny red-haired man asked.

"Yeah, I suppose. We'd better start, then."

"What we digging for?"

"It's big and made of metal."

The man's eyes widened.

"Gold?"

Caniculus shrugged. "I only know it's something important."

The man's eyes flicked towards Aquila.

"Must be, if he's here. Right, lads!"

Soon, the only sounds were the noise of spades, shovels and picks on the stone floors. The mosaics had been fine once, but the fire hadn't done them any favours. Some parts still remained and Caniculus found himself levering up part of a sea monster, its jaws gaping wide. To the side, a large fish was slowly disappearing under the determined blows of his fellows and a mermaid was losing her tail under the relentless assault. It wasn't long before they were down to a layer of sand and gravel, perhaps from when the river was wider or had flowed through a different course. Surely there couldn't be anything under here? It seemed untouched, not mixed together as it would have been if it had been disturbed.

They were several feet down now, widening the hole and lining it with boards brought in for the purpose. It wouldn't do to precipitate a cave-in. Aquila seemed unmoved, watching the labouring men with half-closed eyes and occasionally helping himself to wine. There was no option but to press on, though at this rate they would hit clay and that would slow everything down.

From the mutterings, Caniculus wasn't the only one who was beginning to doubt the wisdom of this whole enterprise. He had resolved to scramble up out of the hole and have a word with the Priest himself, when his spade clanked dully against metal.

Everyone stopped. Caniculus pulled the spade out and angled it, so it scraped against whatever was down there. It was definitely metal, and from what he was feeling, had a slight curve to it.

The other men crowded around, some pulling small trowels from their belts. Aquila's head peered down at them.

"That's it."

"Lord Aquila! It would help if we knew the shape of it," the red-haired worker called up to him.

"It's hollow and bowl-shaped," the Priest replied. "You'll have to empty the inside before you can haul it out of there."

There was nothing for it but to drop to their knees and begin to scrape away the layers of accumulated debris. It was soon obvious that the object was larger than it had first appeared, sunk into the ancient riverbed the Gods alone knew how many centuries before. Several minutes later, the rim was revealed. It was fully eight feet across and Mercury's comment about stew finally made sense to Caniculus. You could have fed an army from something this size.

There wasn't enough room for everyone to dig, so they took it in turns, scooping out sand and gravel from the inside.

"It's not gold," one of the workers muttered to another.

"Why? Did you think it would be?" his pal grinned. "Could be silver."

Caniculus doubted that. Silver would have tarnished in the earth and turned black. This had a sheen to it, as if it had been newly-buried. He decided to test his theory, secretly digging in a little harder to see if he could scratch a little away. It was so big nobody would notice and, if they did, he would claim it was an accident.

His trowel slid over the surface, leaving nary a mark. Whatever the object was made of was impervious to casual damage. He tried a little harder, with the same result. So, not silver then – or maybe it was some magical version, enchanted to preserve it down the years? Whatever, he decided not to press his luck, returning to his task and keeping his head down. His companions had also fallen silent, as if sensing the strangeness of their find.

Slowly, the artefact began to emerge from the confining earth. They had been forced to lean right into it to dig out as much as they could, scoop by scoop. Once it was mostly cleared, they turned their attention to the exterior, scraping and levering the muck away. Even Aquila condescended to heave himself out of his seat to inspect the progress.

"Good work, men." He nodded absently, as if hearing something nobody else could. "Keep going. Oh, and don't worry about damaging it. It can look after itself."

The men shuffled their feet and exchanged glances, the anticipation of treasure switched to a dread of the unknown. Caniculus also found himself reluctant to touch it in any way, relying on his tools to keep it at a distance.

After a good hour of careful digging, it was ready to be lifted. The huge bowl was still covered with lumps of mud and compacted stones, but as they began to lever it up chunks started to fall away, revealing intricate patterns of trees and animals.

Ignoring the hairs rising on the back of his neck, Caniculus added his weight to the sturdy planks they'd managed to wedge underneath it. Finally, it came free.

"We'll have to crane this out, Lord," the foreman said. "It weighs a ton."

Aquila pursed his fleshy lips.

"I agree. I want it done as soon as possible, then bring it to the Basilica. Do not speak of this to anyone."

He gestured to his attendants, who stepped forward, pulling handfuls of coins from purses at their belts.

"Here are your wages," Aquila said. "There will be more where this comes from as long as you keep your mouths shut."

The men took the money, then clustered around the foreman for further instructions. Caniculus sidled up hopefully but was stopped at a word from the Priest.

"Ah, Caniculus. I have another job for you. You have your speechstone?"

"Yes, Lord." He certainly did. A gift from the Gods was not to be abandoned and he had the suspicion that Aquila knew all about his adventures.

"Excellent. Stay here on watch. Nothing must happen to the cauldron until it's time for it to be moved. Should there be any…difficulties, contact me immediately."

"Understood, Lord."

Normally, speechstones only worked between Agents, but this one had been in the hands of a God and Caniculus wasn't about to argue. If Aquila said he could contact him through it, then that had to be the case. Part of him squirmed at the thought, but a job was a job. He could only hope that there'd be more money in it, hopefully enough to set him up for life somewhere quiet on the outskirts of Londin.

"Are you anticipating problems, Lord?"

Aquila grimaced.

"It's possible. The cauldron could be very useful to our enemies."

He beckoned Caniculus closer.

"Trust nobody. Wait for my express command before you permit anyone near it. I'm leaving you in charge."

His eyes bored into Caniculus, who bowed hastily.

"Yes, Lord."

So that was why he'd been sent here. He wondered whose cauldron it was. There were a couple he'd heard of in old tales, both highly magical objects and definitely unsuitable for stew of any sort. Thinking of food made him hungry, but it didn't look like he'd be able to leave his post any time soon.

Aquila's laugh was unexpected.

"Never fear, Little Dog, the Gods hear your plea! Food and drink will be sent to you in abundance, but don't let it distract you! Ah, here are some Royal Guards to keep you company."

The Priest rose, chuckling, while Caniculus was still trying to close his mouth. The steady tramp of marching feet confirmed Aquila's words, as a squad of armed legionaries appeared, armed with muskets. Their officer called a halt, then saluted Aquila.

"You have your orders, Decurion. Carry on." He grinned at Caniculus. "I will see you later, Little Dog. I hope so, anyway!"

The legionaries took up their positions around the hole as a litter appeared, carried by six huge slaves. Aquila rolled himself into it and was carried off, his bearers picking their way over the devastated ground. Caniculus didn't envy them their task one bit.

Guard the magical cauldron. Right. Knowing that he had the power to raise the alarm was only a minor advantage in the scheme of things. He'd have to hope that their enemies didn't mount some sort of surprise attack. Still, several loaded muskets were usually effective deterrents to most sorts of trouble.

He took the opportunity to avail himself of Aquila's chair and made himself as comfortable as possible. All he could do now was wait and hope that the promised meal would materialise sooner rather than later. To be sure, he sent up a general prayer of thanks to any God who might be watching. Caniculus had the feeling that there could be more than one and he could only hope that they were on his side.

As the hours went past, the late summer afternoon gradually shaded into evening and the shadows began to lengthen. The carved wooden chair, so attractive at first, was starting to numb his rear end no matter how he wriggled.

An acolyte delivered the promised food in a large basket, so eating that whiled away much of the time. Caniculus tried not to enjoy himself too much, feeling for once like some sort of aristocrat as he stuffed his face in solitary splendour. As he'd often been on the receiving end of the army's contempt in the past, Caniculus didn't feel at all guilty about eating in front of the guards and he hoped fervently that the smell of hot meat pie was finding its way up each flared nostril. The soldiers had had to settle for cold rations, but Aquila, or whoever had prepared his food, had been more generous.

Now, he was waiting, trying not to doze off and cursing the workers for dawdling. Where had they gone to get the crane? Gaul? They should have been back by now. He was standing, trying to massage some feeling back into his buttocks, when he heard the sounds of clopping hooves and the rumbling of heavy wheels. It was about time.

Two carthorses came into view, led by the foreman. They were towing a crane on wheels and another smaller cart, presumably to take the cauldron away. They pulled up near the hole, the foreman approaching the Decurion whilst his men unhitched the horses. Caniculus thought they must be intending to leave the crane after they'd used it. Perhaps they couldn't find any more draft horses at short notice?

"We're to remove the cauldron. Lord Aquila's orders."

Caniculus sighed to himself and strolled over.

"About bloody time. Where did you go to get it? Caledonia?"

The foreman didn't react, continuing to stare at the Decurion.

"We're here to remove the cauldron," he repeated.

The Decurion, who clearly had been briefed, looked to Caniculus and raised an eyebrow.

"Not without confirmation you're not, sunshine."

"I'll get it," Caniculus replied. He began to activate his speechstone, picturing the High Priest, when a line of red flashed across the Decurion's throat.

Caniculus threw himself backwards, only the wind of its passage telling him of the knife aimed for his jugular. He dropped and rolled, yelling for the guards, only to see them crumpling to the ground or trying to fend off their assailants with their muskets. A couple managed to get off shots, the sharp crack followed by the stench of black powder before they were forced to resort to using them as clubs.

<We're under attack!>

Caniculus leapt to his feet. He was only armed with a knife and trapped by rubble. From the corner of his eye, he saw that one of the shots had found its mark. The creature lying on the floor bore no resemblance to the man he'd been digging with that day.

<They're Fae!>

<Hold on!>

The reply rang in his head and he tensed, waiting for the thunderbolt, the flash of light, anything that the Gods could send at such short notice. All the soldiers were dead now. They had been the prime targets and that left only him. The Fae that was wearing the foreman's face sneered at him.

"You cannot stop us. It is ours now."

His companions were hastening to fasten ropes around the cauldron, speed being more important than dispatching one lone Agent. Caniculus began to edge away, hoping that he could make a break for it. Apparently, he wasn't important enough to kill.

The Fae worked quickly, securing the weight. A couple moved to operate the winding handle. They were wearing heavy gloves, presumably to negate the effect of the metal on their skin. Caniculus could only watch helplessly as the great metal bowl rose slowly from its hiding place, to be swung around and on to the smaller cart. It seemed that there was nothing he could do but watch, impotent, as the magical artefact was stolen away right under his nose.

The carthorses shifted uneasily. A Fae spoke sharply to them, tugging on their reins but they ignored him, ears flattening against their skulls. One reared up, fighting its handler and the other followed suit, their panicked neighs becoming ever more strident.

Caniculus ran for a column, eager to put something between himself and whatever was heading their way. The Fae were conferring urgently in shrill, bird-like voices. Their human disguises had started to fray, features rippling to reveal their true faces. All at once, the horses had had enough. They broke free and galloped off, leaving the cart with its load behind them. Caniculus cursed as they clattered away. It had been too far for him to run, even if he could have bypassed the enemy and now he was stuck in the remains of the throne room with them, and possibly something even worse.

A Fae screamed and pointed. Charred beams and ruined stone shattered as a huge head thrust its way through the wall, stopping only to shake the dust from its tawny fur. Implacable orange eyes surveyed the wreckage before lighting on the terrified Fae.

As one they began to back away, but the beast had already spotted them. All three mouths opened simultaneously, bleating, hissing and roaring as the chimaera charged, intent on the squealing figures.

The lion jaws snapped on one Fae, even as another chanted, throwing gouts of green fire in its direction and the air was filled with the stink of burning fur. The chimaera rolled expertly, putting out the flames and enabling the serpent head to strike at the Fae Mage and crush him in its fangs. Another was impaled on horns and tossed, landing in a boneless heap. Sharp claws ripped out innards in bloody ribbons as the beast whirled, deadly in her power.

Caniculus didn't dare move, flattening himself against the column.

<Report!>

He'd forgotten he was still linked.

<A chimaera's killing them!>

It had to be the same one he'd seen before, the one his uncle had sourced for the arena.

<Good. Get out of there and leave it to do its work.>

Aquila might have been discussing his dinner for all the surprise he was showing.

Caniculus risked another peek. The beast had slaughtered all but one of the Fae, who was making for the exit. He didn't make it. She leapt, claws unsheathed, to crash down on his back and smash him into the floor. Rivulets of pale blood flowed, tracing their way across the remnants of the elaborate mosaic. Caniculus took his chance. Leaving the beast to enjoy herself, he sprinted for the hole in the wall, trying to block out the noise of crunching bone and the Fae's howl of agony. He leapt chunks of masonry, weaving his way out into what had been a corridor. He knew the way from here. As to the cauldron, it had a far better guard now than anything human could provide and the chimaera was more than welcome to it.

He didn't stop running until he reached the safety of his room.

XVI

From her lofty position, everything was laid out before Maia like *tabula* pieces on a board. The unnatural fog concealing the Fae vessels was an impenetrable wall directly ahead, stretching for more than a mile with its boundaries clearly defined. Somewhere in there was an unknown number of enemy, sailing directly for the coast and seemingly unconcerned with anything but this objective.

Parallel to them and flanking them like tracking wolves, her sisters were doing their best to keep up, seeking any weakness they could exploit to their advantage. Behind and falling further back were the inanimates. They had piled on sail and were trying their best, but didn't have the speed of the Ships. A couple of miles away, at a tangent, black shapes cut through the water as the Longships raced to rendezvous with the fleet.

<Fire and Furies! What's that?>

The *Victoria* had spotted her.

<Jupiter's beard! It's a winged chariot!> *Leopard* cut in.

<Is it the Gods?> *Emerald* was awestruck.

<No, it's me,> Maia Sent cheerfully. <Hello everyone! Do you like my new vessel?>

The Ship link descended into babble as everyone tried to talk at once.

<Enough!> The Flagship put her proverbial foot down. <It seems that our *Tempest* is now a...what do you call it?>

<An AirShip,> Maia supplied, helpfully.

<An AirShip.> *Victoria* said the word carefully, as if tasting the sound of it. <Well I never!>

<Greetings, *Tempest*!>

Strangely, *Blossom* didn't sound surprised. She must have been in contact with Plinius all along.

<Hello, *Blossom*! It's good to see you again!>

<I believe you have someone aboard I'd like to have back.>

<I do indeed. Believe me, it was a wonderful surprise to see him and I know he'll be much happier when you're reunited.>

<What? Do you mean he isn't enamoured of flying through the air?>

Maia had to laugh. <Not at all. We just have to work out how to get him to you.>

<Drop down and lower him on a rope,> the old Ship said, ever practical.

Maia glanced at Plinius. It was one thing to climb rigging, but this would be a precision move.

<That could endanger both of us,> she replied.

<Then get your Mages to help. Don't tell me, Heron's fussing around your new devices, isn't he?>

<And Robin.>

<Robin too? Tell them to get their lazy backsides in gear and return my Captain. Right now!>

Maia grinned and relayed the message.

"Heron, Robin, *Blossom* would like the return of her Captain. Immediately."

Heron's head emerged from an inspection hatch. "And I expect she doesn't want to wait another minute, does she?"

"No."

"Typical."

He sniffed and shouted for Robin who was taking notes, probably planning for future improvements to the design.

"Did you hear? Time to practise your levitation spells. Maia, drop to within two hundred feet, if you can."

It was endearing the way he still sometimes called her Maia, as if forgetting that she now had a vessel of her own.

<Captain, Heron wants to levitate Captain Plinius back to the *Blossom*.>

<Really?> Leo sounded dubious. <Still, they know their business. I'm not going to ask whether it's been done before.> <I think they practised in the factory with bales and such,> she answered.

<Wonderful. No worries at all then.>

He turned to his fellow Captain.

"Well, sir, you'll be glad to know that your Ship is insisting you be sent down to her straightaway. Heron and Robin are going to levitate you.

The appalled look on Plinius's face showed everyone what he thought.

"Wouldn't a rope be easier?"

"Ah, Captain." Heron breezed up to him. "No rope will be necessary. We devised certain spells to make transportation to and from this vessel simplicity itself. Saves a lot of time and effort, plus minimises the risk of damaging the cargo. Ropes swing, you know. This will be straight up and down."

He beamed at his audience. Plinius sighed.

"It's a good job I know how capable you are. Just remember that there'll be masts, spars and rigging in the way, won't you? I've no wish to be impaled on my Ship's flagpole."

Maia tried to look reassuring. Leo caught her eye.

<He does know what he's doing?>

<I think so. Besides, Robin won't let him do anything stupid.>

<Ye Gods!>

Heron thought for a moment.

"So, Maia, position us above *Blossom*, with your central belly hatch aft of the mizzen-mast and we'll lower him on to the stern."

"Absolutely not!" Plinius interjected, just as Robin opened his mouth with a look of consternation. "*Tempest*, please ask *Blossom* to lower a boat. You can put me on that, well away from anything sharp and pointy."

"That makes sense," Leo agreed, nodding at his Ship. Maia relayed the request.

<Heron was going to do *what*?>

Blossom was near exploding point. <I swear, that Mage is getting more senile every day!>

<He does love to experiment.>

<Well he can experiment with something that isn't my Captain!>

"*Blossom* is readying a boat now, sir," Maia reported.

"Good. Begin manoeuvres. Crossing her aft seems the best way."

Maia had already decided that was how she would do it. She concentrated on her rudder and side propellers, swinging around in a tight circle above *Blossom* and coming about, whilst the other ships watched with intense interest. She wondered how many of them were already planning their future transition.

The boat was already trailing behind, secured on a long line for added safety. *Blossom* had reduced her speed and temporarily broken formation while the delicate operation was undertaken. Speed was imperative now. Plinius, stoic as ever, waited by the hatch with a Mage on each side.

"Right, Captain. Hold your arms into your body and keep your legs together. Everything secured?"

"One second." Plinius rammed his hat under his arm. "I don't want to lose this. Very well, let's do it."

He closed his eyes, his body becoming rigid as the spell took hold. With matching gestures, both Mages exerted their power and slowly lifted him into the air before swinging him out over the open hatch and down to the waiting boat.

Maia watched as he descended, noting the smoothness of it, almost as if Plinius were standing in an invisible elevator. Robin and Heron were bending over the hatch now, arms tracing invisible sigil after sigil as they made minor corrections. It took less time than she'd thought it would before his boots were grabbed by two crewmen, who guided him the last few feet. Another waved a kerchief, the signal that all was well, so the Mages finished with a flourish. They hadn't even broken a sweat.

"Excellent!" Heron rubbed his hands in delight, before turning to his former apprentice. "See? I told you it would work!"

Robin rolled his eyes. "That's not exactly what you said."

Maia resisted the temptation to snap, knowing the old Mage's sometimes perverse sense of humour.

"Back to your duties, gentlemen. We'll be needing more than a simple spell before long."

Heron's bristly eyebrows shot up. "Simple? *Simple?* She's no idea, has she?"

Robin hustled him away, trying not to laugh.

Maia had already begun to gain height once more, watching *Blossom* and her crew's joyous reunion with their Captain. Cheering drifted up as he was welcomed aboard, an all too brief moment of happiness in their present situation. Now it was time for both Ships to get back into position.

As *Blossom* turned her energies to returning to her place in line, Maia contacted the *Victoria*.

<Captain Plinius is returned, ma'am.>

<Nicely done. Now to business. Can you see the Fae vessels?>

Maia had already tried piercing the mist, but bounced straight back, much, she imagined, as her sisters had done. She might have a new type of vessel, but her senses still operated the same way. There was one thing she was noticing, however.

<Not yet, but I think they've thrown up a wall, rather than an enclosing bubble.>

She passed the message on to Leo immediately.

<We'll try to get over the top of it then. Send to Admiral Vitalianus for authorisation.>

Her Captain gave the order for battle stations as she worked to increase height, pushing her engines to the maximum. The Ships below her dwindled as she rose.

<*Victoria*, requesting authorisation to go over the top of the barrier.>

<Vitalianus approves,> the Ship replied.

The Longships, led by *Wolf of the Waves*, were nearly at their destination. She opened communications.

<Hail, *Wolf of the Waves*!>

<Hah, *Tempest*! A new vessel indeed. You fly like an eagle!>

Climbing a wall of fog. Looking over.

It was easier for her to project the image.

Grinning jaws.

He approved.

Leaving him to make his own overtures to the Fleet, she concentrated on her bearings. She was almost at the mist now and could see that it only reached about two hundred feet in the air. Above was only blue sky. Beyond that…

"I can see them!"

Leo was already on her observation platform, Amphicles by his side.

"There they are!" Leo said, grimly. "Bones of my ancestors, there have to be two hundred or more."

The Fae fleet were moving rapidly in formation and evenly spaced, the antique design with their single sails somehow a glimpse into a barely-remembered past. Even with their magical shields, Maia didn't think the frail-looking vessels were a match for Ships, though they greatly outnumbered them.

<Report back,> Leo ordered, and Maia began to feed information back to her sisters as quickly and accurately as she could.

<Ye Gods! We were told there were only fifty. You must disrupt their castings by any means possible,> *Victoria* told her. <Once the mist is dispersed, we can see where to fire.>

<Understood.>

"Will every enemy vessel have a Mage?" Leo wondered.

"Unknown," Maia told him, "though it is written that most Fae can cast spells. Perhaps their protections are a joint effort?"

"Whatever, we need to act now while we still have the element of surprise."

"It looks like we're about to find out how far they can cast their magics," Amphicles added. "It might be best to maintain height."

"I agree," Leo said. "*Tempest*, weapons situation?"

"All loaded, sir."

Her gun crews were ready and all she needed was the order to open her hatches. Nature would do the rest, so long as her men accounted for the time needed for the bombs to drop.

"We'll aim for the ones nearest the barrier. Logically they should be the ones maintaining it," Leo decided. "*Tempest*, give the word when ready."

A vertical drop was something new, though she knew that Musca would have made the calculations for the cannon. The hatches in her belly were largely untested. Sandbags had been used during training, but not from this height and they had to get this right first time. Already, several men were clustered around the hatches. It was now or never, as she was coming into range.

"Approaching the first of them now, sir."

Leo looked at Amphicles and took a deep breath.

"Fire!"

It was as if Jupiter himself had spoken. Wave after wave of thunder rippled through the decks, sending iron shot out and down towards their marks. The projectiles looked tiny as they vanished, every second stretched to breaking. Musca was counting, his telescope fixed on the scene below, even as his crews were reloading with mechanical efficiency. Then they landed.

Splashes of foam showed where the first three went into the sea, falling short of their targets by ten feet or more. Musca swore. Then the others hit. A sail grew a great, ragged tear, while a black hole bloomed beneath it, throwing up shards of decking like the unfurling petals of some deadly flower. Maia could see bodies cast out like seeds. It appeared that one vessel was holed, but she couldn't spend time watching. There were more to send down to Neptune's realm.

Her guns boomed once more, as she angled herself so that both broadsides would take effect. She was floating over several at once now, so it was time to make a direct attack. Shot fell, trailing sparks like sling stones hurled by giants. The first explosions were more than gratifying, fire taking hold on several vessels.

But the others had seen her. Sickly green fireballs rose up to knock her out of the sky. Most fell but others continued, as if their wielders had greater power. She made a note of their origin.

She added thrust, rising and swerving to avoid the first while simultaneously throwing up her shields. Below, Heron and Robin were adding their Potentia to her own.

"They can't hit the envelope or we're done for!" Heron shouted, sketching a sigil of Power. Beside him, Robin's mouth worked frantically as he poured his own power into the mix.

More and more green trails rose, rising like rotting fingers to pluck her out of the sky and drag her to her doom. First one, then another impacted her hull, barely repelled by the shimmering purple of her shield and, with each hit, she felt her defences weakening. Her only hope was to target her attackers' vessels.

She thrust Potentia into her propellers, speeding until she was directly above the worst of them before slackening off. She'd have to chance staying in position, or there was no way she could hit them.

"Hatch men! Drop now!"

They raced to obey, sailors and marines heaving up the heavy shot and releasing it from her belly. There was no need for finesse, just brute strength and endurance. She stayed as long as she dared before giving the order to cease and pulling away as quickly as she was able.

It wasn't fast enough. A tendril of green snaked through her hatch, seizing upon three marines and dragging them out, even as it faded. They fell screaming to the unforgiving depths.

The lesson was learned too late. She slammed her hatch shut as the others fell back in shock.

<Three men lost, sir.>

Leo's pain was a like stab in the guts. It was a small consolation that the vessel below her was starting to tilt as water flooded its hull.

<Rise!> he commanded. <We need to take stock.>

She obeyed, scanning the towering wall of fog for any sign of weakness. Several vessels had been sunk, but others were closing in to fill the gaps. Had it affected the barrier? That had to be her only concern now.

<We have to keep going,> she Sent to Leo, all too aware of how desperate she sounded, while in her head she prayed desperately for help. Even her mother seemed to have abandoned her now as the air was still and heavy, as if she were floating through treacle.

Then Maia saw it. A looming blackness was forming to the west, split by intermittent flashes of lightning and devouring the blue sky as it spread. It was bearing down on them like the swift shadow of night, faster than anything normal weather could produce. She sounded the alarm to Leo and her sisters, almost screaming it into the link.

<Massive storm to the west, heading directly for us!>

The Ships reacted with consternation, their view blocked.

<More Fae magic?> *Persistence* spat. <If we're all sunk, so be it. We'll go down fighting!>

It was true. One way to end this mess was for the sea to claim them all. As for her, she would be torn from the sky and dashed into the ocean. Maybe the Gods had willed it this way all along?

No, sister.

<Pearl?>

Hope seized her.

I am here. Our Aunt is here. Fly with me!

Abruptly, a silver whirl of agitated air was inches from her face.

Follow!

Maia didn't wait for a command, banking and heading at full speed after the guiding Tempestas.

<What in Hades?> Leo barely braced himself in time, putting out an arm to catch Amphicles, who had stumbled on the tilting deck.

"It's Cymopoleia, sir." Simultaneously, she Sent to the Fleet. <All Ships! Cymopoleia is advancing on our position!>

"Cymopoleia?" Amphicles shot Leo a look of horror. "The Gods must be desperate! She's destruction personified. We don't stand a chance!"

"It depends on how fast we can get out of here," Leo said. "She's favoured Ships before now. Let's pray that she's on our side."

Sister. You will be safe here. I must aid our Aunt.

Pearl darted off, leaving Maia stationary at a good vantage point. She could see that her sisters had heeded her warning, though there was little they could do about it.

<I've met her,> *Patience* said, <off Portus. She spoke to me and said that I had done her a kindness, though I don't know what she meant. Whatever it was, it saved my vessel and crew>

<Use your Priest!> *Victoria* Sent. <She may remember you!>

Maia listened in, knowing that her friend had been spared because of her kindness to her. Still, of all the Gods who could have turned up, she'd rather it wasn't the infamous Lady of Storms. Perhaps in her own way, Cymopoleia was trying to help? The ancient deity wasn't known for her sense of reason or restraint, like a furious old neighbour woman who would stand

299

in the road and scream at passers-by, except Cymopoleia's outbursts could topple trees and rip off roofs.

"How are the Fae reacting?" Leo asked.

"They aren't," she replied. "Perhaps they think they won't be affected."

The great wall of thunderheads, black and purple as a newly-made bruise, swept up to the Fae's position, pushing the sea into turmoil as it whirled closer. White-capped waves began to slam into the sides of the Fae vessels, rocking them violently like the cruellest of hands. Figures gesticulated as the Fae Mages turned their attention to protecting their flanks, throwing up ripples of green power in an attempt to deflect the worst of Cymopoleia's rage. Maia could see that they were trapped between two barriers now, the ocean running up both sides as if they were in a gigantic bath, mounting higher and higher. The rocking grew more violent. Masts tipped and sails began to tear.

Maia reported it all, even as she swung around to get a better view. Leo was trusting her to protect herself, something no mechanical device could ever do. She could hear the Goddess in her head, laughing as she hurled herself against the magical barriers.

The Fae were more organised now, sending up spitting fireballs that punched holes into the heart of the clouds and forcing the Goddess to pull back and coalesce elsewhere. Cymopoleia dodged and darted to avoid them, her airy body sustaining damage, but still she pushed ever deeper into the heart of the Fae fleet.

Maia continued to report, knowing that there was nothing she could do to help. Her Aunt was seriously inconveniencing the Fae, but not actually sinking them. It was as if she was playing some sort of game, baiting them then pulling back.

Abruptly, a mighty bolt of lightning shot into the mist wall, spreading across it in a flash of concentrated power. There was a sharp crack, louder than any thunder Maia had ever heard, causing her crew to cry out and clap their hands over their ears. When the light faded, the mist wall had been blown to shreds.

The Goddess's voice rang across the water.

"I have done my part. The rest is up to you!"

After one last manic peal of laughter she was gone, leaving a choppy sea and three fleets in full view of each other.

<Hello, beautiful ladies!>

Wolf of the Waves and his fellows were slipping into position between the Britannic lines, their smaller, sleeker hulls manoeuvring with ease. The sea was calmer now that the Lady of Storms had departed.

<We don't have much time,> *Victoria* interjected. <All Ships, attack!>

The Flagship's guns spoke first, hurling shot towards the Fae to find the range. To her alarm, Maia could see the enemy beginning to respond.

<'Ware magics!> she called, wondering whether to close in herself.

<Maintain height, but ready weapons!> Leo ordered. <I know you want to get into the thick of it, but it's time to let the other Ships play their part now.>

<So I'm just to watch?> she demanded.

<Not at all. Wait until they're occupied.>

Victoria led the way, firing broadside after broadside towards the enemy. Some shot got through, but it was obvious that the Fae were working to restore their shields. A subtle glow began to shimmer on the water, signalling that they were starting to call the mist once more.

<Damn it!> Leo cursed, beside her on the observation platform once more. <They're regrouping.>

She felt his helplessness.

<We should go in and give them something else to think about,> she said, preparing to open up a channel to Vitalianus. She would need authorisation for further action.

<All Ships, engage with new weapons!>

Vitalianus was gambling all on a final throw of the dice. Maia's view was already compromised by clouds of rising smoke as Ship after Ship fired, aided by the Longships' considerable firepower, but it wasn't enough. Nor was this a pitched battle. Enemy vessel after vessel was slipping away, their sole aim to get to land. She could see her sister Ships were constantly being forced to correct their courses. It was unlike the other battles she'd read about, where two opposing forces stayed put and pounded away at each other until one or the other prevailed.

"We have to stop them," Leo was muttering under his breath, "but how, when they won't stand and fight?" Then, louder, "*Tempest*, keep firing! We've as much chance as anyone to score a hit but don't lose altitude."

Maia could hear her sisters calling to each other as they jockeyed for position. The Longships were similarly frustrated, moving closer and closer and itching to attack the Fae hand to hand. Just as it seemed they were getting to grips with the little vessels, the Fae would slip from their grasp like darting minnows, continuing on their path.

<I don't think seeing them is much of an improvement," *Patience* Sent to her, frustration loading every syllable. <I daren't waste my torpedoes!>

<How many do you have?> Maia Sent back.

<Two.>

It wouldn't be enough.

<Maybe if you all fire at once?>

<It might take some of them out,> *Patience* admitted, <but what do we do then? The idea is to try and herd them into a killing ground, but they're too fast. Also, Sandpiper and the other Mages think that they're not all real. We keep getting different numbers.>

Maia could have kicked herself. It could be another reason that her Shipsenses were not up to par.

<Of course! Illusion and glamour. It's what they specialise in! Is there a way of telling?>

<Not yet. It might be easier if we had more Mages.>

On Musca's orders, Maia adjusted her position so that she was just ahead of the lead Fae. Her Chief Gunner was preparing another salvo whilst busily calculating drop times.

<I've lost three men already, so I daren't go lower,> she told *Patience*, <But I'll do what I can.>

She registered the shockwave as her guns roared, the shot arcing down right on target – and punched through the gossamer illusion into the waves below.

Musca, hanging out of the gun port, spat in disgust.

"You saw that, Ma'am! The bloody thing wasn't real! The Gods alone know how many of them there really are."

"I know, Musca. We're working on it. Captain?"

"Get the Mages up here now."

Heron and Robin appeared in short order, blinking in the daylight. Leo wasted no time.

"Too many of their vessels are illusions. You need to work out which ones we can destroy and you need to do it fast."

"Our colleagues are working –," Heron began.

"Your colleagues aren't up here," Leo interrupted, scowling. "We have a vantage point granted to no others and the Fleet is relying on us."

The two men nodded.

"Understood, Captain," Robin said. He and Heron exchanged glances then stepped forward to peer down at the scene, speaking urgently to each other in low tones.

Maia left them to it, focusing instead on the Fae vessels. From her great height, they looked no more than toy boats constructed to sail on a pond for some child's amusement, populated with unmoving ranks of little stick figures made from scraps of wood and cloth. It was hard to believe that they were a deadly threat to civilisation as she knew it. The great warships keeping pace with them were clumsy in comparison. She tried to pick out any distinguishing features, but the vessels all looked similar with nothing much to tell them apart. Even their pale woven sails were the same colour and none of them bore any marks of rank or allegiance. There were no colours, flags or banners here.

She made a quick count, dismayed to see that another vessel had appeared in place of the illusion she had destroyed. Was it real, or yet another trick? There wasn't even a shimmer of magic around it, no way to tell if it was solid or simply Fae glamour. Besides her, Heron was shaking his head in frustration.

"I can't tell," he muttered to Robin. "It's too subtle a working. Any ideas?"

"Short of targeting all of them and seeing what sinks, no. Are you going to tell the Captain, or shall I?"

Neither looked enamoured at the prospect. Leo was already chafing at the restriction.

"Well, gentlemen?"

Heron took a deep breath.

"I regret to say that there are no markers we can see, sir. This is Fae spell craft at its finest."

Leo's lips thinned.

"Then we've no choice but to give them everything we've got. *Tempest*, resume bombardment. Some of them are real. You choose the targets."

"Aye, sir."

Maia scanned the vessels, all too aware of the growing line of land on the horizon. They were running out of time. Her previous attempt to stop them made her doubt that the leaders were anything more than a perfectly-crafted feint, so she decided to aim for the ones tucked in behind. Surely one of them must be in charge? Perhaps they needed a new angle of attack.

"Heron," she began, "What do you think the range is for casting a glamour of this magnitude?"

She remembered reading in the Navy manual about required distances for Mages in battle. Her memory obligingly provided the diagrams showing the angles and vectors. Perhaps the Fae had the same limitations?

The old Mage, already halfway back to his beloved engines, rubbed his chin in thought.

"Ah! They'd have to be fairly close for this type of work. Maybe a hundred feet? They will probably be working in concert."

His eyes widened as his bushy eyebrows shot up.

"That's it! We need to work out which are Mages!"

"And what do they look like?"

His face fell again. "Not sure," he admitted, but we know they're hierarchical and tied to the land. Maybe they wear symbols or something to display their rank?"

It was as logical a guess as any. She magnified her sight to maximum and began to examine each vessel.

At first, the armed warriors standing motionless on the deck seemed identical, helmeted and clad in corselets of some silvery metal. Most hefted spears, the leaf-shaped points glinting in the sun, whilst others bore swords of an antique design. They didn't seem to be communicating with each other, or the rest of the vessels for that matter, and nor were there many crew. She spotted a helmsman operating a primitive form of tiller at the stern, like pictures of early craft from a thousand years before, but there was nobody in the rigging. The single sail couldn't account for the speed or manoeuvrability of the vessel either. None of it made sense to her.

Perhaps everything they were seeing was an illusion, designed to distract? Maia could feel the frustration building as she searched for anything that would give her an edge.

<All Ships!> The *Victoria*'s call broke into her concentration. <You are ordered to intercept. Break the line, use your weapons, ram them if you must! This ends now.>

Vitalianus was upping the stakes with a decisive throw of the dice. Slowly the great Ships began to turn, tacking towards the enemy to plunge into the thick of battle in a choreographed move. With one part of her mind directing the bombardment from above, the rest of her hunted with desperate intent through vessel after vessel.

There! One of the figures wasn't wearing armour at all. It was dressed in a plain robe, a necklace of twigs, feathers and bone around its neck and swirling tattoos snaking around bare arms. When she stretched her abilities to their utmost, she thought she could see his mouth moving. What had Heron said? They drew their power from nature and the land. She'd found her Mage, now to get at him.

Maia had no doubt that this vessel would have more protections than the others, but the Fae were relying on concealment to get them through. She angled around, positioning herself to allow Musca and his crews to fire a broadside.

The shot bounced, repelled by the same green flare she'd seen when she fired at the *Regina*. Maia cursed the fact that she had no torpedoes this time. Her armaments were useless and this same feeling of helplessness swept over her as she watched her sisters bravely sailing to what could be their doom. Green shields sprang to life about the vessels, as the mist began to rise once more.

<Sister! Help me> she screamed into space. <Mother! Where are you?>

In answer, an image rose up, surfacing from the depths of time and memory. Maia recoiled, but it loomed closer, every detail sharp as grief. A Ship, smiling, her blue eyes full of intent and her arms spread wide to hold her.

Child! Fire and mind! My gift to you!

Gone was the rotting, crumbling wood, the charred remnants. This was the *Livia* in her prime, the regal Ship she had once been. Maia recoiled, but the *Livia* would not be denied. She pressed close, her face thrust into Maia's, and in the depths of her gaze some sanity remained. Wherever she was, and whatever her torment, whether she was a fragment of implanted thought or a sending from the Gods, Maia couldn't tell.

Use our gift! Strike!

They were two Ships, then they were one, bound by the magic of the Mother and the strength of ancient oak, armed with the Potentia of the land and the gift given to the First Ship and passed to her successor. Behind her she could sense the shadow of another, a Ship known to her only through the paintings in the Academy and in the oldest of books. Armed with shield and spear, mail-clad, the *Britannia* stood guard over her sisters. Though long in the earth her spirit yet remained, pulled from beyond in this hour of need. The three of them were joined, bound in sisterhood, but only one of them could act now.

The responsibility was hers. The *Livia* at one shoulder, the *Britannia* at the other, Maia struck, her gift arrowing through the air and into the mind of the Fae mage. His essence writhed in her grasp, twisting and shrieking as she sank her barbed fangs deep into his spirit, holding him fast and siphoning his Potentia in a gleeful rush.

Now!

Even as he crumpled like a withered leaf, she released the energy she had taken, converting it to the element she had been granted. A wash of flame bloomed outwards like deadly petals, consuming the vessel.

There had to be more. Her gaze was a searchlight, raking the fleet. Another and another met the same fate, their shields and castings counting for nothing, swept away by cleansing flame. Illusions collapsed as Mage after Mage died screaming, leaving vessels bereft of their protectors.

Three Ships watched as weapons were launched at last, streaking underwater to hit hull after hull with deadly precision and sending shards of wood, rope and cloth skywards before tumbling to patter like scattered rain on to the surface of the ocean. The Longships added their firepower to the Britannic vessels, some boarding the defenceless craft to hack at the Fae who were desperately trying to save themselves. She could hear their howls, snorts and roars as they spilled blood, laughing at the glory of the battle in their own way.

Barbarians.

Livia did not hide her contempt.

Useful barbarians, Britannia corrected.

They are my friends, Maia told them firmly.

Already, she could feel herself straining to pull away, as if they were moored together and she was releasing her ropes one by one. The distance began to grow. She could almost feel the water beneath her hull again like a cherished reminder of her first vessel and the loss was an ache in her heart. Still, she had to leave them both behind.

Well done, my sister. Remember me. You too will find someone worthy when the time comes.

Britannia raised her weapons in salute before fading away. *Livia*'s smile had vanished and her face was troubled, as if the memory of her crime along with her sanity had only now returned to her.

Forgive me. I did love my Captain, she whispered. *But I would never have hurt him of my own free will.*

Maia, herself once more and overcome with pity, enfolded the unyielding Shipbody in her arms.

We were both used, she told the ghost. *Your duty is done and I forgive you freely. Be at peace now.*

The *Livia* drew back and Maia could see the woman she had once been. She had to ask the question.

What's your name? I'm Maia Abella.

The blue eyes flickered in confusion as she struggled to remember. Then her brow cleared.

I'm Antonia Silvia. I remember now!

Cracks began to appear in the smooth wood of her Shipbody, growing wider and more pronounced, until with a cascade of tiny flakes it disintegrated and fell away.

Antonia Silvia stretched and ran her fingers through her hair. She laughed in delight, then turned and walked away into the distance, off to some place Maia couldn't follow.

There was a moment of silence, then suddenly Maia was back in the real world, leaving behind whatever strange dimension she'd found herself in. Not three Ships but one, alone, flying over smoke, fire and tangled wreckage. The occasional boom of cannon was punctuated by cheering and shouts as her sisters and their allies finished off the enemy.

Leo was standing next to her, his face alight and waving his hat to the Ships below.

"Well done, men! The Mages came through for us!"

Musca and his crews were slapping each other on the back and even Osric was looking cheerful for once. Old Hyacinthus and Monkey were doing a jig, while Big Ajax clapped. It seemed that the whole fleet was celebrating.

The link was full of Ships talking, exchanging congratulations on their victory. Maia listened in, feeling herself apart for the first time since her installation. Checking her chronometer, she realised that the encounter with her predecessors hadn't taken much time at all. She'd truly been in another place.

A loud chant told her that Danuco was by her altar, praising the Gods for their triumph. Maia resisted the urge to scream. It was only now that she could see the damage their jealous rivalries had wrought on the lives of those close to her. Her Aunt had helped a little to be sure, Vulcan had had a hand in designing her new vessel and she'd met Jupiter, Mercury, Juno and Athena Minerva, but were they really the ones to thank? Were they only involved because of their own self-interest? She'd been right when she told Antonia Silvia they'd been used. The woman she'd glimpsed at the end was nothing like the rage-filled, murderous Revenant she'd been fated to become. Maia could only hope that her soul was at rest now, her trials over.

Maia would have to hold her peace and keep her thoughts to herself. The gift she had been given was a secret not even her sisters could know. And, when the time was right, it would be up to her to pass on this legacy to a Ship not yet born.

308

< This is *Victoria*. All Ships, report!>

<*Imperatrix* reporting. Eight destroyed.>

<*Diadem* reporting. Five destroyed, picking off survivors now.>

<*Dragon* reporting. Six destroyed, two sinking.>

<*Swiftsure* reporting. Eight done for. No survivors.>

<*Persistence* reporting. Blew five to Hades. Watching 'em drown now!>

<*Leopard* reporting. Seven accounted for. No survivors.>

<*Blossom* reporting. Four destroyed. Captain Plinius sends his regards.>

<*Jasper* reporting. Three destroyed and picking off stragglers in the water.>

<*Farsight* reporting. Three destroyed and likewise.>

<*Emerald* reporting. Two destroyed and just finishing off another.>

<*Patience* reporting. Three destroyed and another crippled. It's sinking now.>

Maia listened to her sisters' triumphs in silence. She couldn't have honestly said how many Mages she'd obliterated, though she knew she'd managed to account for a few. There had been upwards of sixty Fae vessels once the illusion had been shattered.

Her men were still full of jubilation and starting to relax a little now that her guns were secured, though a few marines were still taking pot shots at figures struggling in the water. Normally enemy survivors would be rescued, but not this time. There could be no mercy for these invaders.

The Ships were making a thorough sweep, pushing through the flotsam and jetsam in an orderly pattern as their Captains dictated, to make sure that all threats were eliminated. Maia ran through her equipment checks automatically, taking refuge in the steady stream of figures that was as natural to her now as a heartbeat. She'd settled on a lazy circuit of the battleground, affording her officers the best view.

<Well, that's that. I'm glad our Potentia trumped theirs,> Leo told her.

<Yes, it did,> she replied.

He was puzzled at her lack of response.

<Are you alright? You sound tired. That shouldn't apply to a Ship though.>

She was tired, not physically, but with a deep weariness of the mind. It was as if all her life had caught up to her at once, revealing the dark meddling that had guided her every step.

<It's nothing,> she reassured him. <A lot's happened lately, that's all.>

He was immediately solicitous. <I know. Losing your vessel, then this. Still, you've done so well. Everyone's pleased with your performance!>

Maia bit back a caustic reply. Of course her performance was what they judged her on now. They didn't know the half of it. She kept her mental voice neutral.

<I'm glad I fulfilled expectations.>

Leo's brows drew together, as if he suspected her sarcasm, but wisely decided not to pursue the matter.

<I'm happy with the eight we sunk. Carry on.>

Amphicles had come to make his report. Maia listened with half an ear, letting her thoughts glide effortlessly like a soaring gull. The ability that the *Livia* had unlocked, passed to her from the *Britannia*, lay coiled inside her mind like a sleeping serpent, dormant but ready to wake at her command. Fire and mind. Deadly weapons indeed, but never to be used lightly. The *Britannia* had had no way of knowing that her successor would be compromised. There were still so many questions and Maia realised that she might never know the answers. The *Livia*'s God-given madness had to have compromised her abilities, or she could have wreaked havoc on her captors. Also, where had they come from in the first place?

Had the *Livia* returned as a Revenant solely to pass on her gift?

The thought was disturbing. Maia pushed it from her, knowing that she was going around in circles when she should be concentrating on the present. She only realised that the litany of sunken vessels had ended when she was addressed directly.

<*Tempest*, report!>

<Eight vessels sunk. Awaiting orders.>

She took refuge in the standard phrases, still feeling that a part of her was detached, whilst in the rest an anger was building. She would have to let it out at some point, but now was not the time. How could she possibly hold the Gods to account anyway? One well-aimed thunderbolt would finish her off for good.

Naiad and *Vanguard* were busy comparing strikes with *Jasper*, while *Persistence* and *Swiftsure* sounded like they'd started parties of their own. It was rare for there to be so few casualties in a battle, though she had lost three of her marines. It was time for her to do her job.

Maia left the platform and found Osric on the lower deck along with his men. They were cleaning out their muskets, emptying the foul-smelling water through a hatch, but snapped to attention at her presence.

"My condolences," she said. "They were good men."

He nodded. "They were, ma'am. I'm just relieved it wasn't worse."

She raised an eyebrow. "I'm still aloft. How are you finding it?"

Osric grinned mirthlessly. "Gives us a better position to shoot from, ma'am. We got a few of the creatures and had our revenge."

"You did. Carry on."

He saluted and her marines returned to taking care of their weapons.

<*Victoria* to *Tempest*. You have new orders.>

She alerted Leo immediately, glad of the distraction.

<You are to proceed south-east at maximum speed. Pendragon is engaging the enemy and you must support. May the Gods aid your flight! Co-ordinates to follow.>

This was it. The sea battle had just been the prologue. They had thwarted whatever workings the Fae had planned here, but now the real fight was on land.

She was the only Ship who could help her beloved Admiral now.

XVII

One second Milo was staring in horror at the stones that were all that remained of Ceridwen and her daughter; the next he was hurled into Stygian darkness. The transition was abrupt, but he was grateful he landed on his feet. Nor was he alone.

His companion was to his left, her face averted. He swallowed, trying to get his brain back into some sort of focus and looked around to get his bearings.

It was yet another cave, its floor smooth as if made by the slow passage of water over millennia. The sides rose above him to a rough ceiling and the air was cold and dry. The little pool of light illuminating his surroundings came from a simple ball of Magelight overhead, which negated any shadows save for the cracks and crevices in the walls.

He took a deep breath, then chided himself. There was no way of telling how far underground they were or how much air there was, though he wouldn't have thought that Julia would endanger them for no reason. He must have made some movement, for she turned to him and he was struck again by the uncanny light in her eyes, as if something inhuman lurked just beyond her features.

She regarded him steadily for a few moments before speaking.

"Can you guess where we are?"

He shook his head.

"No idea. I hope you know."

That earned him a smile, making her look more like the woman he'd known.

"I do. In fact, no-one's been here for a very long time. It's in the nature of a storage facility."

He looked around, puzzled.

"Oh, not here. This is just the antechamber. Come on, there are people we need to meet."

Milo watched with dismay as she stepped lightly towards a blank section of rock. It looked no different from any other wall, with no evidence of human hands. The talk of people was somewhat alarming as well. Who, or what, could possibly live down here? He swallowed his fear and followed her.

Julia halted and stared at the wall, tilting her head this way and that, until her face cleared.

"Got it," she said with satisfaction. "Even Emrys hadn't been here for quite some time, but his memories are clear. I know what I have to do."

She raised her arms and spoke a few syllables in no language Milo had ever heard, almost a song rather than a spell, then tapped out a rapid pattern on the surface.

Immediately, the rock vanished, revealing a circular tunnel about three times Milo's height, as if some God had taken an apple corer and carved out a huge plug. Julia strode forward confidently, the light detaching to bob at her shoulder. Milo hastily trotted after her.

The tunnel led them straight ahead, and not downwards as Milo had anticipated. They must have been pretty deep to start with and, after about a hundred feet by his reckoning, they came to another blank wall. This one was smooth and glistening, like a gigantic drum skin and he could feel the magic embedded in its fabric. Whatever was behind it was protected by some seriously heavy-duty spells. Undeterred, Julia sang out once more. The doorway shimmered and parted, clinging to the outside like a silver hoop.

Julia grinned at him.

"Are you ready for this?"

"Ready for what? I'd really appreciate it if you told me what was going on, you know."

She raised an eyebrow.

"Some old friends who have been waiting a very, very long time."

She led him through into a great hall. It looked more like a castle chamber than a cave, with stone vaulting arching above him and oak panelled walls. Ranged along these and evenly spaced was a succession of chairs, high-backed like thrones. Five of them were occupied by seated figures.

At first Milo assumed they were statues, but on closer inspection he realised they were human. Above their heads, colourful banners were mounted on poles; an oak tree, a leaping fish, a boar, a gorgon's head, a lion, while weapons of antique design were propped against their seats, ready to hand. They looked more like sentries who had fallen asleep at their posts, or ancient warriors who had passed out after a hard night's drinking.

Julia moved from one to the other, much as an Adept checked a ward of patients, peering into faces and nodding to herself.

"Good. The spells have held. I did have my worries."

The voice was hers, but the words were not. Milo repressed a shudder, then realised that a subtle thrum of energy was flowing through his body. Excalibur, Caledfwlch, the Sword of Britannia, was waking up. It recognised these men. He corrected himself instantly. People. At least one was female, her helmeted head sunk on her breast. Her emblem was the head of Medusa, designed to strike fear into the hearts of her enemies and he knew exactly who she was. Who they all were. They had been waiting in the dark for a very long time.

"The horses are through there," Julia said. "I'll check on them too."

She sounded so matter of fact that Milo nearly laughed. It was only then that he realised that his mouth was hanging open. He licked suddenly dry lips and edged forward to get a better look at the warriors. He could see that there were many empty spaces, as if the chamber had been intended for many more than five. After so many centuries, he would have expected there to be dust and signs of age, but there were none. Everything looked bright and newly-made, somehow defying the passage of time.

One chair was more imposing than the others. A roaring dragon was carved across its back, wings unfurling and talons outstretched. He touched it gingerly, feeling the grain of the painted wood against his fingertips and the subtle edges of each scale. The man this had been created for was now no more than an ancient skull on Coventina's altar. Whatever power he had once possessed was dead along with him, save for the glory of his name.

Milo was beginning to feel thoroughly daunted, when Julia reappeared.

"They're fine," she said.

He watched her warily, his hand still on the throne. He still wasn't sure how to take this new Julia, or was she purely Owl now? She grinned at him.

"Fancy that one, do you?"

He snatched his fingers away and she laughed. "I suppose it could be yours by right. It would have been Artorius's but he refused it. There had to be a sacrifice to power the magic, and he was already failing with a tumour eating him on the inside. He preferred to die quickly for his people."

Milo mastered his revulsion at the talk of human sacrifice, anathema to any civilised person, before finding his voice.

"Why?" he gestured around the hall.

"The Gods granted him a vision of the Fae's return, so he called for Emrys and his surviving Companions and together they came up with this plan. Not everyone wanted to go along with it. Most of his original Companions were already dead or wouldn't leave their families, but these few agreed. The spell has preserved them at the height of their strength, to fight the Fae once more."

"And then?"

"Oh, they don't expect to survive. For that matter, none of us might. Nothing is certain. I can't promise you victory, but we'll have a bloody good shot at it."

"I'm not my ancestor."

"No-one expects you to be," she said, "but they'll pledge their loyalty nonetheless. You do look quite like him, you know. You and Cei both."

This time Milo couldn't suppress the laugh. "I look nothing like the statues!"

"Those? Oh, they're based on some Roman Emperor or other, including the heroic pose."

He snorted. "My nickname's Ferret."

She shrugged. "It fits. A certain amount of guile is always necessary, plus the ability to slip out of tight situations. You'll do. Now, there's only one thing that can break this spell. Draw the sword."

Milo braced himself and slipped Excalibur from its scabbard. It sat snugly in his grip as if made for it, emanating contentment.

"It feels happy," he said.

"I'll bet. It's going to meet up with old friends and then they're going into battle. What more could a magical sword want? Now, touch each Companion on the shoulder and that will do the trick."

He glanced at her. "What do we do when they wake up?"

She shot him a look.

"They'll probably need a few minutes, then we can say hello."

Milo rolled his eyes at her, then looked around at the immobile figures. Which should he choose first? He thought he knew who each one was, but tales changed over centuries.

"Just do them in order," she suggested.

The nearest was the one with the emblem of an oak tree. Milo rummaged through his memories of childhood schooling to match it to a name. He'd always loved the old tales. The image came to him as he'd seen it last, printed on the pages of his old textbook.

Gawinius, or Gawain in the British tongue. He was a big man, his face hidden by an elaborate helm topped by a red, horsehair crest. Intricate designs scrolled around the brim and the steel was set with cabochon jewels. It looked an expensive piece of kit, and he realised that part of his brain was busy calculating what it would fetch on the open market. He then added to the sum because it was antique, then chided himself for being so mercenary. There truly was nothing heroic about him, he decided, ruefully. The heavy winter cloak, fastened with an annular brooch, would have fetched good coin too.

"When you're ready," Julia remarked.

Milo took a deep breath and raised Excalibur. The blade clicked as it came into contact with the golden corselet of scale. *Lorica squamata*, his mind supplied, the standard armour for a cavalryman. Whether it would stop musket fire, he didn't know, but then again Fae didn't use muskets. It would certainly be good against edged weapons.

He felt the enshrouding spell release like a soap bubble bursting, and held his breath, staring intently at the warrior's bearded chin, the only part of him he could see clearly.

"Do the next one," Julia ordered. "We haven't got all day and it will take a little time for him to surface."

Milo glared at her in irritation, thinking she sounded more like a crabby old man than ever. Julia could be waspish, but he'd be glad to have her back, if she ever managed to get out from under the spell Emrys had placed on her.

He gave in and moved to the next, who had a banner with a lion. If he remembered rightly, this one was the foreign Companion, Lord Palamedes, who'd come from the Mediterranean somewhere. His helm was plain, though it had a red crest like Gawain's and his cloak was fur-lined. His beard was dark and curling, the coarse hairs spread over a gorget that protected his throat. Milo hoped that they wouldn't all wake up with neck ache and stiff bones. He repeated the procedure, keeping one eye on Gawain, but apart from the dissipation of magic there was no other sign.

Next was Bedwyr, or Bediverius as the Romans insisted on calling him. His sign was the leaping salmon, showing strength and perseverance. He had been one of Artorius's closest friends, surviving many battles and hardships at his King's side, so it made sense that he would be here now. Instead of scale armour, Bedwyr was wearing a shirt of mail, the interlocking rings gleaming and well-maintained. His pointed chin rested firmly on his chest. The next place was Artorius's so he moved on, not without a shiver, to the female warrior.

Nobody knew what her name had been originally, but now they called her Britomartia. Some tales said that she'd been a slave, others that she was a lady of high birth who had followed her true love into battle, gaining the skills to be a fearsome fighter, though he personally thought that a bard's invention. She was also wearing a plain steel helmet with heavy cheek guards. Her long red hair spilled down her mail as if refusing to be confined. Perhaps now he would find out the truth about her origins? Or maybe he would let someone else do the asking. He touched her shoulder and continued on.

Drustanus was last, his emblem an eagle like the ones carried by the legions since time immemorial. His father had been a general, and the son had continued his family's military service, remaining faithful to the end. He was shorter and stockier than the others, and had a good selection of weapons propped at his side to complement the sword across his knees. Milo tapped his shoulder then stepped away quickly, having the sense that the man would wake up ready to fight.

It was sad really. Emrys must have prepared this place thinking there would be many more, but time and circumstance had left only these.

"I don't know what they can do," he said. "Five against an army aren't good odds." He was about to add, 'if they actually wake up', when Bedwyr's head twitched and he grunted, like a man disturbed from sleep.

Milo gripped Excalibur even tighter and took two steps backwards.

"Hold Excalibur before you, point down!" Julia urged him. "They need to see it!"

That made sense. They would be waking up to two strangers with no idea of how much time had passed and had plenty of weapons to hand. He quickly took up position where he would be in view when they raised their heads. It was only then that he wondered what on earth he was going to say to them. 'Did you have a good sleep' just didn't seem right. With any luck Julia would do the talking, or whatever bit of Emrys was left in her head.

Abruptly, Bedwyr straightened, his helm rising as he shifted in his seat. Milo could see him blinking furiously as he came to. Slowly, the others followed suit. Milo stood his ground, Excalibur held before him like a protective talisman and praying that they would have the sense to recognise him as a friend. The weapon was giving off vibrations now, a subtle thrumming that he could feel through the soles of his feet, as if encouraging the warriors to awaken. He hoped that they would recognise it now it had adapted itself from its previous form.

Five pairs of eyes locked on to him. Bedwyr heaved himself out of his chair, his armour rasping as he stood and his mouth splitting into a smile.

"Arthur!"

Then he stopped in confusion, the smile fading. Julia stepped in.

"This is Gwydre, Heir to Caledfwlch. Welcome back, noble Companions! Your long wait has ended and your youth is restored!"

Off to the side, Gawain stretched and rolled his shoulders.

"About bloody time," he said. "It's good to be able to move without my joints creaking! How long have we been asleep?"

The Companions looked from Milo to Julia, waiting for the answer.

"Long enough," she said, tactfully. "It is many years since Artorius was King."

She was speaking Classical Latin. Milo had studied it, but it was usually only used for official business these days. Most people spoke a bastardised version of it containing dialect that told you where they came from. Gawain's speech had a pronounced Britannic accent, though Milo could follow it easily enough.

"And who are you, Lady?" Palamedes's voice was smooth, his Latin excellent.

"I am Julia Victoria Pendragon, descendant of Artorius. Merlin passed his power on to me before he departed for the Summer Lands. I am now to be known as Mage Owl."

That answered that question, though Milo didn't miss the flicker of uncertainty in the Companion's eyes.

"So, Merlin's gone for good?" Gawain asked.

"Yes. He's gone and you are needed. Caledfwlch has awoken because the Fae have returned."

Gawain swore, Bedwyr's lip curled and the others looked to their weapons.

"So, the King was right," Gawain said.

"Did you doubt him?" Palamedes asked.

Gawain shook his head. "Would I be here if I had?"

"Just tell me where they are so that I may kill them."

Britomartia's voice was harsh. She was already hanging her sword at her side and reaching for her spear.

"That's the spirit!" Owl said. "Don't worry, there will be plenty to keep you busy."

She quickly introduced Milo as Gwydre, son of Julius and updated the Companions on their new situation, finishing with a warning.

"Many years have passed, and Britannia has changed."

"I'm sure we'll be seeing that for ourselves." Bedwyr's gaze raked over Milo, stopping on Caledfwlch. "Somehow, I know that's Excalibur," he said, "but why does it look different?"

"It's changed with the times," Milo told him. "When I found it, it was a rusty old piece of metal sticking up out of a bog. I took it without knowing what it was, or who I was for that matter."

"You carry Caledfwlch and that's good enough for me. You're a royal prince, then?"

Milo felt his lips twist. "I'm a Crown Agent and spy. I never knew I was a prince until a few hours ago. My mother was the High Priestess at the Heart of Albion."

"A sacred marriage," Palamedes said, nodding. It was like being under questioning and Milo tried not to squirm. "Have you brothers?"

"A half-brother. He's the Lord High Admiral of the Fleet, but he's on land preparing to fight the Fae."

"And it is his son who killed his cousin, the rightful king?"

Drustanus's deep voice had the lilt Milo associated with Kernow.

"It is."

"Treachery!" Bedwyr muttered. "That's not good. Seems that we're needed, my friends!"

"Before we leave this place," Owl interjected, "do you swear to follow the holder of Caledfwlch?"

"Why hasn't he tried for the Sword of Kingship yet?" Britomartia demanded.

"We've not had time. It's stuck in a column of the Londinium Basilica, waiting. It can wait a little longer. Do you swear?"

Bedwyr relied instantly. "I swear."

The others answered in the affirmative one by one, even Britomartia, though by the look on her face she had doubts.

"Enough talk," she said bluntly. "Let's go and find your army. Where is my horse?"

Britomartia was impatient to see action. Armed with a sword, shield and spears, Milo decided that she did look like her statues. Britannia personified. From her speech, she came from somewhere in the north, perhaps Brigantia. Fierce blue eyes glared at him.

Following her true love my arse. More likely to have joined up to get revenge on someone, or just because nobody dared argue with her.

"They're where you left them," Owl said, unfazed by the woman's belligerent attitude. Britomartia nodded curtly and strode off to the stables.

"Don't mind her, Lord. It's just her way," Gawain said to Milo.

"It's not a problem," Milo answered. "I know she can fight."

The Companion burst out laughing. "I wouldn't like to take her on. She'll drink you under the table too. I wish we'd had more like her. Boudica reborn. You've heard of her, right?"

Milo smiled back. "Oh yes. And all of you as well."

A strange look passed over Gawain's face.

"We are remembered?"

"In many tales of heroism. You're legends."

"Hey, everyone!" Gawain called out. "We're legends!"

"Does that mean we get free drinks?" Drustanus rumbled.

"Absolutely. And all the pies you can eat."

Drustanus and Gawain cheered. Bedwyr shook his head.

"I never set out to be a legend."

Gawain threw an arm around his shoulder. "Tough luck, my friend. You are one!"

"And Arthur is long dead." Bedwyr walked back over to the throne and bowed his head. Without turning, he asked, "You haven't told us how long we were asleep. What year is this?"

Here it was. Owl had gone with Britomartia, so this was all on him now. He sheathed Excalibur carefully before replying.

"It's two thousand and forty nine years *Ab Urbe Condita,* from the founding of Roma."

All he could hear were the sharp, indrawn breaths. He knew it would be a shock.

"Gods in heaven!"

Palamedes spoke first. "It was twelve hundred and ten when we came here." They were all staring at the throne that had been made for their King. "We were so old. Do you remember? Everything hurt. I could barely walk. My sons begged me to stay, but I wouldn't listen. Better to die in battle against the Ancient Enemy than wither in my dotage. Arthur sacrificed himself for us. Do you know how it happened?"

Milo realised that he was being asked. He shook his head, dumb in the face of such grief.

"His own son killed him, according to the old ways. Blood had to be spilled. How we all begged to take his place, but he wouldn't change his mind. 'I am the King,' he said. 'It must fall to me. When you awaken, follow whoever has taken my place. Be faithful to him as you were to me.'

Though his voice was level, tears were pouring down his face. Drustanus was trying not to sob, comforted by Gawain. Bedwyr was as still as he had been when Milo had first entered the chamber, his mute back a testament to his feelings. So, Pendragon had killed Pendragon before, but in a highly ritualised way. The history books hadn't said anything about that.

"We were already here," Palamedes continued, as if nothing was amiss. "But we knew when he died we would leave this world for a while and return renewed. Alas! If only he could have come with us!"

Drustanus sniffed loudly.

"He said there'd be a new king and it was right and proper that this should be so. But there isn't, is there?"

"Hopefully there will be one again soon. It will probably be Cei," Milo said. "After all, Caledfwlch could hardly get to him while he was at sea, could it?"

"That makes sense." Palamedes said.

He pulled a fine handkerchief from a sleeve and wiped his eyes.

"You brought handkerchiefs?" Gawain said.

Palamedes waved a hand. "Of course. I'm not a northern barbarian."

Gawain laughed, just as the sound of hooves heralded the return of Britomartia and Owl, the former leading her horse. Milo thought the grey looked more like a pony. She stopped, her hand on her hip, surveying her friends.

"Why are you all crying like babies? By Epona, I can't leave you for a minute, can I?"

Gawain pulled a face at her, while Drustanus hastily wiped his eyes and nose on a fold of his cloak. Palamedes pursed his lips at him.

"I have another handkerchief if you want to borrow one."

"Piss off."

They grinned at each other.

"Go and get your mounts," Britomartia said. She rubbed her horse's nose affectionately. It seemed lively enough for having been asleep for eight hundred and thirty nine years.

"Yes, Auntie."

Britomartia rolled her eyes at Palamedes, swatting at his backside as he passed her. Milo repressed a smile, well used to banter amongst old comrades, then turned his attention to the horses as they were led out. To his surprise, there were two extra.

"Did Emrys know?"

Owl shrugged. "Probably. Either that, or he thought they might not all survive. It's always prudent to have spares."

"Before we leave," Bedwyr said, "we cannot have the wielder of Excalibur riding out unprotected, can we?"

Milo eyed him.

"That's true. He'll need armour and weapons."

A look flashed around the group, before they reached a silent consensus.

"I'll get them," Gawain said. He disappeared in the direction of the stables.

Owl cocked her head, and her eyes grew distant. Then she spoke.

"If there's anything else you need, get it now. We won't be coming back."

The Companions busied themselves with their weapons and checking tack, all except Gawain. Milo felt even more like a spare part.

"Here, my lord. These are for you."

Milo saw the dragon first. It crouched on the helmet as if it was about to spring into the air, wings unfurling and mouth agape. Then his eyes took in the scaled corselet and the cloak with its elaborate brooch. He swallowed.

"Suppose it doesn't fit me?"

Gawain smiled.

"I think it will. Arthur would want you to have it."

Milo could only stare dumbly. This wasn't ceremonial gear. He could even spot some repairs, though skilfully done. Now everyone was looking at him and he knew he couldn't refuse. He shrugged into the armour, but tried to refuse the helmet. It seemed too personal, as if he were invading the great man's space.

"Put it on." Owl had no such compunction. "He has no more need of it. You do."

There was a harshness in her voice that was at odds with her usual demeanour and Milo thought he heard the echo of another, one who had seen his friend ride out many times before.

"Give me a minute."

He could tie it to the saddle or something. He already felt like he was a child in a fancy Saturnalia costume.

"Here, Lord."

Gawain was offering him the reins of a handsome black gelding. He didn't have to be told whose horse this was. It presumably came in a set along with the armour.

"Um, thank you."

The horse seemed placid enough, though its accoutrements were like something out of a museum. The first thing that Milo could see was the difference in saddle design. He soon found out why that was when he saw the others mount, throwing themselves up and over with practised ease.

There were no stirrups.

"Is there a problem, my lord?"

"It's not what I'm used to," he replied. "Things have changed."

Gawain's broad forehead creased.

"What, horses?"

Actually, he was right. These beasts were half the size of standard cavalry mounts, but he didn't want to get the Companions' backs up. These were obviously the best of their time period and no doubt cost a fortune.

"Something like that," he prevaricated.

"Don't tell me you ride elephants into battle!" Palamedes joked.

"Our horses are... bigger. And the saddles are different. We have things for our feet to go in so that we can direct the horse more easily."

There, he'd said it.

Drustanus whistled.

"Bigger horses? I'd like to see that!"

"Looks like we're going to," Bedwyr said. Britomartia was having none of it.

"I'm not changing my horse."

"Nobody will expect you to," Owl interrupted. "Now can we please get moving? Is there anything else to get?"

The horses were now loaded with weapons, each having their particular place though of course there were no saddle holsters for pistols. Instead, several spears were slotted into holders, ready for use.

"I have need of one more thing." Bedwyr strode to Artorius's throne and reached behind the dragon banner. "We're not going anywhere without this."

Milo knew what the object was instantly. The standard of Artorius. It was in the ancient style, as was the rest of their equipment: a red and gold dragon head on a tall pole, jaws open, with a tail of cloth made to look like scales trailing down to the ground. In a charge this tail would stream behind it to rally the troops and it would whistle to unnerve the enemy. Bedwyr lovingly straightened the cloth, shaking it to untangle it.

"I am *draconarius*."

Milo realised his eyes were moist.

"Of course you are."

For some reason, the *draco* standard suddenly made everything feel more real. He was going into battle under his ancestor's standard, alongside people from history.

Then there were a few moments when he could see nothing at all. Voices came to him from a great distance.

"My lord?"

"What's wrong?"

"Give him space."

The floor was hard against his back and his legs were being raised.

"By Mithras, he's fainted on us!"

There was more, but he couldn't understand the dialect.

"I said, give him space!"

That was Owl.

"Get him some wine."

"We haven't got any."

"Lay Caledfwlch on his belly. It might revive him."

Milo opened his eyes. His view of the ceiling was blocked by helmeted heads and a horse's muzzle, rapidly pushed aside by Owl. His first emotion was one of total embarrassment. Some war leader he was turning out to be.

"It's a side effect of the magic."

Owl brushed their concerns aside, glaring around. Nobody contradicted her. Perhaps she was trying to save his face, or maybe she was telling the truth. Either way, it helped. His leather flask was thrust under his nose and an arm across his back raised him to a seated position. He took it and drank gratefully.

"He hasn't eaten for a while either," she added. "We've been a little busy."

"Perfectly understandable," Drustanus rumbled. "Come to think of it, neither have we. How about we all get out of here and find some decent rations, eh?"

From the response, everyone thought it was a good idea. Milo put down the almost empty flask and struggled to his feet.

"Sorry about that. Don't know what happened there."

"It's the shock of meeting this lot," Britomartia said, unexpectedly supportive.

"We'll grow on you," Palamedes said.

"Yes, like tree fungus."

Palamedes gave her a mock bow. It was a small joke, but lightened the atmosphere and gave Milo a bit more time to recover. He was certainly hungry enough to have eaten one of their little horses, hooves and all. His main worry was that they would think less of him for flaking out like that, but then dismissed the thought. He was what he was. He hadn't asked for any of this and it was way beyond what any Agent could be reasonably expected to put up with. If anyone had a problem, they could take it up with Owl. He took a deep breath and straightened his shoulders.

"So, what happens now?"

The Companions re-mounted, heads swivelling towards the Mage. She had scrambled onto a bay with a plaited mane and was adjusting her robes, stockinged legs dangling on either side. She must have changed when she was with Britomartia, Milo thought. Had Emrys left them for her, or had she conjured them out of thin air?

He gripped the saddle and swung himself up and over, settling himself between the high pommels and cantles at the front and rear. They held him comfortably, making him feel a little more secure, but the lack of support for his feet was unsettling. Presumably, the horse would respond to changes in bodyweight and pressure from his knees. Even so, this style of riding wasn't something he would choose and he decided to swap for a modern steed and equipment as soon as possible. In the meantime, he wasn't intending on walking out of here, so he'd have to do the best he could and try not to fall off.

He'd ridden a pegasus, so surely he'd be able to cope with this?

Owl nudged her horse alongside his.

"How are you feeling now?"

"Fine," he answered, with as much assurance as he could. She nodded.

"Good. Just put on the helmet and try not to fall out the saddle." She raised her voice to address them all. "I had hoped to take you to meet my uncle's forces, but there's no time. I'm going to open a portal directly to the battlefield. Prepare yourselves!"

Great. He was going to ride into battle, leading legendary heroes and carrying an equally legendary sword that looked nothing like the one people were expecting. His day was just getting better and better. As to what Caniculus would think of it all, Milo had no idea. Probably wet himself laughing.

Already, he could sense the air thickening as it became charged with Potentia. A thrill ran down his limbs, settling in his belly as, despite himself, his excitement grew. The Companions formed up around him, guiding their mounts so that he was surrounded, with Owl to his left and Bedwyr, standard raised, to his right.

The horses tossed their heads and whickered, to be soothed by pats and gentle words.

Then Owl spoke and the portal opened before them.

XVIII

It felt like they'd been waiting for days instead of minutes, seconds dragging themselves across his brain like wounded soldiers. Overhead, Helios's chariot had long begun its unstoppable descent into night.

Cei was already sweating under the unaccustomed weight of the steel helm that had been impressed upon him, while beneath him his horse stirred restlessly, as if he knew that his rider was less than prepared for what was to come.

It wasn't as if he would be leading the charge, he thought ruefully. He had officers to do that while he and his generals stood on this high point and oversaw the battle, directing runners with orders or passing them through Raven to the Mages who stood with spells at the ready. He was more of a rallying point, the fulcrum of the whole apparatus, rather than a moving part.

The lines looked impressive enough. Cavalry and infantry were lined up with the artillery behind, the latter ready to lay down covering fire the second the enemy came in range. Dotted among the troops were the standards and banners of each legion, hanging limply in the still air. It had been as hot as Vulcan's forge that day and, as predicted, the Fae had laid low, waiting for the cool of the evening. It was a less than ideal time to fight a pitched battle, but there was no way Cei was sending his troops into the depths of the woods.

On the whole the ranks were silent, though there was a low hum of conversation from the Amazons who sat easily astride their horses. They would be used to fighting in all conditions.

Likewise, the Centaurs waited patiently, weapons slung around their stocky torsos. Technically they were the fastest troops, but he doubted they'd charge in regardless of their own safety. Better to wait and let the ones who were doing it for love of country and their own people to take the brunt. In their place, he would do the same. There was no point in earning money that you had no chance of spending.

It was time for his pre-battle speech.

"I'd better get on with it. Raven, with me."

He waited until the Master Mage was mounted, then they left the assembled officers and rode through the lines. He only stopped when he was reasonably sure that most of the army could at least glimpse him. Even if they couldn't, Raven would amplify his voice. Cei told himself that it wasn't any different to the speeches he'd made before sea battles, even if this time the enemy was something they hadn't faced before.

Mighty Jupiter, give me strength!

Then *tubae* sounded, their blasts shattering the silence like shrieks of defiance.

Cei took a deep breath. This was it.

"Men of Britannia!" he began to say, then his eye fell on a dozen women, standing to one side and armed to the teeth. They had the look of professional fighters, perhaps gladiators, answering the call to protect their families. Then there were the Amazons, assembled in a body to his right with Dioxippe to their fore. He corrected himself hastily.

"People of Britannia! Honoured allies!"

He saw their knowing smiles and a couple raised their arms in salute.

"All of you here know of me, though it has not been fated that I come among you before today. I confess that I am more at home on Neptune's realm than on land, but here I am, as the Gods have willed it."

A low murmur greeted his words, quickly stilled.

"I will soon lead you against our ancient enemy. The Fae believe that we will flee before them like sheep. They are sorely mistaken!"

A few ayes sounded from the ranks.

"Over eight hundred years ago, Artorius the Great drove the enemy from these lands. This time I, Cei Pendragon, will finish what he started! Are you with me?"

The roar that greeted him filled the heavens.

"Our Gods are with us! Mighty Jupiter, Greatest and Best is with us!"

The noise drilled into his eardrums as the legions cheered.

"Mars, Lord of Battle is with us! Now let's teach these invaders a lesson they'll never forget!"

Whether they heard him or not, he no longer cared. He'd said his piece and now it was time to wait for the return of a mythical sword, a powerful Mage and a deadly enemy. He raised his hand in salute and galloped back, even as his mind turned to the Fleet.

Back in his position, a deep rumbling caught his attention. Off to his right, fifteen heavily armoured fighting machines puffed their ponderous way on to the field, white clouds of steam shooting from their funnels. Named *testudines*, after the famous Roman testudo, or tortoise shield formation, they could hold twenty musketeers apiece in their hulls. Cei thanked the Gods that there had been little rain lately. Dry ground favoured them as they could be useless in the mud.

"I see that our Artificers have been busy, though I wish we had more of them," he remarked to Raven.

"I think these new devices will do some good, Raven agreed. "From what I know, the Fae still can't bear the touch of iron, so even if they're shielded the machines will give them pause."

"We can always send them in first," Cei mused. That might break their lines."

"Possibly, but remember not all our enemy are Fae."

It was a sobering thought. Nobody knew how many rogue Mages and other creatures might be bolstering the Fae forces, and they weren't afraid of iron.

"This is always the worst part," Felicio said. "Once the fighting starts there's no time to think of anything else."

"It's the same at sea," Cei said, shortly. "Just different tactics."

His thoughts returned, unbidden, to his fleet. The news of its victory had come through before midday, lifting a weight from his mind. His body might be here, landlocked, but his heart was forever on the ocean with his Ships. He'd been taken aback at the involvement of the Alliance Longships, but not altogether surprised. It made sense to unite in the face of a common enemy.

"Thank the Gods we won't be dealing with them on two fronts," Felicio said. "Still, the majority of their forces are here and –,"

A shout cut him off as a scout galloped up.

"General, a mist has been sighted. The enemy are approaching!"

"About time. Pass the word on, soldier."

The scout saluted and dug his heels into his foam-flecked horse.

"Raven –,"

"Already informing my Mages, General. They report that everyone is awaiting orders."

"I suggest we send in the Amazons first to do a bit of scouting and possibly some hit-and-run. It's the tactics they prefer and I'd rather not risk an out-and-out charge until we have more information on their disposition and numbers."

Cei agreed.

Let's hope it's more hitting and less running. You can never tell with mercenaries, honourable though these appear to be.

"Very well. Have our infantry in readiness to move though. I want the cavalry to try and flank them too, hit them from the side. If they can."

Felicio saluted and beckoned to a runner, drawing the man aside.

"What do you think of these tactics?" Cei asked Raven.

"Sound on an open field, but problematic if the enemy keep to the tree line."

Cei turned his head to watch Felicio. "Well, at least one of us knows what he's doing. Any update on *Tempest*?"

"She's making good headway, sir, but there's a fair amount of ground to cover."

"Her arrival will give the enemy something to think about," Cei said. He stared across the fields to the line of trees beyond. It had been the best place to pick for a fight, but they would have to draw the Fae out. He could see tendrils of mist reaching out from the shadows of the woods like questing snakes and the horizon was already blurry and becoming less defined. The enemy was massing.

An eerie ululation rose from the distance and the horses shifted uneasily.

"That never came from human throats," Felicio muttered.

The woodland was completely blotted out now as the mist swept towards them, advancing rapidly on their position.

"Seems they're trying the same tactics as before," Raven said. "The Mages stand ready."

"Launch a few spells to try and break it up," Cei ordered.

Almost immediately, three streaks of purple flashed westwards fizzing as they went, only to disappear into the void. Cei strained to see if there were any explosions, but it was as if the greyness had simply absorbed them.

"No effect, sir." Raven said. He pursed his wrinkled mouth. "It's too soon for shielding."

Cei waved Felicio over.

"What are the Priests saying?"

"They're praying." Felicio didn't sound impressed. "I thought the Gods were on our side. We could do with a thunderbolt or two, if Jupiter has a mind to help."

They both looked up, but the sky was clear.

"It seems we're on our own for now."

For all their protestations and assurances of support, the Gods were fickle entities. They were probably waiting to see what happened before committing themselves. Not all were ready to offer help openly. Cei thought for a moment.

"Direct the Priests to keep up the sacrifices. It will keep their attention, if nothing else."

The mist was creeping ever closer. They couldn't see the line of trees now and the horses were tossing their heads, uneasy at what was approaching.

"It's the same problem the fleet had. How can we aim if we can't see them? Also, it's not getting any lighter."

Felicio squinted ahead.

"I wouldn't wait for them to get any closer," Raven observed.

He was right. It was time for action.

"Order the guns to fire into the heart of the mist. Let's see if we can break it up, or maybe punch holes in it.

The order went out. Behind him, the cries of 'have a care!' were the only warning they got before the enormous cannons spoke. It was as if some mighty creatures heaved themselves awake underground, shockwaves rippling through the earth. Now Cei was glad of the helmet to protect his ears, though the pulse made his guts tremble.

Heavy shot flew overhead in great arcs, falling into the greyness. Their landing was muffled but unmistakeable. It was impossible to tell if there was any damage.

"Keep firing!"

They'd set up a rolling barrage now, making the ground shiver and heave.

"We can't send anyone in yet, sir. Give the guns time to soften them up."

Felicio sounded calmer than Cei felt, but there was one thing he'd noticed.

"Can you see? The mist has stopped its advance."

It was true. He could see the swirls in it now, like creamy milk stirred with a spoon. Was it becoming patchier?

"Excellent." Raven lifted his arms and pursed his lips. Instantly, he was joined by his fellow Mages, all whistling in a continuous thread of sound that was both unnerving and compelling.

The first finger of breeze ruffled his horse's mane, growing in strength. Behind the lines, the Priests had switched to naming the winds as their knives rose and fell and the altars burned their grisly offerings.

"Gods of the Air! Aid us as you did our Ships," he prayed aloud. "Do this, and should I live, I will build you a temple and make offerings in your name!"

It was a generous offer. He reminded himself that it would have to be on a remote hilltop, where they could do the least damage. He repeated his offer to the major Gods, promising rebuilding, refurbishments, sacrifices, anything to get them on Britannia's side. The mist thinned as the breeze became a wind and then a gale, battering at the mist even as it tried to coalesce and hold its shape.

The whistling stopped, but Raven had to shout over the rising tumult.

"It looks like the major Winds have answered! See?"

He flung out a skinny arm, pointing. There were forms in the mist, suggestions of limbs, bearded heads with round cheeks like the illustrations he'd so often seen on nautical charts and maps. For the first time, Cei dared to hope that they could come out of this alive.

"This'll let the dogs see the rabbits," Felicio called to him. Cei nodded absently as the mist thinned, ripped into shreds and tatters like a mouldy shroud. He was eager to see what was lurking in the trees when he saw the huge shadows, vaguely humanoid and taller than any warrior.

"Are those giants?"

At first he hadn't realised he'd spoken aloud.

"Bigger targets, sir."

It was only as the final wisps melted away that he saw in disbelief the front lines of the Fae army and what they had brought with them.

*

Maia flew on at high altitude, every gear, chain and linkage straining as she poured as much Potentia as she could into her vessel without rupturing something. Her crew worked ceaselessly, cleaning and checking the weapons after their first battle. Heron and Robin monitored her engines, taking notes and muttering incomprehensibly to each other.

Musca was surveying her stores of powder and shot.

"We have enough, don't we?" she whispered in his ear. A new hand would have jumped a mile but her Chief Gunner simply raised his eyebrows.

"I hope so, ma'am, what with the added supplies we took on from the *Victoria*. There's a limit to what you can carry, you know."

"Of course. I have the feeling we'll need all of it before we're done."

She left him to it, watching Big Ajax, Hyacinth and Monkey giving their cannon a good clear out. Black powder residue would clog barrels and touchholes if allowed to build up. It was a dirty job, but essential. Her hold already stank of sulphur and rotten eggs, though they were doing their best to scrub everything down. Grimy faces and clothes bore witness to the last encounter with the Fae and now they were plunging into another one.

"I hope the Admiral's routed them already," Monkey said, holding a bucket to catch the sludge as it drained.

"We can hope, lad, but I don't think it'll be that easy," Hyacinthus said, plunging a wet swab into the barrel. "They'll be throwing all they've got at him. The Gods know what sort of nasty allies they'll have brought along."

Monkey looked at him in alarm. "Such as?"

"Don't know, lad. It's been so long since we fought 'em, nobody knows."

The boy gulped.

"Could be worse," Hyacinthus continued. "We could be down there with 'em."

Big Ajax nodded, but Monkey grimaced, unconvinced.

<Tempest.>

Maia switched her attention away from her crewmen and focused on her Captain. He was standing with Amphicles, perusing a large-scale map. It was strange to see the land masses instead of a nautical chart, but she could read it well enough.

"I think we're about here," Leo said, jabbing a finger on the thick paper. She checked.

"Yes. We've been mainly following the old Londinium Road, but we'll divert just before we reach the capital."

"It's a great pity we can't just fly over the portal site and bomb it to Hades," Amphicles said.

"It would save a lot of trouble, but we've been ordered to steer clear and swing in behind our forces," Leo replied. He didn't sound too happy, but personally Maia thought it was wiser to detour. She had already discovered what deadly Fae magic could do.

"I only hope we get there in time to do damage to their ground troops, though we'll have to watch out for offensive magics," her Captain added. *"Tempest*, what's our estimated time of arrival?"

Maia had already calculated a rough time, based on wind speed and power output.

"About forty-five minutes, sir."

Leo straightened up.

"Keep an eye open for anything suspicious on the ground and, unless ordered otherwise, relay our position directly to the Admiral. I've a feeling he won't want second-hand reports."

She could only agree. To tell the truth, she was looking forward to contacting him. It had been a wrench leaving her sisters behind, even though she knew that they were safe for now. He would be a point of normality among all the strangeness. On Leo's command, she opened the link.

<*Tempest* to Admiral Pendragon.>

<Report, *Tempest*.>

<Captain Valerius sends his greetings, sir. I'm about forty minutes away and flying as fast as I can.>

<Excellent.> The relief in his voice was palpable. <Please return the compliments and continue at full speed. The attack has begun, now dusk has given them the advantage. Be prepared. You may come under attack sooner rather than later, especially if their command has intelligence on your whereabouts and capabilities.>

That didn't sound good.

<I'll be vigilant, sir.>

He paused. <The Gods go with you, *Tempest*.>

He broke the link, but not before she knew just how afraid he really was.

Maia took a moment to compose herself. Pendragon never let anything like this show. It had to be her unwanted ability probing for cracks and weaknesses, despite her increasing loathing of it. The *Britannia*'s legacy seemed designed to exploit vulnerabilities, and she had no wish to see what anguish lay buried in yet another mind.

Leo reacted as expected. She issued the command to battle stations, using her Shipsenses to scan her surroundings. Who was to say that the attack would come from the ground? There were legends aplenty and the Gods alone knew what fell creatures had been conscripted to their ranks. Everyone insisted that there were no more dragons, but hadn't she seen one with her own eyes? It had appeared to be friendly, but you never knew.

Heron and Robin left off fussing over the engines and came to join her Shipbody. Their main function now was as battle Mages, throwing up shields and hurling spells and Maia stood ready to link her Potentia to theirs. Ships and their Mages worked hand-in-glove in situations like this and she would have to rely on them. Firepower might only do so much.

A brief vision of Raven flashed across her inner eye. He was down there, alongside Pendragon, fighting alongside the legions. She could only hope that the powerful magic the creature had inflicted on him with so long ago would save his life, but then again could he survive the deadliest of wounds? She was sorely tempted to open up her private link to him but forced the urge away. He had enough to occupy him and so did she.

The minutes ticked on, the land rolled away beneath her and she concentrated on small things. The pressure of the air. The thrust of Potentia into her engines. Holding to her course.

She would have to trust in the Gods, adding her prayers to those of her Priest and crew.

Pearl, where are you? I wish you were here.

There wasn't much further to go now. She braced herself and powered on, the setting sun casting her racing shadow over the land.

*

There were more of them than he could have imagined, spread out just in front of the treeline, as if the pressure of those that followed had forced them out into the open like pus from a wound. The splintered tangle of broken trees raised jagged spear points towards the sky, pale heartwood lighter patches in the dimness that hung over the whole area now the sun was disappearing. If he'd had the power to cause Helios to turn his chariot, he would have, but Cei doubted that even Jupiter could do that. The artillery barrage had ceased for now, as had the eerie cries, and an unnatural stillness held sway, as if the scene was a colourful fresco painted on a villa wall.

Cei scanned the ground carefully, squinting in vain through his telescope for casualties, or any indication of the effect of his heavy guns. Beside him, Felicio was doing the same.

The Wind Gods had departed, racing away to their assigned compass points having done everything they could. Being wild elementals they couldn't be contained for long, ever restless and seeking the horizon. It was a wonder that the Mages had managed to summon them at all, and it was clear that the effort had cost them.

"Raven, status?"

The old Mage seemed to wake from his trance.

"The guns did a little damage, but not enough. I fear the trees bore the brunt of it, which will further anger those spirits roused to fight by fear of fire and axes. Still –,"

He stopped mid-sentence, his body tensing.

"They're advancing."

Cei's stomach clenched. It was true. The shapeless mass was seeping through into the field, bringing its darkness with it. The Fae had apparently more than one form of concealment and they were using it to their advantage. He strained his eyes, but could make out nothing clearly, which in a way was worse.

"Send in the *testudinae.*"

The armoured devices were an excellent vanguard and would act as shields for the rest of his forces. For a second, he'd debated whether to keep them back as a reserve, then dismissed the idea. It was essential to pile on as much firepower as he could while the Fae were still at a distance, giving the rest of his forces a chance.

Felicio gestured to a rank of *tubicen*, who promptly blew a shrill series of blasts. The answer was immediate.

Rhythmic puffs of steam, increasing in speed and frequency, told him that the *testudines* were on the move, rumbling onwards and leaving great swathes of flattened grass in their wakes. The legions cheered as they clanked into view, steam whistles screaming like the souls of the damned in Tartarus. Gun barrels protruded from ports in the armoured sides as men crouched within, ready to fire at anything identified as a threat.

"They're magnificent!" Felicio shouted. "There are a few last-minute modifications too."

Cei wished he could share the man's enthusiasm for the new machines, but he didn't think for one second that the Fae would be ill-prepared. Their ability to withstand cannon shot from his Ships had taught him that they too would have modifications of their own. He gripped his reins tightly, eyes fixed on the armoured vehicles as they traversed the open land, and waited for the response.

The *tubae* sounded again and a signal flag was raised, causing the *testudines* to halt with a hiss of escaping steam. The metal juggernauts sat in the open, dark shapes in the rapidly fading light and Cei winced inwardly at the thought of what their crews had to be enduring. It was bad enough in an enclosed gun deck.

In response, a lone figure on a horse left the tree line, cantering smoothly to meet them and holding a branch above its head. Cei adjusted his focus and the indistinct shape resolved into a man, heavily tattooed and naked from the waist up.

"It's Kite."

Raven's voice held nothing but disgust and contempt for the traitor Mage.

A dozen questions sprang to the forefront of Cei's mind. The last he'd heard, Kite had been his son's chief ally, yet here he was. Was Marcus with the Fae army, or still holed up in Greenfields? He would give much to know.

Kite reined in his horse at a respectful distance from the nearest *testudo*, every eye on him. Satisfied that he had their attention he began to speak, projecting his words across the battlefield so that he sounded more like a God than a man.

"People of Albion! I am Kite, First Druid of the Ancient Land, and I bring you a message!"

"Gods protect us! We don't need his ilk again," Felicio spat.

"He sets out his stall from the start." Cei answered.

"Aye. It'll be human sacrifices face down in a bog, or carted off to the Fae Court for sport before we know it."

"You have been lied to! The Fae come in peace, to restore the ancient rights of these islands and to liberate you from the Roman yoke that has held you in thrall these past centuries. There is no need for blood to be spilled this day! Lay down your arms, and you shall be granted all the rights and privileges of a sovereign people, lost to you since the invaders came to these shores over a thousand years ago. I am Kite, and I speak the truth!"

The words slipped into Cei's ears like nesting serpents seeking a safe burrow. They had the ring of sincerity, laden with sweetness and the promise of joys to come. He shook his head to clear it, momentarily confused.

"And I am Raven, pupil of Merlin himself, and I say you lie!"

The Master Mage's voice pierced his befogged senses like a battle cry, stripping it clean of the subtle Fae glamour. Around him, the legions stirred and muttered as the spell was broken.

"I see you, old man," Kite sneered. "Still hanging on and giving out bad advice. You know you haven't a hope of winning. Submit, or I can't promise you a peaceful death."

Enough, Cei thought. He cleared his throat, knowing that Raven would work his magic.

"And I am Cei Pendragon, of the line of Artorius. I know you lie. You are naught but a murderer and traitor to your people. Crawl back to your foul masters, worm!"

Cei was used to his voice being amplified, but this time it was almost deafening. Raven gave him an approving nod. Encouraged by their leader's defiance, his men began to shout taunts of their own, adding rude gestures for good measure. Kite sat impassively for a few seconds, then threw the branch he'd been carrying on the ground. He shrugged theatrically, swung his mount's head around and returned whence he'd come, jeers and curses trailing after him.

Cei signed to Raven and, when he next spoke, his voice was normal again.

"Do you think my son is with them?"

Raven chewed his lip. "I'm not sure. I think if he were, Kite would have used that information to cause you pain. It's what the Fae and their lackeys do best. I think you can take it that he isn't, but don't count on it."

"Well said, sir. You sounded like the wrath of Mars himself there," Felicio said.

"Thank you, general. Talking of Mars, have we any word from the Priests? I would like the support I was promised."

"Aquila has just arrived," Raven said. Cei almost choked. The High Priest of Jupiter rarely left his temple in Londin and was certainly in no shape to fight.

"Where is he?"

"In your command tent, frightening the servants."

Cei didn't bother asking Raven how he knew.

"Has he a report for me?"

341

"Yes. Apparently, Marcus has left Greenfields, but nobody knows where he is. He apologises that he can't give you more information. He's going to attend to the sacrifices personally."

Cei bit back his reply. Cursing the Gods for their lateness would do none of them any favours. They would help in their own time, either subtly or overtly, but he would bet that they would want blood to be spilled first. His people would have to prove their worth before any intervention was forthcoming. There were many forms of sacrifice, but death was the most powerful.

"I will leave him to his task and pray to Fortuna that he is successful."

Felicio pulled out an amulet on a thong around his neck and kissed it reverently, before returning it to its place. Cei knew that he was invoking the Goddess, though she could be a fickle deity indeed. He mentally added his own prayer.

"Let's hope she smiles on us and that Mars lends us his strength."

He'd made his own sacrifices to the God of War. If Britannia fell, there would be no more worship and the Olympians would have to retreat further east. How could they want that?

He glanced at the skies, where clouds were massing. Kite would have made his way back to the enemy ranks now and the tension in the air was building. The *testudines* were holding their ground, but would it be too much of a risk to order them to advance? As if reading his mind, Felicio answered the question.

"We should wait for them to come for us, sir. Never give up the high ground."

"Indeed. But suppose they decide to leave us here to wallow in the dark?"

"We'll know soon enough. I pray we can fight before then."

Leather creaked as Cei shifted in his saddle. His backside was already growing numb.

"The Mages stand ready to flood the place with light if need be."

"Something's happening."

Raven's dry voice alerted them and he raised his telescope once more.

Bit by bit, the covering veils were lifting from the Fae troops. Images swam into view, blurred outlines becoming distinct and details springing into sharp focus. Cei fought back a wave of nausea as the Fae revealed their hand and they had their first sight of the Ancient Enemy.

He'd faced storms, Northmen and savage monsters from the deep, but this was different. There were creatures in their ranks straight out of winter's tales that lingered on as stories to frighten children by the fireside, things of shifting shapes and primeval heritage. Things that had not been seen in civilised Britannia for centuries.

Haughty Fae Lords and Ladies sat astride huge quadrupeds with talons for feet and single horns rising from their foreheads. Their coats gleamed unnaturally in the gloom, as if they emitted their own light, and he could hear low snarls as they readied themselves for battle. The front ranks consisted of blocks of armoured Fae, interspersed with creatures that looked like wolves one second, bears the next, pawing the ground and swaying in anticipation of the charge. Behind them, the trees themselves seemed to be moving, branches writhing as they clutched at the sky.

"If they bleed, we can kill them."

"Sir?"

Felicio had moved up next to him. On his other side, Raven stood as silent as any statue.

"I said, 'if they bleed, we can kill them'."

Unexpectedly, Felicio grinned.

"Your ancestor had it right, sir. Magic can't protect them all the time."

"Artorius had his Companions, Merlin – and Excalibur. What do we have, Felicio?"

"Let me see, sir. Tortoises and a whole lot of gunpowder."

"Then that will have to be enough."

Their conversation was interrupted as the shapeshifters raised their muzzles and howled.

"Looks like this is it, sir," Felicio remarked.

"I think you're right. Order the *testudines* to advance and hit them head on."

The rumbling and clanking of the heavy machines almost drowned out the ear-splitting screeches as the Fae surged forwards, shifters rapidly outpacing the Fae mounts and throwing huge clods of soil and grass in their wake. Cei braced himself, waiting for the first of the new devices to be deployed.

The foremost *testudo* commander didn't hesitate. A long streak of orange flame arrowed from its foremost nozzle, bursting on to the first ranks and setting them alight. The screeches grew shrill as fur and flesh burned under the onslaught. More machines moved in, spraying deadly liquid fire in high arcs, the swivel-mounts covering the whole of the front line. Simultaneously, the guns spoke, sending iron shot ripping into the enemy. Blackened bodies writhed in agony and the stench of burning hair and the meat beneath hung in the air.

"Tell them to aim for the trees."

Cei spoke quietly, but with deadly purpose. If the enemy's cover could be burned, that would be half the battle. He could already see that some of the tree spirits were retreating in fear, unwilling to risk the flames, but the others were pressing forwards, all save the Fae. So, the Masters were more willing to risk their allies than themselves. It made sense. He'd be sending in the mercenaries as soon as the field was clear.

The dry summer was once again in their favour. The grass had caught too, the flames bowing and twisting into bizarre forms as both sets of Mages fought to control them to their advantage.

"The commanders report that they're running out of Greek fire, sir," Felicio told him.

Cei watched as the shifters that had avoided the flames were mowed down by gunfire.

"Order them to recommence the barrage and send in the Centaurs and Amazons."

Felicio saluted, calling to a runner who galloped over. After hurried instructions, he turned and headed off to the ranks of foreigners. They would be earning their money this day.

War cries echoed as Dioxippe received her orders and led her women in a headlong charge, flanked by Centaurs, bows at the ready. The hybrids' faces were grim, but the Amazons were laughing as they attacked, eyes alight with the joy of battle and fortified by their faith in the Huntress. Arrows flew and creatures fell by the dozen, collapsing over the bodies of their fellows in a tangled heap of fur and claws.

The Amazons and Centaurs began to harry the front lines, loosing arrow after arrow and firing muskets. Fae fell, but were pushed aside as others took their places. The line began to move, marching steadily towards the Britannic legions.

"Should we advance?"

Cei spared Felicio a glance, but the General was firm.

"No, sir. We can't see the full extent of their forces. I'll get the mercenaries to flank them, then we can aim for the centre."

It took endless seconds for the orders to be relayed, but eventually the Centaurs peeled away, galloping in a body to the left flank, while the Amazons mirrored them on the right.

"I don't understand it," Felicio said. "Why aren't they engaging our cavalry? There's no point in riding down our infantry while we have horse still in play."

Cei didn't understand either. There was something about this battle that wasn't right.

"Pull them back! Pull them back now!"

Raven's hoarse voice had risen to a shout.

Cei was confused, until he followed the Mage's pointing finger. The sky was full of dark winged shapes, growing larger by the second. He raised his telescope.

"What in the Gods' name are those?"

"Strange allies indeed," Raven answered. "Sir, I need to gather the Mages."

Cei didn't hesitate.

"Do whatever you think necessary."

He'd never seen anything like them. Huge black wings, talons like birds of prey and with red, glowing eyes, the creatures were starting to swoop down on the Amazons. The women had broken away and were spurring their mounts back to safety, shooting as they went, but they weren't all quick enough. The bird-things dived like stooping falcons, snatching them bodily and soaring aloft. Cei couldn't see any beaks, or even any discernible heads, just the red eyes glaring balefully like the eyes of Cerberus himself. When they were high enough, they dropped their captives. Bodies rained down like ripe plums. A few Amazons had drawn their swords and fought mid-air, stabbing and slashing at their captors. Woman and monsters fell together like stricken harpies, crashing to their mutual doom. Mage spells trailed purple sparks as they zoomed towards their targets.

And still the creatures came, some with feathers aflame, expressionless and unnatural.

"They were stalling!" Felicio called. "The Fae have no intention of engaging and risking their precious hides."

They had to be constructs, Cei knew, some evil mixture of roc and Hades knew what else, bred to kill.

The musketeers were firing now, angling their weapons upwards to try to get a good shot, but the bird things were more manoeuvrable, dodging and croaking defiance like unearthly crows. One snatched a legionary standard, swooping upwards as its protector hung on grimly, desperate to protect it. It let go, but only when it was too late to save the man.

"Hold your ranks and files!"

Felicio's order rang out, but the legions were trapped between the advancing horde and the aerial attack. Several of the flying creatures angled out, toward Cei and his bodyguard. He drew his pistols and began firing. Two screamed and fell, smashing into the ground while spells blew the others apart into greasy smoke that mingled with the fog of discharged powder. It was getting harder to see the black shapes swooping above him and there was no time to reload.

Raven was at his side and a shimmering shield sprang up above him. Felicio was by his side.

"That's my last pistol shot, sir!" He reached for his sword.

"I'm out too," Cei yelled back. ""Keep moving!"

"Yes, sir!"

He urged his horse over to his legions, his guards scrambling to keep up, too angry to even curse the Gods, the Fates and all the others who were so eager to watch while his people died. He almost missed the shouts from the front lines.

"Giants! They have Giants!"

He'd been right. Another ancient enemy had indeed come for revenge; twenty foot tall creatures with stone clubs that could obliterate a house. The guns fired and one fell, but it wasn't enough. Nothing was enough to stop this.

He reached the front lines and focused on his soldiers. Suddenly, everything was clear.

"People of Britannia! Are you with me?"

By some miracle, Raven's spell still operated. Those who weren't fending off the deadly birds answered him with a roar.

"Then let us fight together!"

He dug his heels into his mount and charged down the hill, the might of Britannia at his back.

XIX

Pendragon had engaged the enemy.

Maia could have cried with frustration. Even at her fastest speed, powering her way through the endless blue, she wouldn't reach him in time. Leo stood on her observation platform, his hands gripping the rail so hard she could see the white of his knuckles, while Heron, eyes glazed, relayed the information from his speechstone.

She had one ear on him and several others listening around her vessel, when a silver streak appeared from nowhere, coalescing right in front of her Shipbody.

"Pearl?"

Sister. There is danger! You will be attacked!

Pearl's features shimmered in and out of focus, but there was no mistaking her urgency.

"By whom?" Maia demanded. Pearl looked confused.

I don't know what to call them. Mother says they are unnatural creatures devised by the Fae. They are busy attacking your Admiral's troops and will attack you, too.

"Thank you, Pearl. Thank Mother too."

The battle is not going well. The Fae have summoned many creatures that are no friends to humans. We will do what we can. The Winds helped a little, but they had to move on.

"Can you call them back?"

Her sister's nebulous face split into a smile.

You have the Potentia. Use it.

It was true that she'd dealt with the Fae at sea. Could she do the same on land?

She saw the fog of battle first, hanging above the treetops and lit with flashes of purple fire. The Mages were busy.

"Enemy sighted, Captain."

"All hands! Battle stations!"

There was woodland in the distance, the thick canopy broken and splintered from heavy shot. Figures were moving beneath it, scuttling between the trunks, but she was forced to swing around so quickly she could barely make them out.

"Reduce speed to half!" Leo ordered. Then they were out in the open, drifting above a sea of sulphurous smoke. Black powder residue hung in the air while below her she could hear the boom of heavy artillery and massed ranks of muskets. All else was concealed.

At first, Maia thought the ascending winged shapes were carrion crows, startled from their feast on the field of battle. It was only when they got nearer she realised they were something else entirely and definitely not friendly.

"Enemy incoming!"

The marines were already firing, knocking the fell beasts from the air with practised skill and sending them plummeting into the fog which swallowed them whole. But still they came flocking like birds dodging her cannon shot, swift, silent and with deadly purpose. The muskets seemed to be having more luck with them, but it was only a matter of time before they caused some real damage. Maia knew that her envelope of gas was the most vulnerable part of her new vessel. They would have difficulty breaking into her hull, but the propulsion systems were another matter.

"Robin, Heron! We need to shield!"

She saw them concentrate, lips moving as they evoked Potentia to link with her own. The rush of power through her hull was a blessed relief and she seized upon it, plaiting the double strands into her own to form a continuous flow of energies. It was a matter of moments to direct them upwards and around her envelope, protecting it.

Several bird-things flung themselves against her defences, breaking bones and scattering feathers like pigeons against glass.

She paid them no mind. The shield was holding and it would give her time to do what she had to. Pearl darted among them like a whirlwind, twisting necks and ripping off wings with a ferocity Maia wouldn't have believed. The Tempestas was staunch in her defence, flitting so fast that she was nothing more than a brief flicker of movement in one place before moving on to the next victim.

Throughout all, the marines kept up a steady rain of shot, the heavy lead musket balls tearing into the creature's bodies. There was no blood. Whatever animated these things had nothing so ordinary.

After an age, the bombardment stopped and there were no more. A few battered feathers spiralled through the air, but the bird-things were gone.

<That was unpleasant,> Leo remarked, <but I fear we've more to come. Was that our friendly Tempestas I saw?>

<It was.>

<We owe her our thanks once again. Can you sense any more of those things?>

Maia scanned her surroundings.

<No. I think that was all of them.>

<Thank Jupiter for that. Ask her if she can clear the air for us, will you? We have to have visibility, even if it means revealing our presence.>

She could only agree. It was vital to know what was going on. Evidently, this was the Fae's favourite trick.

"Pearl! I can't see a thing down there. Can you help?"

Watch me!

The Tempestas dived gracefully into the fog, which rippled away from her like spilled water. Gradually, the battlefield became clearer to Maia, allowing her to get her bearings. A cool, breeze sprang up, fresh and filled with the scents of summer as Aura manifested to aid her daughters.

It was carnage. Scarred earth, littered with burned and bloodied bodies surrounded the smashed remains of machines. Several were retreating, their weapons spent, while another was being destroyed by a colossal, hulking figure. Each blow of its club caved it in further and Maia could only pity the crew within. She opened her belly hatch, watching as several grenadoes plummeted down and on to the Giant's head. It was blown apart, showering the earth with brains and skull fragments, but the damage was already done.

Past the devastated machines, she spotted the main melee. Pendragon and his legions were fighting for their lives. Guns had given way to hand-to-hand combat in many places. There wasn't much time to reload, so it was a job for swords and axes. Amazons and Centaurs circled, getting in as many shots and arrows as they could while trying not to hit their allies. It was impossible to tell who was winning, such was the noise and confusion. Standards told where each block of fighters was standing its ground. The disciplined legions marched in step, stabbing as they went, each legionary protected by his fellow's shield. The red and gold of the Dragon banner drew her eye, but she couldn't risk dropping bombs or firing, as she could as easily kill friend as foe.

Then a new wave of creatures burst from the treeline.

"What are those animal things?" she asked Heron as he approached her Shipbody. The Mage grimaced.

"Shifters. People mutated by spells to be slaves to the Fae. They've always been used as shock troops."

"Aim for the outliers," Leo ordered. "We can make it as difficult as possible for them to deploy reinforcements."

Maia adjusted her course to take her directly over the advancing Fae as they raced towards the beleaguered blocks of fighters. Soon, craters bloomed like scattered flowers, mingled with blood and ripped bodies.

<Maia.>

It was Raven. She looked for him, but couldn't see him in the surging press of bodies below.

<Raven? Where are you?>

<Defending Cei. Listen! You can't help here. Find the portal the Fae are using and destroy it. It's about three miles to the west. You'll see a greenish light.>

<How? Will bombing it work?>

<It's worth a try.>

<But you…>

<Never mind about me. Go!>

Maia responded immediately, reaching out to Leo through their link. Although she would have rather stayed to defend Pendragon, she knew that she and her crew were the only ones who had a chance of getting to the portal now. If nothing was done, there would be no stopping the enemy advance. She adjusted her course immediately, barely waiting for Leo's command, when someone materialised next to her in a flash of purple.

"*Tempest*. Head for the portal. Now!"

Leo automatically raised his pistol, then he recognised their boarder.

"Princess?"

"I am Owl now," she said.

"On my way," Maia acknowledged.

Everyone's mouth had fallen open. Maia didn't need further orders – she was already hurtling over the enemy lines towards the strange glow that had to be the Fae portal. She could only pray that her weapons would make a difference when she got within bombing range. Going down in flames was not an option she wanted to consider.

*

There wasn't time to think, never mind be afraid. Milo's mount charged forwards, carrying him into an expanding tunnel. Sound and vision vanished, leaving him in blackness, though he could feel the movement of his horse and sense the others nearby. Just as he was about to cry out, the world burst in upon him and he was charging towards a line of distorted creatures across a trampled meadow with the stink of black powder invading his nostrils.

He couldn't remember drawing Caledfwlch, but it was in his hands, shining brighter than any sun. It was all he could do to hang on, feeling the air against his face and the Potentia that channelled up from the earth beneath him, while before him the Enemy fragmented into dust and ashes wherever the light touched. Time stretched, then stopped, becoming one endless moment of brightness as he hung suspended, every cell in his body bursting as if he was filled with a radiance from somewhere beyond. Caledfwlch's power raged through him, his body its channel and, for the first time he could remember, he was at peace.

This was what he had been born to do. Nothing else mattered.

*

Cei's arm was growing heavy, yet still he slashed and stabbed at one looming shape after another, the features blurring until they were no more than targets for him to demolish. He knew if he stopped he was finished, so he dug in his heels and urged his horse onward through the mass of bodies.

The gelding valiantly stretched his neck, using his body weight to slam into the enemy. Ahead, Cei could see the Fae Lords astride their creatures as his forces approached. One raised a hand and foot soldiers shot out of the tree line, hurtling with leaps and bounds through the cavalry towards the dwindling band of defenders. He couldn't tell whether the screams ringing in his ears were those of his own men or the unnatural shifters meeting their doom. There was no time to think, even as he spitted another of the monsters, then wrenched his sword free in a bloody arc.

A bass roar echoed through the clash of metal and crack of musket fire. A Giant crashed to the ground, but the price was high. Dead warriors lay in piles, felled by his lethal club. To his left, Amazons and Centaurs were harassing another, but it was slow work.

Cei cursed the Fae Lords. They were staying out of musket range and Kite's turncoat traitors were busy repelling cannon shot as fast as his gunners could fire. Powerful green shields were springing up, causing the view to shimmer and waver like heat from a griddle. Raven and his Mages were doing their best from the rear, purple lances striking the domes of force without much effect.

The realisation hit him. Whereas Britannia and the Empire had concentrated on improving their machines, the Fae had refined their magics to counter cold iron and the traditional spells they had all come to rely on. Now it was looking like that had been a fatal mistake. Technology alone wouldn't win this war and Cei knew it. The magic that had stopped his Ships' weapons was in full operation here and he couldn't think of a way past it without resorting to hand-to-hand.

Maybe if he could break through and kill the enemy leaders, he would stand a chance of turning the tide of battle? He swung his horse around and retreated just enough to give himself a chance to rally his men, knowing that his bodyguard would follow. There were a lot fewer of them than there had been but it was their only chance.

He waved to an officer who galloped over, his *tuba* at the ready.

"Sound the call!"

Several blasts brought the ragged line of cavalry together. Cei was about to order the charge when more and more Fae appeared in massed ranks, freshly arrived and ready to fight. Fell creatures paced among them in their hundreds, more than the eye could easily count.

"Sir!"

It was Felicio, his helmet spattered with gore. He grabbed for Cei's reins.

"We must retreat!"

Rage exploded in Cei's breast, until he thought his heart would burst with the force of it.

"Retreat? Where to? I'd rather die here. All forces! Advance!"

If this meant his death, then so be it. He'd be forever damned if he turned tail and ran. He owed his country that much.

"Sir!"

A sudden burst of white light lit up the centre of the field like a thousand suns, leaving them all dazzled. Cei blinked, his vison full of after-images as his eyes adjusted.

"What in Jupiter's name?"

He forced himself to squint through the pain, painfully aware that all sound had abruptly ceased. The air was thick like syrup and time itself had slowed to a crawl. Was it more Fae trickery?

The intense radiance was coming closer, brighter than any Magelight he'd ever seen. Vague figures were at the heart of it. They seemed like people on horses, not the foul horned monstrosities the Fae used. Cei's heart leapt. Were the Gods finally answering his prayers?

Then their leader came into view more clearly. He was wearing armour of antique style and holding a sword, while above his head a great dragon banner flew proclaiming his house. Cei gasped in disbelief.

The weapon flashed and the Fae foot soldiers shrivelled like leaves in a fire. Hybrid beasts howled and dashed back into the cover of the trees, clawing and trampling any in their way. Their Lords yanked at their mounts' heads and tried to flee, many rearing in panic as the strange riders blasted their way through rank after rank, leaving nothing but flakes of burning embers as body after body was sucked of life and obliterated. The air around Cei was full of drifting remnants, spiralling gently down to the churned and bloodied earth.

"It's Artorius," Felicio whispered, then he let forth a great shout.

"Artorius!"

The leader raised his sword in salute as he and his Companions mowed down the opposition, leaving none behind. They swept past the stunned Britons and into the woods, in pursuit of the routing Fae.

Another shout and a huge warrior in Greek armour sped across the field, moving faster than any man could. Behind him were two others, like satellites dragged in his wake, both armed to the teeth and heading after the riders. Mars and his sons, Phobos and Deimos were laughing as they disappeared into the shadows to begin the slaughter.

As the cheers began, Cei heard someone sobbing. It was a moment before he realised it was him.

*

Julia, or Owl, wasted no time in taking charge.

"Your mission, Captain, is to destroy the Fae portal. Don't worry about the battle. All is being taken care of. *Tempest*. Do you see it?"

"Yes, coming up on it now."

355

"We must take up position above it and fire. Heron. You and Robin must throw up a defensive shield. The Fae will try to blow us out of the sky, so be prepared. I will help you as much as I can. *Tempest?*"

"Aye, ma'am."

Maia had already spotted the portal, set in a clearing at the edge of the woodland. The trees around it were leaning as if trying to get away from the alien thing in their midst and scorched patterns radiated from the centre like a poisonous web on the tainted ground.

Behind it was a void from which a steady stream of creatures, both Fae and other things, were pouring. Lining the way like an honour guard were chanting Mages, their Potentia keeping the portal open. Maia did a quick count. There had to be over a hundred of them, both Fae and human, the latter recognisable by their robes.

"Filthy traitors," Leo muttered. Robin ran in and saluted, his birthmark vivid against the paleness of his skin.

"Good lad," Heron said. "Let's get that shield sorted, shall we? They haven't looked up yet, but it's only a matter of time."

Robin glanced at Owl, then gave him a brief nod. Maia could feel the strain it was putting on both her Mages. They had been forced to use too much Potentia lately and it was depleting their systems. It would be up to her to make up any shortfall and protect her vessel while directing her weapons.

The change in air pressure told everyone when her magical defences snapped into place once more. Using her magnification, Maia could see the upturned faces as they registered her presence.

"They've seen us, sir."

Leo's eyes flicked to Owl.

"Now, Lady?"

The Mage's face was furrowed in concentration.

"Yes."

"All weapons! Fire!"

Maia's crew scrambled to drop as many grenadoes as they could, hurling them through hatches as her guns erupted in a rolling barrage towards the glowing wound in reality. Device after device impacted, but still the gateway remained defiant, impervious to the force of the explosions.

<They're having no effect I can see,> she reported, desperately scanning for any change in its appearance.

<Keep trying.>

She relayed the order with an ever-growing sense of dread.

"Continue barrage!"

To further her dismay, Maia could a see a group of Mages detaching from the main body and clustering in a formation that boded ill for her. She didn't hesitate.

Reaching out with her mind as she did before, she began probing for any weak spots, digging and twisting like a determined gardener to expose the roots of their Potentia. It was like grasping vicious brambles that twisted and screamed, sharp thorns stabbing and slashing in their attempt to escape. She hung on, tugging with all her strength until she could rip them free from their anchors and hurl them far away, their magics sputtering and dying. There were two Maias once more: one, the Ship, guiding and protecting her vessel, the other a wild thing of elemental power that was tearing into her enemies. She watched as this new self whirled through the enemy Mages like a tornado, blasting their bodies and searing their minds to oblivion. All the fear, all the pain, released at last in raging destruction.

Sister! Enough!

Pearl was there, her presence cutting through the madness. Maia forced herself to pull back, fighting with all her strength the mad urge to destroy. It was a terrible effort, but at last she dragged it back to that place deep within her where it had lain unnoticed for so many years. She could never allow it to win.

She was the *Tempest*. She was a Ship, not some wild thing let loose to attack and rend. If she had been human, she would have sobbed aloud. Instead she stood, anchoring herself to her vessel, her Captain and crew who were all shouting orders and observing the battle. Nobody had even noticed what she'd done.

"Well done!" Leo was saying to Heron and Robin. "Good work there. Now let's get that portal closed, shall we?"

She had managed to protect him from that side of herself. A safety feature perhaps, though one that had worked against her father. One day, she might have to tell Leo just who and what he had bound himself to, but today was not that day.

"We'll finish this now," Owl said.

She stepped past Leo, turning her face to the Shipbody. In that second, Maia looked into her eyes and saw the full knowledge of what she had done and, in return, Maia knew that Julia was changed forever. They were both so much more than they had been, and there was no going back for either of them.

<Ready?> Owl asked.

The two women smiled as one.

<I am,> Maia answered. <Let's end this.>

The ancient magic of Britannia and the power of the Olympian Gods combined as their hands and minds linked. Together, they stepped to the edge of the observation platform and looked down on the invaders. The words came unbidden to Maia's tongue as the spell took shape.

The gateway flickered, slowly, then more rapidly. The sickly green edges began to crackle and pulsate as it vanished in and out of existence. Maia felt her Potentia rise within her, not wild and untamed as it had been, but controlled and guided as they chanted. She was a source of pure power. Owl was siphoning that power, forging it into a weapon strong enough to aim at the heart of the Fae spell and smash it to pieces.

Even as the rearmost Fae turned in alarm, ahead of them a terrible light began to filter through the trees. Something was approaching from the direction of the battlefield. Maia could see mounted figures, the foremost holding aloft something that shone like an exploding sun. At its heart, she could discern the outline of a sword.

After one final surge aimed at the portal, she felt Owl softly pull away with the sense of a job well done. Their link ended and Maia felt her Potentia return to normal levels, settling once more in its accustomed channels through her vessel.

"What's that light?" Leo was demanding.

"I'd guess it's Excalibur," Heron said cheerfully.

"Thank the Gods! About bloody time. *Tempest*, it seems the portal's done for. Increase elevation to five hundred feet in case it goes up with a bang."

She obeyed. It was very satisfying to watch as, caught between the sword and the collapsing gateway, utter panic swept through the enemy ranks. Creatures and Fae Lords fought to retreat in their terror to get away from the implacable power of the artefact and its deadly light.

The screeching roar from the portal stopped them. A snarling, reptilian head began to force its way through, followed by a huge, elongated body. Armoured scales gave off an eerie glow and malevolent yellow eyes swivelled as it took in its surroundings. Heedless of its allies, the wyrm's sinuous coils crushed all in its path in its eagerness to emerge before the way was blocked. The portal was failing rapidly, but not quickly enough. The creature's tail flicked clear, even as the counterspell took hold and the gateway flashed once before vanishing.

The monster screeched in triumph, then prepared to launch itself skywards, leathery wings unfurling. Maia realised in horror that she would be its first target.

"All guns, fire!"

Her crew poured shot down like rain, but the creature merely shook its head, as if only stung.

<What do we do now?> she asked, ready to push as much Potentia as she could into her shields. To her surprise, Owl's confidence was unshaken.

<We call in the really big guns.>

A speck appeared above her, shining like a star in the indigo of the evening sky. It rapidly resolved into a helmeted figure descending at great speed. At the last instant, it slowed and landed gracefully. Maia gaped. It seemed the Gods had come at last.

Athena Minerva strode through the routing enemy, holding her shield before her. Maia couldn't see her face, but the Fae were screaming and cowering, frozen in place as they were struck down. The Goddess paused before the wyrm, arm outstretched, and Maia pulled her sight back instantly.

"All crew! Close your eyes! Close your eyes!"

They were far away, but she wasn't taking any chances. She knew the range of her guns, but not this weapon.

The wyrm reared up, wings beating fiercely. Its jaws gaped wide, displaying teeth the length of a man's arm and seemingly determined to swallow the Goddess whole. Maia kept her eyes firmly on Athena Minerva's back and watched in fascination as the creature suddenly recoiled like a salted slug. Its bulging eyes opened wide, wings crumpling as it saw what no living creature could withstand. Slowly, inexorably its body solidified, transformed by the power of Medusa's gaze.

Maia looked away as the Goddess began to turn, concentrating instead on making sure her crew were doing as they were told.

"Heron!"

The Mage had been unable to resist, about to sneak over to get a better look. He shot her a guilty look.

"Seriously?"

He shrugged. "It's interesting."

"It's deadly, you idiot!"

Her frustration with her eccentric Mage was the thing that brought her back to herself.

"I wasn't going to look closely," he argued. "I doubt it would work at this distance anyway. I was merely observing the effects."

Now everyone was scowling and Leo was having none of it.

"Heron, close your eyes! Shield status?"

"Maintaining, sir," Heron replied, quite unabashed. Robin had a thoughtful look on his face. Maia was willing to bet that the pair of them were wondering just how the process of turning flesh to stone actually worked.

She risked a quick peek using her Shipsenses. The Goddess was standing, her spear in one hand and shield in the other, surveying a field of statues. Fixed to the centre of the shield was a head, neatly severed. Maia could see that the woman had been beautiful once, but now there was nothing human in that mad gaze, frozen at the moment of her death centuries before. A few snakes still twitched.

She looked away, feeling a ripple of unease, but that was all. The ancient oak that formed her Shipbody was immune to the Gorgon's stare. As Heron had said, that was interesting and she stored the knowledge away for future reference. Then the Goddess and her deadly weapon vanished. Leo's strained voice snapped her back.

"*Tempest*. What's happening?"

"It's all clear, sir. She disappeared. I think most of the Fae are dead."

"Good. Lower shields."

Leo bowed politely to Owl, who nodded solemnly to him.

"Well done, everyone," she said. "I must go now."

There was a brief flash of purple light, and she vanished as well.

Leo swallowed.

"I suppose we'll find out what happened sooner or later. In the meantime, get Danuco up here in case the Goddess decides to pay us a visit."

The Priest arrived promptly. He looked drained, as if the constant rituals had sapped his energy, but there was no mistaking his joy. He saluted Leo, almost falling over himself to make his report.

"The Gods answered our prayers, sir! You saw what Athena Minerva did to our enemies, and she isn't the only one. I've had reports of thunderbolts and Mars himself in the fray, along with his sons."

"We thank the Gods for their aid," Leo said, formally. "What's happening now?"

Danuco's eyes glazed as he connected to the network of Priests.

"The Gods are tracking down surviving Fae and their allies. The Huntress is leading them."

Maia felt a chill run through her at the thought of Diana's proximity. Even though they were now on the same side, too much had happened for her to feel comfortable at the thought of possibly seeing that Goddess again. Was it her imagination, or could she hear the faint belling of hounds as they sought their quarry?

"We must return to the main battlefield," Leo decided. "There may still be some resistance and we'll need to report in, I presume directly to Pendragon."

He raised a querying eyebrow at his Ship and Maia hastened to agree.

"It makes most sense, sir, though I can contact Raven if you'd rather?"

"Try for Pendragon first."

Tentatively, Maia reached out through the link. There was a pause in which she could sense the presence of her sisters, then the Admiral came through.

<*Tempest*! I'm informed that you destroyed the portal. Well done.>

<Thank you, sir.>

<Are you undamaged?>

He must have been exhausted, but his mental voice was as strong as ever.

<Yes, sir. The operation went well. Do you know the Gods appeared?>

<And that's not all. I will take your full report later. Now I must talk to legends. Pendragon out.>

He broke the link abruptly, leaving her puzzled. Legends? No doubt she'd find out his meaning soon enough. Maybe Artorius Magnus himself had returned? After today, nothing would surprise her. She nearly contacted Raven, but decided to leave it. There was too much going on and they were best left to it.

She reported back to Leo, who was as puzzled as she was.

<Legends?> Her Captain shrugged. <Personally, I think the Gorgon's head is enough for one day. Proceed to the camp and we'll make anchor. We all need to rest.>

She ran through her tasks automatically, all the while aware of the new part of her, sleeping now but ready to wake if needed. Pearl was near, hovering just out of vision as was her mother, and now she felt closer to them than ever. Was she still a Ship, or would she become something else?

Would she have a choice at last? She couldn't decide if the thought was a comfort or not.

*

It was over. Cei's muscles ached from gripping his horse's flanks and he was soaked with sweat. He wanted nothing more than to throw himself out of his saddle and into a cool bath, but that wouldn't be happening any time soon.

The brief contact with *Tempest* had heartened him, but the day was only getting stranger. All anyone had eyes for was the band of warriors who had appeared in the midst of the battle. Their leader had wielded a sword of light that Cei knew in his bones was Excalibur. Did this mean he was no longer in the running for the throne? He devoutly hoped so.

Another figure was approaching. It appeared to be a young man, dressed in the robes of a Mage. Cei wasn't so exhausted that he didn't see the deference shown to him by the other Mages.

Blast it! He levered himself gingerly off his horse, and straightened up to greet him. This had to be someone important. As the person drew nearer, the figure's features became clear.

"Julia!"

But why was she dressed like this. Was it a disguise?

His niece was smiling.

"Uncle!" she called, picking up her pace. She stopped at arm's length, and it was only then that he noticed the strangeness in her eyes.

"Julia! How…what?"

He could barely articulate the words.

"It's a long story. The upshot is that I'm now Mage Owl. Merlin left me his powers and a lot of his memories. He's gone you see, but somebody has to keep fighting."

While Cei struggled to process what he was hearing, Raven appeared and greeted her warmly.

"Well, Princess Owl. Seems you finally got your wish."

Julia nodded gravely. "In a way. I have a lot of work to do, starting yesterday." She turned back to her uncle.

"Dear Uncle. I'm sorry. There won't be any marriage for me, but here's somebody you really need to meet."

Cei could barely speak. Relief at seeing his niece safe was almost too much.

"Who's that then?"

She gestured, and a man stepped up. His face shadowed beneath the ancient helmet, he was indeed a legend brought to life.

"Prince Cei. I'm glad to see you again."

The stranger carefully lifted the helmet off his head.

"You…you're the Agent I charged with protecting the Princess!"

His niece spoke.

"Milo. Yes. It turns out that he's actually your half-brother. His true name is Gwydre."

Cei swallowed, lost for words. His eyes lit on the sword, sheathed and quiet now, as Julia explained what had happened. He met his new brother's eye, noting that they did look alike. It was obvious when you knew. Gwydre looked nervous, and no wonder. Maybe neither of them wanted the responsibility.

"I thought you were Artorius returned."

Gwydre winced. "Sorry, sir. I did bring some of his Companions though. Found them asleep in a cave where Merlin had left them."

Cei blinked as each was introduced. It all felt like a dream.

"My Lord Prince," Bedwyr said. "Do we have your permission to continue the hunt? I fear that some of the Enemy still remain."

"You do indeed, noble warrior," Cei said, grasping to retain his composure. It was all getting too much. Britomartia flashed him a smile, eager to return to what she loved best. He thought she would have made a good Companion for Diana. They mounted up, storybook tales come back to life, and thundered off in pursuit of more adventure.

"What now?" he asked.

"Now we thank the Gods and wait for more news," Raven told him, ever practical. "I think you need to sit down before you fall over, sir. A drink for Prince Cei!"

He could be loud enough when he wanted to be. A page ran over, bowed and offered a flask of wine. Cei offered it first to Gwydre, who waved it aside, then drank, wishing it was water so that he could pour it over his head. It had been a very long day.

"I need to check on my men."

"May I come with you?"

His new brother sounded hesitant, as well he might. The troops were still expecting Artorius.

"Of course. Please, have a drink."

Gwydre smiled. "I will now that you've had one, Your Highness."

Cei found himself returning the smile. He may have lost a son, but it seemed that he had gained a brother. It was a strange sensation.

"Let us review them together and make sacrifice."

Another, welcome voice activated his link and he seized upon it eagerly as something familiar in an unsettling new world.

<*Tempest* reporting. I am approaching your position, sir.>

<I'll see you shortly.> "That was *Tempest*," he explained. "She'll be here soon."

Gwydre's face creased in puzzlement. "Here?"

"She's an AirShip now," Raven explained.

Cei almost laughed at Gwydre's expression. "It seems we have a lot to catch up on."

"It's been a trying day," Raven said. Cei couldn't resist.

"Really?"

The Legions were already marching back to their tents, Felicio at their head. Adepts were tending the wounded on the field then sending them back in a steady stream to the makeshift hospitals that had sprung up in the camp. Pendragon made for them first, hiding his discomfort to give words of praise and encouragement to those able to receive them. His niece joined Raven in helping where they could, augmenting the prayers and medicines with spells. After a moment, Gwydre joined them.

"You have some skill?" Cei asked as the former Agent bandaged a slashed arm, muttering a simple spell of pain relief.

"I trained as a Mage for a time, plus I'm used to injuries," came the reply. Cei admired the way he dealt with the men, speaking softly and field-dressing wounds with the ease of long practice. "They're usually my own," he added with a wry grin.

It was a while before Cei could finally return to his tent and allow his servants to strip off his blood-spattered armour and stained tunic. There was no bath, but there was warm water enough to get the worst off. He'd insisted that Gwydre join him, attended to with all the deference due to royalty, before they sat down together to share a meal. His niece had vanished, off on some tasks of her own, and Cei knew better than to question her. She was not the woman he had come to know, not anymore, and the will of the Fates had overruled any plans he might have had for her. Time would tell where her path lay. In the meantime, he had enough to do thinking about what the Fates had in store for them all.

Everything had changed. Milo found himself ushered into a campaign tent, which he suspected had been hastily vacated by one of Pendragon's generals, and was suddenly surrounded by servants addressing him as 'Lord'. He'd never been anyone's Lord before.

He removed Excalibur carefully and placed it across a cushioned stool to keep it out of the way while he was washed and dressed in a fine tunic, which he suspected belonged to his new brother. All he had to do was stand there and occasionally lift his arms as the men cleaned off the grime. He reckoned he must have smelt pretty bad, as he couldn't remember the last time he'd had the chance for a proper bath. A quick sluice down didn't really count, not to a civilised Briton who was used to regular and leisurely bathing.

At last the servants left him standing in his borrowed finery, taking away his armour and undergarments to be cleaned. His old underwear would probably end up in the refuse pile judging by the quality of what he was wearing now. The new clothes were comfortable enough, but it was disconcerting to be wearing someone else's. He insisted on keeping his boots. Heaven knew whether Pendragon had the same size feet, but he'd be damned if he was going to give them up. They'd cost enough and were less than a year old. The servants had to be contented with giving them a good clean.

"My Lord, General Felicio wishes to pay his compliments."

Milo took a deep breath.

"Send him in."

The slave bowed and scurried off to draw aside the tent flap. A second later the general appeared. He was still wearing armour but had evidently made some effort to neaten his appearance, though his eyes were shadowed with fatigue. He came to attention before Milo, snapping off a sharp salute. Milo responded automatically, then remembered that he should be the one to speak first. That was weird too.

"General Felicio. I'm pleased to meet you."

He'd seen the man before, but as Milo had been lurking in the shadows of a large hall on surveillance duty at the time, he didn't expect to be remembered.

"My Lord Gwydre. It is my honour to greet you on this day of victory."

"No, it's my honour, General."

He almost added, *I'm just the idiot Excalibur chose,* but thought better of it.

"I have come to escort you to Prince Cei's tent," Felicio continued. Milo searched his face for clues as to his thoughts, but the man was good. Nothing showed past his formal attitude. It was only as Milo started forward that Felicio's eyes slid to where Excalibur rested on its cushion.

He'd nearly forgotten. It wouldn't do to leave the blasted thing alone in a tent. Milo picked it up and buckled on the sword belt, aware of Felicio's scrutiny the whole time. It was true that Excalibur, Caledfwlch, wasn't half as pretty as its mistaken namesake. There was no fancy jewelled hilt, just some gold thread on the pommel and a leather wrapped grip. Hardly anyone would give it a second glance under normal circumstances. Perhaps that was what it wanted? Milo remembered thinking he could strip the gold off it to sell and almost laughed.

"Lord?"

It must have shown on his face. He had to be more careful.

"I was just thinking how strange all this is."

Felicio's impassive features split into a grin. "I know what you mean, Lord. I'm fixing on the fact we won, not that there are Gods and Companions running around out there chasing Fae through the woods."

This time Milo did laugh, shaking his head.

"I can't believe it either. Please, lead the way."

He followed Felicio, both of them escorted by an armed guard that fell into step as they marched across the parched ground to the largest tent, the one with the dragon banner displayed prominently outside.

Pendragon was waiting to greet them. He stepped forward immediately to clasp Milo's arm. They were of a height and once more Milo met dark eyes, so much like his own. Indeed, if it wasn't for his brother's grey hair and weathered face, they could have been twins. It had to have been some special magic to stop anyone seeing the resemblance.

"May I present the Lady Drusilla, wife of our dear and most lamented Senator Rufus?"

He'd heard of her, of course. He was quietly shocked when she curtsied to him and he had to think quickly. "I'm honoured, my Lady. The Senator was a great man of glorious memory."

"Thank you Lord Gwydre. The Admiral has told me that he has a new brother. It gladdens my heart to meet you."

The other people present needed no introductions. Aquila had stood when he entered, smiling broadly. Milo wondered just how much he'd known all along. The other was Raven, as imperturbable as ever. Milo turned to Aquila first.

"Greetings to you, Lord Aquila."

"Lord Gwydre! Delighted to meet you."

"I offer my prayers and thanks to Jupiter, Best and Greatest," he replied, seeing the approval in the Priest's eyes.

"I will pass them on," Aquila answered, "though it seems that you have the favour of more than the Olympians."

Milo was conscious that everyone was looking at the sword.

"I have been blessed indeed."

Blessed or cursed. Who can tell?

Aquila raised an eyebrow. Damn it, could the man read thoughts?

"All things shall be as the Gods and Fates decree."

Aquila was nothing if not diplomatic. As Milo would have to be from now on.

"And I believe you know our Master Mage?" Pendragon was saying.

"Oh yes."

Raven bowed politely. "Lord Gwydre."

So that was how he was playing it. Milo decided to join in. "Master Mage. I trust you are well?"

"I am indeed. I see you found a use for your rusty piece of metal?"

The others looked at them both in bemusement.

Pendragon couldn't resist asking.

"Rusty piece of metal?"

368

As Milo told the tale Felicio's eyes widened, but the Prince just laughed.

"Like that, was it? It appeared the sword played us all for fools."

Milo had to agree.

"I'm afraid so."

"Come, let's have some food and you can tell us more."

Milo thought he didn't have much appetite, but the sight and smell of the dishes that were brought made him aware of just how empty his stomach was.

He was given the place of honour next to Pendragon, with the Lady Drusilla to the other side and Aquila, Felicio and Raven opposite. It was hardly a formal dinner party, but Milo still felt awkward. Fortunately, the others had plenty to talk about while he ate and listened.

The first topic of discussion was the hunt for survivors.

"Those that are left will be pursued and destroyed," Felicio assured everyone. "Mars himself told me so."

There was a brief silence as everyone digested this news.

"I heard that the Gods manifested," Drusilla said. "Indeed, the Priests report that Athena was seen on the field, wielding the Gorgon's head, no less."

"We can be glad that none of us saw that," Felicio said with a straight face.

Milo ducked his head. He didn't know the man well enough to know whether he was joking, but then is brother rolled his eyes and Raven groaned.

"The Lord Mars led my legions himself. Did you hear his sacred trumpets?"

This time the General wasn't joking.

"I didn't hear much over the sound of the muskets," Pendragon admitted, before turning to Milo.

"Did you hear them, brother?"

Milo shook his head.

"I can't remember much." *Except the joyous feeling of destiny fulfilled.*

Caledfwlch had its own agenda. Maybe he'd been chosen to be merely an appendage. He could barely feel the weight of it, but its unceasing presence was still there at the back of his mind.

"I told you the Gods were on our side. Did you doubt them?" Aquila deftly speared several slices of meat onto his plate.

"Never," Pendragon answered.

"They came when needed, true," Raven said, "but we all know they have their own ways of working."

"It all ended so fast," Felicio said. "Once the portal collapsed, that was it. Let's hope there'll be no more of them for the foreseeable future."

"What of the ones up north?" Milo asked. Aquila smiled.

"They'll provide much sport for a while. The Gods move fast when they desire." His bland words belied the carnage that even now had to be taking place. "They will keep no footholds here and have been much weakened. It may be the end of them in these lands – and I mean Hibernia too. Oh, the lesser Fae will remain, both friends and foe, but I can't see the Major Fae staying."

"Where will they go?" Felicio leaned forward, fixing the Priest with interest.

Aquila shrugged. "To lands beyond the ones we know. They are not creatures as we are."

"Personally, I don't care so long as they don't bother us again," Drusilla said.

Milo was feeling better as the food filled his stomach, though he still had to pinch himself. Lord Gwydre! It seemed ridiculous in more ways than one.

There was more talk, but he found himself drifting in and out of the conversation. Everything was becoming more dreamlike. He started as a hand was laid on his shoulder.

"You were dropping off there," his brother said.

"I think we could all do with a rest," Raven said, though to Milo's eyes he didn't look any different. Did the old man ever sleep? "We need to be fresh for the tasks ahead."

Like finding out what the Sword of Kingship intended for the pair of them. Milo's heart sank.

"True words indeed, my old friend." Pendragon rose. "I will meet you all tomorrow."

"I'll go and check on the troops, sir," Felicio told him. "Reports will be coming in through the night." He raised a hand to forestall the Prince's protests. "You know I'm used to it."

"Wake me if necessary."

"I will, sir."

Milo retreated to his tent in a daze. Perhaps when he woke up, he'd be back at The Anchor and it would all have been a dream?

As the servants undressed him and he was escorted to his warmed bed, all he could he think of was that it had to be.

XX

The Ship link was alive with gossip.

Maia was relieved to plunge back in and update her friends, who had been chafing at being left on the side lines. It didn't last long. *Imperatrix* was particularly cross with her.

<You didn't keep us updated! How are we supposed to know what's happening if you don't tell or show us?>

<I was a little busy fighting the enemy,> she replied, wishing that she could have linked with somebody less prickly. <Do you want to know what happened or not?>

<We've already heard things,> *Imperatrix* replied.

It was all Maia could do to keep her temper.

<So you'll know all about what Athena Minerva did. The wyrm was massive!>

That set everyone talking at once, until *Victoria* exercised her authority.

<Be quiet, all of you! *Imperatrix*, stop needling *Tempest*. Go on, *Tempest*.>

The older Ship backed off for once, much to Maia's relief.

<Thank you, *Victoria*. As I was saying, the Gods turned up.>

She told them an edited version, with more emphasis on the role of the Gods and Owl than her own. That was something she still had to keep private.

<Where are you now?> *Blossom* asked.

Maia surveyed the camp from above. She was anchored to the tallest and sturdiest trees she could find, glad to have the respite after all the frenetic activity.

<At the camp. It's settling down now, but the last of the Fae and other things are still being mopped up.>

<How's the Admiral?>

That was *Leopard*, direct as usual.

<Fine, so far as I know. He's in his tent. Apparently Excalibur has turned up in the hands of a bastard half-brother.>

She hadn't believed it when Raven had told her who he was. He'd warned her about releasing that information as well. Who would have thought an Agent would be the one to wield the mystical sword?

<We heard!> *Jasper* was beside herself. <And Artorius's Companions as well! Have you seen them all? What are they like? Fancy the other sword not being Excalibur!>

<Yes, no, don't know and imagine that,> Maia replied.

<Really, *Jasper*!> *Dragon* was dismissive. <How can *Tempest* see anything much from up in the sky?>

<Well, I don't know to be sure. She might have seen him!>

There were a few sniggers.

<You're our eyes and ears now,> *Victoria* said firmly. <Be sure to relay anything important, *Tempest*! We're all making good speed down the coast and should be rounding Kernow soon on our way back to Portus.>

<I will,> she promised, already determined to tell them only what she thought they should know. There was enough going on to keep everyone happy for now and they would have their work cut out for them making such a speedy voyage. Already she could sense Ships from further afield beginning to talk about returning. Those who were on far postings, or whose Captains had refused to commit, would be returning to port. There would probably be some sort of reckoning for the latter.

Maia opened up her private channel to *Patience*. Her friend responded immediately.

<*Tempest*! It's good to talk in private! You wouldn't believe some of the tales that have been flying up and down the link!>

So, the news wasn't all coming from her.

<Such as?>

<A dragon sighted flying low over the western coast and attacking Fae positions. Strange lights in the sky and thunderbolts destroying buildings!>

It was true that Ships had ears everywhere.

<Which buildings?>

<The palace in Londin! Burned to the ground, they say. Unfortunately, Marcus wasn't killed. He fled to Greenfields, but nobody knows where he is now.>

<Maybe the Gods have caught him already? Wherever he is, he can't get far. His Mages are dead and his forces are broken.>

<Even so, watch yourself,> *Patience* advised. <Don't assume it's all over, because they still might have some nasty surprises waiting. Remember, the Fae are known for their treachery, and Marcus was an apt pupil.>

That was her friend all over. Briseis was both cautious and wise and Maia loved her for it.

<I'm floating above the treetops,> she Sent. <If I don't look down, I could be at anchor in some harbour. Most of my crew have left for the night and are camping on the ground. Only my Captain, a few marines and the Mages are left.>

<Shore leave, eh? Except it's vertical.>

<Yes. Nobody can expect them to stay cooped up here for too long, even though they're used to being cramped. I'm not able to store as many supplies as I did.>

<Do you think you'll stay like this, or will it be temporary?> Patience caught herself immediately. <Oh, don't answer that one. I'm sorry I asked.>

Maia thought for a few moments. The questions didn't bother her as much as she thought they might, though she could tell that *Patience* was embarrassed that she'd blurted everything out so directly. It was unlike her, so Maia knew that the thought must have been uppermost in her mind for a while.

<It's all right, honestly it is. It's been strange, but there are compensations. Do you know, I'm not sure. It won't be up to me anyway. They might want more of us. What about you? Fancy flying?>

Consternation shot through the link and she had to laugh.

<It would be different,> *Patience* admitted. <I'd certainly consider it if they asked. This vessel isn't too bad, but it's not really mine. It all feels borrowed, if you know what I mean.>

<I can imagine,> Maia agreed. <I had that feeling at first, even though there's a small piece of my original vessel in here to

help things along. Also, it's newly built, without any existing baggage.>

<And you don't have the former commander looking over your shoulder and being a pain in the stern.>

<No! Really?>

<Don't worry, he soon got his marching orders. But if you ever come across Tetius Micianus, give him a wide berth. The man's an ass.>

<He'd have a long drop if I did.>

Patience laughed.

<I should have pushed him overboard.>

Maia remembered some of the conversations she'd had with the older Ships especially the *Persistence*.

<I believe accidents do happen. He won't be the last annoyance you come across.>

<You're right, unfortunately! I'm glad I have Fabillus. How's Leo?>

Maia groaned.

<Still besotted with the new technology. He's currently snoring in his bed. No proper cabins up here, I'm afraid, I haven't the room.>

<It all sounds fascinating! Being able to be above the land as well. What's happening now?>

<Apart from the guards on watch, nothing much. Everyone's grabbing some sleep while they can. It's quite pretty, with all the little lights and the campfires. What about where you are?>

<The wind's getting up,> her friend reported, <and the watch are in for a soggy night. If it gets any worse, we might all have to shorten sail, but so far, so good.>

<Safe journey and I'll be in touch again soon.>

The conversation ended, and Maia settled down for the night. She kept one ear on the Ship link, but she'd already heard most of the gossip and the speculation was wearying. It was nice to have some time to herself before the inevitable demands for information began again.

She resisted temptation for a full two hours before opening the link to Raven. It had been a while since they'd spoken properly and she hoped the dead of night would be a good time to catch him, as she knew that he didn't sleep much. She pictured the red thread in her mind, imagining its smoothness before gently travelling along it to its destination.

<Raven?>

The barest whisper into the dark, just enough to catch his attention.

<Maia? Hello!>

<So you are up. I didn't want to wake you.>

She felt him sigh.

<I think I've got out of the habit of sleeping more than a couple of minutes at a time, and it seems to be growing worse.>

He sounded resigned.

<Whereas I don't sleep at all.>

<No, you don't. It's good to have company in the dark. How are your sisters? Bombarding you with questions, by any chance?>

<Very cross with me for not relaying everything the instant it happens.>

<That's Ships for you, especially when they've no action of their own.>

<I can see their point, though.> Maia felt she had to defend the others. <None of them is in my position.>

<True. So, have you got them all up to speed?>

<So far as I understand it. What happens now?>

He paused and she could picture him, hands tucked into the sleeves of his robe.

<In the morning most of the army will break camp and march to Londin. There's a small matter of the Kingship to resolve.>

<And two candidates? I take it Marcus is well and truly disqualified?>

Raven snorted. <Oh yes. If that one's got any sense he'll have left the country by now, though I don't know where he'd go, except to Hibernia. The Empire has a long reach and he's burned all his bridges. I suppose it's too much to ask that he falls on his sword in time-honoured fashion.>

<But you don't know where he is?>

<No.> Irritation crept into his voice. <He was holed up at Greenfields by the Thamesis, but he's not there now. He could try to escape to the New World I suppose. The Fae will have no

use for him now that their plans have failed. Kite's dead, along with all the turncoat Mages. The Gorgon's head saw to that.>

Maia had seen the statues, like some mad sculptor's workshop abandoned in the trees. She didn't think anyone would want to walk in those woods anytime soon.

<I saw it happen,> she admitted.

<Really? It must have been spectacular. How much did you see?>

If she couldn't trust Raven, she couldn't trust anyone.

<It had no effect on me,> she admitted, <but I think we should keep that quiet.>

<I agree. Interesting. I presume the Gods are immune too. It must be a legacy of your heritage.>

<Or the fact I'm made of wood. It was still terrifying. I had to stop Heron looking, you know.>

<Good Gods! He doesn't get any better.>

Maia thought she caught the word 'idiot' as well.

<It's a good job Robin has some sense. They're both here with me now. I don't suppose I can keep them?>

<That will be up to the new Prime Mage, when he's appointed. Or I should say they. There's Owl to consider.>

<I know. I couldn't believe what's happened to the Princess.>

<Neither can anyone else,> Raven answered, drily. <It's come as a shock to all, including me and I trained her. There are a lot of unknowns here. The Fates haven't finished with us yet.>

<Then there's Agent Milo. I like him, but I never thought he was a Prince.>

<According to Roman Law he isn't, but Britannic Sacred Law's another thing. Cei has ordered that he be referred to as Lord Gwydre. Personally, I think the poor lad's in shock. Neither of them wants to be King, you know.>

That wasn't good, but she could understand why.

<We all want our Admiral back.>

<Of course you do. He wants to *be* back, but that's up to the Sword of Kingship.>

<The one stuck in the column of the Londin Basilica?>

<That's the one.>

<Am I coming with you to Londin?>

It was best to be prepared.

Raven was amused.

<Oh yes. You're a star attraction.>

<Can't say I'm thrilled,> she admitted, <but it will be nice to get a good view of everything.>

That would annoy the *Imperatrix* even more. To her irritation, he seemed to divine her thought.

<Don't forget to relay!>

<I won't!> She decided to change the subject. <Have you seen any more Gods?>

<No. they're somewhere else, doubtless wreaking vengeance on the remnants of the enemy. Artorius's Companions are off on adventures of their own.>

<What will happen to them?>

He thought for a few moments.

<Another unknown. They'll either adapt to this world, or leave it. Every single person they knew died centuries ago and they were old when they went into the cave to be enchanted. Maybe the Gods will take pity on them, one way or another. At least they have each other. It could be a fresh start for them.>

<There weren't even any Ships around when they fell asleep,> she marvelled.

<No. Britannia came later. They're even before my time, believe it or not. It was a pity Merlin couldn't stay as I would have liked to say goodbye.>

Maia thought he sounded tired.

<You can visit me, if you like,> she offered.

<You know, I might just fly up with you to Londin, if Cei's agreeable,> he said, and her spirits rose. <I'll ask in the morning. Now, there are some things I have to do before then, so we must sign off for now.>

<I understand. Speak to you later.>

Reluctantly, she withdrew from the link, tucking the thread back into the braid until the next time.

Londin! She hadn't been there for so long. And now she would have a whole new perspective.

She began to check her systems once more, accompanied by the less than melodious snores of her Captain, Heron and several exhausted marines. Three hours until daylight and the dawn of a new era.

378

Would it be King Cei, or King Gwydre? And what had happened to Marcus?

*

Milo awoke to the sound of water trickling. For a moment, he thought he was back in Coventina's temple watching the Goddess arise from the waters, then he remembered.

The bed was more luxurious than it had a right to be, curtained with heavy brocade and embroidered with mythical beasts. He could see each tiny stitch, expertly worked and threaded through with gold and silver, highlighting claws, wings and eyes. All that work for bed hangings.

Then they were drawn back and a whole group of slaves and servants stood ready to take him in hand. It was a far cry from rolling out of bed, splashing his face with stale water and slouching off to the nearest food stall or tavern for his breakfast, or worse yet, crawling out of whatever ditch he'd found to sleep in for the night.

Milo allowed himself to be ministered to, still feeling that he was caught in a dream he couldn't escape. He even had someone to bring his chamber pot, and he definitely wasn't used to that.

"My lord, Prince Cei has invited you to breakfast with him."

He nodded at the servant, before strapping on Excalibur and following him out into the freshness of the summer morning. It was his favourite time of year, though short nights made skulking in the dark more of a challenge. Perhaps those days were gone forever now.

Around him, the camp was waking up. Savoury smells drifted on the breeze, as well as less pleasant ones that told of thousands of people living in one place without regular sanitary facilities. It would be better when they moved on. Another few days in the heat and the place would be stinking even worse.

Cei was waiting for him with a smile.

"Good morning, brother! Sleep well?"

"I did, thank you. And you?"

It was true. He'd slept like the dead, and if there'd been any dreams, he couldn't remember them.

"Well enough, though my body's still on Ship time. I wake for the watch change."

Cei smiled ruefully, gesturing Milo over to a table loaded with bread, meat and fruit. He helped himself, appreciating the freshness of the loaf. After a few moments, Raven appeared and Cei greeted him cheerfully.

"Good morning, Master Mage! Please, join us."

Raven bowed politely and settled himself on to a couch, though he waved away the offer of food.

"Thank you, sir, but I've already eaten. I've come to report that everything's ready. General Felicio is supervising the packing up and I've had half-a-dozen Mages checking the forest, just in case anything slipped through that we should know about."

"Good. Find anything?"

Raven smiled.

"An awful lot of statues. I was wondering whether you wanted to bring any along. They would serve better than heads on poles."

And certainly less messy, Milo thought to himself.

Cei chewed on a piece of bread, thinking.

"If there are any that are recognisable, we could have them set up in the Temple of Athena Minerva as a salutary lesson. Maybe next to Echidna?"

The old Mage's smile grew wider.

"I'll arrange it. There's a certain ex-Prime Mage who deserves a place of ignominy. I don't think we can transport the wyrm though, unless we chisel its head off."

Cei nodded.

"Do it. We'll approach Londin in strength. I want a triumphal parade." He stopped. "What I mean to say is, we *need* a triumphal parade. That way everyone will be reassured and we can pay honour to the Gods. What do you say, brother?"

So, he was going to be consulted. Milo was quick to agree.

"It's an excellent idea. The people need security and a show of strength."

"And we'll have our new AirShip," Cei said, his pride evident.

Milo hadn't been able to miss the huge craft hovering over the camp. It was hard to believe that it was the same Ship he'd known and not some device of the Gods, though the rumour was that Vulcan himself had had a hand in her design and manufacture.

"It seems like we're all on the same page then," Raven said. "I'll order the arrangements, though hauling an enormous stone head will take time. It depends how quickly you want all this to happen. The land needs a ruler sooner rather than later."

He raised a warning eyebrow.

"Very well. We can have the official triumph later," Cei decided. "It will be enough to have the legions and a few statues." He turned to Milo. "Everyone will be waiting to see you anyway, plus the Companions, if we can persuade them to return."

"They want to see Excalibur, you mean."

"Don't sell yourself short! You carry it, not I."

Milo sighed. His brother echoed him and they both laughed briefly.

As they finished, Milo was left to wonder just what the Fates were spinning for him. Would they be cruel, or kind? He resolved to pay a visit to as many altars as he could before they left for Londin. He'd need as much divine help as possible to get through the next few days.

*

The preparation for the army's departure took longer than everyone had hoped, in part because Raven and Owl insisted on checking the site of the Fae portal thoroughly, in case anything malefic had been left.

Milo wholeheartedly agreed with their suspicions and, after some persuasion, had managed to wangle himself a place on the small investigating party. Cei was less than thrilled at the idea, but Milo was having none of it.

"I'm a trained Agent with the ability to detect harmful magic," he protested. "Besides which, if anything nasty should appear, this should take care of it."

He patted the sword, watching as his brother's eyes lingered on the hilt. There was no envy there, only respect.

"It does make sense," Raven interjected. "Also, Caledfwlch should give warning if there's anything major about."

Cei frowned. "Very well. I do see your point, but don't take too long. We're almost ready to go."

His brother had been loath to leave before the majority of his troops, even though it would have made getting to Londin so much quicker. Milo had the nagging feeling that Pendragon was putting off the pivotal moment for as long as possible, just in case he was lumbered with the Kingship. He could see why. The terrifying possibility hung over his head too, like a great weight about to drop at any moment.

"Let's get on with it," he said.

"The Companions have returned," Raven said. "They can accompany us. With your permission, sir."

"Very well. Go. But be careful."

It was a relief to leave the activity of the camp and ride into the trees. The results of the bombardment were evident in the shattered and splintered foliage, though a lot had already been cleared. He spotted several Mages doing their best to repair some of the damage, but the landscape would bear the scars for many years to come. It would probably be renamed too, as the site of a major battle.

Raven and Owl went first, followed by Milo and the Companions who were all cheerfully taking it in turns to regale him with their exploits. They'd had the chance to wipe out several pockets of resisting Fae and even caught sight of some Gods.

"I heard that the Lord of War and the Huntress were in the region," Milo said, when he could get a word in edgeways.

"True. Britomartia spoke to the Huntress herself, didn't you?"

Britomartia, riding at ease, nodded. "I did."

She didn't vouchsafe any more information, and Milo didn't feel like asking her. Still, it was as well to know who they might come across, though he would bet that the Olympians had moved on by now to celebrate in their own way. There were certainly enough sacrifices being made to satisfy all of them. Armies had a lot of stomachs to feed.

The devastation continued as they went deeper. Blasted craters showed where *Tempest*'s aerial bombardment had done its work, and the familiar smell of death hovered in the air. Milo tried not to look too closely at the scattered bodies, or parts of them anyway. Gunpowder had proved very effective here.

"Not smelt that for a while," Palamedes remarked, wrinkling his nose.

"The smell of victory," Britomartia said, grinning.

"This victory needs clearing up," Raven remarked over his shoulder. "It will all be burned soon. Look! Here we are."

A cart was approaching them, pulled by heavy horses and escorted by cavalry. Owl hailed them and the driver drew the animals to a stop.

"What have you got there?"

The officer cantered over and nodded respectfully.

"We've orders to gather some of the, erm, statues, Lady."

"Show me." Owl's voice was quiet, but the men hurried to pull back the tarpaulin. Several figures lay prone beneath the oiled cloth, awkward in their wrappings. If he hadn't known they'd once been living, Milo wouldn't have guessed. The only oddness was the clothes they were wearing, which hadn't been transformed by the Gorgon's lethal glare. Stone faces stared back, caught in expressions of surprise and disbelief. They hadn't even had time to be afraid before the spell took hold.

"Is Kite there?" Raven asked.

Owl stood up in her stirrups for a better view.

"Oh yes. Not so proud now, is he? He'll have pride of place in the triumphal procession along with the other traitors, then we can put them all somewhere there are a lot of pigeons."

She gestured, and the cloth moved itself, hiding the grisly remains.

"Carry on, gentlemen."

The officer saluted and resumed his position, while the driver snapped the reins, eager to get away with his grisly load, Milo decided. The soldiers tried to keep their eyes fixed ahead, though most of them sneaked a glance at the ancient warriors riding past. It was interesting to see the differences in armour and mounts and once more Milo was struck by the incongruity of it all.

"Must get some of those stirrups," Gawain muttered.

"And a pistol," Britomartia added. "Possibly three."

They were entering a clearing now, lined with more statues. Many of them were equipped with Fae armour, riding what Milo could only describe as carnivorous looking horses. They certainly had sharp teeth, bared in final paroxysms of terror as they were overtaken by death. Many lay toppled where they'd fallen as they reared, their riders thrown or, in some cases, crushed by their weight. Other creatures lay scattered, some on two legs but most on four. He couldn't tell if they were wolves or bears, as they seemed to have characteristics of both. He supposed he'd seen them on the battlefield, but his memory remained a stubborn blur.

A gasp from Drustanus made him look round.

"Jove's bollocks, but that's bloody enormous!"

Towering above them was a massive stone shape, blocking out the light. Milo squinted to make it out, waiting for his eyes to adjust.

The wyrm had been caught mid-pounce. Its jaws were agape, showing the razor-sharp fangs and ribbed palate poised above a sinuous belly armoured in overlapping scales. It was a wonder that it was still upright.

"It'll be a job to break that up," Gawain remarked. "Might be better leaving it here."

"That will be up to the logistics team," Raven said. He sniffed, as if unimpressed.

"Seriously, it's very big," Drustanus told him. "I know you can't see it, but it is."

Milo laughed before he could stop himself.

"He's a very old Mage. Don't be fooled."

"Don't spoil the illusion," Raven said, while Drustanus looked confused. Then his face cleared.

"Oh yes. Magic. I see."

Raven grinned.

"So do I."

Gawain clapped his friend on the back. "Mages, eh? Some things don't change!"

"Talking of Mages," Owl said. "Behold, more traitors."

She pointed to several robed and hooded figures. Milo dismounted and went to look, wondering whether he'd be able to identify any of them. He'd dealt with Lapwing personally, but Kite had managed to turn others to his cause.

"What are you doing?"

Milo answered Gawain without turning.

"Seeing if there's anyone I know."

He moved from figure to figure, glad he was wearing gloves as he tugged the hoods from the Mages' heads. The first was instantly recognisable, as he'd been a classmate for the brief time he'd been a pupil at the Collegium.

"Yellowhammer," he called to Raven.

"Never liked that one," the Master Mage replied. "Always ready to grab on to any coat tails he thought would advance his position. He was one of Bullfinch's lackeys, but he must have switched to Kite. I bet it wasn't difficult to persuade him to betray his friends."

There were a few he didn't know and some he did.

"Buzzard."

"Never liked him, either."

The Companions watched, uneasily.

"They sided with the enemy and deserved all they got," Bedwyr said. "They should be broken up and used to pave the roads. Come on, let's check the portal so we can return to camp."

"I don't sense anything untoward," Owl said. "Lord Gwydre, what does Caledfwlch tell you?"

Milo thought a moment. The sword rested quietly on his back.

"Nothing."

"Then there's nothing here. Let's get back."

Milo cast a look around the blighted clearing and its silent occupants. It was like a cemetery, but with the dead above ground instead of below it. Even the birds and woodland creatures were silent.

"Yes, let's."

He mounted and the company retraced its steps, leaving the oppressiveness behind. Privately, Milo thought Bedwyr's suggestion to break up the statues was a good one. He'd be the first to swing the hammer.

As they reached the outskirts of the camp, he came to a decision.

"Go on ahead, he said. "I'm going to the altars to give thanks."

He wouldn't be making his formal sacrifices until later, but he could offer up prayers and a bit of incense. It would be nice for the Gods to forget about him, but while he carried Excalibur he knew that wasn't going to happen. He rode off before anyone could protest, or demand that he wait for a guard. He'd be damned if he would spend every waking moment chaperoned like a spoiled princeling.

Now he had to work out how to be relatively incognito. Concentrating, he drew on a spell that had served him in the past. Not quite a disguising spell, more of a 'this person is ordinary, nothing to see here' masking effect. He'd lost count of how many times it had proved useful. Milo waited until he felt the effect settle around him before he continued on through the partially-dismantled camp and up the slight hill to where the Priests had set up places of worship.

There were more than he'd imagined. All the Olympians were represented, plus some Britannic Gods that hadn't joined their worship to the major Deities. Some Eastern Gods were on the edges, as well as a few African ones that he wasn't particularly familiar with. All had Priests of both sexes and acolytes around them, some more than others.

He made a beeline for Jupiter's first. There were several Priests in attendance, foremost being the familiar bulk of Aquila, who was supervising the butchering of several bulls. Greasy smoke billowed from the heaped piles of bones and fat, rising upwards in the still air to please divine noses and not, he was glad to see, into the camp.

He was going to take his place in line, when the High Priest spotted him and sent an acolyte rushing over. The youth skidded to a halt before Milo's horse and bowed.

"Greetings, Lord Gwydre. Lord Aquila sends his regards and invites you to worship."

No hastily muttered spell could fool the High Priest of Jupiter. Milo sighed, handed his horse to the acolyte and strode up to the altar. As he approached, Aquila heaved himself out of his chair and nodded.

"Lord Gwydre, welcome!"

To give the man credit, his eyes barely flickered to Milo's hip.

"Thank you, Lord Aquila. I've come to pay my respects and give thanks to Jupiter, Best and Greatest."

Aquila's eyes crinkled as he beamed.

"Excellent. We've been sacrificing on your behalf, as you can see. The God is pleased with the outcome of events and is ready to bestow his favour upon you."

Milo went through the ritual motions, scooping up a handful of incense and casting it upon the flames. For an instant, the sweet smell almost masked the stench of burning fat.

"Hail, Jupiter, *Optimus Maximus*," he chanted, arms raised. "I thank you for your beneficence and beg for your support in the trials that are to follow. All praise to you, mightiest of Gods!"

A tingle crept up his spine as he finished his devotions and the sword twitched on his hip, as if trying to alert him. There was someone behind him, watching with ageless eyes and he could sense the heat of his presence. He froze, then turned slowly, but it was only Aquila.

"The God is well pleased," the High Priest said. Tiny specks of gold twinkled in the man's eyes for a second, then faded. Milo smiled weakly.

"I am honoured."

He bowed to Aquila, then walked off as quickly as he could without appearing to hurry. Sometimes the Gods got too close.

He prayed at Mars's heaped altar, this time without the unnerving feeling of being watched. The Priest in charge was a large, brawny man and clearly an ex-soldier. He blessed Milo without comment, then moved on to the man behind him, greeting him by name. He was at ease in this company, as well he might be and, if he had seen through Milo's ruse, he gave no indication of it.

Milo moved down the line, noting which Gods were more favoured than others. Some people had their own preferences, Gods to whom they felt they had a personal connection, while others were receiving everyone's attention. He couldn't even see Athena Minerva's altar for the crowd.

He smiled to himself. There was nothing like turning up in person with a deadly weapon to guarantee the choicest offerings. Several Priests were busy accepting gifts, anything from baskets of food and wine, to weapons, clothing and even pieces of armour. Others had fashioned wreaths, or gathered fruits. All the food would be distributed later, adding to the Goddess's prestige. Worshippers from all over the Empire stood ready to pray, and already a babble of Britannic, Latin, Greek, and other more exotic languages filled the air. Some clutched statuettes or amulets ready to be blessed.

Milo watched the general bustle and debated what he could offer. It was all very well his brother sending gifts on his behalf, but he felt he owed the Goddess something more personal. The trouble was, he didn't have anything much that was truly his own. He contented himself with standing in line to pay his respects. It was all very well being a lord, but he was sorely in need of funds. He could only hope that the Goddess would bear with him until he found a more suitable offering.

The final altar was Diana's. There were already two attendant Priestesses waiting, so once more he queued to greet them. It seemed an age before he reached the front. Everyone knew that the Huntress was in the vicinity and had fought on their behalf. Like her cousin, Athena, she was one of the most petitioned, even though there were few females in the camp.

"Hello again, Milo."

He could only stare in astonishment as the women turned towards him. The last time he'd seen them had been out at sea, on the deck of *Wolf of the Waves.*

"Latona! Bodil! How are you here? It's good to see you again," he added.

"We serve the Goddess," Latona said, laughing at his amazement. "As to why we are here, we wouldn't have missed this fight for the world, would we, Bodil?"

"Oh no," Bodil said. Now he could see her properly, he noticed the sword at her hip. Latona was similarly armed.

"I thought you lost, along with the crew."

Bodil nodded slowly. "We were prepared to die fighting, but it was not our fate. The Goddess decreed otherwise, and so we are here. Have you come to worship her?"

"I have and to offer my thanks. I believe she was an implacable enemy to the Fae horde."

Latona smiled. "Indeed. She smote many, before Athena and Mars turned up and slew the rest. Still, there is sport to be had chasing any that remain. We've just finished for now, haven't we, Bodil?"

She placed her arm around the taller woman's waist and pulled her in for a hug.

"Yes. Now it is time to feast!"

They shared glances of mutual affection.

"Then I won't keep you. I've come to pray and I promise to make a proper sacrifice as soon as I can," Milo said.

"The Goddess hears you," Latona said, her eyes sparkling. Milo had the sense he was missing part of their story, but he was glad that Julia's former slave had done so well for herself.

"The Princess is here, but she's a Mage now."

Bodil's eyes widened, but Latona didn't seem surprised.

"So I've heard. She's very powerful and has the Goddess's favour."

"I'm sure she'd like to see you," he said, remembering what he had seen in the Heart of Albion.

"I'm sure we'll bump into her at some point," Latona agreed.

They watched as he scattered incense.

"I'm glad you're both well and I hope to see you again soon," he said when he'd finished.

"We hope so too," Bodil said, smiling.

As he walked away, he wondered what the joke had been. Maybe they were simply glad to be alive?

He'd only gone a few paces when his stomach began to remind him that it was past time he ate something. All that riding had left him hungry and, for once, he was glad that someone else would be providing the food. It would be nice to have a wash as well. Mio quickened his pace, threading his way through legionaries packing their leather tents and belongings on to carts, ready for the march up to Londin. The rest they would carry themselves, heedless of the weight.

The unexpected blow caught him in the back, as if he'd been punched by a giant's fist. Milo found himself pitching forward on suddenly weak legs, the yellowing grass rising to meet him. After a moment of confusion, he was surrounded by voices.

"Dear Gods, it's Lord Gwydre!"

"He's shot. Move aside!"

Someone was yelling for an Adept. Numbness had set in, though he knew that the pain would hit any second. He tried to murmur a healing spell, but his mind slid off the words. Then hands were lifting him.

"Get him into the tent!"

He didn't recognise the voice, but he could see an Adept's robe from the corner of his eye. A man was shouting out in agony and, after a moment, he realised that it was him. Then he knew no more.

XXI

Maia had her figurative hands full. What with taking on supplies and rounding up her very hungover crew, it was as much as she could do to remember to relay everything back to her sisters and keep the communications going between land and sea. Being the only Ship on the spot meant that these duties were hers alone. It was like being in the middle of an ant's nest and she found herself wishing that she could be on her way, flying above it all.

The first she knew of the shooting was an urgent message from Leo. He'd been on the ground with Pendragon, discussing details of her flight to Londin.

<*Tempest*! Recall the crew and make ready to weigh anchor immediately! We have to get to Londin as soon as possible. Lord Gwydre's been shot.>

Lord Gwydre? He meant Milo. She'd seen him about the camp and heard the tales that were growing by the minute. Who'd have guessed how important the Agent would become?

<Why can't they treat him here?>

<The arrow was poisoned by Fae magic. Raven says the only cure's in Londin and they daren't portal him.>

That answered that question. And she'd thought she had enough responsibilities. Now her speed was all they had. She summoned Amphicles, who got to work bellowing orders. Looking down, she could see Leo striding over to the scaffold they'd erected, complete with ladders, that served her makeshift platform. If she was going to have a more permanent berth, something better would have to be devised. Hot on his heels, two marines were carrying a stretcher. She could see Milo's pale face, the rest was covered with a blanket. Accompanying him were two Adepts, together with Pendragon, Raven and Aquila puffing along in the rear.

"Heron, Robin, you'll have to get him up here," she ordered. Her Mages were already waiting by her belly hatch. "Can you manage the others as well?"

"Those that can climb must do so," Heron muttered. "I don't know about Aquila. Perhaps Jupiter can grow him some eagle wings or something."

Robin frowned at him, then both were too busy concentrating to speak. Slowly, the stretcher with the stricken man rose into the air, ascending smoothly until it hovered above the hatch. Hyacinthus and big Ajax grabbed the handles and guided it in to where Hawthorn was waiting.

"Get him to the upper deck," her Adept said. "I'll do what I can, Ma'am, but Fae magic is beyond me. I'll try to alleviate the symptoms."

"There are other Adepts coming up," Maia said. She could see them now, but what caught her eye were two figures rising through the air. Raven had hold of Aquila, transporting them both towards her.

"More passengers arriving, sir," she informed Amphicles. "Raven and Lord Aquila."

"Lord Aquila?" Her second-in-command's face was a picture. "Get Danuco to greet him. What's our status?"

Maia checked her levels of Potentia.

"Engines fully charged sir. Just waiting for the word. Here's the Captain now."

She alerted her crew.

"Captain on deck! All crew to stations! Ready to cast off, sir."

Leo was red-faced and breathing heavily, sweat running down his forehead from under his hat.

"Good. Weigh anchor as soon as everyone's aboard." He turned to Pendragon, who had just made the ascent and saluted. "Welcome aboard, sir. I wish it was under better circumstances."

"Indeed, Captain Valerius. So do I. My compliments, *Tempest*."

She returned his salute automatically.

"Thank you, sir. I'll do my best."

"I know you will. Proceed with all speed."

On the surface he was perfectly self-possessed, but she knew him too well. He was terrified his brother would die. It was a cruel twist of fate if he was to lose both his son and his new-found brother. As to his niece, Julia had passed beyond them all. Was he to be the only true Pendragon remaining?

She dismissed her speculations and waited for orders.

<*Tempest*, report. What's happening?>

It was *Victoria*. She'd missed her designated contact time.

<Lord Gwydre's been shot with a poisoned arrow. I have to get him to Londin as soon as possible.>

<Dear Gods help us!> the Flagship said. <It's the same trick they pulled with Artorius. Why isn't he dead already?>

<I don't know. Maybe it's because he carries Excalibur?>

<Do your best and keep me informed. We're approaching Portus now. Our prayers go with you.>

Victoria ended the Sending and Maia busied herself with unmooring, powering up her engines and gliding slowly away above the treetops. Below, the camp continued to break. The army would follow as fast as it could, but it would be more than a day before the vanguard would reach Londin, even with a forced march.

With any luck, she would make it in under two hours.

*

In the meantime, a consultation had started on her upper deck. Space was tight, especially with so many new passengers and the only privacy was a flimsy partition. A seat was found for Aquila, while most of the others opted to stand around the table. Like most other items it was bolted to the floor, but she did have some moveable things to draw on for emergencies.

Pendragon waved away the offer of another chair, though Raven accepted one, settling himself into it with one hand resting on his staff. Amphicles was dispatched to take charge of operations to allow Leo to attend. Danuco and Heron made up the rest of the company, though Hawthorn was expected to report in as and when, using Maia as a channel. He was busy conferring with his fellow Adepts, both of whom feared the worst.

"We're keeping him as comfortable as we can for now," Hawthorn told her. "I fear that whatever they've used is unknown to us."

"I know you'll do your best," she said.

She'd asked her mother for help and was being aided by a brisk southerly breeze that was just enough to increase her velocity without damaging any of her structure. It seemed that communication with her immortal family was becoming easier. Maia tried not to be too reliant on it or take it for granted, but if anything counted as an emergency, this was it. Her crew were being as quiet as possible, so as not to disturb the patient, though from what she could see, Milo was deeply unconscious.

Sister!

It was Pearl, shooting out of the clouds.

<Pearl! Good to see you!>

I have a message from the Gods. Make your way to the Forum. A mooring is being built for you there. Hurry!

Before Maia could reply, Pearl streaked off, disappearing into the distance. Maia shrugged to herself and adjusted her heading. She'd be flying into the heart of the city. Why, she didn't know. She opened her link to Leo and relayed the information.

<Which God was it?>

<Gods, plural,> she said. <I didn't get time to ask which ones.>

<Do as she said.> Leo ordered. <I'll tell the others. Maybe it's because the Sword of Kingship is there?>

It had to be. She left him to concentrate on the meeting.

"It's definitely Fae work?" Aquila was asking as she listened in.

"It is," Raven answered. "If he hadn't been carrying Caledfwlch, Excalibur that is, he'd have been dead almost instantly. The sword is keeping the worst at bay, but its magic can't resist indefinitely."

"Just like my nephew," Pendragon said.

Raven nodded. "The same, except this time some sort of dart was used, possibly blown through a pipe like they do in the New

World. Easier to conceal. The assassin wasn't caught, but I fear they might be human."

"Hiding in plain sight?"

"We think so. No Fae could have got through the camp perimeter without alerting the warding spells we laid down. This speaks of human agency."

The look on Pendragon's face boded ill for the perpetrator.

"Then we shall have to make the hunt a priority. Lord Aquila, is there any help the Gods can give us?"

The High Priest laced his hands across his ample girth.

"The Huntress herself is investigating, ostensibly on her father's orders though I have to say she is most eager to see justice done. The malefactor will have to have more than Fae protections on their side to escape her."

Maia remembered her own meeting with the Goddess and knew that to be so. If she hadn't been the instrument of Jupiter's plan to chastise his wayward daughter, she would never have made it past her trials. It was a close run thing as it was and the memory of Diana's rage still frightened her. It was good that they were on the same side now.

"I understand Lord Gwydre is holding on to life," Aquila continued, "but Fae poisons and magic Britannic swords are not part of my expertise. Raven, what do you know?"

All eyes turned to the Master Mage, whose milky eyes were fixed ahead of him as if seeing things nobody else could.

"There is a way of restoring him," he said at last. "Much has been happening behind the scenes, and that is why we are heading for Londin. The Gods have been busy making alliances and calling on their various aspects. Aquila, you will have heard of the search for an ancient artefact in the heart of Londin?"

"You mean a certain very large and powerful cauldron? I was sent to find it. Now I understand why."

He couldn't disguise his smugness, and Maia wondered what the Gods had been up to when nobody was looking.

"What are you talking about?" Pendragon wasn't in the mood for any delays. "I think we've had enough of riddles, though I know our Master Mage enjoys them."

Raven sighed.

"Forgive me, sir. The Cauldron of Ceridwen has been unearthed from beneath the old Londin Palace."

"Was that why Jupiter sent his thunderbolt?"

Aquila answered.

"It was. Jupiter was showing his displeasure, and paving the way for an excavation. An Agent was sent to guard it and foiled an attempt by Fae infiltrators to carry it off."

"And why wasn't I told this sooner?"

"You had other things to think about," Raven said and Aquila nodded in agreement. "This was the Gods' business. Now we need the Cauldron to restore your brother to health. That and the Sceptre of Britannia."

"Which is where?"

"Safe. The same Agent retrieved it, with the Gods' help."

<He's been busy, whoever he is.> Leo Sent to Maia. <What do you think of all this?>

<The Gods have their own agendas,> she replied. <I know that to my cost. All that time we thought they weren't doing anything, they were preparing for this.>

<Scary, isn't it?>

<Very.>

<How are we doing for time?>

Maia checked her internal chronometer.

<We'll be there in just under an hour.>

<Then I hope they're ready for us.>

Maia hoped so too.

*

Caniculus had been hanging about all day, waiting along with all the other inhabitants of Londin for news of the battle. Those that hadn't fled had spent the past hours arming themselves with anything they could get their hands on, or making weapons if they didn't possess anything. Spiked clubs and long knives strapped to shafts to make a sort of pike seemed to be the favourites, but he doubted they'd have much effect on well-armed Fae. It was safer to cluster within the old Roman walls and pray that nothing got through.

After a short internal debate he'd decided to make his way to the Forum, where most of the temples were. The new Temple of Jupiter beside the river was bound to be packed solid, and he fancied his chances more with one of the smaller ones. After all, he'd met a few of the Gods personally now, so he might be able to count on Mercury, Athena, or maybe, at a pinch, Mars. It was a pity that he hadn't become a devotee of Mithras as then he could have hidden underground, but he'd never fancied being drenched in bull's blood, for all the contacts you could make in high places.

As he pushed his way through the crowd, all with the same idea, he reflected that if Pendragon lost the battle they were all doomed anyway. It might be better to break into a handy wine shop that the owners had temporarily left unguarded and drink his worries away. The growing darkness would help in that regard.

"Ho! Caniculus!"

His hand automatically went to his knife. Nobody here should have recognised him. Then he saw who it was.

"Lord."

Mercury stepped away from the wall he'd been leaning against and grabbed his arm.

"Over here. Now, I've one more job for you."

"Yes, Lord."

Caniculus did his best to look enthusiastic, though he didn't think he was fooling anyone.

"Mars is busy, as you can imagine," Mercury said easily. "Don't worry, we Gods have everything in hand – or almost everything. You know how it is. You think it's all sorted, then an Oracle throws a spanner in the works."

He made a disgusted noise.

"An Oracle?"

"Yes, and a reliable local one for once. None of the usual ambiguous mumblings like they do at Delphi." He rolled his eyes dramatically. "She says you must get the cauldron and transport it to the Forum as soon as possible. Oh, and you'll need to take the Sceptre as well."

Caniculus swallowed.

"Er, you do know that there's a chimaera guarding the Cauldron?"

Mercury raised an eyebrow.

"I do. Good job your family knows all about them. I think they'll want her back." He winked. "Off you go!"

Then he wasn't there anymore and Caniculus found himself literally staring at a wall.

"Right," he muttered. It was hard to tear himself away from the fascinating patterns on the bricks, but his options were limited. It was time to call for help, and not of the divine variety.

He squared his shoulders and turned about face, heading back to his bolt hole. A quick calculation had told him that he'd be better picking up the Sceptre first before going to get his family. He didn't think they would have left the city, not with all the animals and their livelihood on the line.

He was almost at his front door when distant cries and running feet put him instantly on alert. He ducked into an alleyway to listen, uncomfortably aware of his pounding heartbeat. It was time for news.

The shrieks grew closer.

"We won! We won! The Fae are routed! We won!"

Other voices took up the cry, interspersed with cheers and whoops of celebration that spread through the streets faster than a horse could gallop. The wave of noise washed over and past him as he crouched in the grimy alley, his head on his knees and tears of relief sliding down his face.

"All right, sir?"

He raised his head to see a concerned face peering down at him, outlined against the streetlights. He sniffed.

"I think so."

"A large hand clapped him on the shoulder. "No need to be afraid now. Pendragon got the bastards, and I heard Athena Minerva turned the rest to stone with Medusa's 'ead!"

Now that was news. Caniculus realised his jaw was hanging open.

"She did *what*?"

"Yeah! I didn't believe it either, but the Priests say it's true." The slave's face split into a huge grin. "Up you come. "

Caniculus scrambled to his feet.

"Thank you. Here, have this for being the bearer of good news."

He gave the man some coins. After a pause, the man slipped them inside his purse. "Very kind of you, sir. I'll put it to good use. Nearly got enough for my freedom."

Caniculus clapped him on the arm and wished him luck as he set off again, still shouting the news. If every citizen gave him a tip he'd be free by the morrow, but Caniculus felt better for doing it. Hadn't he been blessed? It was only right he should pass on some of his good fortune.

Renewed by the general cheer, he slipped back into his room and felt under the mattress. His fingers closed on a hard cylinder. Good. For one moment he'd worried that the Sceptre had been gone, despite what Mercury had said. The place was full of thieves looking for opportunities. He'd have to carry it carefully, as pickpockets would be out in force. It was a pity he'd had to give the helmet back.

He withdrew the Sceptre and gazed at it thoughtfully before stuffing it under his tunic, adjusting his belt to take the weight. It was safer to keep it next to his skin rather than in a bag that could be snatched. Right, now for the cauldron.

He tried to take routes less travelled on his way across the city. The main streets were full of people singing, dancing and doing other things in dark corners that he didn't look at too carefully. It seemed that everyone was determined to enjoy themselves now that the threat had passed. He was glad he wouldn't be one of the city street sweepers in the morning.

Soon, the familiar gates of the yard appeared in view. They were closed, as was usual, but he abandoned all caution and rang the bell for entry.

A sliding panel drew back and eyes peered out.

"We're closed tod – Brocchus?"

"Aulus! Can I come in?"

"Yes, of course!"

The panel closed and there was the sound of bolts being drawn before the smaller door set within the larger one swung open to reveal his big brother. Caniculus scurried inside and Aulus shut the door after him, making sure it was secure. Caniculus stood for a moment, breathing the sounds and smells of home. They were a little more pungent than usual, largely because of the enormous dung pile in the corner.

"What's happened here?"

Aulus grimaced.

"Couldn't get it hauled away because of all the trouble. Looks like things will be back to normal soon, I'm happy to say."

"I hope so. You've heard, then?"

Aulus nodded. "Yes, thank the Gods. There are lots of strange stories doing the rounds. Pa heard some off the local Priest, but they seem a bit far-fetched. Come on. Ma will want to see you."

"And feed me, I hope, unless she's in bed."

He hadn't had time to grab more than a quick bite earlier in the day, and it was getting on to midnight now.

"No, she's going to see you starve," his brother replied. That was the cue for an arm punch. "Ow!"

"You deserved that. You've no idea what I've been through."

"Ah, the glamorous life of a Government Agent."

"Beats shovelling crap all day."

"Now boys! Behave, the pair of you!"

Valentina was on him in a second, giving him a hug before examining him closely.

"You look tired, Brocchus. I'm so glad you're back! Come and tell us what you've been up to."

In no time at all he was seated at the table with a large bowl of stew and some bread, telling his family an edited version of events.

His cousin, Silo, was sceptical.

"Seriously, the Gods gave *you* orders?"

"You can believe it."

"I do," Balbus said. His uncle had appeared from the yard. It seemed that nobody was sleeping this night. "There are stranger stories doing the rounds. So, we're to retrieve the chimaera? I wondered where she'd got to."

"The old palace. We're to get her and take an old cauldron thing to the Forum. I'll need a cart and some help."

His mother fixed him with a look.

"An old cauldron thing? What's that when it's at home?"

He shrugged.

"Something that was buried ages ago. Apparently it's needed again."

"I heard Jupiter blasted the palace with Marcus in it. Is he dead then?"

Caniculus shrugged.

"Don't know," he mumbled through a mouthful of stew. "Probably scarpered."

His uncle nodded. "That sounds about right. He's a dead man whatever, royal or no royal."

"Hello, son!"

Caniculus stopped eating long enough to greet his father and younger brother. They came into the kitchen beaming, with wet hair and red faces from a scrubbing after working with the animals. Novius kissed his wife and seated himself next to Caniculus.

"To what do we owe the pleasure?"

Caniculus explained his mission and Novius brightened.

"Hear that? The Gods themselves want us to have our chimaera back! I bet the poor girl's hungry. Aulus, finish your food and nip to see what meat stocks we have left. If I have to buy a cow I will, but that'll take time. You say we have to do it quickly, Brocchus?"

"Yes. As soon as possible."

Caniculus wiped his bowl with the last of the bread and belched quietly. Mercury hadn't chosen his mother's stew recipe for nothing.

"Right. We'll get on with it now. Let's see. She'll need to be fed first, then drugged when her belly's full."

"Unless she's already eaten," Balbus said, meaningfully.

"She killed a load of Fae, but I don't know if she ate them."

Novius paused. "Well, she'll want more, unless someone's been stupid enough to bother her. Let's eat up and go and get her, shall we?"

"And the cauldron."

"Oh, yes. That too. It'll be a two cart job, then, unless we can get the beast to pull the cart."

"Don't be daft!" his wife swiped at him with a towel. "You take care now. Don't forget how dangerous she is. Let Baro lead. After all, he's the one who caught her in the first place."

"True," Novius said. "He'll be back soon, along with Caius. Crocodiles," he explained to Caniculus. "Never know when someone will want to flood the arena."

"We'll have to stock up, Pa. The new King will want games."

"Lots of games, Aulus!"

Novius rubbed his hands. "This will be good for business, whoever he ends up being!"

Caniculus caught his mother's eye and smiled. Some things never changed.

*

Londin was in the distance, its features growing more distinct as she approached at speed. Maia could already make out some important landmarks and glints of silver from the great river Thamesis. The golden statues on the roof of the new Temple of Jupiter shone like beacons in the summer sun.

"I can certainly smell it." Leo was standing beside her on the observation platform. "This heat won't be doing the populace any favours."

"I expect normal service has been disrupted somewhat," Raven said, from her other side. "The sooner they get the new system up and running the better, before we all drown in the stink."

Leo grunted in agreement. Below them, fields and woodland were already giving way to more urban areas, including some industrial complexes clustered around major road arteries, though for once the chimneys weren't pumping out their usual loads of smoke. It would take a while to get back to full productivity.

"Can you see the Forum yet?" Leo asked.

"Yes, I've got a bearing," Maia replied. She extended her Shipsenses and focused on the centre of the city, relying on the knowledge she had absorbed from maps to add a mental overlay to the scene before her. This way it was easy to pinpoint where everything was.

There. She could see a structure rising above the Forum like a weird skeletal tower. It had to be her mooring site, built with the help of magic for speed and stability.

"It looks like they're ready for us."

Leo squinted down his telescope. "Oh yes. Can you believe they've built it so quickly?"

"I expect the Chief Artificer had some tricks up his sleeve," Raven said. He winked at Maia.

"He's certainly very capable," Maia replied, trying not to grin. Despite the rumours, hardly anyone was aware of Vulcan's exact contribution to the war, and it seemed he wanted it that way. She opened the link to Pendragon, who was below watching over his brother.

<Making the final approach now, sir.>

It was true. They were passing over crowded rooftops and streets filled with people all looking up at this strange vision. Maia had adjusted her speed before they crossed the river, using her braking mechanisms and nudging herself with her propellers into the correct position. She was passing over the roof of the Admiralty Headquarters now, while further to the north she could see the blackened remains of the Old Palace.

She set her nose towards the mooring tower and glided forwards, using her Potentia to give herself extra manoeuvrability. This was the tricky part. Maia blocked out everything and concentrated on making a successful connection. Fortunately, the wind had calmed so her bowline dropped without incident, enabling the ground crew to attach it to a crank. Slowly, she was reeled in and secured.

"Drop anchors," Leo commanded.

This part was familiar. She had several anchors as before, though now they would be attached to the ground instead of letting them snag on the sea bed.

"It's going to wreck the paving stones," she warned.

"I don't think anyone cares. At least they've had the sense to clear folk out of the way," Raven remarked.

As the last anchor bit, she assisted the men in working the crankers, feeling them drilling in to hold her fast. It was heavy work, made easier by her Potentia. She received the signal when all was done.

"All secure, Captain."

"Well done! Anyone would think you'd been doing it for ages."

She could tell he was relieved that everything had gone smoothly.

"It was easy this time," she said. "I wouldn't like to do it in a force eight gale though."

"Yes, that would be tricky," he admitted. "Inform the Admiral we've docked and can begin disembarkation."

"Aye, sir."

She opened the link to Pendragon immediately.

<Docking completed, sir. Ready to proceed.>

<Thank you, *Tempest*.>

He sounded preoccupied, and no wonder.

"I'll go and supervise," Raven said. "Don't forget to relay to your sisters."

"Oh, yes."

With everything going on, it was easy to forget. The Ships had agreed to not to contact her unnecessarily, so it was up to her.

<*Tempest* to all Ships! I have docked in Londin. Opening the link now.>

Maia reached along the Ship link, expanding her vision and transmitting. Instantly, the comments flooded in as the Ships got a whole new view of the capital. Gasps of amazement filed her mind.

<Look at all the people!> *Jasper* said. <I haven't seen that many – well ever!>

<It hasn't changed much in two hundred years,> *Dragon* remarked. <I thought they were building new temples?>

<You're right," *Leopard* agreed. "The Basilica's looking a little shabby. Where's the sword, then?>

Maia turned her attention to the largest building and scanned the columns.

<There it is!>

The jewelled hilt gave it away.

<So, either the Admiral or Lord Gwydre has to pull it out.> *Victoria* didn't sound thrilled.

<Or somebody else!> *Persistence* cackled. <It should be all comers, like it was with the original Artorius. Get the women to have a go. Where's Julia?>

<She's a Mage now.> Maia said.

<So? She could still rule.>

The discussion moved to who would pull out the sword. Maia left them to it, watching as Milo was moved gently down to her hatch. Raven, Robin and Heron had already sent Aquila and Pendragon ahead. She left them to it. Her part in this was over now. She'd done her best, and that was all anyone could ask for. It was time to watch the show and pray for a happy resolution.

XXII

The sun was rising higher in the sky by the time Caniculus and his family accomplished their task. Baro and Caius had been summoned from their crocodiles to join the team, the former eager to reclaim his prize catch. As Novius pointed out, these things took time and you couldn't rush animals, added to which they'd had to cross half of Londin.

The chimaera was surprisingly docile, happy to devour the several sides of beef that Novius had procured and lap up a tub of water laced with calming herbs. There was no sign of Fae, only chewed up bits of suspicious-looking cloth, so it appeared she had found them to her taste after all.

"Where she comes from, it's likely she'll eat anything," Baro said, standing over the beast like a fond parent.

She was already sleepy when they encouraged her into the closed cart, chaining her to the floor just in case.

The cauldron was still where it had been when Caniculus last saw it, so it was simply a case of hitching up a horse to the other cart. It wasn't too long before they were rolling through the streets and heading for the Forum. They could already hear the noise of the crowd.

"We'll need to clear passage," he said to his father, who had insisted on taking the reins. They made a strange convoy, though soon Baro would head off back to the yard with the chimaera. Aulus, Caius and Silo stayed with him to help, while Novius remained with Caniculus, despite his son's protests.

"I'm the head of the household," he stated. "If anything goes wrong, it's on me. I'm not leaving you to shoulder the Gods' demands on your own."

Caniculus gave up arguing. There was little point when his father had made his mind up on something. As well try to move the statue of Jupiter with a toothpick.

"If you must," he grumbled, unwilling to give up without at least a token show of resistance. He was hot, sweaty and thoroughly fed up.

They'd gone about a quarter of a mile when Novius broke the silence.

"What's that?" Novius was staring up at the sky, shading his eyes with one hand. "It's not one of those rocs, is it?"

He'd never managed to capture a roc, though he would dearly have loved to. Caniculus followed his father's gaze.

"That's not a bird. It's sort of flying machine hovering over the Forum."

He started as a voice boomed in his ear. He'd forgotten about the speechstone.

<Caniculus? What's happening?>

Aquila was impatient.

<I've retrieved the cauldron and am heading down the Magna Via,> he Sent back, hastily. <We might need help getting through the crowds.>

<I'll arrange an escort.>

<Understood.>

Caniculus took a deep breath.

"Pa, Lord Aquila knows we're coming and is sending people to clear the way."

"Right," Novius said, sucking his teeth. "It'll be the City Watch, or maybe some soldiers."

He snapped the reins to urge the drowsy horse into a trot. Caniculus glanced over his shoulder, but the cauldron was secure. Looking at it made him wish it was full of wine, enough to swim in. He'd need that much to slake his thirst when they were finished with all this.

Hoofbeats up ahead heralded the arrival of a full troop of mounted cavalry. At the front were two warriors who looked different from the others, in old-fashioned helmets and armour. They drew up alongside the cart and saluted.

"Greetings!" one said. "We have come to escort you to the Forum with all speed."

"Thank you," Novius answered. He glanced at Caniculus, who shrugged.

"I am Bedwyr, of the Companions," the man continued. "This is Palamedes. We will keep you safe."

"Er, right. That's nice."

The cavalrymen arranged themselves into an honour guard, some in front to clear the way, with the others keeping watch behind. Despite himself, Caniculus was impressed.

"Why are they dressed like Artorius's Companions?" Novius whispered to Caniculus.

"Because they are," the nearest soldier said. "Don't ask," he added. "Apparently some have returned, but not Artorius. There's another chap carrying Excalibur now."

"Fancy that," Novius sniffed. Caniculus hid a grin. Few Londiners would let on they were impressed by anything.

The streets were busier as they trundled closer to the Forum, but anyone in the way soon moved at the sight of a heavily-armed troop of horsemen heading in their direction. It wasn't long until Caniculus could see one of the gates up ahead. A path lay open to them, lined with thousands of people.

They passed underneath the shadow, welcoming the momentary relief from the blazing sun, then they were in the huge open space and heading directly for the Basilica. This close, they could see the aerial machine clearly and Caniculus gaped at the huge gas-filled bag with what looked like a vessel underneath. He was too far away to make out the name, but if they had flying Ships now, that was extraordinary enough in itself.

Guided by their escort, Novius pulled up in front of the Basilica steps. Caniculus could see the sword, still stuck in the column where he'd unwittingly thrust it all those weeks ago and he prayed that its true owner would pull it out. The thought that he'd carried it with him made the hairs on the back of his neck stand up.

Aquila was waiting to greet them.

"Ah, Agent! Congratulations on the completion of your task. You will be well rewarded. And this is?"

"My father, Lord. He helped remove the chimaera and provided the cart."

Novius bowed.

"Gaius Sylvestris Novius, at your service, Lord."

Aquila regarded him benevolently.

"You have done your country a great service, both of you. I'll take it from here. You can leave the cart and take the horse. I believe you have something else for me?"

Aquila held out his hand. Caniculus had got so used to the hard lump inside his tunic that he'd almost forgotten about the Sceptre. He rooted about inside his tunic, then dragged it out, placing it in the High Priest's palm. Aquila hefted it and nodded.

"Excellent work, Agent."

He turned away, dismissing them. Caniculus grabbed his father's arm and hustled him away into the crowd which, with many a curious glance, parted to make a space for them. He finally felt that a great weight had been lifted and he could go back to being just another anonymous face, like any good Agent. Hopefully this was the last demand the Gods would make of him.

They had a ringside seat for what was going to happen and Caniculus was determined to make the most of it while he could. Then it would be time for wine. Plus they'd better remember to pay him. A lot.

*

Leo took up position on Maia's observation platform, and was soon joined by Amphicles, Osric and Musca.

"You're not disembarking, then?" Maia asked them.

"Not bloody likely, ma'am," Musca replied, with a grin. "We've got the best view in Londin from up here."

She had to agree. The rest of her crew were peering from gun ports, or down through her belly hatch. Some were waving back at the crowd, who seemed delighted with the novelty. Ships were always popular, in whatever form they came in. Maia listened in to the Ships link, which was fully active as everybody was watching now.

<They're happy to see you,> *Diadem* said.

<Course they are. People love us,> *Jasper* said.

<We're passing the mouth of the Fal now,> *Patience* Sent. <Lots of people have turned up to watch.>

<Wish we could stay here for a bit,> *Emerald* said, wistfully. <I like it here. It's near where I grew up.>

<Didn't know you were a Kernow girl.>

<Oh yes.>

<We've been ordered to Portus, and that's that,> *Victoria* interrupted. <We'll be sent off on new assignments soon enough, so let's enjoy being together.>

<I'm looking forward to anchoring at Portus, I can tell you,> *Dragon* said, to general agreement.

They broke off as horsemen rode into the Forum, escorting a laden cart.

<What's that on the cart?> *Jasper* asked.

<It looks like a huge silver bowl.>

<What do they need that for?>

<It's the Cauldron of Ceridwen,> Maia said. <They're going to use it to try and heal Mil – Lord Gwydre.>

<You know more than you're saying!> *Jasper* accused.

<I might.>

<More than you, anyway,> *Persistence* sniggered.

<Oh, blow it out your porthole, you old bag!>

<Now then, ladies!>

<Don't spoil the fun, *Victoria*!> *Leopard* drawled. <*Jasper*'s so funny when she's cross.>

Maia sighed. Leo caught her expression.

"What is it?"

"Ships!"

He chuckled. "Arguing again, are they?"

"There's always something."

"Shows they're happy," Musca said. "They're all kindness when it's trouble, but as soon as that's finished they love nothing better than having a good snipe at each other. Ain't that right, Osric?"

"It is," her Sergeant of Marines replied. "Especially with the Harridans around. Love a good scrap, those two."

"Are they leaving the cauldron on the cart?" Leo wondered.

"Looks like it. Everyone can see that way."

A woman emerged from the Basilica. Dressed in simple green and brown robes, her head adorned with a crown of leaves and flowers, she walked down the steps accompanied by four other women carrying ewers.

"She must be the High Priestess of the Mother," Amphicles said in awe.

Maia stared at the woman. She was dressed like the High Priestess, but this wasn't Ceridwen. What had happened? Then she recognised Arianrhod, one of the Priestesses she'd met during her stay at the Heart of Albion, just before her Trials. So, there had been a change at the top. Raven's fears about Ceridwen's loyalties must have been well-founded. Of course, Aquila couldn't be expected to officiate this time. This was an older, Britannic mystery.

Meanwhile, the horse had been unhitched from the cart and a ramp was fixed from the Basilica steps to the lip of the cauldron. The women processed up the ramp and emptied the ewers into the Cauldron. It looked like plain water to Maia, but she supposed that it had been made sacred in some way.

"That won't do much to fill it," Leo said, but as they watched, the level began to rise, bubbling up as if the bottom were connected to a spring, until it began to overflow. Silvery sheets of water poured from the lip to vanish into the ground. The crowd sighed as one.

Arianrhod leaned over and raised her arms, speaking in ancient Britannic.

"Hail to you, Lady of the Life and the Living Waters! Grant us the power of your healing powers, we beseech you. Accept this offering and restore the line of Pendragon!"

She lowered her arms and waited. Out of the shadows came two other people. Maia recognised Julia in Mage robes, her long hair unbound down her back. The other was Pendragon, wearing ceremonial robes in his capacity as Royal Pontifex. He was carrying something in his right hand.

"That's the Sceptre of Britannia," Leo announced. "I've seen it before."

"I thought it was stored away somewhere?" Amphicles said.

"It was." Leo said. "Artorius took me into the strong room once and showed me all sorts of stuff."

It was a happy memory for him, but Maia knew that he still missed his friend more than he could say.

"They've trotted it out now for the coronation," Musca said.

"It makes sense. Do you think the Admiral will try for the sword now?" Amphicles was agog.

"Not until they've sorted out his brother. It wouldn't be fair. I expect he'll have first go as he's the elder," Leo said.

Pendragon and his niece approached the High Priestess and bowed as the crowd watched in silence. Maia could sense the eyes stacked behind hers, taking in the sight. More Ships had joined the link now. All of her sisters were waiting to see who the new ruler would be.

Pendragon took the Sceptre and carefully unscrewed the end. He withdrew a lump of something that looked like a black piece of stone, then handed the casing to a waiting attendant. Maia had never heard that it came apart. The outside had to be just for show, but what significance could the rock have?

Pendragon looked at it for a few seconds, then passed it to his niece, who ran her fingers over it before nodding.

"The Luck of Britannia is intact!" she proclaimed.

Maia gasped. Everyone knew about the Luck, which had healed the land and its peoples of the Great Blight all those years ago. She didn't know how many people knew who had discovered it, changing his life in the process. Raven was standing off to one side in a group of Mages. He didn't react, but she had to know.

<Raven,> she whispered.

<Yes, Maia?>

He sounded calm enough.

<Is that the stone you found in the cave?>

He paused before answering. <Part of it, yes. It was broken in pieces and buried throughout this island to provide protection. This is the core of it, shaped to fit inside an outward show of power and authority.>

<What will it do?>

<It will augment the healing power of the waters and combat any foul influences. Hopefully, the two things combined will

heal Milo. After that, the water will be distributed to the Adepts for healing purposes. A lot of good should come from this day.>

Julia stepped up the ramp and dropped the Luck in the Cauldron. Instantly, the water began to shimmer and sparkle.

"Bring him."

Milo was borne up on a stretcher, then Pendragon removed Excalibur from where it had lain on his body. Clad only in a loincloth, Milo was lifted and lowered gently into the sacred vessel.

Everyone held their breath. This had to work.

*

The first thing Milo noticed was the sound of running water. It was more than a trickle, but not as powerful as the sea. The next thing was a flood of warmth that ran through him, spreading from his core, a flow of energy that filled every space in a rush of well-being. He felt weightless, as if floating in a great lake, soothed and comforted by a presence that seemed familiar even though he didn't know where he was.

Return and fulfil your destiny, my son.

The voice was clear, subtly feminine. It was like his mother's yet he knew it wasn't hers. This was older, more powerful – and could not be denied.

I hear you, Great Mother.

He opened his eyes. He was suspended in a churning, bubbling whirl of water, but his mind was at peace. Then the tumult ceased and he was drifting on the surface, looking up at the endless blue of the sky. It was a moment of perfect calm.

Suddenly, his view was blocked by a head. He smiled up at it, not knowing who it might be, but quite at one with the world.

"Brother! Take my hand!"

Memory returned in a rush. The last one was of falling on to sun-parched grass. He'd just been to the altars and was going back to his tent. What had happened?

He looked down at himself, but there was no wound to be seen.

"What?"

"Let's get you out of there." He placed the voice. It was Admiral Pendragon. The head turned away. "Give me a hand."

"Here, Uncle."

Another hand gripped his arm, and Milo was pulled upwards. His feet touched a smooth, metal surface, and he saw that he was in some sort of circular bath. He didn't have time to reflect on the strangeness of it all before his head cleared the rim and he saw that he was nearly naked. In front of thousands of people. In the middle of the Londin Forum.

"Gods of Olympus!"

He stared around in bewilderment, acutely embarrassed, before two attendants rushed up to throw a large towel around his shoulders. They helped him clamber out of the water and down a ramp on to the steps.

"Welcome back, Gwydre!"

All Milo could do was stand in confusion as he was dried off, conscious of the eyes fixed on him. They then removed his wet loincloth and dressed him in a linen tunic and embroidered robe, lastly fitting gilded sandals on his feet. All the while his brother stood next to the Princess, who, he remembered, was now a Mage. She was smiling, which made her look more like the Julia he'd known.

"What happened?" he stammered.

"You were shot full of Fae poison," Pendragon said, moving closer so they wouldn't be overheard. "If you hadn't been carrying Excalibur, you would be a dead man. As it is, we had to dunk you in Ceridwen's Cauldron to heal you."

Milo swallowed. "Fine, but did you have to do it here?"

"We had to get you to the Cauldron, here in Londin," Pendragon answered. "As to the how, look up."

Milo looked up.

"*Tempest*! You mean that I rode in an AirShip and can't remember? How annoying!"

"Go on, give everyone a wave. You had us all worried."

Pendragon was grinning openly now. Milo faced the crowd and lifted a hand.

The noise was deafening.

"Behold, the Prince Gwydre Pendragon, son of Julius Pendragon and chosen bearer of Excalibur!"

414

Owl's amplified voice proclaimed his lineage for all to hear. She was there at his side, offering him the familiar sword. He took it as a man in a dream, feeling the burden of it and wondering if he would have to carry it for the rest of his life.

The soldiers on the crowd line raised their weapons and cheered, though even that was lost in the general roar of an ecstatic population. Milo thought that he'd survived his wound only to be deafened by all the excitement. It took the brassy notes of massed *tubae* to bring back any semblance of order.

"I'm sorry to put you through this now," Pendragon murmured in his ear, "but this must be decided today."

Milo frowned, trying to work out his meaning, until an arm around his shoulder guided him to look in the right direction.

There was a sword stuck into a column.

"*Merda!*"

"Quite."

He'd seen it before, as had half the country. It was the one everyone, including himself, had thought was Excalibur. He glanced down at the real thing. There was no comparison. His didn't look half so showy.

"The Sword of Kingship."

"Yes. The one Artorius pulled out."

"And you want me to try for it."

Pendragon raised his eyebrows.

"I'd go first, but I think you've more chance."

Milo looked back at the sword, then at his brother.

"But you're the elder." Then his eye lit on his niece. "Maybe she should have a go? She's got more power than all of us put together."

"It's not for me." Owl said, clearly.

Milo mentally ran through every curse word he could think of.

"I don't want it."

"Neither do I," Pendragon said. "I want to go back to my Ships."

Milo stared at him helplessly.

"Come on, what have you got to lose?" a familiar voice said at his elbow. Raven had sneaked up on him. "If you're not meant to be King, it won't budge."

"Seems a stupid way to choose a ruler," Milo said stubbornly. "Can't we have an election or something, like they do in Athens? Throw all the names in a pot?"

"That will be later in the year when we vote for the Senate and the municipal councils," Pendragon said. "Go on. Think of it as a purely ceremonial position."

Milo shot him an exasperated look.

"I hate all these people looking at me. I'm supposed to be a secret Agent!"

Nonetheless, it was best to get this over with, before what was left of his resolve drained away completely. He strode over to the steps, climbed up and took hold of the hilt.

The grip fitted into his palm like it was made for him.

He tugged, and it slid out, several feet of gleaming, magical steel.

"*Merda!*"

It seemed like he was the bearer of not one sword, but two. Excalibur's subtle thrum of approval vibrated in his bones and he felt a little relief. It wouldn't have been good if they'd clashed. Perhaps the same person had made them both?

Whatever. He was doomed to glory. Milo raised the sword in approved fashion and resigned himself to his fate.

*

Caniculus was delighted to have a good view of proceedings. It wasn't every day that there were such momentous events, besides which he had the happy feeling that his part in them had come to an end. It was about time he had a little holiday and the chance to spend time with his family. He could already almost taste his Mum's cooking.

His mind had wandered to the thought of fountains running with wine and other free handouts, when he saw the supine figure being brought out and placed in the cauldron.

"See," he told his father. "I knew it was magical."

If he never saw another artefact again in his whole life, it would be too soon. First the Sword, then the Helmet, then the Sceptre and now the Cauldron. He'd collected the whole bloody set!

The crowd held its breath, waiting to see what would happen. Then Lord Gwydre stood up. Dried and robed, everyone's eyes were fixed on the Pendragons. Then, after a short delay, Gwydre pulled out the sword.

The cheers were deafening. Novius was waving his arms, finally impressed, while all around him people were clapping each other on the back or crying with relief that there was a king once more.

Caniculus stood in shock, mouth hanging open for the second time in as many hours.

"What's the matter, son?"

Novius was peering at him.

Caniculus raised a shaking hand.

"I know him!"

Ferret had a lot of explaining to do. And he'd better remember his old mate Dog, king or no king.

*

Milo was the King. Maia could hardly believe it. She watched as the Royals disappeared into the Basilica, presumably to get some respite from all the attention, though Raven remained behind with the Cauldron. The magic-infused water was being ladled out by several Adepts, who were pouring it with infinite care into a series of tiny vials for later use.

The fleet was beginning celebrations of its own. Her crew were clapping each other on the back and cheering and Leo had already ordered the rum barrel to be broached. How long she'd be moored here, she couldn't tell, but it seemed that she wouldn't be going anywhere in a hurry so it didn't matter if everyone ended up legless. Thinking fast, she ordered everyone to stay away from the hatches, and sealed them firmly. It wouldn't do to have drunken sailors falling from the sky like acorns in autumn. That would certainly spoil the festivities.

"Fancy it being him all along," Musca was saying. "I thought he was just a servant."

"Nah," Osric corrected. "He was guarding the Princess, and you don't have just anybody doing that."

There was further speculation in the link.

<He does look like a Pendragon, now you come to think of it.>

Blossom was leading the discussion, as the Ships tried to work out what that would mean for them. Many were already delighted that it would mean their Admiral's return.

<I've kept his cabin just as he left it,> *Victoria* announced. <The odds are that he'll be back just as soon as King Gwydre is settled.>

<Some people will 'ave a lot to answer for as well,> Persistence muttered

Maia knew that the Ships who had initially sided with Marcus, then left to avoid the conflict, were watching too. These included the *Justicia*, but she and the others were keeping very quiet. They would have their own peace to make with the new regime, and were probably already formulating their excuses. It was even possible that a few Captains would be replaced. Maia let it all wash over her. What was the use of bearing grudges?

She kept relaying as the Britannic crown was brought out on a cushion and lowered on to the new King's head by Arianrhod. The High Priestess of the Mother always crowned the sovereign. The compact between the ruler and the land was back in force and every Briton would sleep more soundly for it. As to what sort of ruler Milo would be, Maia had the feeling that he'd be a good one. Being brought up as a commoner helped.

Keeping one eye on her increasingly boisterous crew, most of whom were waiting eagerly for shore leave, she opened her private link to Raven.

<Hello Raven. What happens now?>

<Bored already?>

She Sent him a rude noise, but he simply laughed. <The King and the Royal Party will process through the city to stay in Senator Rufus's town house, as the Old Palace is no longer available. I suppose it will have to be rebuilt sooner rather than later.>

<He was a great man,> Maia said. <He and Lady Drusilla were very kind to me.>

<They were good friends indeed. Lady Drusilla is on her way up to Londin from the camp and I hope to see her shortly.>

She didn't know if she should ask, but did anyway.

<Is there any word on Marcus's whereabouts?>

<No. It was thought he was with the Fae, but that doesn't appear to be the case. He outgrew his usefulness to them, even as a hostage. Who'd want to ransom him now? They would do worse to him than we ever could. Macro was picked up trying to cross the Britannic Ocean at Dubris. He'll be for the arena, I expect. The last we heard, his master was at Greenfields, but he isn't there now. I suspect he's fled to a port to try and escape the country.>

<Where would he go?>

She saw him shrug for her benefit.

<Maybe the New World. Even we don't know what's in the interior, though I don't think he'll find feather beds and fine horses. We'll catch up with him sooner or later, and I hope the same goes for the assassin. Now, there are more important things to think about. Anything else you want to know?>

<Are they going to put the stone back in the Sceptre?>

<Immediately. We'll keep it for the parade and the official Triumphal procession, then it will go back into the strong room for safe keeping. They've got to get the water out first and that will take some time. I'm staying here to keep an eye on it.>

There were ten Adepts around the Cauldron now, with four others at the bottom of the steps. Tables had been set up and already queues of the afflicted had formed, hoping to get a taste of the healing water.

<I don't think they care that someone's already bathed in it.>

<Would you? It won't restore missing limbs, but there are enough ailments to keep everyone busy. I suppose it will be first come, first served, but a lot will be sent elsewhere. Some will be stored, in case of emergencies.>

It was a wise proposition, so long as it was well-guarded.

<Seems we're both hanging around.>

<Seems that we are. I may as well sit down.>

He arranged himself on the steps, and leaned on his staff. A servant brought him a cup of wine, which he drank with relish.

<They haven't forgotten you, then,> she teased.

<They wouldn't dare.>

<Who do you think will be Prime Mage now?>

He thought for a moment.

<Probably the scariest Mage around, and for once I don't mean me. Owl might want it. It will keep her near the King and I think she should have a say in things, don't you? Plus, she has all the accumulated wisdom of Merlin to draw on.>

<Do you think she'll ever go back to being the person she was?>

<So many questions! I'm not a soothsayer!> He was back to his snappish self. <Honestly, I think she'll achieve balance. As she adjusts, I imagine she'll be able to compartmentalise her personae, though the marriageable princess is gone forever.>

<She'll be happy about that.>

<It seems nearly everyone has been changed lately. Think of it. Milo is King. You're an AirShip. Julia is a powerful Mage. Cei has lost his son. Only I remain as I was.>

It was true. None of them was the same, only him.

One of the Adepts gathered up his robes and descended the marble steps to where Raven was sitting. Maia couldn't hear what he said, but Raven put down his cup and stood.

<It seems they've emptied enough for me to get the stone and replace it. Give me a moment.>

Another Adept brought the Sceptre's casing. Raven climbed the ramp and leaned over the edge of the Cauldron. Maia could see the stone cylinder, black against the silvery metal and lying in the few inches of water left in the bottom. They'd have to siphon the remainder out, or tip it up to get at it.

Raven gestured and the stone rose slowly, gliding purposefully towards his outstretched hand. It didn't look like the rough lump it had been when he found it. The memory of his ordeal in the cave that she had relived through his eyes had stayed with her ever since. The eyeless, alien creature he'd killed had had its final revenge and he still lived with the consequences.

Raven's outstretched fingers grasped the dripping stone and pulled it towards him. He examined it for a moment, as if in wonder, then crumpled like an empty sack.

"Raven!"

Maia's scream alerted the Adepts, who looked around in puzzlement, before seeing the stricken Master Mage. All Maia could see was her friend lying in a heap on the ramp like a bundle of old clothes, the stone still gripped in his gnarled fingers.

<Leo! Something's wrong with Raven!>

Her Captain came clattering on to the platform, slightly the worse for wear.

"What?"

"He picked up the stone and was struck down!" she wailed. Part of her wanted to detach right now and rush to his aid. Helpless, she called to him, her mind to his, desperately trying for a response, but there was no answer.

Two Adepts were bending over him, one of whom was Hawthorn. Raven had fallen face down and they were attempting to roll him over so they could examine him.

"Go down and see how he is, please!" Maia begged Leo.

"The Adepts will care for him," Leo said. "What can I do?"

"You can tell me what's happening!"

She felt like shaking some sense into him, then, something stirred, like a tiny flutter through the private link.

"He's not dead!" She could have sobbed with relief.

They'd got him on his back now, so she could see his face. His eyes were closed and though she couldn't see if he was breathing, the thread that connected them gave her hope.

Without warning, the Adepts stood up, consternation on their faces.

"Why aren't they helping him?"

Maia raised her voice and yelled down at full volume.

"Hawthorn! What's happening?"

Her Adept raised his face and spread his arms. She could read his lips as he mouthed.

I think it's magic!

Something wasn't right. The Master Mage's face was rippling, the wrinkles becoming shallower and smoothing out before vanishing. Frail strands of white hair thickened, changing in colour to jet black and fanning out around his head, while his robes fluttered as the body beneath grew in size and musculature.

Raven was growing younger in front of her eyes.

Maia was transfixed as the ancient Mage was restored to youth. He took a deep breath and opened his eyes.

They were blue, like cornflowers. And she knew them well.

This time she was unable to stop the sobs.

"It's fine, he's not dead," Leo was saying, while every Ship demanded to know what was going on. Maia could hear nothing, do nothing but stare at the face of her dream husband. The one the Huntress had offered her. A perfect man for a perfect life that could never be.

Her Quintilian.

Had she forced herself to forget? But she'd known his voice, been inside his memories, lived a part of his life, the best and the absolute worst. He was her mentor, her guide and had been from the beginning of her strange, magical journey.

Of course Diana had picked him to tempt her, then somehow twisted things so the knowledge was beyond her grasp.

<Maia! What is it, my dear?> *Blossom*'s pleas finally penetrated her shock.

<It's Raven!>

<Is he dead?>

<No...>

<Then get a grip, girl! You're a Ship, not a hysterical maidservant!>

<It was him all along,> she gasped. <He was there all along and I didn't know it! And now it's too late!>

Sister!

A funnel of swirling air swooped down to envelop her, as tight as if she were a swaddled babe. The pressure helped, though she still felt as if her heart had been ripped out, leaving her hollow like a rotted tree.

Leo had flattened himself against the bulkhead, his eyes wide as Pearl formed before him. The mass of air withdrew from Maia and solidified, becoming a semi-transparent figure.

"Who are you?" he whispered. Pearl turned to him.

"I am her sister. I am your cousin. I am Pearl, daughter of Aura and Lucius Valerius Vero, born into the divine as Maia was born into the human world. Forever one, yet forever separate, by Jupiter's decree."

Her words hit home like hammer blows. Leo nodded slowly. "Now I understand. Not all, but some. This is a secret, isn't it, linked to her strange abilities?"

"Yes. And you will keep it."

Frantic knocking on the doors told them the crew were trying to gain access.

"It's all right!" Leo shouted and it subsided.

Maia looked at her sister. Had she doomed them both with her confession?

"I don't care," Pearl whispered. *"None of this is fair. Now, remember who you are. I don't know whose doing this is, but you are strong!"*

"The Huntress."

Pearl's face darkened. *"Then she will pay."*

Maia shrugged. "How can Gods pay? I'll have to live with her revenge."

She pulled away, running her awareness through her vessel, along each plank, bolt and strut. Outside the platform, Musca was waiting with an axe to break down the door if needed, backed up by Big Ajax, worry on their faces. Automatically, her hand slipped inside her wooden breastplate to touch the little dog he'd carved for her, when she'd been a Candidate with dreams of becoming a Ship. It was the only thing she owned, now that her necklace was gone.

The pain of memory threatened to overwhelm her again, so she closed her eyes and called on the strength within the sacred oak of her Shipbody, tracing it back to the Great tree in the Grove of the Mother.

She had no breath to regulate, no pulse to slow, no tears to dry. She was a Ship and her duty called to her. With an effort of will she sank deep into the peace of the forest, letting her pain pass through her and sink into the earth to lie buried with her old body, deep underground and safe in the soil of Britannia.

Lady Gemma Valeria had never truly existed. It was time to let her go.

<*Tempest*! Report!>

The voice snapped her back.

<This is *Tempest*. All is well, Admiral Pendragon.>

Maia opened her eyes. Pearl hovered in front of her, like a glass vessel filled with milky liquid, constantly moving.

"Are you better now?"

<I will be. Thank you, my sister. I hope you won't get into trouble."

Pearl tossed her head in defiance.

"I am owed favours," she announced. *"As are you. Don't forget that. And if I should see the Huntress, I'll get the clouds to rain on her!"*

It was a very Pearl thing to say.

"You do that."

"Farewell. To you also, cousin!"

Her form dissolved into vapour and vanished, leaving a freshness in her wake. Leo straightened up and blew out a breath.

"Someday you'll have to tell me the whole story."

"I will if I can," she promised. She opened her clenched fingers to see the little dog grinning up at her, tongue lolling. She stroked it gently and tucked it away again.

"Big Ajax made it for me," she said. "You won't tell, will you?"

Leo smiled.

"Not a word. About anything."

She looked down into the Forum. The shadows had lengthened now and it was almost eight o'clock. The Cauldron of Ceridwen had been emptied. Raven, unrecognisable from the man he had been, was slipping the stone back into its housing. There didn't seem to be anything wrong with him. He replaced it on a cushion to be taken away, then looked up at her.

<Right, Maia. What's going on? I heard you screamed the place down!>

His mental voice was the same, at least.

<I thought you were dying.>

A half-truth was better than a lie. He'd have sniffed that out immediately.

<So you frightened everyone out of ten years' growth? Honestly, I can't leave you alone for a second, can I?>

<You are as I remember you,> she said.

He paused, a slight frown appearing on his handsome features.

<What? Old, grumpy and impatient?>

Where could she start? By keeping things the same.

<Exactly. What will you do now?>

He folded his arms and regarded her sternly.

424

<Well, for a start I'm going to have some dinner, in the company of the great and good. There will be several glasses of the finest wine. Then I'll see about getting my assignment back. I fancy flying over Britannia and looking down at the world. That's if you want me, naturally.>

<Oh? I'll have to think about it.>

<Will you now? See you soon. And I do mean *see* you!>

He strode off, his robe flapping around his knees.

<You need to get a new robe!> she Sent, watching him slip away into the shadows of the empty Forum.

He raised a hand and blew her a kiss, eyes dancing.

"Will you please tell me what's going on?" Leo asked in exasperation.

Maia smiled.

EPILOGUE

It was over. All his dreams for the Kingship, his alliance with the Fae, his future. Every scrap of power he'd once had was dust and ashes.

The only thing he could do was run.

He was on his own now, except for one of his slaves he'd bribed with most of what he had managed to get out of Greenfields, plus the promise of freedom. Even Macro had deserted him, not that he was to be trusted. He might have tried to use his ex-commander as a bargaining chip for immunity against prosecution, though as his henchman had slit Rufus's throat in cold blood, his pleas were unlikely to have been heard.

His only chance was to get a vessel to the New World and disappear into its vast territories. A set of old clothes had to suffice as a disguise. There was no way he would dress as a slave, but a countryman's hooded cloak served to hide his features.

He was supposed to have joined Kite when the battle was won, but the link had snapped abruptly, leaving him flailing. The Mage that had been left with him as a go-between had turned pale and fled. That was the moment he knew something catastrophic had happened.

Now here he was, standing by the stinking banks of the Thamesis, waiting for the tide to come in along with the boat that would carry him away. The river was wide and sluggish as it came to the end of its journey to the sea, filled with rotting hulks and everything the city discarded. Even the water looked unclean.

He huddled into his cloak, as the night air was chilly despite the heat of the day. The star-filled sky above him carried its own menace, though he didn't dare enter one of the disreputable taverns that served this stretch of the river. They looked rough and the clientele were worse. There were rumours of robbery and murder here at the edge, where the law rarely reached. Scum from all over the known world washed up here and nowhere was safe.

He leaned against a crumbling wall and waited for his slave to return with supplies, the rough texture of bricks through cloth unpleasant against his skin. The man was taking his sweet time about it.

A shadow silhouetted against the lamplight made him start.

"Sorry, sir. I did as you asked."

"Give it me."

The slave had procured a greasy pie, along with some thin wine. He took a swallow and grimaced at the bitter aftertaste.

"This stuff's disgusting. Didn't they have anything better?"

"No, sir. Sorry."

He was tempted to throw it at the man's head, but quelled the impulse. He had to keep his companion sweet if he had any hope of getting out of here. Two armed men were less of a target than a solitary traveller.

"What's the news?" he asked, biting into the pie. That was vile too, but it would serve to keep body and soul together, plus it was still warm.

The slave hesitated.

"Out with it!"

"Everyone's saying Excalibur has returned. Your grandfather had a bastard son no-one knew about and he's got it."

Marcus nearly choked. When he managed to swallow, he growled, "That's bollocks, Syriacus. The sword's in Londin."

"That wasn't Excalibur," Syriacus said. He sounded like he was starting to enjoy himself. "That was the Sword of Kingship. It was never Excalibur."

The man was becoming more irritating by the minute. "Go on."

He may as well hear the full story.

"The Gods descended. Athena had the Gorgon's head and wiped most of them out. The Huntress and the Lord of War did for any that escaped."

The Gods. *Merda!* Icy fingers trailed their way down his spine. Who could he pray to now? He had no Gods left.

"They're putting the statues in the Temple of Athena for all to see."

They'd be next to Echidna. He remembered the menacing figure, stuffed and mounted in the flickering light. Even moth-eaten and past her best, she'd been magnificent. He'd been promised monsters – even a great wyrm. All stone now, as dead as his hopes.

"Who's King?"

"He's called Gwydre. The bastard I told you about. Someone shot him full of poison, but they healed him with magic."

For one glorious moment, he'd thought it could be him. If he could only have pulled out the sword, there would have been no need for any of Kite's deceptions. It had always been his dream, to claim the sword as his birthright and finish with the thrice-damned, interfering, arrogant Romans once and for all.

Now some by-blow had it and he was doomed.

"Look, sir!"

The lights of a vessel were approaching, sailing in on the tide. His mood lifted a little.

"This will be our transport."

He threw away the half-eaten pie in disgust, wiping his fingers on his cloak. Once they were well away, he'd order finer fare.

"Get our belongings. We want to be ready to board as soon as possible so we can stay under cover."

He glanced up at the sky, half-expecting to see a thunderbolt, then smiled. The Gods weren't all-knowing and he'd covered his tracks well. Even if the vessel was searched, he'd bluff his way out. He always had. Failing that, there were plenty of ruffians ready to bloody their hands for a few coins.

The vessel glided up to the dock and he squinted at it through the darkness. It seemed to be barely bigger than a fishing boat, and definitely not an ocean-going craft. The crew were huddled at the stern. As they reached the quayside, a couple jumped on to the dock to tie up.

"This can't be it? Syriacus?"

He was alone. The bundle of their belongings had vanished too. He'd been too preoccupied watching the boat and now he was abandoned. He swore, cursing the slave to a gruesome death. His fingers fumbled inside his pockets for the pouches that held gold and other valuables. He wasn't destitute yet and the small craft was still an escape. Perhaps it would take him to a larger one, further out to sea? He wasn't sure how it all worked, but he knew that some vessels couldn't always get everywhere. It was ironic that his father could have told him and he damned himself for not making the arrangements personally.

"You're waiting for passage to the New World?"

The man sounded as though he was from Gaul.

"Yes."

"The wise man knows which way the wind is blowing."

It was the sign he'd been waiting for.

"It blows from the west."

The man nodded. "Come."

He led the way over to the vessel and up the gangplank. It really was quite small, he thought. There was no way it could undergo a voyage across the Atlantic. It had to be a transfer.

He expected to have to wait for the tide to turn, but to his amazement the man abandoned him as his fellows cast off.

"Hey!" he called. Who would operate the vessel? He didn't know the first thing about sailing, despite his family's efforts to shove him in the Navy.

The boat drifted into the current that would take them back into the heart of Londin.

He ran to the rail, debating whether to risk plunging into the filthy water and trying to make it back to shore, his cries unheeded by the crew. What was he to do? There was a sail but it was furled and even he knew, despite his ignorance, that he wouldn't be able to make any headway against the rushing river.

A slight noise behind him made him turn, heart racing. A figure was standing at the bow where no figure had stood before. Had someone stayed to help him after all? He started forwards, then stopped as the boat's lamps snapped on one by one.

The woman moved toward him. In the flickering light he could see her fine clothes, the crown on her head and the slow, stiff way she had of walking. As she drew nearer, the light gleamed not on flesh, but on the wood of a Shipbody.

He backed away, until his path was blocked by the wheelhouse and he could go no further.

"It can't be you! You were sunk!"

The Ship regarded him, her lips twisting in contempt.

"Yes, my vessel was destroyed, but I survived to learn of your lies and treachery. You never intended to keep your promises, did you? A Fae wife! What a fool I was! But no more."

"Get me out of here and I'll give you anything you want –."

"Oh, I'm getting you out of here." *Regina*'s smile was triumphant. "We'll be taking a little trip back to Londin together. Not how either of us imagined, I'm sure, but I know everyone will be delighted to see you again."

She moved closer and he found himself fascinated by tiny details. The glint of light on her paintwork, the smoothness of her wooden skin.

"Do you know that my father fell on his sword on learning of your failure? He was a fool to believe you too. Also, you made me kill my brother. I'll so enjoy watching you being executed in the arena. Taking you in will help me to be forgiven. Minerva herself told me so, and her I do believe. Britannia needs every Ship she can get, even a renegade like me."

A hand shot out, clamping down on his arm like a vice. In the silence, the snap of bone sounded like a pistol shot.

He screamed and sank to his knees, gazing up at the Ship in horror even as the sail unfurled and the little boat slipped into the current.

Upstream, fireworks showered bright stars into the skies as the celebrations began.

AUTHOR'S NOTE

There you go, that's Book 5 finished. Thank you so much, Dear Reader, for sticking with me through the whole series. I hope you enjoyed it!

There will be other stories of the Ships, as they assure me that they have more tales to tell in the future. These might be in short story form rather than novels, but who knows? I have little control over this process. I set out to write a standalone book in 2020 and it turned into five!

I would be very grateful if you could **write a review, however short, on Amazon and Goodreads** as we indie authors rely on them to get our books seen in a very crowded market. A few lines are all that's needed to give people hunting for their next reads a flavour of what you thought.

If you want to catch up on Twitter/X, you can find me @EKkoulla or on fb #ShipsofBritannia. My website is **emkkoulla.com**, where you can sign up to my monthly newsletter, plus you'll receive a **FREE novella** about the early life of the enigmatic Marinus.

In the meantime, I wish you calm seas and a fair wind!

ACKNOWLEDGEMENTS

Where to start?

Writing this series has been an amazing (and sometimes terrifying) four and a half year journey into the unknown. I have learned so much, most of all not to give up even when things seem impossible to accomplish.

There are so many people who have supported me along the way, friends both in person and online. They are the ones who spurred me on, comforted me when I wailed in frustration and encouraged me to be the best I could be.

My husband, Stephen, who promises that he will read my books 'one day'.

Thea Magerand, my amazing cover artist, who has been with me from the start. You can find her website at **ikaruna.eu**.

My wonderful friend, Dr Madeleine Campbell-Jewett, who is an extremely knowledgeable editing and proofreading guru. It's thanks to her and her husband, Bob that I attended my first ever SFF convention, which just happened to be Glasgow Worldcon. Nothing like starting with the biggest! Any irregularities you may find are solely down to me.

My beta readers, Jane and Perry in the UK and Robyn in New Zealand. Your unfailing support and enthusiasm for the world of Britannia is wonderful!

Lesley Affrossman and Natalia Richards, wonderful fellow authors, for all their help and advice.

Tracy Clark at PublishNation, who does all the tech stuff like formatting and making sure that my books conform to the rules. I'm getting better at the technology but I still need help!

I absolutely must give a massive shout-out to the fantastic Indie Author Community on Twitter/X. They brighten my days with their conversations, observations and witty memes about what it's like to be independent/small press writers in the 21st Century. They are the best, and may their sales and page reads never cease!

Also, thank you to all the book bloggers, reviewers and sale/competition organisers who work tirelessly for the writing community. They are so often the reason readers find our books and change lives for the better. I always say that marketing is like pushing an elephant up Mt Everest while wearing stilettos, and I truly appreciate their help with the heavy lifting.

Last, but definitely not least, to you, Dear Reader. If these books have entertained and diverted you for a while, then my work is done.

Printed in Great Britain
by Amazon